PRAISE FOR
THE LIGHTHOUSE AT THE END OF THE WORLD

"A wonderful magic show . . . Marlowe's fictional exploration of Poe's life and creative vision is accomplished with great panache, providing fascinating insights into the nature of dreams and the workings of the imagination." —*Los Angeles Times*

"Astonishing. . . . This was the book I enjoyed most this month, perhaps this year." —Robin W. Winks, in the *Boston Globe*

"Wonderful . . . a horror-filled exploration of a madman's mind."
—*Richmond Times-Dispatch*

"Marlowe is a historical novelist of the first rank, with a deliciously supple and fluid prose style. . . . He makes Poe come alive in all his mad glory." —*Publishers Weekly* (starred review)

"Brilliantly written . . . more lyrical than a literary biography, subtler than a mystery. . . . Marlowe's magic realism equals that of the very subject he explores." —*Cover*

"This is a remarkable novel, beautifully written, cunningly constructed, and dense with subtle clues and allusions."
—*Ellery Queen's Mystery Magazine*

"A marvelous journey into what may well represent Poe's mind as he created. . . . Historical fiction at its best." —Newport News *Daily Press*

"This extraordinary novel helps us to see the mysterious figure of Poe more clearly than ever before." —James Dickey

"*The Lighthouse at the End of the World* held me in its thrall to the end. Tautly shaped and finely written, this novel hovers daringly between fact and fiction, bringing Poe and his imaginative world to life with ease and gumption." —Jay Parini

STEPHEN MARLOWE was born in New York and educated in Virginia. He founded the writer-in-residence program at the College of William and Mary. Author of the internationally acclaimed bestseller *The Memoirs of Christopher Columbus*, he was awarded the French Prix Gutenberg du Livre in 1988. He has lived in some twenty countries and was last seen in Paris.

Stephen Marlowe

THE LIGHTHOUSE AT THE END OF THE WORLD

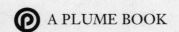

A PLUME BOOK

PLUME
Published by the Penguin Group
Penguin Books USA Inc., 375 Hudson Street, New York, New York 10014, U.S.A.
Penguin Books Ltd, 27 Wrights Lane, London W8 5TZ, England
Penguin Books Australia Ltd, Ringwood, Victoria, Australia
Penguin Books Canada Ltd, 10 Alcorn Avenue, Toronto, Ontario, Canada M4V 3B2
Penguin Books (N.Z.) Ltd, 182–190 Wairau Road, Auckland 10, New Zealand

Penguin Books Ltd, Registered Offices: Harmondsworth, Middlesex, England

Published by Plume, an imprint of Dutton Signet,
a division of Penguin Books USA Inc.
Previously published in a Dutton edition.

First Plume Printing, October, 1996
10 9 8 7 6 5 4 3 2 1

Ⓟ REGISTERED TRADEMARK—MARCA REGISTRADA

The Library of Congress has catalogued the Dutton edition as follows:

Marlowe, Stephen.
    The lighthouse at the end of the world : a tale of Edgar Allan Poe
/ Stephen Marlowe.
        p.   cm.
    ISBN 0-525-94049-9 (hc.)
    ISBN 0-452-27556-3 (pbk.)
    1. Poe, Edgar Allan, 1809–1849—Fiction.   2. Authors,
American—19th century—Fiction.   I. Title.
PS3563.A674L5   1995
813'.54—dc20   95–15477
                                                                CIP

Printed in the United States of America

PUBLISHER'S NOTE
This is a work of fiction. Although historical figures appear in their natural settings,
any actions, motivations, or opinions attributed to or about real people in the book are
purely fiction and are presented solely as entertainment.

BOOKS ARE AVAILABLE AT QUANTITY DISCOUNTS WHEN USED TO PROMOTE PRODUCTS OR SERVICES.
FOR INFORMATION PLEASE WRITE TO PREMIUM MARKETING DIVISION, PENGUIN BOOKS USA INC.,
375 HUDSON STREET, NEW YORK, NEW YORK 10014.

For Annabel

Is *all* that we see or seem
But a dream within a dream?

One

Oh, outcast of all outcasts most abandoned!—to the earth art thou
not forever dead . . . and a cloud, dense, dismal, and limitless, does
it not hang eternally between thy hopes and heaven?
—"William Wilson"

"You are Mr. Edgar Allan Poe, are you not?"

I should, to be prudent, have said I was not. With his one twin-
kling eye—a patch covered the other—and his florid cheeks and the
tracery of burst capillaries that colored his bulbous nose a violent
purple, the captain of the steamboat *Columbus*, bound from Norfolk
for Baltimore, was all too obviously a convivial man.

But how seldom I basked in the light of recognition! Besides, it
had begun to rain and my deck passage did not entitle me to pass
through the saloon's bat-wing doors, now almost filled by the captain's girth.

A sudden roll to larboard decided the issue by propelling me at
him. Sidestepping nimbly for so large a man, he draped a meaty
arm across my shoulders and convoyed me into the saloon before I
could say a superfluous "I am." But make no mistake; I did say it.

He said, "I never forget a face" and "portrait in the *Southern Ar-
gus*" and "not that I'm much for fantastical tales or poe-etry, ha! ha!
ha!" as we penetrated blue streamers of cigar smoke and a clamor
of masculine conversation that almost drowned out the thump of
the paddle wheels.

When we reached the oak bar, most of the crowded room was

not visible except in the back-bar mirror, and for an instant this gave me the vertiginous notion that we, here on this side of the mirror, were the reflections, noisy and noisome in our imperfection, of a reality that, from behind the Negro bar steward's white-jacketed back, saw a sullied semblance of itself in the image of which I was a part. The notion passed, as such foolishness does, in the time it took the captain to introduce me to a fellow with Little Van side-whiskers and another whose name sounded like Rum, which by then I was drinking.

Just one drink, I assured myself. One convivial drink with the convivial master of the steamboat *Columbus*, Pompey Gliddon by name—for how could I prove to myself I could stop unless I started?

I wonder, have I started this narrative at its beginning or close to its end? These are the two accepted places, and they are mutually exclusive, so the point ought easily to be resolved. But the more I ponder it, the more I see how elusive the answer is.

I disembarked in Baltimore on the evening of September 28, 1849. I would never see the year 1850, nor even November of '49. Is it not then evident that the beginning I have made must be very close to the end indeed? And yet, I have used the word "narrative," and by it I mean no autobiographical maunderings. No, these pages are rather an attempt to account for those five days during which I disappeared, in my forty-first (and final) year, to be found by a publisher of my acquaintance on the floor of a tavern frequented by Irish immigrants and known as Gunner's Hall. Close to the end of my life though they are, did not those five days begin the moment I walked, rather to my surprise still ambulatory after imbibing most of a bottle of rum, down the gangway of the steamboat *Columbus*? But then how mutually exclusive *are* beginning and close-to-end?

The answers to certain other questions would be helpful. Where had I gone, those five days? And what done? And in whose company? I had been on binges before. Surely that was the sum and substance of it, a not very mysterious mystery. But then why, in hospital, in what little remained to me of afterwards, did I sometimes call myself Mr. Peacock?* One question begets another, and on the wall behind the troglodytes the flames of their meager fire fling flickering shadows while the story-teller pursues his rhythmic, mesmerizing *and-then-and-then*, so like the beat of *Columbus*'s paddle wheels (is not a tale a journey?), hoping to beguile his audience, or at least himself, into forgetting those unknown horrors lurking outside the cave long enough to confront the familiar horrors *inside*. For the story-teller knows this: A nightmare does not give rise to terror; rather, it is the other way around.

A tavern, then. I can be seen at the far end of the bar, hunched and shivering with the unseasonable cold. My white linen suit, so dapper when I lectured at Richmond and Norfolk, is now rumpled and sodden.

I am drinking gin and hot water, my fourth—in *this* tavern. That I have already spent or, in fumbling thick-fingered for it, possibly lost the money intended for my passage in the railroad cars to Philadelphia, now seems important only in that it means I cannot pay for my drinks. I have found myself in such predicaments often enough. The usual solution is to pass out. Pass out and they will search your pockets to ascertain that you are penniless before depositing you with no intemperate violence in the gutter or, better, summoning the police, who will deposit you in a cell, if not warm then at least dry, for the night. And the morning, with luck, will see to itself. Does this strategy bespeak a certain lack of *amour propre*? Perhaps. Yet why *not* pass out? Oblivion, however temporary, is the objective, after all.

The man tending bar has a dissipated face with dark unhealthy pouches under the eyes, rather like my own. A hazard of both our occupations? He wordlessly holds a hand out, palm up, a gesture both jaded and theatrical. Once in a similar situation I recited some lines from "The City in the Sea"—or was it "Ulalume"?—in the

---

* It cannot be said with any certainty whether or not Mr. Poe knew that the word for "peacock" in Old Norse is *poe*. (Editor's note)

hope that someone would pass the hat. But I was hooted down and deposited outside rather more vigorously than had I merely pretended to pass out.

Aside from myself, a single patron remains in the bar-room, as if determined to outwait me for some reason I am too besotted to grasp. On the bar at his elbow stands a tall beaver hat, and his stone-gray topcoat is in the latest French fashion. Have I ever visited France? Alexandre Dumas insists, in writing, that I have been to Paris, venturing forth only at night like the Chevalier C. Auguste Dupin, but we shall come to all that.

I squint at the bar-tender's large, chapped hand. The index finger gestures—pay me. The bar-tender is a big man, and the hand becomes a fist. I begin to worry. As I have said, there are degrees of being thrown out.

Another hand, this one well manicured, enters the small space from which I shall soon be forcibly evicted. Deftly it inserts coins into the large red fist.

When I try to thank the altruist in the French topcoat, he waves me to silence. "I know what it is to be down on one's luck. Do you need a place for the night? Come, get your coat."

But I have no overcoat. At the door he unfurls a large umbrella and goes outside, where he waits; I can hear rain drumming on taut fabric. Soon I join him.

Sometimes anywhere is better than here.

A labyrinth of alleys. From the mouth of one I see by the light of a reluctant dawn the water of the harbor, flat black and oily under the rain, and on it a row-boat half sunk, or half afloat. My benefactor steers me by the elbow across a board-walk to a brick building. The ground shifts underfoot. I step warily back. But it is only a scale. The place is, or has been, a warehouse. Charred beams, once part of the roof, lie about, mute testimony to the fire last year in which more than sixty buildings were gutted. The door hangs by a hinge. Someone comes out, short, burly, in navy-blue reefer.

"This makes six for the night, I believe?" says my benefactor.

"Not until he says he's willing." The burly fellow appraises me in the dim dawn light. "He Irish?"

"You know me better than that," says my benefactor.

"Native-born, are you?" the burly fellow asks me. "Where?"

"Boston."

"Can you sign yer name?"

"I can."

"Or any other name?"

I shrug.

"Give me one."

"Rufus Griswold," I say.

"That *yer* name?"

"No."

"Give me another."

"Neilson," I say.

"*That* yer name?"

"No."

I am standing on the scale. It moves. It seems to be weighing me. Does it find me wanting? As my cousin Neilson has?

And Rufus Griswold?

"A roof over yer head, most of a roof, leastways," says the burly fellow. "And victuals. Well? Yes or no?"

"Why not," I say.

"There, you heard him. Six," my benefactor says.

"Five, weren't it?"

"Six, including this one."

I hear the clink of heavy coins. Five. But the first had nothing on which to clink. So, six. Including me.

"The food won't poison you. I eat it myself sometimes," the burly fellow tells me with gruff compassion. "There's gin to drink. Rum if you like."

"What crime must I commit?"

"Vote. You will vote in the Congressional election."

Sound bubbles from me, a kind of laughter, to be inundated by the slosh of water against pilings and trod upon by my benefactor's retreating footfalls. The exhilarating prospect of the unknown—and all it is is a Whig coop, from which, more than once no doubt, I shall exercise my right to vote.

The burly fellow averts his face from the puff of stale breath begot by my laughter. The laughter is all the volition I have left. I am literally unable to move until he shoves me, will-I, nill-I, into the building.

T<small>WO</small>

It is now rendered necessary that I give the *facts*—as far as I comprehend them myself.
                    —"The Facts in the Case of M. Valdemar"

I wish I could write that I heard, rising from the susurrant semi-darkness, snores, whimpers, wheezes, gnashing of teeth, maniacal cachinnation, and cries to chill the blood—auditory melo-dramatic artifice, in short, suggestive of some extravagant Gothic adventure in which I would play a stirringly heroic role among the homeless, despairing souls in that coop. But truth constrains my pen.

The burly fellow's shove sends me reeling into a vivid stream of invective as the sleeper whose straw mattress and outstretched legs I have stumbled over comes exploding to his feet. Soon I find myself hemmed against the brick wall by a half-circle of threatening derelicts who study me as they might a specimen mounted in a museum where they have gone only to keep warm but which interests them in spite of themselves. It is the white suit, of course. Sodden, rumpled, stained, it never the less is eloquent of a bespoke bedizenment that awes them. I am utterly alien. I could have come from the antipodes. Or the moon.

Their awe spawns resentment; their resentment, anger.

"That be silk?" asks one.

"Nope. Linen," says another.

"He a sporting man, or whut?"

"Whut you want here, sporting man?"

"You sartin it's linen?"

"I know linen when I see linen."

"She-it." This scatological skeptic takes a sleeve of my coat between thumb and fingers. I consider an orderly retreat, but my back is already to the wall.

"Feels genu-wine," the skeptic allows, and my coat is stripped off me. Reaching to reclaim it, I see dawn seeping in through three small windows high on the harbor side of the building; see bearded faces; see black teeth and no teeth; see scars and mutilations; see, worst of all, in rheumy eyes, enjoyment.

"Give it here," says one.

But my white coat makes the rounds, seeming for a while to have quite disappeared until it surfaces on a corpulent man whose bulk splits it up the back.

My tormentors now are silent, and more frightening for their silence. My white stock goes next, its appropriation almost strangling me. My white shirt follows in two pieces, not including the lower half of one sleeve, the right, which still clings to my arm. I am shoved again against the wall, then yanked back amongst them. Tripped, I tumble onto my back, struggling to no avail as both my shoes go. They are old shoes, but under caked mud they are undeniably white. Who among my tormentors has ever worn white shoes?

"A mite skinny in the shanks."

"Give them trousers here."

A tug-o'-war, which the white trousers cannot possibly survive, begins.

Those not participating flop me over, face down, and now I do hear one of those cries to chill the blood.

In the silence that follows, a voice speaks. The words are few. "That will be enough now. You've had your fun."

It is no loud voice, nor is its tone commanding. Rather, it conveys a burdensome ennui.

Muttering, one by one my tormentors remove themselves.

The agency of my deliverance is a tall man deep of chest and broad of shoulder. Looming above me, he looks a giant.

As he helps me up, I see on his face a welted scar, crescent-shaped, that runs from the corner of his eye to his chin.

"Pretty, is it not?" he says.

I make a meaningless sound.

"You've been hazed, but that's the end of it," he tells me. "It's too early in the morning for such a hullabaloo. Here, these came off a dead man."

A pile of unspeakably filthy rags is thrust at me, and the scar-faced man withdraws without further word.

Meanwhile my tormentors have formed two disorderly ranks that shuffle toward a trestle table at the far end of the room, where the burly fellow in the reefer presides over a great steaming pot. It occurs to me that perhaps the meal, not the scar-faced man, has been responsible for my succor. But then I see him stride past the waiting men, see those closest to the table immediately make room for him.

He is, I learn later, a merchant seaman called Monk. Any group of men, however ill-assorted, will acknowledge a leader, and here it is Monk. In matters of discipline, even the fellow in the reefer—are they shipmates from another life?—defers to him.

I scrutinize my new wardrobe: a gray flannel shirt; trousers of grayish and patched—and befouled—cassimere, too large; a frayed rope for a belt; an out-at-elbows coat of once-black alpaca; and a pair of venerable boots, their soles coming apart and lined with folded newspaper like rotting *papier-mâché*, their stench worse than that of the trousers. But as I am cold—have never been so cold—I put on these garments, redolent of how many elections past I have no wish to know.

Oh, yes; I almost forgot. I was hatless, but now I have a hat. Of the cheapest sort called palm-leaf, with no band and badly soiled. I study it, as these men have studied me, like a specimen in a museum, then clap it—a good fit—on my head. And I laugh.

A hat. I have more than I started with.

———

I shuffle forward between two charred stanchions to the feeding trough, in my nostrils the stink of the rags I wear, the stink now of myself. For clothes make the man, do they not?—like the terrifying figure in "The Masque of the Red Death." Unmasked, he is nothing. Literally. The costume is all there is. That, and death to those who strip it away. I know another story about a masque. When the clock strikes midnight and the revelers reveal their faces, a woman asks her partner to remove his mask too, the most frightening mask of all. And he says, still dancing with her in his arms, I wear no mask. Does she drop dead of terror? I am uncertain of the ending, for it is someone else's story. Endings often trouble me, whether mine or others'. Endings, it has been said, are my weakness. Because I believe a tale should not close at the end, but rather open, like a morning glory to the sun? Then why have I not written many tales that do so? Perhaps I shall.

Is the end of something not the beginning of something else— even the most endful of ends, death, the beginning of all that time when you will *be not*? But I must desist from such speculation. For I can see the words of the critic, like the handwriting on the wall: "Poe will never command the wide readership his genius deserves because he leaves beneath and behind him the wide and happy realm of the common and cheerful life of man to deal in mysteries of 'life in death.'" And death in life, I suppose?

That wide and happy realm of the common and cheerful life of man; of a single individual, let us say; of me, or of you—can you see it, perhaps as thousands and thousands of daguerreotypes flashing by, each one establishing irrefutably that you exist because you were *there* when the camera's shutter opened; each one as unique as the moment it records because, like that moment itself, it cannot be duplicated?

In barely a decade, how Monsieur Daguerre's fabulous invention has revolutionized the world! And yet. And yet—isn't the very uniqueness of each daguerreotype a drawback? Daguerreotypes cannot be broadcast like seed grain, or reprinted endlessly like the written word. Well, you say, there is a competing process developed in

England, less pin-sharp but capable of endless reproduction. Yes, but. (Is there not invariably a yes-but wherever science is concerned?) The competing process, called calotype, produces an original image that reverses reality, making of darkness light and of light darkness. Or have our senses deceived us until now?

The advent of the photograph and the steel pen almost exactly coincide. Is there a warning here—again the handwriting, or photograph, on the wall—that words and pictures are doomed to battle for the minds of men?

However that may be, M. Daguerre's fabulous invention, or that of his English rival, will supersede mere human memory, and a good thing too. For is not memory the most capricious of servants, storing chaotically the minutiae of every human life in a filing system with no rhyme and less reason, so that something you see or hear, be it singular or commonplace, even something you smell, say the aroma of molasses, dark, thick blackstrap, which I can smell now as I reach the trestle table on which remain a few chunks of bread slathered thickly—something you see or hear or smell sends you to plunge into those thousands and thousands of daguerreotypes inside your head to withdraw one.

Three

There arose in our pathway a shrouded human figure, very far larger in its proportions than any dweller among men. And the hue of the skin of the figure was of the perfect whiteness of the snow.
—*The Narrative of Arthur Gordon Pym*

Soot-darkened red brick flanked a spotless white stoop, the marble glittering in a sudden shaft of sunlight that seemed for a moment to greet my arrival before the clouds closed in again, turning the sultry afternoon to virtual night.

Thunder crashed and I let the door knocker fall. The door opened to reveal a girl of nine or ten who looked up at me and screamed.

At the thunder? At my smile?

Was the smile perhaps suggestive of a death's head? In the four months since I had been drummed out of West Point I had eaten little, become emaciated.

The door shut in my face. Rain came down in torrents, in buckets. The door opened. The little girl said, "Hen—Henry? But you're upstairs in bed!"

I inserted my foot to prevent the door from shutting a second time.

"Henry is here in Baltimore? My brother Henry?"

The girl's oval face tilted up at me. "You're Eddie? My cousin Eddie?"

"Virginia? Who is there?" a voice called, and my cousin Virginia called back, "A man, Muddy—he says he is Eddie."

"Land, child! Then bring him in."

The voice, deep for a woman's, belonged to my aunt Maria Clemm, my dead father's sister.

I went in dripping wet behind the child. My aunt Maria wore a white widow's bonnet and a black dress, much pleated. She was tall, with the broad shoulders and broad, beetling brows of a man. Some have said she looked like my grandfather, General David Poe, who had been a friend of Lafayette and, possibly, of Washington himself.

Maria Clemm took both my hands in her strong square mannish ones. "Let me look at you." She looked at me. "Have you been starving yourself?"

"Well," I said, "it was not my plan to do so."

I soon was seated on a hard-backed chair at a bare wood table, envisioning platters piled high with thick slices off a pork roast, and cold veal, and meat pies. I was twenty-one and still an optimist and, as my aunt had surmised, starving. My stomach growled. Virginia giggled. My aunt Maria cut slabs of dark bread, yesterday's, and slathered on the blackstrap, then stood behind me toweling my hair while I ate. Virginia sat wide-eyed with elbows on table and chin on hands, watching me.

"Bring your cousin coffee."

It came thin and bitter in a chipped mug, but steaming.

Maria Clemm clucked her tongue. "You are so thin the cords stand out in your neck." Her hands were gentle. My aunt was, the evidence of her appearance and voice to the contrary, a very female person.

"We do not have much, Eddie," she told me, "but until you get back on your feet you will share what we have."

"That's what she told Henry," my cousin Virginia said. "Last winter."

"Virginia," her mother admonished.

"Are you as ill as he is?" Virginia asked.

"Now, Virginia, that is quite enough."

"Mr. Jeffries says Henry leads a untemprelate life."

"Young lady, you are not to listen to the idle talk of our boarder."

"Mr. Jeffries says that is why he has the consumption. Henry."

Maria Clemm slapped her daughter, not hard, on the side of the head. Brown braids swung. Virginia wailed.

"Bronchitis," my aunt said. "Henry has a touch of bronchitis."

He sat up in bed, wearing not sleeping attire but a black shirt and stock. We both usually wore black, my brother Henry and I; I cannot say why. Perhaps the dignified look it imparted belied "untemprelate" living.

Henry—or William Henry Leonard Poe, to give him all his names—did not rise. He laughed his greeting at me, a happy sound that ended in a deep, rolling cough that contorted and reddened his face. "Drink," he managed. There was a water jug, a tumbler. I poured, offered. He shook his head and coughed. And coughed. His eyes, of that indeterminate color neither gray nor hazel, looked beseechingly at me. I had not the faintest idea what to do until his hand groped toward the floor. There, under the bed, I found the corked bottle of corn liquor. I poured a more than generous measure into the tumbler and he drank it off, and, magically, the cough subsided and the redness left his face except for the hectic spots in his cheeks.

"And they say whiskey is bad for you," he observed. Weak but still mellifluous voice. Broad Poe forehead and wide-spaced Poe eyes under heavy brows. Aquiline, almost Hebraic, nose, small mustache, no side-whiskers. We looked like brothers; or like the same person.

My brother always claimed he could remember our father, a hard-drinking actor who deserted the family when I was not yet two. It is possible; Henry would have been four then. Our mother, an impecunious but acclaimed actress, died of consumption while playing in Richmond the following year. Henry was raised by General Poe and by the general's daughter, Aunt Maria, and went to sea young; I was taken in by admirers of my mother, the Allans. At any rate, the woman was an admirer. I shall have more, alas, to say of the Allans later.

Henry looked at me mockingly. "Are you a general yet, like Grandpa?" He offered me the bottle. I drank.

"Aunt Maria allows you whiskey?"

"Friends bring it. She pretends not to know."

I returned the bottle. Henry drank.

"I have been court-martialed," I said.

Henry laughed his happy laugh. No cough this time. "I never expected you to graduate from the Point. You were too long in the ranks, hating officers, ever to *become* one."

He returned the bottle. I drank.

"I wished to resign, but Mr. Allan would not permit it."

"So you arranged your own court-martial."

The bottle moved, was offered, tilted, returned. Before long it was empty and Henry pointed floorward; farther under the bed I found another.

"There were in all twenty-three charges of gross neglect of duty and disobedience of orders, over a period of twenty days. Also, I became inebriated at Benny Haven's Tavern."

Henry laughed; no cough. The corn liquor had given his eyes a liquid sheen. I felt light-headed.

"And did you derive any benefit from it?" he asked.

"The court-martial?"

"The Point."

"I can dissemble and clean a Hall carbine in pitch darkness."

"I assume you mean 'disassemble.' "

"What did I—oh."

We were both smiling when Henry withdrew from behind his pillows a cumbersome firearm with an oversized hammer and a cluster of barrels. I threw my arms up melo-dramatically.

"Ever seen one of these?" he asked. "My good-luck piece. A barhammer pepperbox pistol manufactured by the gunsmith Elisha Haydon Collier in the early twenties. Not many were made."

"Why your good-luck piece?"

"Because when I was in Marseilles I survived its best efforts to kill me. There was a girl, a most beautiful girl named Nola. . . . Well, I shall tell you about it some time." Henry replaced the Collier pistol behind his pillows. He was like that; he often did not finish a story he started. He said: "Mr. Allan is still richer than Croesus, is he not?"

"He inherited substantial parts of the Commonwealth of Virginia."

"And you are destitute?"

I shrugged.

"Why not go and see him?"

"My foster father is a businessman. He has an intense dislike of 'geniuses.' "

"I still say see him."

"Perhaps I shall, at the right moment."

But there was never a right moment for me and John Allan.

"You have been writing?"

With a wave of my hand I dismissed the question.

"Writing," said Henry, "is another way of traveling. More difficult than mine, perhaps, but not so easily prey to the frailty of the flesh."

Henry was for several years a seaman aboard the frigate *Macedonian*, sailing to the Mediterranean and South America. He began to reminisce. In Caracas an Indian had tried to sell him a white three-toed sloth with a red ribbon in its hair. He had smoked hashish in a den on Mount Pagus above Smyrna. He had dallied with Italian signorinas and Irish colleens. He had seen Montevideo, Uruguay. This seemed as distant to me as the planet Venus.

"But," he told me now, "my traveling days are over."

"Nonsense. You will recover." I tried to sound confident.

"Not a hope," he said.

We stared at each other. My eyes filled. This time Henry shrugged.

And told me about a seaman who said he had sailed to the frozen continent of Antarctica with the *Flying Dutchman.*

The months passed. Henry grew weaker. I wrote a tale, a fantastical tale about the *Flying Dutchman* and Antarctica,* and it won a contest in the *Baltimore Saturday Visiter.* I bought a joint of beef and two bottles of Henry's favorite claret to share my triumph with the family.

"You should not spend your prize money on such luxuries," Maria Clemm told me as we sat to table. But above her freshly starched collar, a faint proud smile lifted the corners of her long thin mouth.

"Fifty dollars will put a lot of roast beef on the table," Henry said, and laughed his happy laugh. A dry, crepitating sound escaped his lips, too inconsequential to call a cough.

"What is keeping Mr. Jeffries?" Maria Clemm asked. "The soup will grow cold."

"He is not in the house," I said.

"Where is he?"

"In his new accommodations, I imagine."

"But he seemed satisfied to board here. The front room is comfortable."

"I told him to leave. We need no boarders now."

Henry moved down to the front room the next day.

A week later he hemorrhaged. I ran to the doctor's house and returned with him in his buggy. We all waited for him to emerge from Henry's new room.

"He is sleeping. He will pull through. This time."

* "MS. Found in a Bottle." (Editor's note)

I had to walk. Anywhere. On a busy downtown street I encountered the editor of the *Saturday Visiter*. He touched the brim of his hat. I interpreted this as a mock salute. He knew I had been court-martialed, dismissed from the Point.

"You, sir, are a son of a bitch," I said. I think I was smiling.

There were further words. He punched me and I punched him. We circled each other awkwardly. Blows flew, most of mine, I fear, ineffectual. Passers-by separated us.

"Who blackened your eye?" my aunt Maria asked.

When I told her, she said, "I am so pleased you recognize the importance of good relations with your publishers." In her deep voice I could detect not the slightest edge of irony.

"What?" I said.

"The Poe men are not large but they are wiry and strong. Had you wished, you could have thrashed him."

Virginia watched her mother apply a cold cloth to my eye. Water ran down my cheek and under my collar.

"Let me feel your muscle," said Virginia. "Please?"

I flexed it and she touched it and endorsed the wiriness and strength of the Poe men with an exhalation of awe.

"The incident was unavoidable?" Maria Clemm asked me.

"The *Visiter*'s contest was not only for stories but for poetry as well. The editor submitted a poem of his own under a *nom de plume* and saw to it that he was awarded first prize. Which I should have won."

"Nonsense," said Maria Clemm. "You brawled because your brother is ill."

Winter came; Henry worsened; his cough seemed to shake the flimsy walls of the house. At night, waiting in the darkness for the gush of blood that would choke him to death, he was afraid to sleep. I sat up with him, listening to him talk, first about places he had seen, then about places he had not.

When he slept, if he slept, I would go to my room in the attic to write. I was struggling with a tale I had begun about an author who had started to write a story about the end of the world, which may have been only the end of his own life. The author had trouble with the plot and could not finish the story. But neither could he get it out of his mind. It consumed all his waking hours. Nights he dreamed a recurrent nightmare about an author who wrote, or had begun to write, a story he could not finish. The author in the nightmare let himself be so dominated by the intractable story that he forgot every thing else. He never left the house. He ignored his wife. He did not eat. The author who dreamed the nightmare soon experienced the same difficulties. All else was forgotten by him too, was lost to him. No more able than the author-protagonist to finish what had become a horror story, I burned the manuscript.

Those nights I wrote, the house was still. Sometimes I would hear a soft footstep on the stair.

"What do you want?"

"I like to watch you."

And Virginia would sit on the floor in her thin shift, clasping her knees.

The scratching of the pen fascinated her. "I can hear the words," she said.

"You must go back to bed. You're shivering with cold."

"What are you writing?"

"About a remote, decaying, gloomy building on the edge of a swamp where in dank underground vaults frightening things happen among armorial trophies to busybodies such as you. Now go to bed."

"You can't scare me. What's armorial trophies?"

Downstairs, Henry began to cough. I hurried to him. I propped him higher on his pillows. From their now deep sockets, his trapped eyes looked at me. I gripped his hand, tight. When finally he slept I returned to the attic. Virginia had not moved. In the candle light I could see the plume of her breath. And tears on her cheeks.

"I'm afraid," she said, and I took her in my arms and felt the pounding of her young heart.

In January it rained steadily for two weeks.

"I wish it would be over with," Henry said.

"The rain?"

"Every thing."

I pretended not to understand. "Spring cannot be far off."

"Can you not give me something?"

Again the pretense: "I shall read to you."

But he shook his head. Then began to cough.

A month into the new year, a spurious spring came cruelly to the city. Oaks and sycamores thrust out pale green shoots. There were premature buds. Orioles darted here and there, flashing orange and black, gathering twigs. Their hanging nests could be seen in every tree. Henry took a remarkable turn for the better. His color was good, he regained his appetite, he got out of bed to take a few steps about the room, leaning on my shoulder at first, soon unaided. Then one night a howling blizzard brought winter back. The next day there were snow-drifts taller than a man, and deep frost. The premature buds and shoots withered; the orioles sat forlornly on lifeless branches, their feathers puffed up against the cold. Henry was unfazed. "I wonder," he said, "if they might take me back aboard the *Macedonian* when my lungs are healed. I'm an experienced seaman. There are lands I would see."

"Where?" I encouraged him.

"Everywhere."

And Henry laughed his old happy laugh, and in its wake was no fit of coughing.

I was, untypically, exhausted the night after the blizzard. Blaming it on the change in the weather, I retired early and dreamed of a city so far east it was west, a city sunk beneath the waves of a lurid sunset sea, a city of spires and domes, of minarets and one gigantic tower, time-eaten, a city where my brother Henry ran lightly, weightlessly, through deserted submarine streets, and all at once I knew how to finish the tale that neither I nor my protagonist nor his dream-self had known how to finish, but when I woke I no longer remembered the ending.

I woke to a candle flame. It was not yet dawn. Maria Clemm stood over my bed.

"It is Henry," she said.

"I know," I said.

Four

If there is any thing on earth I hate, it is a genius. Your geniuses are all arrant asses.

—"The Business Man"

What boots it to tell of the series of boarders who paraded through the house, each more obnoxious than the last, so that Maria Clemm could make ends meet?

"Eddie, please do not provoke Mr. Hoad," my aunt said.

"Mr. Hoad, he looks like a toad," Virginia chanted.

"Virginia! Did Eddie teach you that?"

"No, but he does look like a toad, Muddy."

I grinned. "He is undeniably built low to the ground, and with those bow legs and broad bottom—"

"Eddie, for pity's sake! Not in front of the child."

"There is a tub in his room for bathing, I believe? Why does he not use it? Toads are amphibious."

"Virginia, you will leave us."

With an impish look at me, the child did as told.

"Eddie, do try to be reasonable. The money Mr. Hoad pays each week puts the food on our table."

"And a good thing, as he eats most of it."

"He works hard all day."

"And I do not?"

"Eddie, don't put words into my mouth. I am well aware that, for one who follows his Muse, should inspiration not strike . . . why, then . . ." But my aunt was honest, and aware of no such thing, no more than I was, and her voice sputtered off in confusion.

"Mr. Hoad is a common laborer," I said. "To place Virginia in proximity with him is not wise."

"A harness maker is a skilled laborer. A craftsman. Sometimes I think it is you who are the bad influence on Virginia."

I rose. My face was hot.

"Eddie, I'm sorry. Why do you not try to find work?"

"I have my work."

"But other writers, do they not work at . . . *work*, in order to subsidize their . . ."

"Avocation?"

"I fear I am making matters worse."

"There is no reason why an author," I said with a pomposity barely excusable in a man of twenty-four, "should not be able to support himself entirely by the efforts of his pen."

"But none do so."

"No, none do."

"Eddie, I am not suggesting that you find work in order to support us or even yourself. I am suggesting"—here my aunt bit her lip—"that employment might be beneficial to your character."

"Henry!" I heard myself shouting. "I am as old as Henry when he died! Older!" I saw my hands flailing air, as if I were observing someone else, some wild and delirious madman. "*He* was ill," I said, my voice plummeting to a whisper, my hands falling to my sides. "I have not the same excuse. You are right. I have been a parasite."

"I never said you— Where are you going?"

I went to Richmond. Walked the entire way, except for a ride in a farmer's cart south of Fredericksburg.

I was five days on the road. Thirty miles a day is not an unreasonable pace, for one in a hurry. So, a hundred and fifty miles. Winter miles, the road mostly deserted, here a silent farmhouse, there a scarecrow guarding nothing, over yonder a village wreathed in wood-smoke. North of Ashford a darkie came out of the woods with a brace of hare. He ran when he saw me. Drop one, I pleaded; drop one. But he did not. I stole food where I could: eggs from a chicken coop, turnips and carrots from a root cellar. I was chased by dogs. I drank from icy streams. My boots fell apart.

Henry had said, go and see him. So I went and saw him.

My haste ended at the northern outskirts of Richmond, the city where, until then, I had spent most of my life. You enter Richmond gradually, uncertain whether the countryside has intruded into the town or the town encroached upon the countryside. You see a straggle of buildings among the fields, and soon more buildings and less field, buildings of brick and of white clapboard and of weathered wood, and beyond the hills the gleam of the river, and you hear a rumbling, clattering, shouting, whip-cracking din of carts and drays, calashes and phaetons, buckboards and gigs hurtling along the rutted, unpaved streets. But it is no big city like Baltimore. Not including slaves, there are some twenty thousand Richmonders.

I found one I knew, Ebenezer Burling. I had known him since childhood, since before the Allan family's removal to London, where for two years John Allan tried to establish an English branch of Ellis & Allan, dealers in fine Virginia tobacco, and I attended school at Stoke Newington. Neither venture had prospered. I smugly became convinced of my superiority to my provincially educated compatriots. As for John Allan, he sank into debt, where he remained until the timely death of an uncle made him one of the richest men in the Commonwealth.

"Eddie? Is it you?" cried Ebenezer Burling. When we were children I had been his idol. Now I saw a tall man of one-and-twenty, tow-headed and freckled as the day I had taught him to swim. And *he* saw a man of middle height who, despite his bloody-footed limp, carried himself erect—the legacy of West Point—but otherwise looked, "I swear, like an escaped convict," said Ebenezer Burling. He saw a face so badly in need of a shave that it was difficult to tell where side-whiskers left off and five-day smear of beard began, saw a large head covered with dark and matted hair, saw a worn and dusty black coat buttoned to the neck over a black stock, no overcoat, no hat, no gloves, "Good Lord, no boots," cried Ebenezer Burling. "Look at your feet, Eddie, come in, come in, are you back to stay?"

"I am in Richmond to see Mr. Allan."

Ebenezer led me to the kitchen of the two-story frame house, where he worked the pump handle, bending his head unnecessarily to the task. Then he looked up. "Mr. Allan is no longer young, Eddie."

"He is not well?"

"They guard their privacy. It is said he suffers from the dropsy."

By then I was wrapped in a blanket. A darkie girl had borne off my clothes to attack them with carpet beater, brush, sponge, and flatiron while I washed with cold water and a bar of strong soap and shaved with Eb's razor.

"All the more reason to see him."

"Well, it might be wise to stop here until you have recovered from your journey."

Eb fetched coffee, a whole pot, also the better part of a pecan pie. Watching me wolf it down, he smiled suddenly. "Remember the pecan pie we gave my sister, topped with 'whipped cream,' only it was shaving soap?"

I smiled at his smile.

The darkie returned with my clothes. Eb helped me don them. "You look almost respectable," he said, "from the ankles up, anyways."

"If I might borrow a pair of boots," I said.

"Mine? My feet are the size of canal boats."

"Mine are swollen."

"*And* bruised, *and* bloody," he said as he brought the boots.

I sat to lace them. When I rose, a wave of dizziness almost made me sit down again.

Eb said, "You ought to stay the night."

But I shook my head.

Did I wish to present a pitiable figure to my foster father? I do not think so. Exhaustion, like drink, imparts to the tongue a glibness; sufficient, I hoped, to persuade John Allan of the virtues of generosity until I was established in my career.

Ebenezer Burling gave me an ebony walking stick with silver ferrule. I tried for a jaunty stride.

I was walking with a slight limp along a sycamore-lined street halfway from the Burling house to the Allan mansion at the corner of Fifth and Main when a carriage came to a stop perhaps fifty feet ahead. Its dappled horse wore a gay scarlet plume. The Negro driver hurried down, but the carriage door opened before he could reach it and a boy of four or five jumped out.

"Alex, you will wait for Amos to assist you."

"But Mommie I can open the door I'm a big boy," declared Alex.

"None the less, you must learn to wait."

The Negro coachman by then stood holding the open door.

I ducked behind a tree. I could feel the blood pounding in my ears, my throat.

The day was warm for mid-February. The little boy wore a dark tunic cinched at the waist by a leather belt and flaring over minia-ture nankeen trousers. I saw his mother's black patent-leather boots and a swirl of petticoats and a flat, beribboned hat and then her face.

"One hour, Amos," Elmira Royster—no, Elmira Royster Shelton—said. Taking the boy's hand, she went along a walk bor-dered by boxwood and climbed onto a porch and disappeared into a house.

And I stood a long time pressed against the sycamore's scabrous bark. Well, I knew that she had married, knew that she had a son (and a daughter too, who would be a babe in arms), knew that her hair was the darkest color you still could call amber, knew that her eyes were blue, her nose but slightly retroussé, knew that her thin, downward-curving lips, so suited to her patrician, almost haughty face, once had parted avidly under my lips, knew . . .

"Charlottesville is not so far," I had said.

"Write to me often."

"I shall."

And I had, in the beginning. But she had not in turn written.

I watched Amos fill the muzzle bag, then continued on my way to the corner of Fifth and Main, trying to convince myself that not very much had happened.

The mansion was called Moldavia and stood on a hill overlooking the river and the woods beyond. The portico rose two stories, and on the upper porch John Allan had installed a telescope, to spy, some said, upon the activities at the state capitol. Of out-buildings there were eight among the flower gardens, fig trees, and grape vines. Moldavia always put me in my place: less a member of the family than a dependent with cap in hand, ready to tug his forelock.

I pulled the bell, heard footsteps inside, expected a liveried darkie, was surprised when a white woman dressed all in black like me (was she in mourning?) opened the door. She was not small, but the vast doorway made her seem so.

"Oh! I was expecting Dr. Provis."

"I must see Mr. Allan on a matter of urgency," I said, looking at a jowly face, its bulbous nose and fleshy lips set in the parentheses of deep grooves of discontent. But perhaps, on the subject of her plainness, I protest too much. I met her only that one time and our interests did not coincide.

"It is not possible that you see him."

"He is ill?"

"He is very ill, I fear. Not to be disturbed under any circumstances."

I said, "I am Edgar Poe," and her dull eyes widened. Before she could shut the huge door I pushed my way inside and swiftly mounted the mahogany staircase, and went along the corridor to my foster father's bedroom. Gas lamps had been installed, and were lit against the dimness. Such a harsh glare and offensive smell of gas would never have profaned Moldavia in the days of the first Mrs. Allan. For her the only proper indoor lighting was an old-fashioned astral lamp, an Argand, that glowed soft as moonlight through its ground-glass shade. But again it may be that I protest too much. Frances Allan had always treated me as a son, had *loved* me as a son is loved, whatever my differences with her husband.

At the door to the sick-room, the second Mrs. Allan caught my arm. I turned. In the gas light, *like* the gas light, her dull eyes glittered. I shook her off, and with a cry she stepped around me to bar my way. I raised a hand. It held the ebony stick. She cowered and I went in.

John Allan was rising with difficulty from an armchair near the tall window. I could see the glossy green leathery leaves of a tulip tree behind him and the still tightly closed purple fleshy buds.

"What do you want here?"

Had I prepared a glib speech craving his financial support? Did I intend to improvise? Now that I stood before him, I had no words. I may have reached out a hand importunately. At any rate, why I was there could be seen on my face, and he shouted past me: "How many times have I told you, no niggers and no beggars?"

He had always the visage of a hawk, the keen, small eyes under shaggy brows, the hooked nose that made the jaw so negligible, and his disease accentuated this. His thin hair had gone white and stuck up like ruffled feathers, his eyelids were swollen hoods, his head darted in pointless motion on the stalk of a neck.

"No niggers," he repeated.

The woman made a sound. Then she went around me and was at his side.

"Leave us," she said.

"Sir, it's Eddie," I said.

"Eddie? Eddie? Sent the little bastard to school at Stoke . . . Stoke, yes, and that did him no good, by God. Sent him to the University of Virginia, where he drank himself into a continuous stupor and got himself horsewhipped for cheating at cards. Sent—"

"Sir, that is not true."

"*Sent* him to West Point, thinking that would make a man of him, but the little bastard's nature rebels at discipline. Should have known. Eating his poor aunt Maria out of house and home, last I heard. Last he *wrote.* How I abhor geniuses . . . arrant asses . . . eccentric prattling fools . . ."

"Sir, I have come to—"

"Make a man out of a genius? Might as well try to get money from a Jew."

"*Will* you leave?" said his wife.

"Geniuses and niggers," said my foster father.

I heard a heavy tread along the corridor. A portly gentleman appeared in the doorway.

"Mrs. Allan," he said with some asperity, "visitors can do the patient no good, no good at all."

"It was not my idea, Dr. Provis, that he have one."

"Sir, you will do us the courtesy of leaving."

I did them the courtesy.

"Like trying to make a nutmeg from a pine knot," said John Allan, his voice following me along the gas-lit corridor. "Niggers and geniuses. You tell him if you see him, boy, hear?"

Five

There are certain themes of which the interest is all-absorbing, but which are entirely too horrible for the purposes of legitimate fiction. . . . As inventions, we should regard them with simple abhorrence.
—"The Premature Burial"

Sometimes anywhere is better than here. . . .

I must learn not to believe every thing I write.

For what is anywhere but another here, waiting to happen? And why should I expect the next here to be better than the last? Or why, of a multitude of possible anywheres, does this one, and not some other, become the new here?

Once Elmira asked me, "Why do you move so much without *going* anywhere?"

"Because I cannot pay the rent," I said. That was an answer I knew would satisfy her.

In the anywhere I have happened upon, now my new here, I sit, feverish, my back against the damp brick wall, palm-leaf hat tilted over my eyes, pretending still to sleep. A grubby gray dawn smears the high small windows. There was a commotion last night, my second in the coop. Running footfalls, shouts. Something banged. A lamp flared, searching. Faces leaped out of the darkness. Voices complained. Now the lamp still burns. During the night one of us prisoners—for what else are we?—

escaped. The banging was of a door, a small door in the rear of the building.

"Picked the lock," says one prisoner admiringly, "easy as you'd pick yer teeth. From the *outside.*"

"The outside?"

"He was already out."

"How'd he *git* out?"

"Winder."

"Way up there?"

"It was the one they call Sweeps on account of he used to be one."

"One whut?"

"Chimney sweep. He clumb up to the winder."

"And gits out and picks the lock to come right back in?"

"The way I see it, he wanted back in to git something he forgot, or else there's two of 'em wanted out, and the second ain't no chimney sweep."

The burly overseer, acting on the first possibility, is ransacking the warehouse with the help of an inmate named Lionel Lilly. Lionel Lilly is a big man, almost as big as Monk. I see Monk sitting at the base of a stanchion, a lazy smile on his scarred face. Because he disdains the search, the inmates are uncooperative.

"Give us a hand," says the burly overseer.

"I have lost nothing," Monk says.

Every verminous pile of straw is poked and prodded, every man's clothing gone through. There will be no thin coffee this morning, no gin and water. The coop is crowded now, its population doubled since my arrival. Each newcomer has been greeted by rough and raucous hazing that stops always short of violence. But each, within an hour or two, is accepted. They belong. I do not belong. Even if I now wear the befouled rags of a dead man, I am still the man in the white suit. And do not forget the white shoes! In their eyes I am of another class. They will never trust me.

Yet among my own kind I am déclassé—an irony they would not understand here.

Once, my very good friend Rufus Griswold was happy to relate, Horace Greeley said of me: "We know what he is."

Did he mean a drunkard?

Or a danger to women (and adolescent girls)?

Or not just unworldly but unearthly (as another friend would say of me)?

Rufus Griswold did not specify.

A shoe pokes me. I tilt up the palm-leaf hat to see Lionel Lilly. They say he killed a man in the prize ring in Perth Amboy, New Jersey, after 120 savage rounds, and never fought again. His is a battered ruin of a face, so what they say could well be true.

"On yer feet."

My straw is not just prodded, but taken apart.

"Out of yer clothes."

No one else has been ordered to strip.

With a will that surprises me, I fold my arms across my chest and shake my head. Lionel Lilly grabs me by the throat. Other inmates, their own lesser indignities forgotten, offer vociferous encouragement.

"Shut up, the lot of you!" a voice shouts; Monk's voice.

"What are you looking for?" he demands of Lionel Lilly.

"I reckon I'll know when I find it," says Lilly.

"You have it?" Monk asks me.

I manage to gasp, "Have it? I don't even know what it is."

"Let go of him," Monk tells Lionel Lilly.

I am slammed back against the wall. I slide down. Lionel Lilly moves on; Monk, back to where he was seated.

After the search uncovers nothing, the burly overseer hunkers next to me. "You're a man of education," he says. "What do you make of it?"

I shrug.

"What worries me," he says, "he could of been one of Ryan's boys."

"Who is Ryan?"

"Believe me, you will learn who Ryan is if his boys find us. It is a question, plain and simple, of politics. Like every thing else. There's eighty of you, and you will vote in the elections unless Ryan's boys stop you."

"How would they stop us?"

"How? Brickbats, cudgels, is how." He looks at me. "What are you doing here?" he asks me. "A gent like you?"

"I'm on ice until the elections, same as the rest."

He gives me another look. "You ain't forgot your addresses?"

"I assure you," I say, "that I am capable of remembering three names and three street addresses."

"Long as you remember them when it's time to vote. If Ryan don't stop us first. Yep, all a question of politics."

Once I had an appointment to see President Tyler in Washington City. Would the other prisoners here believe that? Missed opportunities are commonplace in their lives. So is bad luck. So are influential men who can bring you down with a word spoken or withheld; or treacherous men, with chicanery. Palm-leaf hat tilted over my eyes, I have heard them speak of these things.

I have heard: "Mr. James Gordon Bennett of the *New York Herald*, as was always Cock-eyed Jimmy to me. Why, all I need to do is knock on Mr. James Gordon Bennett's door in New York, where I used to be in newspapers, and he'd ast me in to cut his mutton with him and give me a gold eagle to boot. Because he knows it's only luck—with luck I could be settin' where he is and him settin' here 'steada me. Cock-eyed Jimmy."

And I have heard: "I was a-saving up to buy me a quarter section of that *un*credible Mississippi bottomland, soil so rich you can't keep up with how fast the cotton grows, but I got swindled by a land jobber right here in Ballimer."

I have also heard: "Oh, that P. T. Barnum. Smooth? Talk the stripes clean off of a tiger. He sez to me, exhibit your General Tom Thumb with me—see, I started out being the little feller's manager—and I'll make you rich. The upshot being, he takes the midget away from me, and my other half runs off with the sword swallower in his show. P. T. Barnum. Yessir. Talk the stripes clean off of a tiger."

I have it on good authority that, armed with my invitation to see President Tyler, I passed two hours at the President's House. But that is a long way from becoming Minister to Spain, like Washington Irving.

"What is the worst thing you ever did?" Palm-leaf hat tilted down over my eyes, I hear this question asked. Not of me. The details of my biography are writ to their satisfaction by the white suit. Would it change their perception of me if they learned I habitually wore black?

The worst thing you ever did in this life. Well?

It is a question they almost seem to enjoy answering. Perhaps, like missed opportunities and bad luck, like influential and treacherous men, to answer is to explain why they are here. Who can argue with divine retribution?

Lionel Lilly's answer is easy. He beat an opponent to death while thousands cheered in Perth Amboy, New Jersey.

(Once I took the railroad cars with my wife from Philadelphia to Perth Amboy. We crossed the Hudson by steamboat to New York and she waited aboard while I found us lodgings in Greenwich Street.)

The one who calls himself Peto confesses to deserting his wife and five children during the Panic of '37. He returned two years later to learn that all his children had died of diphtheria.

(My bride was a child, but it was not diphtheria that would take her.)

Monk, who usually keeps to himself, surprisingly enters the conversation. He tells a story well, the ennui gone from his voice. Fingering the scar on his face, he relates how, drinking with a shipmate one night in the only seaport on an island in the Malay Archipelago, he heard talk of an aboriginal people reputed to possess a great treasure. Monk and his shipmate hired a Malay guide, and in the central highlands they found the Yaanek, a tribe who worshiped a stone idol which, Monk tells us, resembled a statue of Poseidon he once saw in Athens—except that instead of a trident the Malay god carried a huge parang the exact crescent shape of the scar Monk would soon have on his face.

After a few days among the Yaanek, Monk and his shipmate determined that their hosts had few possessions and no treasure. Monk's shipmate owned a bar-hammer pepperbox pistol, which one of the aborigines stole. On finding the thief, Monk was content to thrash him, but his shipmate, perhaps angry that they had come so far for nothing, insisted on teaching the aborigines a lesson. Loading the unwieldy pistol, he discharged all seven chambers at the stone god. There was, Monk says, a blinding flash stronger than sunlight. When it faded, there remained no sign that the idol had ever been, except for a few shards scattered on the altar where it had stood.

The aborigines were stricken with such horror that they did nothing to stop Monk and his shipmate from leaving. When they reached the camp where the Malay waited, Monk found he had a crescent scar—it looked an old scar and was quite painless—on his face; his shipmate, who had carried off one of the shards of the shattered god, had begun to cough blood. They returned through the jungle to the coast.

On his next trip to the Orient, Monk learned that the tribe, fasting in the hope of persuading its shattered god to return, had starved itself almost to extinction.

(As far as I know, my brother Henry never sailed to the Malay Archipelago. And although few were manufactured, the bar-hammer pepperbox pistol he showed me can hardly have been unique. Still, I cannot bring myself to ask Monk the name of his shipmate, to ask him whether he twice came to my rescue because I remind him of Henry.)

A pugilist who slaughtered his opponent in the prize ring.

A father who abandoned his children to a frightful death.

Two seamen (one my brother?) who, by shattering a god, annihilated an entire tribe.

What links them? Death is their common denominator, their benchmark, their touchstone.

So, were I to speak, it hardly would surprise anyone if I said that I had killed my wife.

Six

. . . the agonies which are, have their origin in the ecstasies which might have been.

—"Berenice"

A single memory of my cousin Virginia—Virginia sitting on the cold attic floor in her shift, hands clasping her knees, listening to the scratching of my pen and saying she could hear the words I was writing—this single memory, I often think, is what kept me from completely unraveling in the months after John Allan died.

My foster father's rejection of me was as complete in death as in life. I had not expected a grand legacy, but I had expected *something.* Even a token from one of the wealthiest men in the Commonwealth of Virginia would have been of help to one of the poorest. But I was not mentioned in John Allan's will.

I cadged money where I could, and I slept rough until I slept in the back room of the Alhambra Tavern, where in return for washing up I could drink as much as I wished, and I developed a cough and was mildly curious to see if it might become the consumption which had killed my mother and my brother Henry (who, I would learn later, may have killed a god), but the cough ran its course, and Ebenezer Burling chanced upon me at the Alhambra and took to taking me home to dinner, and I stopped drinking sufficiently to apply for a position as a teacher of English at the Richmond Academy, but the job went to someone else. And all of this, I suppose, is what a biographer means when he writes that his subject disappeared from history—"from biographical view" is a fancier locution—for some months. Or years. Invisible to history, I still saw that image of my cousin Virginia by candle light, hands clasping her knees as she listened to the scratching of my pen, and I saw it still when I got work with the *Southern Literary Messenger,* published by a self-educated, inoffensive printer who shall remain nameless here,* who aspired to elevate the taste of literate Southerners, and especially of literate Southern travelers who required something easily disposable to pass the time during long rail journeys. Hidden from biographical view, I corrected the *Messenger*'s proofs, I dealt with the correspondence, I wrote the critical notices. I was paid fifteen dollars a week, which did not deter me from disputing his taste-elevating theories with the Inoffensive Publisher.

"If you wish to increase your circulation," I would suggest, "lighten the type-face of these funereal columns."

"Fill the paste pot, Edgar," the Inoffensive Publisher would say.

"To be influential, you must be read," I would opine. "And to be read, you must offer sensational subjects in a style that will dazzle, that will mesmerize your readers."

"We need a filler for page seven, Edgar." And the Inoffensive Publisher would rise from his chair, both creaking, to approach me and say, "Your counsels, Edgar, I have observed, are, alas, abundant when you have been drinking."

And before I could concede that he might be right, he would pronounce, sweating and florid in the heat of a summer morning in the cramped office of the *Messenger*, "No man can do a reliable day's work who drinks as you do."

For the Inoffensive Publisher was a devoted subject of Her whom he called "that chaste empress, Temperance," and he would often cross to the side of the room where I sat, away from the window, and sniff the air like a hound dog and nod and mumble acerbically, "Knew it."

Sometimes, brandishing the latest issue of the *Messenger*, he would shout, "The South is awakening!" and I would say, "If you hope to keep it awake, the merely strange should become the mystical and marvelous," and he would sigh and tell me, "Answer the correspondence, Edgar," and I would answer it, glaring at him from time to time as we both sweated in the sultry afternoon, and when he glared back it was inoffensively.

If I was frustrated by my work I was never the less glad to have

* Thomas Willis White. (Editor's note)

it, and nights at the boarding house where I rented a small room I wrote tales in which I tried to make the strange become the mystical and marvelous.

One afternoon a tall girl of about eighteen with blond hair and blue eyes walked into the *Messenger*'s office and so enthusiastically planted a kiss on the Inoffensive Publisher's cheek that I half expected and certainly hoped she would do likewise to me. My employer did not introduce her. Whenever she visited, which was often, I simply ceased to exist.

She arrived late one morning a few minutes after the Inoffensive Publisher had gone to have his hair cut. I looked up from the review I was writing of a novel.

"Please don't stop. I had not meant to interrupt you."

With my quill pen I was assailing, even more than the unworthy novel at my elbow, the other reviewers who had shamelessly lauded it because, I wrote, it was the work of one of their own, a member in good standing of the New York literati, that overgrown, self-congratulating flock of complacent magisterial geese.

"Oooh," said the blond girl, reading over my shoulder, enveloping us both in a scent of gardenias.

I continued to write. I fear that my hand, usually so clear, wavered.

"You must be . . . Edgar Poe?"

"I am."

"I'm Elizabeth. Daddy says you are very . . . opinionated?"

She whirled to the window and back. Her blond hair swung, and the ribbons of her broad straw bonnet. She clapped a hand to the crown to keep the hat from flying off.

"He also says your . . . critiques have brought the *Messenger* . . . a goodly number of new readers?"

Whenever she paused, perhaps searching for the right word, she would lick her red lips.

"He also says you are very . . . bold to be so outspoken?"

And she whirled, and her hair swung the scent of gardenias like an acolyte swinging incense. I did not feel very bold.

"Also very . . . handsome?" She smiled. She had deep dimples.

She had long eyelashes. They fluttered. "Not that my daddy said *that*," and she laughed and whirled again to the window just as the Inoffensive Publisher came in the door.

Later he told me, "You will keep away from my daughter."

My cheeks burned. I said nothing.

"No offense, Edgar. But you are a drinking man."

Nights, I wrote less and went to the Alhambra more. Maudlinly I began to pine for the only family I still had, my aunt Maria Clemm, and her daughter, who had been able to hear in the scratching of my pen the sound of my words. I wrote increasingly often to Baltimore, and Maria Clemm wrote back. I would not believe, she said, what a little lady my cousin Virginia, at thirteen, had become. But things were difficult. The state of Maryland, finally taking account of the demise years before of my grandmother, the widow of General Poe, had terminated the small pension that, along with the sewing Maria Clemm took in, kept the wolf from the door. Could I spare a trifle? I sent what I could and day-dreamed of renting a little cottage here in Richmond where my aunt and my cousin could live under my protection. *They* had taken *me* in, had they not?

By and by I found a small house on a slight rise of ground from which you could see canal boats plying the James River. There was a bedroom for Maria and Virginia to share, and an attic for me. In the tiny parlor stood a pianoforte. I could almost hear my cousin Virginia playing it, singing, her deep blue eyes asparkle with pleasure. The rent, though reasonable, was more than half my salary. I would let the estate agent know.

Returning in high spirits to my boarding house, I found a letter from Maria Clemm on the hall table, and in it was devastating news. The next morning, telling the Inoffensive Publisher that pressing family business called me away, I took the stage for Baltimore.

"Guardian? You would willingly abandon your own daughter to him?"

"Your cousin Neilson has money. As his ward, Virginia would live in a lovely home. Look around you, Eddie."

I did. I saw a mean boarding-house room, not much bigger than my own and cluttered with the same cheap furniture worn out by the same failed, anonymous lives. But it was clean; it was spotless; it gleamed. Maria Clemm may have come down in the world, but she was still an impeccable housekeeper.

"Your cousin Neilson would educate her and introduce her to polite society. Here she must help me with that." "That" was a sewing basket and a stack of piecework. "He is a responsible family man who—"

"John Allan was a responsible family man, and I never felt more than an unwelcome stranger, in his house on sufferance. Is that what you wish for Virginia?"

"Neilson is not John Allan, Eddie. Neilson is blood kin to us all. *And*, I remind you, his wife was my husband's daughter. They have called me Muddy for years. I trust him."

"What can he do for Virginia that I cannot?"

"You are not—forgive me—you are not altogether *established*, in Richmond or anywhere. Your cousin Neilson is a lawyer. He owns a successful newspaper. He wishes to sponsor Virginia. Who knows? In time an eligible suitor might present himself."

"It all sounds so crass."

"Neilson would be like a father to her."

"He is hardly old enough. He is my age."

"And twice Virginia's." My aunt's deep-set eyes studied me. "Why do you resist the idea so, Eddie?"

At that moment the door opened and my cousin Virginia burst into the room. Her face was flushed. I saw droplets of perspiration where her dark brown hair fell over her forehead. She brought in with her the faint and contradictory scents of youth and musk. Had she been running? Playing? "Eddie!" she blurted, and I realized as never before how sweet was her voice. Her eyes smiled up at me as she bobbed in a charming little curtsy. When she rose, the crown of her head barely reached my chin, and I am not tall. But she was no longer a child, if not yet a woman. Her figure was plump and pretty. She rose on tiptoe to kiss my cheek, and as she did so I could feel against me the warm contours of her bosom. I stepped quickly back.

Maria Clemm was watching me. Her eyes slid down from my face and up again.

"Oh, Muddy, is he going to stay?" Virginia said.

I stayed for tea, bread, and blackstrap. The subject of our cousin Neilson's offer was not discussed again. Virginia's laughter filled the room. I felt confused and angry. I saw in my mind's eye the little house on its hill in Richmond overlooking the river. I did not want to lose it. But it was no house I needed for myself. What did I need a house for?

Neilson would be like a father to her.

He is hardly old enough. He is my age.

I can stop him, I thought. There is a way I can stop him.

Seven

I was a child and *she* was a child,
In this kingdom by the sea.
                    —"Annabel Lee"

The trap took us at a lively trot from the steamboat landing along Hopewell's single street.

"It's a Morgan," said Virginia. "I think the horse is a Morgan."

"Yes, so it is," said I.

"Are those plum trees?"

"No. Peach."

"Of course. How silly of me."

I announced that it was a fine day, if warm. Virginia informed me that the woods were beautiful. She craned her neck for a last look at the landing. "That's odd," said she.

"What is odd?" said I.

"The smoke from the steamboat. It was a dense black cloud as we approached the landing. But now the boat is leaving and it's just plain smoke again."

"Pitch pine," said I.

"Pitch pine?"

"They throw pitch pine into the furnace to make the smoke black."

"Why?"

"To say 'Look at me,' I suppose."

I looked at her. She wore a poke bonnet with a gossamer white veil, and a sheer white muslin canezou, much embroidered, over her tight bodice. All this finery had been sewn by Muddy.

"Have you been to Hopewell before?" Virginia asked.

"No," I answered.

"No, I did not think so. It's not an especially large town—more a village. But attractive."

"For a stop along the river," said I.

"I can smell the sea," said she.

"The tidewater, actually. The tide rises into the river, you see."

"Aah," said she. "Of course. The tidewater."

The driver asked, "Y'all newlyweds?"

Virginia clutched my arm. She blushed.

"I got a knack of tellin' newlyweds," said the driver, and the trap stopped in front of Hopewell's only boarding house. From the little schoolhouse next door a woman's voice called, "Chil*dren*!" and Virginia looked at once in that direction, where a dozen or so youngsters drifted across the yard and inside.

The driver took down our carpet-bags, and, to the creaking of springs, I handed Virginia out of the trap.

The bed was an enormous four-poster that filled most of the room, and at the slightest provocation it creaked too. I learned this when I set our carpet-bags upon it. Virginia stood with her back to the door.

The chatter in the trap had given way to an uncomfortable silence. Virginia coughed. "Pardon me," she said, and I assured her it was quite all right.

We both listened attentively to the small sounds a sleepy hamlet on the river will make in the late afternoon. I made a show of examining the wash stand, Virginia the wallpaper.

"Some tea might be refreshing after the journey," I said.

"I couldn't face the landlady."

"But why?"

"I couldn't bear her to look at me that way again."

"Which way? I'm sure she thought you a most beautiful bride."

"She was smirking at me. Just like the Reverend Mr. Converse."

The Reverend Mr. Converse had joined us in matrimony in Richmond, in our rooms in the boarding house where we would live with Muddy. The little cottage with its view of canal boats carrying coal on the James had been let to someone else.

"Nonsense," I said. But I spoke the word gently.

"He smirked when he read our marriage bond. The part that said I was 'of the full twenty-one years.' "

I smiled. "Had it said sixteen, he might have questioned it."

"Don't I look even *sixteen?*" Virginia cried.

"Of course you do. More than sixteen. That isn't what I meant."

Virginia suddenly giggled.

"What?"

"Elizabeth. She took me aside and said if there was any thing I wished to know of wifely matters, I had only to ask her."

The Inoffensive Publisher and his daughter had witnessed our marriage. Muddy was in attendance too, of course, snuffling back tears.

"Elizabeth tell me of wifely matters and her not even married?" scoffed Virginia. Then her lips pursed, pensively. "Do you suppose she . . . there are women, or so I have heard, fast women who . . ." And she stopped, flustered.

"Perhaps," I said, "she has friends who are married and talk of such things," and I smiled again, and Virginia said, "She is very beautiful, and so tall."

I said, "Not half so beautiful as you. And as for tall, you are still growing."

"Because I'm still a child. Oh, Eddie!" And my bride began to cry. I crossed the room and produced my handkerchief, and she blew her nose daintily and then hard. As the room's single chair looked uncomfortable, I led her gently to that dominating bed. Obediently she sat, though on its very edge. It creaked. She leaped to her feet. Then sat again.

"Tired?" I asked her.

"No. Yes. I don't know. I did not ask her, Eddie."

"Ask who what?"

"Elizabeth. But Muddy told me."

"Told you—?"

"To do whatever you wanted me to do, because you are my husband. Oh, Eddie, what do you want me to do?"

"I want you to have a good rest. And then we'll eat supper. It's served at seven o'clock."

"I *am* tired," said Virginia.

From the door I waved. Virginia blew me a kiss.

I walked through the village and along the road a mile or so into the piney woods. Returning, I paused outside Hopewell's only tavern. I heard masculine voices, laughter. I walked on. It was later than I had thought. I looked into the boarding-house dining room. The other guests were already eating. Our two empty places were conspicuous. A man at the far end of the table leered at the newlywed. "You will join us?" asked the landlady. Ten minutes, I told her.

But Virginia was asleep. She had unpacked our bags. She slept curled on her side with one fist under her plump cheek. Her face was pretty in repose, if marred by an adolescent's complexion. A feeling of unreality engulfed me. I was married. Why had I married? My bride was a child. Why had I married her? She was my cousin. My father's sister's daughter. But cousin marriages were not uncommon. She was thirteen. I quickly amended that to virtually fourteen, as if the additional almost-year made all the difference. I leaned over the bed and blew softly at the dark brown curls falling over one cheek. She stirred. Her eyes fluttered open and she looked up at me in momentary panic.

"It's supper time."

She sat, pulling the counterpane to her chin. "I'm not hungry, Eddie. You eat."

I told her that I too was not particularly hungry, and I sat on the edge of the bed. Which, of course, creaked. Virginia slid away from me, holding tight the counterpane, but I glimpsed one bare shoulder. She was wearing only her shift.

We talked. I do not remember about what. By and by one of Virginia's white arms emerged from under the counterpane. I took her hand; brought it to my lips. She made a little sound. She shut her eyes. Her lips parted.

Heavy post-prandial footfalls came up the stairs and past our door. Virginia's hand withdrew. Her eyes opened wide and she looked past me at the door, as if afraid it might open. Both her arms were under the counterpane again. I lay on my side, facing her, propped on one elbow. She smiled, and again her hand emerged. I had not removed my boots. Thinking that to do so now might break whatever spell was in the making, I left them on. She reached for my hand.

There came through the window the bellow of a pole-axed steer. Virginia gasped. Her hand dived under the counterpane.

"It's only a bullfrog, yonder by the river," I said.

"I'm such a baby."

"You are my darling little wife."

I wished I had not spoken, wished I could call back my avuncular tone.

The daylight faded. Virginia dozed. Thinking she would be frightened if she awoke in darkness, I rose and struck a lucifer and lit the four candles in the sconce near the door. They did not burn cleanly. Tallow, not spermaceti. I could smell the tallow. This irritated me until I reminded myself that the room, after all, cost only a dollar fifty a day.

From the bed Virginia called softly, "No, please blow them out. And do remove your boots, Eddie." Her voice was small but determined.

The bed, of course, creaked when I resumed my place upon it. In what light remained I could see the rise and fall of Virginia's breast under the counterpane. Her breathing was agitated. I touched the counterpane. Something was different. Something had changed. I could not at first identify it, for the smell of tallow all but overwhelmed that other scent, just the suggestion of which began to excite me. I threw back the counterpane and reached for my wife and she cried out at my impetuosity and I smelled gardenias and imagined her whirling to the window and back, hair swinging scent like an acolyte swinging incense until it filled the room and I know not what might have come to pass had I been more gentle with my child-bride, her dark brown hair spread on the pillow and tears on her cheeks and her plump little body so rigid under me that I rolled off her as she said Eddie oh Eddie what did I do wrong tell me what to do and I will do it but I said you hush now it doesn't have to be now.

In the morning a darkie girl brought up the tray laden with a platter of fried eggs and rashers of bacon and ham, a bowl of hominy grits, steaming pitchers of coffee and milk, and enough buttermilk biscuits for a dozen newlyweds. She set the tray upon the small table and bid us a good morning, tittering as she left.

Virginia had surprised me by sleeping soundly. I know because I did not. But she only picked at her breakfast, while I ate like a horse. Soon we were gazing at each other as if from a great distance, Virginia wrapped in the counterpane and seated on the edge of the bed, I on the room's single chair. A blue-bottle fly flew against the window glass, buzzing frantically. I got up, raised the sash, and let it out. The morning was cool and fresh. A dray loaded with sacks of grain went slowly by. I heard the steamboat's bell, two brazen notes. Dense black smoke rose above the river.

In the schoolyard, girls hardly younger than Virginia were skipping rope and chanting,

> *"Sugar, salt, pepper, cider,*
> *How many legs has a bow-legged spider?"*

"Oh, I know that one," said Virginia, and I shut the window.

The morning crawled by. The room grew warm. Dinner time came. We could hear convivial voices downstairs, and laughter.

"Shall we?" I asked.

"I'm not hungry. They would stare at me. They would make sly jokes."

I had to get out. I needed a walk, I told myself. But I knew I meant a drink.

"Are you going to dinner?"

"No. For a walk. Would you like to come?"

"I'll have a nap."

It was two hours before I returned past the schoolyard, more or less sober. The schoolgirls were skipping rope and sing-songing,

> *"Georgie Porgie, pudding and pie,*
> *Kissed the girls and made them cry;*
> *When the girls came out to play,*
> *Georgie Porgie ran away,"*

and I saw Virginia in profile in the shadow of a magnolia, looking no older than they in her bridal finery, an expression of longing on her face so intense that I had to turn away from it. I was close enough to hear her say, "Do Eddie, do Eddie, do Eddie," in a soft urgent voice, and whether the schoolgirls heard her I cannot say, but when they began skipping rope again they chanted,

> *"Eddie Beddie, pudding and pie,*
> *Kissed the girls and made them cry;*
> *When the girls came out to play,*
> *Eddie Beddie ran away,"*

and that night I said again, "It doesn't have to be now." And it wasn't the next night either, and the day after that it rained all day, and the next day it was still raining as we took the steamboat back to Richmond.

Eight

Through the pale door
A hideous throng rush out forever,
And laugh—but smile no more.
                    —"The Haunted Palace"

Election day dawns—if such is the appropriate word—more like a
bleak December morning than one in early October. The storm-
roiled waters of Chesapeake Bay slap and smash against pilings
outside the coop. The wind blows a fitful melancholy dirge, rattling rain like pebbles against the high small windows. Still, there
is an air of excitement. Today we inmates, or whatever we are,
shall be taken to vote for Congressional candidates about whom
we know nothing, and since our ignorance is utter, each of us will
vote three times. I myself shall vote first in the Fourth Ward under the cognomen of Phidias Peacock, who supposedly lives at 6
Mechanics Row. Then I shall vote in turn as Thomas W. Frederick
of 29 Portugal Street and C. Auguste Dupin (mispronounced *Doo*-
pin so that Baltimore's polling officials will be able to spell it)
of 3 Amity Street.* After exercising our franchises we shall be
dispersed into the streets of the city to confront or flee whatever
problems drove us here to this brief hiatus in our existence. Most
of us were glad to come and shall be as glad to go. Our enforced
camaraderie—I alone exempted from it—will not outlast the elections.

I sit shivering in my now habitual place, drinking thin coffee
laced with Jamaica rum and thinking of a Person from Porlock. How
lucky Mr. Samuel Taylor Coleridge was to have had one! (Or did he
invent him? No matter.) Coleridge awoke from an opium dream

* For Peacock, see footnote in Chapter 1; Thomas W. Frederick is an inversion of
the name of Poe's good friend the popular novelist and song writer Frederick W.
Thomas; C. Auguste Dupin is, to any reader of Poe's work, a name readily recognizable.
(Editor's note)

during which he composed his poem "Kubla Khan," and began to transcribe it from memory, only to be interrupted by this possibly apocryphal Person from Porlock. (Person indeed. Was it man, woman? Child? I do not believe Coleridge ever says.) The poem, with its fantastical imagery and tantalizing symbols, remains incomplete. And this unidentified intruder, not Coleridge the addict, receives the blame.

But then, Coleridge's vice was opium, not alcohol.

You can talk or write, as earnest and philosophical as you please, about an enslavement to opium. Coleridge tells us that he lived three years with a physician in an attempt to break the habit. And not too many years ago in his *Confessions of an English Opium Eater*, Mr. Thomas De Quincey, the late Mr. Coleridge's very good friend, in his sixties and still going strong as I write these lines, expatiated in splendidly embellished prose on his own addiction to the drug. His other addiction is contributing to *Blackwood's Magazine*, but we are none of us perfect.

Now consider the plight of the excessive drinker. He has no such license to wax philosophical, to expatiate in prose too good for *Blackwood's*. Your Coleridges and De Quinceys, so forthcoming about their addiction, are literary lights most welcome in polite society, where, it is presumed, they will not soil the Saxony carpets. The taking of opium is seen as a private affair, whereas the tavern or saloon, with its noise and stink, is a very public place. Does this explain why solicitude is lavished upon the confessional opium eater, and contumely upon the excessive drinker? Excessive drinker! Why not say "drunk," a word so onomatopoetically suggestive of a fall, perhaps from grace, at least down a flight of stairs?

I am a drunk. I must, of course, not write about this. To do so would be to defame my own self. *Why* am I a drunk? Ah, why! Have I come here, come to anywhere, *now* here, to take stock of myself? Do I not owe this to my future second wife, before I return to Richmond to marry her? Does she know of my addiction? She knows. How lucky are we poets and painters that there be women enough who believe that their love and understanding will render drink superfluous. Opium? That is another matter. Perhaps the women of opium eaters themselves become addicts, inasmuch as no opprobrium attaches to the appetite. As for women poets and painters, I cannot speak for their men except to say I am glad not to be one.

The rain slackens and the fellow in tall beaver hat and stone-gray French topcoat who recruited me to thrice do my patriotic duty comes to take a few of us out of hibernation.

"Hello there. Almost did not know you without the white suit."

These words are spoken with a smile, and he has a similar greeting for each of his other charges.

I hear from outside a soft whistle.

"Come along, then," says the fellow in the stone-gray topcoat, and we follow him to the corrugated metal door, which rises just enough for us to crouch through in our mis-matched clothing, as ragtag-and-bobtail a group of derelicts as you will ever see, and so back into the world.

Which is: a black sky; rain falling on a rutted muddy unpaved street; in the harbor the same row-boat, half sunk, or half afloat. But was there not, the night I came, a board-walk here, and a scale that shifted underfoot? Did the door not open vertically, hanging by a single hinge? I stand motionless, disoriented. The others continue forward, unconcerned. Do they not notice the changes? I have the singular notion that I am seeing the print of a photograph made from a plate twice exposed, but it does not last. Reality is reality; memory, faulty; the impossible, impossible. The world is, *must be*, what you see now.

I see now that the others are rounding a corner fifty or so yards ahead of me, and I hurry to overtake them, not from any sense of group spirit but because we all have been promised a dollar of folding money for each time we vote.

Approaching the corner, I hear shouting.

"There they are!"

"He's running away!"

"Get him!"

And back past me at a sprint comes the fellow in the stone-gray topcoat. "Ryan's boys!" he bellows. Ahead I hear more shouting, a single hoarse scream, pounding footsteps, stone striking stone (or brick, brick), and another not entirely dissimilar sound, but less resonant and, once identified, terrifying. This is the sound of hurled brickbats colliding with objects softer than themselves. A man—I recognize him as one of the inmates—comes staggering around the corner, head streaming blood, to collapse at my feet.

The harbor; I must reach the harbor. I am an excellent swimmer. Once I swam six miles in the James River against a strong tide under a boiling summer sun. In the water I will be safe. I whirl, to see that the stone-gray topcoat has fallen, and is trying to rise. I whirl the other way, to see something red and rectangular floating toward me through the rain, turning end over end. So slowly does it move that I will have more than enough time to dodge and see it float harmlessly into the wall, still turning end over end, and an instant later I will be in the harbor, swimming through chill water to safety.

Yet even as I think these thoughts I am aware that the object is a brick, and that nothing as heavy as a brick can remain aloft yet move so slowly. Have my senses been accelerated, then, imparting a spurious slowness to the hurtling brickbat? I step to one side and in my strangely speeded-up perceptions hardly seem to move at all (move and you will ruin the photograph), so that for those who can hear it (I am not among them) there comes that terrifying sound of a brickbat colliding with an object softer than itself.

Nine

What she is *not*, I can easily perceive; what she *is*, I fear it is impossible to say.
—"MS. Found in a Bottle"

I am engulfed, upon opening my eyes, in a bewilderment so total as to make me ignore for fully a minute the insistent hammer striking the anvil that is my head. When finally I reach up to touch gingerly the swelling under blood-matted hair, I conclude that the pain is responsible for my inability to locate myself or even to recall the events that have placed me here, wherever here is.

In appearance it is a muddy street where recently rain has fallen. And it is near the sea, for I can smell the sea. No, it is not the sea I smell; rather it is the edge of the sea. My brother, a sailor by calling, once told me that the open sea has no smell unless an exhilarating purity can be considered such.

My brother—I picture his face, so like my own, and I know that he is dead. Was he lost at sea? I do not remember. Was he . . . did he kill a god once? What does it mean, to kill a god? What god? I do not know the god's name. I realize then, with a sense of shock, that neither do I know the name of my brother.

I lie without moving, listen to the melancholy wind. How can I not remember my own brother's name?

What is *my* name?

I struggle to my feet, supporting myself against a rough surface. It is a wall of brick, red brick. Everywhere I go in this city I shall see, know I shall see, red brick. The city is Baltimore. I am in Baltimore.

My name is Phidias Peacock.

It is with a feeling approaching euphoria that I thus establish to my satisfaction my identity.

My name is Phidias Peacock. And?

But there is no "and."

The euphoria vanishes.

My name is Arthur Gordon Pym. My father was a respectable trader in sea-stores at Nantucket, where I was born. My maternal grandfather was an attorney. . . .

But this is no part of *my* background. Who is Arthur Gordon Pym? He is a fictional character, the protagonist of a long tale by Edgar A. Poe. "Chapter One: My name is Arthur Gordon Pym." But *my* name is Phidias Peacock. Am I a bookish sort of fellow, then, a reader of long narrative tales? Is that a place to start?

To spare time for the reading of such narratives—is that not a frivolous activity for a man of forty years to engage in? Surely I have work to do. But perhaps I am of independent means.

I am clad in rags. I pick up an old, ill-used palm-leaf hat that sits in the mud on its battered crown. So much for independent means.

My name is Phidias Peacock. And?

My name is Phidias Peacock. My father was headmaster of a distinguished preparatory school in New England. He was by avocation a sculptor and named me, his only son, for the greatest of all sculptors, the builder of the Parthenon on the Athenian Acropolis. My mother, a pious bluestocking distantly connected to the Lowells of Massachusetts, objected to the name. Phidias died in prison, she protested, while awaiting trial for sacrilege. Nonsense! said my father. Most great artists, in that they live by their wits in a Philistine society, are outlaws, and if the only crime of which Phidias the sculptor stood accused was sacrilege, he was a very law-abiding artist indeed.

Thus armed with the beginning of a life, putatively my own, I lean against brick and wait confidently for more to come. And more does.

My name is Phidias Peacock and I reside at 6 Mechanics Row.

With this knowledge to guide my steps, I begin at once to walk.

Number 6 is one of a row of identical red brick houses of two stories, each with an identical white marble stoop and an identical white front door, and all facing an identical row of houses across the narrow unpaved road, now a quagmire. I entertain momently the singular notion that there might be a multitude of identical Mrs. Phidias Peacocks, one behind each door.

The white marble stoop indicates no affluence; they are ubiquitous in this part of Baltimore, a neighborhood of drawn windowshades hiding shabbiness, perhaps squalor, within. Is this where I live?

I use the wrought-iron knocker, and wait. I let the knocker fall again. Silence. Might I have a latch key? A search of the rags I am wearing discloses nothing. I try the door.

It swings open.

"Hello?" I call. "Is anyone there?"

No response. I glance behind me and to either side, guiltily, half expecting someone to accuse me of trespassing. The rain has almost stopped; the muddy street is deserted. I try to dissuade myself from feeling guilty. I am Phidias Peacock, and I live here—do I not?

Yet try as I might, I can recall no aspect of the interior of the house.

"Is anyone there?" I call again. "It is I, Phidias."

The entrance hall is long and narrow. I can see a gilt-framed looking glass, a touch of unexpected luxury, as are the candles flanking it, burning in wall brackets. What delinquent housekeeper, departing, would leave them lit?

A third time I call, and a third time receive no response. Candle flames flicker and flare in the draft from the open door.

I square my shoulders and cross the threshold.

I am in no way prepared for what next occurs, even though it enters my mind then, like the memory of someone else's life, that I myself have written fiction containing such inexplicable happenings.*

My awareness of the *outré* commences with the vague sensation of an increased weight upon my shoulders, as if I have absentmindedly donned a coat, and with an equally vague sense of surprise at the clack upon the waxed wood flooring of my worn, paper-stuffed boots. I say vague because my thoughts, for a moment longer, are elsewhere: I still am not certain that the house is unoccupied.

Then I pass in front of the looking glass, and the barrier between the tales I have written and the world we all of us inhabit forever blurs.

Not that the reflection I see is anyone but myself. I see a man of middle height, slender, who carries himself well, as if trained to do so. The broad brow, the dark side-whiskers, the gray wary troubled eyes of Phidias Peacock, the severe line of the mouth—all are the face I am familiar with; *my* face. And still I gape. Do I cry out?

I am attired as follows:

Black frock coat meeting at the throat a black cravat; black beaver

* The reader is commended to Poe's *Tales of the Grotesque and Arabesque* (Philadelphia: Lea & Blanchard, 1839). (Editor's note)

hat; pigskin gloves—a gentleman's respectable if severe costume, complete but for stick, and carefully brushed and cared for.

Perhaps, I tell myself, the looking glass, in some way I cannot comprehend, is responsible for the apparent change in my attire. So I look away from it, and down—to see the gleam of black leather boots.

I raise one foot. The boot sole, although not new, is intact, *and bears not a trace of mud.*

This, of course, is impossible.

But I remind myself that I have recently struck my head or, even, been felled by an assailant. Under such fraught circumstances is it surprising that my senses are disturbed in ways I am at a loss to explain?

Have I myself not written—for so clamors again the memory of what seems another's mind—have I myself not written from the viewpoint of disturbed narrators, to confound my readers' ability to interpret events? Have not critics suggested that by using such artifice I have given birth to a new type of German or Gothic tale, in which uncertainty of perception generates macabre effects?

Now I am ironically aware that this uncertainty, which I have so often inflicted upon hapless characters and readers alike, is in turn happening to me. Perhaps I only *think* I am wearing the accustomed Phidias Peacock black and not the rags in which, on regaining consciousness, I found myself. Or perhaps—is this not more likely?— I imagined the rags. (I have for the moment forgotten the mudless state of my boots.)

Removing my black beaver hat, I reach up to touch the swelling beneath my blood-matted hair, to reassure myself by its presence that the world still obeys those natural laws that keep it from a chaos too fearful to contemplate. But the sound of a horse galloping into the street stays my hand.

I return to the door, which is shut. Have I shut it? I cannot recall.

The horse, by the sound, has ended its gallop outside this very house.

I lift a corner of the window shade to the left of the door and peer out to see, mounting the stoop, a tall, slender young woman in equestrian costume of black silk hat, black satin stock, smoke-gray jacket nipped at the waist, and, peeping out from under a full smoke-gray skirt that billows in the wind, white strap trousers and glossy black boots. Tucked under her right arm is a black riding crop. But I see no horse.

The young woman taps the door with the riding crop to announce herself, thus seeming to indicate she is no resident of 6 Mechanics Row. Am I?

Her blond hair swirls in disarray, and as I open the door, she claps a hand to the crown of her black silk hat to keep it from flying off her head.

"Good day," I greet her.

"Will!" she exclaims with the beginning of a smile that becomes a moue of disappointment. "Oh! For a moment I thought . . ."

"Yes?"

"I was mistaken." She clears her throat; I realize she is nervous. "I've come to apply for the position," she informs me.

"Ah, to be sure," I say, hoping for further enlightenment, but instead she sweeps past me in a studiedly haughty walk. Before following her I look outside to make absolutely certain: no horse.

She stands before the looking glass, angling the brim of her black silk hat just so. Suddenly her eyes, the same smoke-gray color as her riding habit, open wide, and so does her mouth.

"Is something the matter, Miss . . . ?" I ask, a twofold question.

She regards me levelly in the looking glass. Her face is flushed and the floral scent of her perfume all but obliterated by the smell of horse; she has been riding hard.

But then why is her costume as innocent of mud as my boots?

"Miss Tangerie," she says, and launches into a strange *curriculum vitae* in a breathless voice, rather like an ingenue auditioning for a theatrical role. "My family is of English extraction on my mother's side, God rest her, Franco-Italian on my father's. My grandfather made a fortune as a dealer in tropical hardwoods and in Gozo olives,

black Gozo olives I should say, only to lose it in the Panic of '18
. . . You are not listening."

I tell her she is mistaken.

"But people invariably ask what 'gozo' means."

"But I know where the island of Gozo is situated."

She does not ask how I am the possessor of such geographical
arcana. Instead: "Does the position entail travel?"

It seems wisest to answer question with question. "Would that
please you?"

"Oh yes sir! Very much."

During the course of this dialogue her eyes frequently seem drawn
to the looking glass.

"It may do so," I hazard.

"Might I inquire as to the nature of my duties? I assure you that
I am highly qualified."

"But if you don't know what is expected of you, how can you be
confident of your qualifications, Miss—Tangerie, is it?"

"Nolie Mae Tangerie." She pronounces her name in a self-satisfied
tone at odds with the anxious scrutiny she gives her own reflection
—as if to say that no matter how troubled she is by what she sees
in the looking glass, she finds her entire name entirely to her
satisfaction.

And I? For a third time I feel a surge of memory not my own—
is it a kind of hallucination?—which makes me ask: How can I,
creator of characters with such whimsically bestowed names as Dr.
Tarr and Professor Fether, Bibulus O'Bumper and even (how apposite!) His Royal Highness of Touch-Me-Not—how can I cast the
first stone at someone who has come, perhaps honestly, by the name
Nolie Mae Tangerie?

Still I say, *"Noli me tangere?"*

"Nolie Mae, yes."

"Is it too much to hope," I ask her, "that you might have some
small grasp of Latin?"

"Is such knowledge a requirement of the position?"

"It might be."

"I can read Latin. And Greek. And Hebrew. And I have studied all the sciences. I can discourse upon the nebula hypothesis or the voyage of Bougainville to Tasmania; or refute the claim of the Austrian physician Mesmer to have been the first to put his patients into a trance-like state (Paracelsus was that); or tell you who discovered hydrochloric *and* sulfuric acid, or when and by whom the first commercial steam engine was produced (1776, Boulton and Watt), or what Fraunhöfer is famous for, or who invented the kaleidoscope and who the hobby horse. I play the harpsichord and the English horn. I know all the balletic positions and can handle with a fair degree of competence a revolver, flintlock *or* percussion cap. If pressed I can acquit myself well with foil or épée. And, oh yes, I have some skill as a water-colorist." The same breathless, theatrical, auditioning tone. But are her smoke-gray eyes mocking me in the looking glass? "Yes, I know Latin, Mr. . . . ?"

"Peacock. Phidias Peacock. I ask only because your name—"

"*Your* given name, Mr. Phidias Peacock, is Greek, and Greece is not very far from Gozo. I suppose that is how you knew."

"No, it is simply that my brother was a sailor who called at Gozo on more than one occasion."

On hearing this, Miss Tangerie pivots so swiftly to face me that she has to clap a hand again to the crown of her black silk hat to keep it from flying off.

"So *that* explains the resemblance!" she cries. "You do not *talk* as he does and you do not *think* as he does and I daresay you do not . . . *never mind* . . . as he does, but when I first saw you I mistook you for your brother."

"Henry?" I say, remembering then his name. "You knew Henry?"

"William Henry, yes," she says.

My brother's given names, the reader will recall, were William Henry Leonard.

"A *nom de guerre*, I assume," she goes on. "It hardly surprises me. He was always involved—heroically involved—in wildly romantic Byronic adventures. Fighting for the Greeks against the Turks, the Poles against the Russians. Gun-running to Gozo. How *is* Will?" She smiles.

How well I know, in retrospect, that I should have prepared her. But, alas, I did not.

"He is dead."

"Dead? But . . ."

Her head falls against my shoulder, her black silk hat flying off. "Once," she says in a voice softer than the distant echo of a dream, "once in a stolen moment at Marseilles we were lovers."

I stroke her blond hair with an awkward, inadequate hand; she draws away.

"How did he die?"

"I do not remember."

"You don't remember how your own brother died?" she asks, aghast.

Before I can explain, the door bursts open and a violent wind howls into the hall. The candles flare, our shadows leap along the wall, Nolie Mae Tangerie screams. Do I see a *third* shadow, blown swiftly toward us by the wind? The candles flicker, die—and there is nothing but the empty doorway, the gray day outside, and the girl swooning in my arms.

Ten

Out of joy is sorrow born.

—"Berenice"

"*Paon*," I said.

"*Paon*," said Virginia.

"Again. *Paon*—more through the nose. Not that you saw one."

"I did, Eddie. *Paon*."

"There are no peacocks on the outskirts of Philadelphia, Pennsylvania."

"Eddie, I saw it. Plain as day."

We were returning home from an amble in the woods and an attempt, half-hearted on my part, to find her peacock. The house, or part-of-a-house, that we had rented stood on Sixteenth Street near Locust, at the edge of Philadelphia.

Muddy was hanging laundry in the garden, which was located where the rest of the house would have been had its builder not run out of money. "What did you see?" she asked Virginia.

"A peacock. Spreading his tail in the woods not half a mile from here."

Muddy made a scoffing sound.

"Cross my heart," insisted Virginia, not heatedly. In her seventeenth year her pretty face still had a childlike plumpness, its eventual maturity suggested by the Grecian profile and the heavy-lidded deep blue eyes. Her complexion was pale; too pale, Muddy always said.

I said, *"Le paon déploie sa queue."*

Virginia laughed. "I love the sound of French. It is so foreign."

"Too foreign for *my* clumsy tongue," grumbled Muddy, but she was pleased that I had been teaching Virginia the language of diplomats and drawing rooms.

What pleased Muddy even more was the piano in the parlor. Virginia played every afternoon before dinner, accompanying her own singing.

"Le paon," I began again, *"déploie—"*

And Virginia turned the statement into a question: *"Pourquoi le paon déploie-t-il sa queue?"*

I had taught my wife algebra too, or as much algebra as I had retained from my days at West Point. All men, and not many of us make a secret of it, like to play Pygmalion.

"Why, Eddie?"

"Why does the peacock spread his tail? To show off his plumage to the peahen that he hopes will become his mate."

"Eddie," Virginia asked me then, still in halting French, "Eddie, do you ever want to . . . go with other girls? I would understand, if you did. But I would want you to tell me."

"Most wives would not wish to know."

"Most wives are . . . wives. Did you ever . . . go with Elizabeth?"

"No, I did not."

"Did you ever wish to?"

"I may have."

"Was that why we left Richmond?"

"We left because Elizabeth's father resented the fact that my advice was sound and his editorial wisdom wanting."

Muddy harumphed, "You and Sis won't have to speak French if I go and put dinner on the stove," and went inside.

Muddy often called Virginia Sis, and sometimes unthinkingly so did I. This always brought a hurt look to Virginia's face, for she took it as an oblique reproach for the innocent state in which we lived. But I did not intend it as criticism. I would have said or done nothing to hurt her.

"Then if that is why the *paon* spreads his tail," she said, in that way she had of darting from one conversation to another and back again, "there must be a peahen in the woods too."

"Not in these woods, Sis." And I saw the hurt look on her face.

"You still don't believe I saw it?"

"Well, we looked together but could find nothing."

She took my hand and tugged. "Then we must look again."

She found the feather near where we had searched before, on a mossy hummock in a glade in the oak woods.

"See?"

I saw. It was pale gold and blue, with a large spot, deeper blue, that glinted like metal in the sunlight.

"Well, Mr. Know-All?"

I might have suggested that the undeniable peacock feather could have fallen from a woman's fancy bonnet. But why diminish Virginia's triumph? So I merely smiled, gracious in error.

"Eddie?"

"Yes, my dear?"

"I saw the peacock. He was probably searching for his lost mate."

"If you saw him, he probably was."

"He *was.*" And, impishly grinning, she tickled my lips with the feather, then held it behind her back when I reached for it, then surprised me with it in her other hand and tickled my lips again. I caught her wrist, but she twisted free, laughing, and darted among the trees. She was swift and graceful as a dryad. I could not overtake her until she chanted, "When the girls came out to play, Eddie Beddie ran away," and allowed herself to be cornered with her back against a tree. She looked up at me, and I grasped her arms, and she began to squirm this way and that. I expected more laughter, but she did not laugh. I saw myself reflected in her eyes. Then they became heavy-lidded, and her hands, which were against my chest, fell to her sides and she released the feather. Drifting to the ground, it seemed to expand until the moss glinted all metallically blue.

And how had the peacock feather really come here? And why had we waited so long? And did a change truly fall upon all things? Did brilliant star-shaped flowers burst into bloom where before no flowers were? How did the ruby asphodel appear, so early in the spring? She was innocent and artless *and so was I,* and, having at last invented love, together we explored it.

Muddy was very understanding about our long moony silences and how we grinned from ear to ear at each other with only our eyes, and she did no more than raise her thick black eyebrows toward her salt-and-pepper hair when Virginia moved all her possessions—sixteen years, one armload, mostly petticoats—from the room she shared with Muddy downstairs in our part-of-a-house to the low-ceilinged cubicle under the eaves where I slept and where sometimes, if the day was not fine, Virginia would join me for a while, she to sit afterwards and comb her long dark hair, the comb making a crisp crackling sound, and watch me as I resumed writing at the small table near the cot with its straw mattress "hardly big enough for *one* person to *sleep,*" said Muddy; and if the day was fine, "Let us search for the elusive *paon,*" Virginia would say, but our woods had changed, a small murmuring stream was now a mighty river where silver and gold flamingos came down to the bank to drink while, lost in the splendid wilderness of each other, we searched.

I have described Virginia as plump, but rather she was petite, barely five feet tall, and when she disrobed, or when I disrobed her, a measure of plumpness departed with the large full sleeves of her one dress and another measure with each petticoat, and Virginia in her shift in my embrace, that Virginia, she was waif-like, and Virginia testing the water of our river with her toe, that Virginia, she was a willow wand, and Virginia lying on the mossy bank, that Virginia, she had small strong arms and legs for gripping, and if I rose, taking my weight on my hands, to see my wife loving, the Virginia I saw then, that Virginia, she had still of her apparent plumpness only her breasts with their bronzy-colored nipples, and I loved her for being one person to all others but a different one to me, and I would have loved her were that not so. I loved her. I loved her, and time fled.

One day in January of 1842 I returned home early from my odious thrice-weekly chores at the offices of a magazine* because of a hard snowfall that would make the long walk difficult later. Usually, on approaching our part-of-a-house, I would hear the piano. Virginia loved to play and sing in her sweet, true voice popular sentimental songs like "The Sweet Birds Are Singing" or patriotic airs like "Let Me Rest in the Land of My Birth." But that day all was silent until I walked into view (I assume) from the front window, when a rollicking melody came suddenly from the piano. As I stamped my boots free of snow in the doorway, Virginia began to sing in a bawdy voice I had never heard before.

She got no further than "Come blind, come lame, come cripple,/ Come some one and take me away!" when I knew it for the song my mother had sung all up and down the country, the song that made Eliza Poe famous from Boston to Charleston. I stood inside the door, and I listened, and I saw Muddy beaming, and saw Virginia's pretty (deceptively plump) face in Grecian profile, the hectic color in her cheek, and here in the bosom of my small family I felt a moment of perfect contentment that brought a thickness to my throat, even while I smiled at the lyrics.

* *Graham's Lady's and Gentleman's Magazine.* (Editor's note)

"Come blind, come lame, come cripple,
Come some one and take me away!
For 'tis O! what will become of me,
O! what shall I do?
Nobody coming to marry me,
Nobody coming to woo!"

And singing—no, ceasing to sing—Virginia turned to me with a polite little apologetic cough, her own smile—no, look of surprise—engulfed by the flood of bright arterial blood that poured from her nose and mouth.

"Bronchitis," Muddy said, while the doctor examined Virginia. "She has a touch of bronchitis, all this cold weather, it is going around."

"Singing, straining her voice," I said, "she burst a blood vessel."

The doctor did not use the word "consumption" either. To use it was bad luck. One might refer in whispers to the white plague or the death-in-life, though never in the patient's hearing. Still, the patient knew. The patient might be "too young to die," but the patient knew. The patient's face was pallid except for the cheeks, the patient suffered chills and fever and night sweats, sleeplessness and irregular appetite, the patient coughed blood, the patient could not breathe. The patient knew.

The doctor said, "We must guard against another hemorrhage from the lungs." He rubbed cold hands together. "Where does she sleep?"

"Upstairs. There is a little room. The warmest in the house."

"How is it heated?"

"The heat from the cook stove rises," I said.

"She has sufficient blankets?"

Muddy and I looked at each other. We owned but three blankets, none of them heavy.

"She sleeps under my greatcoat," I explained.

"It is very warm," explained Muddy. "Warmer than any blanket."

"An army greatcoat," I elaborated.

The doctor said, "And wholesome food. Red meat. Milk. Fresh fruit and vegetables."

As well might he have said *foie d'oie* and vintage wine.

For an instant I saw in my mind's eye a savagely apposite scene, frozen in time like a photograph—Virginia seated at table in a world she never knew, dressed all in organdie and taffeta with a diamond pendant at her throat, in my cousin Neilson's great house, silver and crystal glittering under the chandelier, a beefsteak oozing blood among the vegetables on her plate, a glass of claret in her hand as she leaned smiling toward the handsome, young, wealthy suitor at her side.

Muddy said, "Fruit and vegetables, in winter?"

"The railroads, my dear Mrs. Poe—"

"Clemm. I am the widow Clemm," said Muddy, clinging in the face of calamity to the certainty of her name.

"—have changed all that. The stalls along Market Street—surely you have seen what can be bought there?"

"Doctor!" I shouted. "We cannot even pay your fee!"

At first, misunderstanding, he dismissed with a gesture his fee. Then in resignation he said, "Get her the best food you can," and as I helped him on with his coat he told me, "I hardly need warn you that for one as ill as your wife, childbearing is out of the question. Moreover"—he lowered his voice—"bodily exertion of any kind entails the gravest of risks, and in this I must include the exercise of your connubial—"

"I understand," I said.

He gave me a small regretful smile. "This prohibition, until the disease has, God willing, run its course, is total."

I yanked open the door to put an end to his insupportable garrulity, and moments later watched him drive off through the snow.

Eleven

I had found the spell of the picture in an absolute *lifelikeliness* of expression, which, at first startling, finally confounded, subdued, and appalled me.

— "The Oval Portrait"

You cannot get lost in Philadelphia even if you wish to—and I wished to. What are cities for but to lose yourself in, for an hour or a day, for a month or a year, for a life?

How I longed, those three days a week I left Virginia entirely in Muddy's care and went to work at the magazine, to plunge into the labyrinthine streets of some unexplored immemorial city, to follow at random this turning or that, for no other reason than the mystery of where it might lead. But I always knew where I was going, and when, and I always knew where I must return. And in the unlikely event of my forgetting, the relentless gridiron of Philadelphia was there to remind me, streets crossing regimented streets, so many yards to the city block—urban regularity simplifying the search for anywhere, wherever anywhere happened to be, if you truly wished to find it.

For resourceful men determined to lose themselves, there was, of course, a solution, and the most resourceful man I knew was Frederick W. Thomas, who when in Philadelphia could usually be found losing himself in the bar-room of the Congress Hall Hotel. Years ago, Thomas had known my brother Henry, and Virginia remembered meeting him more than once when she could not have been six years old. It was difficult to forget that you had met Frederick W. Thomas, because he walked jerkily with the aid of a metal device into which his twisted left leg, result of a childhood fall, was strapped, but none the less he walked faster than most men with two sound legs, and insisted that his lameness not only made him irresistible to women but was a spur to creativity, "as is all illness," he said, "because it reminds you every waking hour of your own mortality."

As a lawyer and as a writer of popular songs and novels, Frederick W. Thomas earned substantial sums—and wished instead for "literary fame like yours, Poe, and the devil take the money," but I do not believe I was famous, not then, nor that he would have surrendered the money in any Faustian bargain. Moreover, he was a political man, a stump speaker for the Whigs, who had rewarded him with a sinecure at the Treasury Department in Washington City that paid him fifteen hundred dollars a year and left him all the free time he needed to cultivate a taste for fine wines and high-priced women.

So it was in the bar-room of the Congress Hall Hotel that I met Thomas, as he had bidden me in a letter from Washington, on a dismal March afternoon. At his table sat a woman, young and pretty and Titian-haired. I expected introductions, but Thomas said only, "Good Lord, Poe, out with no overcoat in such a downpour?" and handed the woman a room key. She departed with a raised eyebrow but without protest.

Thomas was drinking what looked like white wine. He poured some for me.

Virginia, I told Thomas, had curled up under my greatcoat for a nap, and I had not wished to disturb her.

"How is she?" he asked.

"She can take short walks."

"Not in this foul weather."

"The winter is almost over."

"Will she survive another?"

I fiddled with my glass. *Would* he go on? I was sorry I had come.

"Manzanilla," said Frederick W. Thomas, sipping and then holding to the light his wine. "Aged beside the sea in San Lucar de Barrameda, near Seville. Bit of a salty tang that mere sherry lacks, wouldn't you say? They stock it here just for me."

I drained the manzanilla in my own glass, and he poured it full again.

"Can she travel?"

"She is not strong enough at present."

I waited. So also did he. I said, "Why do you ask?"

Thomas said, "I have been in touch with the President through his son Rob. Rob is a poet of sorts, you know."

I knew.

"He believes that, where possible, the United States should be represented abroad by those not untouched by the Muse. Yourself, for example."

I emptied my glass. Again he filled it. "I?" I said. "But—"

"It is quite possible, now that Washington Irving has paved the way."

"Irving's father was wealthy, mine a roving player."

"Which only makes you the more deserving. Let me speak, Poe, as an admirer and a friend. No serious man of letters—excepting Jamie Cooper, and you would not wish to write like Jamie Cooper —can support himself by his writing. This is America, not France or England. Surely it is not your choice to live always hand to mouth, dependent on the charity of others when you are not combing proofs for errors or churning out reviews that appear in some magazine cheek by jowl with fashion plates or banal lithographs of a boy and his dog."

"What have you in mind?"

"I? I have in mind whatever offers. The *President* has in mind postings abroad. Secretary to the legation at Paris, for example. Or Madrid. Irving began as secretary at London, you know. Soon, they say, he will have a legation of his own."

I drank the third manzanilla. Was poured a fourth. Waved a hand in a vague gesture the meaning of which even I did not know.

"Such postings open from time to time. Rob Tyler is a great admirer of your work. He wishes to meet you. Could you slip down to Washington on short notice?"

My gesture, still vague, became vaguely negative. I drank the fourth manzanilla and a fifth. Another bottle, covered with chilled beads of moisture, appeared.

"But I am no . . . diplomat."

"Now *there*," laughed Frederick W. Thomas, "speaks a man who knows himself. You will learn by precept, as all diplomats do. Diplomats are made, not born."

"Nor am I a linguist. Apart from the classical languages, I have only a smattering of French."

"More than a smattering. A good command. And French is the language of diplomacy."

"For those more fluent than I."

Yet even while I was nay-saying, I saw myself as in a daguerreotype seated at dusk of a summer evening outside a fashionable café in the Rue de la Paix watching the lamp-lighter reach up with his long torch to light the illuminating gas. I am not suggesting I imagined this tableau. It was, I was certain, real. I even knew, was certain I knew, what the Edgar Poe seated at the café table with a bemused expression on his face was thinking. He was thinking that he had sat here before, at this same marble-topped table, in this same wicker chair, watching this same lamp-lighter (who dragged his left leg along like Frederick W. Thomas), hearing the same pop of sound as the gas ignited and colors saturated the black-and-white dusk panorama of the busy Rue de la Paix. He told himself that he was experiencing that inexplicable phenomenon of seeing again what he had not seen before—whereas I was aware, from the vantage of the bar-room of the Congress Hall Hotel in Philadelphia, that *he* would think so then only because *I* was seeing it now. I at once tried to drive the idea from my mind. It was dizzying, it was disorienting, and, in some way I could not then understand, it was terrifying in its implications.

"Poe?" Frederick W. Thomas seemed to be calling across a vast abyss.

"What? Sorry, I seem to have been wool-gathering."

"I was saying that you need to broaden your horizons. Washington Irving could hardly have written his *Columbus* or *Tales of the Alhambra* had he remained at home," said Frederick W. Thomas.

And I said, "Irving left these shores not to broaden his horizons but to escape his grief when his fiancée died."

A silence followed. Our eyes met. Thomas sipped delicately his manzanilla. "Leave her," he told me.

"What are you saying?"

"That if Rob Tyler can procure such a position for you, and if your wife cannot travel, go without her."

"Good God! I could never do that."

"This is the only life you will ever have. Only a fool would wait until she dies."

I hurled the manzanilla in his face.

Waiters converged on us. He rose awkwardly, having to drag his twisted left leg out from under the table. One waiter solicitously offered a napkin. Two others made for me with the obvious intention of removing me from the premises. Every eye in the bar-room was upon us.

"No, no; it was an accident," Frederick W. Thomas said. "We are friends, Mr. Poe and I."

With evident misgivings the waiters left us. Thomas sat again, dragging his twisted leg back under the table.

"I am desperately sorry," I told him.

"Perhaps I . . . was too blunt."

"I was beastly."

"I truly do wish to help you."

"I know you do."

"Then keep an open mind, Poe. When Rob Tyler can see you, I shall let you know."

I thanked him and drank another manzanilla and left as soon as I decently could. I was already overdue at the magazine but did not go there directly. The rain had stopped. I walked down to the Navy Yard and stood and watched a forest of masts swaying against a fathomless sky.

Five minutes after reaching the magazine offices, I was at full rant. Was I drunk? I did not feel drunk, and the Dashing Young Publisher* did not accuse me of being drunk.

The Dashing Young Publisher's magazine had a circulation of 25,000, a five-fold increase in only a year. I wish I could say this

---

* George Rex Graham. (Editor's note)

was owing to my editorial sagacity, but unlike the Inoffensive Publisher in Richmond, the Dashing Young Publisher made all his own decisions. I was superannuated office boy, proof reader, review writer—and, if he liked them, the Dashing Young Publisher bought my poems or tales.

He liked, and had scheduled for the next issue, my tale "The Oval Portrait." He handed me the proofs, an amiable smile on his dashing young face.

"Page eleven," he said. "Effective, isn't it?"

Page eleven contained the entire text of "The Oval Portrait" surrounding the etched likeness—in, naturally, an oval frame—of a young, pretty woman in classic profile.

"Who is responsible for this?" I demanded. "Is it John?"

"The etching, you mean?" said the Dashing Young Publisher. "Yes, I own I am pleased. John Sartain at his best. One can see something of Hogarth here, don't you agree? Well, London's loss is Philadelphia's gain."

"It is monstrous!"

"Monstrous? It is exquisite—and very lifelike."

"How dare he? I thought he was my friend. Surely anyone would recognize this as a portrait of my wife."

"Nonsense, Poe. John has never met your wife, has he?"

"You could have described her to him."

"What ever for?"

"What *for*?" By then I was shouting. "You read the tale. Tell me the theme."

"Now really, Poe. Surely—"

"Tell me."

"It is about a painter," he said, "and his beautiful young model, barely more than a child, who—"

"Who happens also to be his bride. And he poses her for long, enervating days, does he not, while he paints an astonishingly lifelike portrait of her, *refusing* to see that with every stroke of his brush he is withering the health and spirit of his bride, *refusing* to see that the tints he spreads upon the canvas are drawn from the cheeks, the hectic spots of color in the cheeks, of his model. And, applying the final strokes to the portrait, he exults, does he not, 'This is life itself!' and, trembling and triumphant, turns to regard his beloved —*who is dead.*"

Panting, I glared my rage at him.

"That is the story, yes. A most effective"—this was the Dashing Young Publisher's highest accolade—"Gothic tale. One of your best."

"The artist killed his wife!" I shouted.

"A brilliant conceit, Poe, that—"

"Virginia! For you it is the story of Virginia and me!"

"My dear fellow, please."

"You instructed John Sartain to make her Virginia's double!"

"Try to calm yourself, Poe."

"*Calm* myself!"

"It never entered my mind. And if it had, then John's engraving is sadly ineffective. For the portrait hardly resembles your Virginia at all."

I tore the proofs across, and across again, and flung them at him. Doing so, I inadvertently struck his shoulder. Lurching backwards, he collided with a table, and the table slid, and he fell in a welter of torn proofs as a voice said from the doorway:

"I fear I have interrupted an editorial conference."

The man leaning against the door jamb, arms folded across narrow chest, legs crossed at the ankles, box coat casually open, was slender and of average height. His high brow was furrowed, his lips fleshy and parted in a moist smile.

With an athlete's grace the Dashing Young Publisher sprang to his feet. As he did so I realized that although I was but three-and-thirty, both these men were substantially younger than I and each already had made his mark in the world of letters. For I had met before in these offices the man who now walked in. He was Rufus Griswold, the critic and self-styled taste-maker—to whom I, of course, was Edgar Poe, the critic and self-styled taste-maker. That he also was a licensed Baptist minister interested me only as the possible theme of a tale. That I also was a fiction writer interested him not at all; poetry was his field.

"I had not expected you so early," said the Dashing Young Publisher.

"So it would appear."

"Mr. Poe and I," the Dashing Young Publisher continued smoothly, "do not see eye to eye on the *placement* of his most recent tale."

"The placement, to be sure," said Rufus Griswold. "Publishers" —he smiled at me his moist smile—"are the enemy. You must learn to turn the other cheek, Poe, like a good Christian. But then you are not, are you? To read your poetry is to enter a world where Christ seems never to have lived, let alone died."

"Thus saith the preacher," said the Dashing Young Publisher, and Rufus Griswold shrugged.

"I used to worry that literary pursuits might be, from the Almighty's viewpoint, frivolous. But I think not. God's hand is, after all, everywhere. *À propos*, Poe"—he paused briefly to savor the sound of his words—"*à propos*, Poe, I am editing the definitive anthology of American poetry, and there might be room for one or two of yours. So, if you would care to submit several?"

I said that I would. It seemed a good note on which to leave, and I shook hands with both of them and shut the door behind me. Standing a moment outside, I heard the Dashing Young Publisher urge Rufus Griswold to forget what he had seen.

"For poor Poe's benefit more than your own, I should say," said Rufus Griswold.

"We all know he has been under a strain."

This did not stop the Dashing Young Publisher from requesting the following week my resignation from his magazine. When the announcement appeared in its pages, he accepted my departure "with warmest wishes for whatever Mr. Poe might undertake."

My replacement as the magazine's factotum and review writer was Rufus Wilmot Griswold.

Twelve

There are moments when, even to the sober eye of Reason, the world
of our sad humanity must assume the aspect of Hell.

—*Marginalia*

I found myself wishing Virginia would lament her lot, would dep-
recate Muddy's or my efforts to make her comfortable, would accuse
us of neglect, would be sullen and cherish grievances or whine and
use her illness as a weapon.

How much easier to resent an invalid who complains!

But Virginia was sweet as any angel.

Still, our lives were dominated utterly by her illness, our time
filled with listening for the creak of a floorboard overhead, the
rustle of her straw mattress, a call or a cough. We climbed the
steep staircase, almost a ladder, and, climbing, hated it. We
looked at the bare cupboard, and hated it. We listened to the
silence and waited for a sound, and hated both. Muddy swept
the yard aggressively, cleaned the windows angrily, scrubbed the
little stoop furiously. I went into town and cadged drinks and got
occasional work through journalists who frequented the taverns clus-
tered at Third and Chestnut, the heart of Philadelphia's publishing
district.

Muddy and I vented upon each other the anxieties we hid from
Virginia.

"This is the third time this week, Eddie!"

"I was only being convivial. I am not drunk."

"If you were less convivial, you could write more."

"They give me work."

"If you wrote more, Virginia could have better food."

"I provide what I can."

"Think of yourself, if not of us. Need I remind you that your
brother died of drink?"

"He died," I said, "of a hemorrhage of the lungs."

And we would both look at the staircase that was almost a ladder, and listen for a cough.

One day in winter when the weather was mild and Virginia felt strong enough, we brought her downstairs, and, bundled in my greatcoat, she went with me to stroll in the woods. Her eyes were enormous, her cheeks flushed. When she smiled she looked like a child still, as if her brief time as woman, wife, inamorata, had been play-acting.

"Isn't this where we found it?"

"Why, yes, it is." I knew without asking that she meant the peacock feather.

She paused to rest on the mossy hummock, her head tilted back, her eyes shut so that she seemed to gaze sightlessly up into the pale, watery sunlight. On her eyelids I could see a fine tracery of blue veins, yet another mark of her illness.

"Remember the first time we came here?"

I said that I did. I wanted to take her in my arms. I took her hand.

"Eddie," she said, and then for a while was so still that in my greatcoat she seemed a porcelain doll with bright painted cheeks. "Eddie, this is no life for you. Cut off from every thing."

"I get out."

"Not enough. You're all cooped up, as if *you* were the invalid."

"When you are well," I said, and smiled, and realized that her eyes were shut, and essayed a laugh that did not sound sincere. "When you are well, we shall regain the time we have lost by living twice as fast as other people."

Her lips moved, but she did not speak.

"Truly, I get out enough."

"You should have friends."

"I do have friends. Don't I tell you about them?"

"Oh, Eddie! I don't mean to drink with. I mean . . . friends."

"No woman," I said, "can ever appreciate the camaraderie of the bar-room." My lightness of tone was forced, but Virginia did not seem to notice.

"In this masculine camaraderie of yours, do you *speak* of masculine things?"

"Like hunting and fishing, do you mean?"

"Like women."

"The topic does on occasion come up."

"And you?"

"And I what?"

"Eddie, you are young still—" Her voice dropped so as to be almost inaudible, and, were her eyes not tightly shut, I was certain she could not have continued. "Young and . . . vigorous. It is not normal not to have a woman, Eddie."

I chose to say, but again alas with that tell-tale laugh, "How do you know I have not?"

"Then have you?"

"No," I said after a while. "You are all the woman I need."

So unconvincing. And so untrue.

"I am no woman at all."

I raised her small cold hand and kissed the fingers one by one. I kissed the V-spaces between her fingers, kissed her palm, her wrist. I kissed her eyelids with their stigmata of her disease and tasted the salt of her tears. I kissed the hectic rose of her cheek. She made a sound at once less and more than speech. Her fingers entwisted in my hair and she pulled me down.

"Eddie, I don't care, I don't care what happens!"

But I stood. And said, "It is late, Sis, we should go." And when we got back to our part-of-a-house Muddy handed me a letter.

That night I woke from a dream and listened to the rafters creaking like the timbers of a ship, listened to field mice scurrying in the wall, listened to the soughing of the wind, to the many-fingered tapping of a tree branch against a window, Virginia's tiny window upstairs. Would it wake her? My dream was of sweaty limbs entwisted like pythons and a moist red mouth like a carnivorous plant and an immemorial rhythm like jungle drums and a sibilant sound like the sea as it races as fast as a galloping horse across a sand beach below a cliff on which stands a turreted castle, and I was running, running for my life, but the sea was swift.

I jumped, nearly levitated, when a hand touched my shoulder. It was Virginia.

"You must not come downstairs alone in the dark."

"Eddie, I had a bad dream." She was trembling. I held her. She was wearing only her shift. "You were on a wild shore under a cliff, Eddie, and a great wave broke, and you ran but could not outrun it. Oh Eddie, Eddie, I have dreamt often of my own death, but never before of yours."

While she spoke I wrapped her in my frayed old blanket and my hand brushed accidentally the softness of her breast and then not accidentally the narrowness of her waist and flare of hip. I lay down with her in my arms and felt the hot bellows of her breath on my shoulder, and I lay rigid, twice rigid, and in the morning I left for Washington City.

Thirteen

I have great faith in fools. Self-confidence my friends will call it.
—*Marginalia*

I crossed the lobby of Fuller's Hotel on Pennsylvania Avenue with a change of clothing in my carpet-bag, and in my wallet a ten-dollar bill which Frederick W. Thomas had sent with his letter.

Yes, a room had been reserved for a Mr. Edgar A. Poe; no, Mr. Thomas was not receiving.

"But I'm expected."

"Perhaps if you would inquire later, Mr. Poe? Boy!"

A slave took my carpet-bag and I was soon ensconced in room 13 on the second floor in back. The room overlooked a fenced yard where chickens scratched and female slaves with kerchiefs on their heads were festooning clothes-lines with laundry. The fence separated the yard from an empty field, and beyond the field I saw a road, a broad paved road innocent of buildings and traffic. Far beyond the road was the glint of the river, and beyond the river the green of the Virginia shore.

I stood a while looking at the purposeless road, long, straight, and empty. I would, I decided, wait an estimated hour—I had long ago pawned my repeater—before going downstairs to inquire again about Frederick W. Thomas. But why not wait in the lobby? Was there a bar-room? I craved suddenly a glass of beer; went to the wash stand, poured water from the pitcher into the glass, and drank. My eyes were drawn again to the meaningless road. I half expected not to see it. But it was there, waiting.

I went downstairs. The lobby was crowded. Men sat in deep leather chairs impatiently turning the pages of newspapers without seeming to read. Others with distorted faces stood conversing and spitting. Spittoons were everywhere, but careless streams of tobacco juice splotched the floor yellow. One man spat with virtuosity into a spittoon inches from my boot. There were no women. Most of the men wore their hats, and many of these were coonskin. There was a gamy smell like raccoon too. I saw no familiar face; knew no one. Had no more reason to be in this city than had that absurd road beyond the yard. If offered, I would accept no overseas posting. How could I? I could go nowhere except back. But meanwhile I was here. I went into the bar-room. Sawdust covered the floor. The din was prodigious. A barricade of shoulders several rows deep blocked my way to the bar. I saw a slave holding a blackboard overhead. On it printed in chalk was my name.

Next to his boots on the rack inside the door was Frederick W. Thomas's leg brace. Thomas called a weak greeting from the bedroom of the suite of rooms he kept at the hotel, and I went inside.

A fire blazed on the hearth. The room smelled of alcohol and mustard, of camphor. Propped on three pillows, Thomas lay sweating under a comforter. His cheeks looked sunken, his complexion jaundiced, his eyes bloodshot. He placed a hot limp hand in mine.

"They cupped me and blistered me," he groaned. "They insist, despite the fever, that I shall live. At the moment, *for* the moment, I should prefer it otherwise. You look well."

I thanked him for paying my passage from Philadelphia, for the ten dollars.

"Make it last. Your room here is paid for, but you will not see the President until tomorrow night."

"Tomorrow night?" With Thomas ill, the prospect of being on my own in a strange city made me uneasy.

"There, on the night stand."

It was an invitation in my name to attend the "levee" at the President's House, March 11, 9:00 P.M. to midnight.

"A levée, at night?"

"You see, your French is superior to the President's. Or, I should say, to his daughter-in-law's. It is young John's wife who serves as hostess. But it is Rob Tyler who procured the invitation. Have you and Washington Irving ever met?"

I said that we had not.

"He will be the guest of honor, marking his departure for his post as Minister to Spain. The circumstances could not possibly be more auspicious for you. Irving likes what he has seen of your work. A position in the Customs Service is as good as yours."

Frederick W. Thomas sneezed explosively, coughed, turned red in the face, hacked, and spat into a cardboard box. The Customs? Doubtless he meant diplomatic; probably his fever made him misspeak himself.

"Unless," he said, and smiled. "Unless it is your custom to hurl your drinks in people's faces," and I realized that midst the coughs he was laughing. "Poe, do for pity's sake leave me now. If I look half as bad as I feel, I would sooner maintain a dignified privacy on my deathbed."

We shook hands, and I told him he would be better before he knew it. And so he was; but I was not.

I supped meagerly on soup and hot buttered biscuits, then drank a glass of port wine after my coffee. A second glass followed, and a third. I began to wonder how I could decline, to his face, the President's offer. Perhaps it would be better to decline formally in writing after I returned to Philadelphia. Levée, at night; I smiled indulgently and drank more port. By the time I left the dining room for the bar-room, I felt maudlinly regretful that I must refuse my posting abroad. Over a first bourbon I persuaded myself that the President would be sympathetic to my situation. Over a second, I began to suspect that I should not have a third. Over a third I felt a sudden desire to walk that vestal road that must wait, with more patience than I, for the city to reach it.

I paid for my drinks, tipping the bar-tender lavishly. A hackney cabriolet pulled up in front of the hotel at my signal. Climbing in, I asked: "Do you know the road behind this hotel, the completely empty road, not a building on it, that, I imagine, starts at the same nowhere as it ends?"

"I know it, yes," said the hackie from his perch behind the raised hood. "It's nothing special, in Washington City." He flicked his whip and the horse began to trot.

"In that case," I said, before the wicket shut behind my head, "take me to a bordello."

"No?"
"I'm afraid not."
"Is it something I did?"
"No."
"Or failed to do?"
"No."
"If you don't like me, you can have another girl."
"But I do like you."
"You are sweet," the girl said. She lay with her hands clasped behind her head, jet hair fanned on the pillow. She was young—

how young I wished not to know—and of a reminiscent plumpness. Her cheeks were rouged a bright red.

"We could try again in a little while."

"No, I think not. But thank you."

"There is still some champagne."

She leaned past me across the bed to turn the lamp up, then poured the champagne. Elsewhere in the house I heard masculine laughter.

"Is this your first time?"

"In a bordello? Yes."

"We are like other girls, you know, only more honest."

"You are part Negro," I said suddenly.

Her face closed. "Surely that is not why—"

"No, of course not. I just now noticed."

"Most men choose me because I am. It excites them."

"You are free?"

"Here?" She almost smiled.

"I mean manumitted."

"My mama was. She saved the cap'n's baby's life."

"Tell me about it."

I had never written of a manumitted slave; or of a prostitute.

"It better if you try again. You a manly-lookin' man."

"Why are you talking like that?"

"Sayin' yo' manly-lookin'? Yo' is." The darkie dialect thickened. "Yo' *is*, cap'n."

"Stop talking like that."

But she knew what she was doing. She had become someone else. She chuckled, a deep and lusty summons to arousal. Her head swooped down. Her mouth was hot. My excitement grew, but when her mouth came away and she drew me to her with a hand on my shoulder like Virginia's hand last night, I pulled back. After that, try as we might, I could not do what I had come here to do.

I had paid for the girl before going up, but when I came down they demanded two dollars and a half for the champagne.

"I don't have it," I said.

"Now, sir," chided the very large, very black man in a deep soft gentle voice.

"That was vintage champagne," said the woman. She had a round chinless head like a turtle's.

"It was swill," I told her. We were in a small, red plush sitting room. Mirrors covered the walls, reflecting a table laden with bottles.

"Poisonous swill," I elaborated.

"Lower your voice," said the woman.

"Swill!" I shouted.

A piano had been playing somewhere nearby. It stopped.

"See if he has the money, Obadiah."

Obadiah sighed and came toward me. I snatched a bottle up by its neck and smashed it on the edge of the table. A greenish liquor that smelled like cheap hair tonic sprayed the room. I faced Obadiah with my improvised weapon, the jagged glass catching glints from the chandelier. Obadiah shook his head with great sadness and proceeded to close the space between us. I wanted to damage something. Not someone, I assured myself—some*thing*. But Obadiah was there, available. With my free hand I snatched up another bottle and hurled it at him. It went sailing past his head and smashed into a mirror. Glass shattered; shards cascaded to the floor. The piano began again to play, sprightly and loud. I threw a few more bottles randomly. The turtle-headed woman dove under the table, or tried to, but the bulk of her crinolines impeded the process. Her efforts distracted Obadiah. I broke for the door, opened it, ran along a dim passage to a larger sitting room, same red plush, same mirrors. The pianist played a final thunderous chord and looked up. He was a bald brown man, pate and face shiny with sweat. In three identical armchairs three white men sat, none young, all well dressed. One had a girl on his knee and his hand up her gown; the others were smoking cigars and scrutinizing the girls lounging at the bar. They scattered as, with a forearm, I swept the bar clear of bottles and glasses. In the mirror behind the bar Obadiah loomed. I turned and his big black hand closed on my wrist. I dropped the neck of the bottle. Obadiah seemed to be bleeding from the ear. I tried to kick him. He backed away and stood for a moment, fists on hips, shaking his head. He smiled as melancholy a smile as you will ever see and punched me in the stomach. I at once became frighteningly aware of an inability to breathe. My knees hit the floor. I gasped; vomited. Some time passed. I saw my wallet in Obadiah's big hand. The turtle-headed woman gave him something she had been reading.

"Great day in the morning," said Obadiah.

"Exactly," said the woman. "But look at this room. I would like to kill him."

"Well," said Obadiah.

"In a manner of speaking."

"To be sure," said Obadiah.

"I would like to flay the hide off him with a horsewhip."

"Uh-huh," said Obadiah.

My impression was that they had had this conversation before. But I was fuddled and cannot vouch for the accuracy of the words and sounds I set down here.

"But he has *that*," the woman said. "Who are you, Mr. Poe?"

"I? I am nobody."

Let her draw her own conclusions.

"They do not invite a nobody to the President's House."

"As you say."

"Give him back his wallet, Obadiah."

Obadiah complied.

"And the invitation."

"Oh, I hardly need that to get into the President's House," I said.

Obadiah returned it none the less.

A young Negress appeared at my side holding a cloak. It was not mine; I did not own a cloak.

"It is not mine," I said.

"He come in wearin' it," said the girl.

Black cloak, red silk lining. I donned it with a flourish. The red silk swirled. My stomach hurt.

Obadiah escorted me out. I thought he would leave me, but a coachee was waiting, side lamps glowing golden in the rain. We climbed in and I heard the driver's muted shout and we were underway. No word passed between Obadiah and me as we rode. Rain fell steadily; the windows misted over. At last the coachee slowed to a stop.

"Who are you really, Mr. Poe?" Obadiah asked in his soft voice.

"I don't know," I said.

Obadiah laughed. "Whoever you are, I hope you are a good walker."

"I'm to walk?"

"To the President's House or to Cincinnati, Ohio, it is all the same to me."

The driver opened the low, narrow door on my side of the coachee and I crouched to go through. Obadiah gave me the gentlest of shoves. It was enough to send me tumbling to the ground.

After the coachee drove off, I sat huddled in the cloak an hour or so on the edge of the road and by a profound effort of will forced dawn to touch the eastern sky at its ordained time. The road, I then saw, was macadamized and ended here in a muddy field of corn stubble.

I began the long walk back. The road ran straight into the gloomy dawn. The rain fell harder. There were no crossroads, no buildings. But I knew where I was. Soon I could see the city. From the pristine road, blackly gleaming with rain, it was the city that seemed absurd. I left the road at the right place and walked through more corn stubble and climbed the fence into the yard of Fuller's Hotel.

Fourteen

Words are murderous things.

—Marginalia

The first face I recognized at the President's House belonged to a man I had last seen seated in an armchair, a girl on his knee and his hand up her gown. Our eyes met. He raised a quizzical eyebrow, then turned away to accept a goblet of champagne from a passing waiter.

The second face I recognized belonged to Washington Irving. I had seen his likeness often enough in magazines. The famous writer was a portly gentleman in his fifties who, especially here, could have been mistaken for a politician. I wondered if he ever longed to be again the slender young adventurer who had traveled the roads of Spain on muleback. Would I in my fifties be portly and poised, with an undeniable air of command? It seemed unlikely. It seemed unlikely that I would live into my fifties. Or forties. Or even until tomorrow. My skin was on wrong; my hair, as the French say, hurt.

Admirers and well-wishers surrounded Washington Irving. A man half his age joined the group. He had plump cheeks and long hair. The great man shook his hand warmly, introducing him to two senators, a general and the Secretary of State, Daniel Webster. The young man was the English novelist Charles Dickens, already as famous on this side of the ocean as Washington Irving was in England. Seeing them together drove home to me their success. Dickens was *here.* Irving had been *there.* He had spent more than half his adult life abroad—beginning, I could not but recall, after the death of his fiancée. Irving and young Dickens would converse of things to which I, in my insularity, would be a stranger. Oh, I had lived in England as a child, had been schooled there. But it was not the same. As a man I had yet to lose my geographical virginity. How different had been my brother Henry! He could have joined their conversation; he would have fit. He had wanted to be both writer and wanderer, but had had time in his short life only for the latter. Had he lived longer, what might he have written? Had I traveled wider, what might I? But I was still young. Or at least not yet old.

Still young, or at least not yet old; I recited silently again the litany, and grabbed a goblet of champagne off a passing tray. I drank several more in rapid succession and went out to the hall, where a military band was playing in fast duple time an unmilitary melody. It conjured images of Vienna, of the lingering twilight in the garden of a *Heurigerstube* on a summer evening, couples dancing under the arbors, the young pale wine like nectar, or of the Opera Ball, the music of Mozart and Waldteufel inside, and outside the snow falling on monuments to heroes I could not name, nor ever would, for Vienna was a distant, unattainable dream. There was champagne in the hall; and bourbon. I drank; I drank. Still young, not yet old.

From the East Drawing Room came a burst of laughter. I walked back in. President Tyler was there, mingling easily with the crowd, his face mild, pleasant, touched with care, not unhandsome. He clapped Washington Irving on the back, spoke a few words, and walked on. But Irving called out something which made the President turn and, laughing, rejoin the group around its luminary. And I knew why I was drinking. I was drinking because I knew that if offered an overseas posting—which I could not accept—I would not, could not, refuse.

"Poe! Edgar Poe!"

On the edge of the crowd I saw Rufus Griswold, slender, his satin-collared box coat casually open. His fleshy lips parted in a moist smile as he joined me. "I didn't know that you and the man of the hour were acquainted," he said.

"We aren't. I am here to see the President's son."

"Rob? Aha! Applied for a government posting, have you? God knows," said the Baptist divine, "writers need all the help they can get. Is it the Customs House? A plum, Poe. Others have entered their names, but if you have the support of Rob Tyler they have done so in vain. Well—today your cup runneth over. I bring more glad tidings."

I told him that such were always welcome.

"I am including some of your clever little efforts in my anthology. Not front of the book, perhaps, but it cannot possibly harm you to appear in the company of such shining young talents as Isaac McLellen, Jr., Lydia Sigourney, and Anna Peyre Dinnies. You see . . ."

His condescending congratulations droned on, but I did *not* see. Or rather, all I saw was Rufus Griswold's teeth. Why had I never noticed that his teeth, over-sized, evenly spaced, resembled tombstones in a crowded churchyard?

I looked, perhaps pointedly, away from him—to see the room slowly begin to spin.

Faster the room whirled, and faster yet. The President's guests began a mad dance to the beat of a polka from the military band in the hall, heedless of the risk of being flung into space by centrifugal force. I alone stood still, a studiedly casual look on my face, as if nothing untoward were occurring.

Soon, without surprise, I found myself capable of stopping and starting that madly whirling room, as a child can change what he sees in a kaleidoscope by giving the tube a twist.

I could, if I wished, inspect one by one the colorful shards in the kaleidoscope simply by holding the tube steady. The colorful shards were segments of faces—a pair of angry eyes; a nose bent off true (possibly by a blow); sallow cheeks and rouged; mouths that opened, shut, nibbled, dribbled, spat the pronoun "you" and lingered lovingly on "I."

This observation carries no moral judgment. Catching only bits and pieces of conversation, it might have been "eye" and "yew" I heard.

Had I eyed a yew hedge in the garden? I stifled an impulse to laugh. Ought I to have a walk in the garden? Would it clear my head? How drunk was I?

If I went outside, would I return? Or leave forever unclaimed the cloak with the red silk lining?

I did not go outside. For simultaneously the vertigo passed and I heard someone speak my name.

Eyes, noses, cheeks, mouths reassembled themselves into faces.

It was Daniel Webster I had heard speak my name. Thumbs hooked under lapels, eyes focused on the middle distance, jaw a slab of New Hampshire granite, Daniel Webster was holding forth:

". . . mistake to mention Edgar A. Poe in the same breath."

I expected more, and he did not disappoint me.

"Now, Bryant and Longfellow," he went on, "*and*, for all his turgid style, the prolific Fenimore Cooper—is he here? no?—all sing of the open spaces of America, of the frontier, of men on the move, of freedom if you will. Whereas Poe—is he here? yes?—"

"This is Edgar Poe, Mr. Secretary," said Rufus Griswold, and I took an awkward step forward, all too conscious of being studied, and not just by Daniel Webster.

He shook my hand. " 'The Murders in the Rue Morgue'! I congratulate you, sir! I would take an oath that the Chevalier C. Auguste Dupin, that master of ratiocination, is as real as our new Minister to Spain here."

I basked.

"However," said Daniel Webster. And paused. And resumed, "However, sir, I cannot but wonder why you insist on writing of tombs and vaults, of being buried alive or walled up, of murders and mesmeric horrors, of medieval dungeons and vampires—"

I may have said, "No vampires."

"—of portrait painters that leach the life from their subjects. Sir! All this, this Gothic, this German . . . claustrophobia when our country resounds with the clarion call of the West, the great beckoning wilderness—opportunity that a brave man can seize in his two strong American hands. Bryant! Longfellow! Sir, they shape America even as America shapes them!"

"Claustrophobia," said Washington Irving thoughtfully, tasting the word, judging. "And yet, it is a claustrophobia where horror lurks behind a mask of beauty and beauty behind horror, where—"

"Too subtle for a simple New Englander like me," said Daniel Webster disingenuously. "Now, you take Cooper—"

And I spoke. And found to my surprise, to my dismay, that— sobriety lurking behind a mask of drunkenness (or the reverse)—I could deploy structured sentences, giving crisp and clear voice to my thoughts.

My thoughts, it seems, were these:

"James Fenimore Cooper, sir—perhaps you can tell me why it is the invariable recourse of Mr. James Fenimore Cooper, should his work be reviewed unfavorably, a not infrequent occurrence, to sue the offending editor for libel?"

Under the circumstances, I think you will agree this was a marvel of nouns and verbs and modifiers, all in commendable syntactical order.

"Has Mr. Cooper brought litigation against you, then, Mr. Poe?"

The question pleased me, acknowledging as it did my status as a critic to be reckoned with. I smiled also and said:

"Such litigation, is this the opportunity you spoke of, sir, that a writer can seize in his strong American hands? Publicity via pettifoggery, not the printed page? If so, only the writer who inherits wealth, as Mr. Cooper has done, can win fame by hounding critics through the courts. Litigation is costly."

"Then he *has* brought an action against you?"

"He has not. But should he, I would know how to deal with it."

"And how, pray tell, would that be?"

"Sir, I would need only read aloud in open court some examples of Mr. Cooper's America-shaping prose."

Why was I saying these things?

Was I prey to some evil genius, a genie released from a bottle— a champagne bottle?

Or did I know exactly what I was doing?

"But Cooper would be present in open court, sir," said Daniel Webster, "and he is not present here."

Before I could say with what pleasure I would debate his litigiousness with Mr. Cooper, should we meet, the room again began to spin. In an instant my vertigo was so severe that I had to grab something, any thing, and hold on. I grabbed, and I held, and what I was clutching in both hands proved to be a broad and well-tailored shoulder, property of a man of some thirty-five years with a great prow of a nose and a jutting shelf of brow and the aura, as insufferable as it was unmistakable, of the privileged, patrician Bostonian.

With me adhering to his shoulder and staring from no great distance into his at once recognizable face, Henry Wadsworth Longfellow said with aplomb, "I do not believe I have had the pleasure, sir," and the room erupted in laughter.

When he could be heard, Secretary of State Webster pronounced my name and I made haste to release the Longfellow shoulder so that I might grasp the proffered Longfellow hand. But it was not to Longfellow I spoke; I directed my remarks to Daniel Webster.

"Here is another America-shaper I believe you mentioned, sir. None other than Professor Longfellow of Harvard."

How providential for me, I remember thinking, that Henry Wadsworth Longfellow was here, unlike Cooper, so that I might say what I thought freely and frankly.

"Professor Longfellow," I said freely and frankly, "why, Professor Longfellow has his own way of seizing opportunity in his strong American hands, has he not? He borrows it whenever the need arises. This is known in Boston as 'paying homage'—and he pays so much of it that it becomes difficult to know where Tennyson and Milton and Coleridge leave off and Professor Longfellow begins."

This charge, I ought to say, had been leveled before. Longfellow's admirers, who were many, generally offered the following in refutation: Mere similarity of two works does not signify plagiarism; on the contrary, the more the works resemble each other, the less possibility of plagiarism, for what man of letters would destroy his credibility by obviously copying another's work?

Daniel Webster, apparently an admirer of Longfellow, dismissed my words and myself from consideration by turning away—to address the young man at his side, who I realized was the President's son Rob. And what did Rob Tyler do? Rob Tyler, exchanging a glance with his father, turned up his hands to show their innocent palms.

Washington Irving studied me with a sphinx-like smile.

Rufus Griswold? There had been, until then, an occasional warning pressure on my elbow from Rufus Griswold's fingers, but I felt it no more; Griswold had taken up a position some distance from me.

Voices urged Longfellow to defend himself.

But in a mild tone, some would afterwards say murderously mild, he said merely, "I have always thought life too precious to waste in a street brawl with a drunkard."

The next thing I remember, I was outside and marching resolutely

from the President's House to the fading music of either "Lillibu-
lero" or "The Radetzky March," or some other rousing tune, or
perhaps just silence, my plagiarized cloak protecting me from the
night wind despite being worn inside out.

The following day disappeared. I have no recollection of it. Later
a friend—had I any left?—would say that, encountering me aimlessly wandering along Pennsylvania Avenue, he gave me fifty cents
to buy a hot meal. If so, this did not prevent me from being rav-
enously hungry on materializing at the door, the back door (had I
walked that absurd road again?) of Fuller's Hotel. It was Mr. Fuller
himself who admitted me, no doubt concluding from the reversal of
my cloak, red silk still outermost, and my stubbled chin and blear
eyes—were my hands trembling?—that I was indisputably not at
my best.

Upstairs, I flung myself across the bed and waited for sleep but
soon heard the rapid thumping drag of Frederick W. Thomas's crip-
pled left leg. He pounded at the door and entered carrying his greatcoat over one arm. I sat up.

"Will you remove that ridiculous cloak? You look like a disreputable circus performer."

"I fear I may have acted like one."

"So they tell me. Poe, what is the matter with you? Nothing on
this earth would have met your needs better than to be a customs
inspector at Philadelphia. Nineteen hundred dollars a year, man—
and all the time you need to write."

"Philadelphia?"

"It took some effort to persuade Rob Tyler that, for you, an overseas posting would not suit, but only one at home."

Frederick W. Thomas put on his greatcoat.

"You ought not to go out on a day like this," I told him.

"I must see Rob. You have squandered my credit with him."

Thomas, sighing, relented. "Have something to eat. Charge it to
my account. And no alcohol. I'll see to your fare home in the
morning."

But perhaps he had not relented. Perhaps he only wished to rid himself of me.

I had no such option.

Fifteen

There was something, as it were, remarkable—yes, *remarkable*, although this is but a feeble term to express my full meaning—about the entire individuality of the personage in question.
—"The Man That Was Used Up"

Nolie Mae Tangerie—what a name! It cannot be real. And yet the person indisputably is. I am all too conscious, carrying her limp form into the parlor, of the warm weight of her thighs on my arm, of her head lolling against my shoulder, of the long spill of her blond hair catching highlights from an antique lamp standing on an octagonal table of gold-threaded marble far too opulent for 6 Mechanics Row. Who has lit the lamp? It casts a soft light on the many portraits—of whose ancestors I shall never learn—hanging in gilt frames on the silver-gray papered walls. Twin sofas, of rosewood upholstered in crimson silk, face each other. Heavy silver drapes bracket the recessed window that looks out upon a garden, its privet hedges neatly clipped and gleaming greenly in the rain.

Why do I go on about all this?

Why but to gain a respite for reflection.

What does one do with a woman, a most attractive young woman, who has swooned in one's arms? Especially if her name is Nolie Mae Tangerie?

I place her supine upon a sofa, but she is so long of limb that her legs, encased in white muslin strap-trousers, dangle over one crimson-upholstered arm.

"Miss Tangerie," I say softly, and then louder, "Miss Tangerie." She does not respond.

I remember learning this at West Point: *See that the patient*—or had the word been victim?—*can freely breathe. Loosen tight clothing.*

Fumblingly, I liberate her throat from the confinement of the black silk stock—only to realize that her smoke-gray jacket is itself constricting. I unfasten the top three buttons, ready to pull my hand back from proximity to her breast at the faintest indication of her return to consciousness. A pulse is clearly perceptible in the side of her throat. I lay a finger against it. A steady beat, almost exactly one per second. Counting, I observe her face close up. It is fine-boned, the cheek-bones high, the eyes widely spaced. I see a tiny mole, of the sort called a beauty mark, at the corner of her mouth. I resist an impulse to trace lightly the shape of her lips. Instead, less boldly, I run my finger along the line of her jaw to her ear. A firm tug at the lobe might bring her around.

Her eyelids flutter.

I pull my hand back and stand erect, looking down, with a not entirely unjustified twinge of guilt, into her smoke-gray eyes.

She lifts her arms. "Will? What happened?"

"No, I am Phidias."

"But Will, he—"

"You have had a fright."

"—he was here!"

"The wind blew open the door," I tell her, "without warning. The door slammed against the wall."

"That was when he came in. Like—like a wind-blown shadow."

I point out in a cool and logical voice that the wind has no effect on shadows except as it moves the objects that cast them. This fails to persuade not only Miss Tangerie but myself, for I recall my own fleeting awareness of something—a shadow in addition to our own?—when the wind fluttered the candle flames.

Miss Tangerie is now seated with her long legs drawn up, folded to one side and half tucked under her—a position which women apparently find comfortable and which I have never seen a man attempt. She fingers her loosened stock and the unfastened buttons of her jacket; looks at me.

"I know I saw him."

"That is not possible. My brother is dead, Miss Tangerie."

"I have only your word for that."

She stands; we are the same height. She glares at me. Skepticism I am prepared for, but not anger. "And I have only your word that he is your brother."

"It was you who remarked the resemblance, not I."

"How can you not remember how your own brother died?"

"Henry was a sailor. He traveled the world. It is not at all unusual that I don't know the details of his death."

"That is not what you said. You said you did not remember."

By then I have followed her into the hall.

"How convenient. Am I also to believe that you remember nothing Will might have said about Panchatan?"

I have never before heard the name. But then how do I know it is an island, part of the Malay Archipelago?

Confused, I shake my head.

"Did *you* kill him?" She is at the door.

My mouth flies open. So does the door. She descends the three steps to the street, turns, mounts the stoop to brush past me and back inside.

"My hat," she says, and retrieves the black silk hat from the hall floor and claps it on her head. Her smoke-gray eyes give me a defiant look.

"If you think you will find it without my help, you are grossly mistaken," she says.

"Find what?"

"The Shard, Mr. Phidias Peacock. If that is your name."

She is at the door again, about to disappear forever.

For some abstruse reason I wish this not to happen, but all that occurs to me is to say, "What shard?"

"Tell me you would not kill for it. Anyone would. A saint would. *I* would."

"Kill for a . . . shard? A shard of what?"

"*The* Shard. If Will Henry is dead, he died trying to recover it. He always spoke of trying."

"Not to me."

"Then that proves you are not his brother."

Since I see no way to prove I am, I let that pass. "It was stolen from him?"

"By a shipmate, yes."

"A shipmate called Monk," I say, to my own surprise.

Miss Tangerie's response surprises me more. She grasps the lapels of my frock coat. "You know him? Where is he? Is he here in Baltimore?"

I nod. "He was this morning."

"You saw Monk this morning? Where?"

How can I tell her that it was in a Whig coop for penniless drunken drifters?

How do I even know of such a place?

"I do not remember where."

These words sound mendacious, even to me.

"You have the most convenient memory of any man I ever met."

There is a silence, not necessarily profound but troubling to me. I wish to tell her that I have met with an accident which has left my memory riddled with lacunae but I am afraid she will scoff at that too.

"For the man who can lead me to the Shard," she says, "I would do any thing—any thing. And never mind my name."

Her smoke-gray eyes smolder, her face blurs as it converges with mine, her hands release my lapels to clasp behind my neck, her mouth speaks against my mouth.

"Are you that man, Phidias?"

When I tell her a regretful no, she whirls from my embrace—or, rather, her embrace of me—cries "Oh!" and rushes out the door, clapping one hand to the crown of her hat to keep it from flying off.

Miss Tangerie aimlessly wanders the streets around the harbor. The afternoon grows late, the daylight fades. She hurries down narrow alleys, strides along rain-swept avenues. An occasional carriage rumbles by, or a wagon. Miss Tangerie begins to climb the road that leads to

Druid Hills, pausing to turn and gaze down at the harbor. She sees, as I would if I turned in the same direction, the tall masts of Baltimore clippers in the China trade, the French, the Argentine. Is her wandering less aimless than it appears? Does she know I am following her? I flatten myself against a brick wall. She resumes walking, makes two more turns, rapidly, the second into a narrow way awash with rain water. She raises her skirts. In no time the white muslin trousers are mud-splattered. I am too close; I drop back. The way intersects a broad avenue, where Miss Tangerie walks swiftly to the left. Ahead of her I can see trees and, rising above them to its impressive height of 160 feet, the white marble Doric column which supports Baltimore's most famous landmark, a statue of George Washington looking, some complain, almost Napoleonic. Miss Tangerie plunges into the little park. I follow, running. Why do I wish not to lose Miss Tangerie? Is it because she knows something about my brother?

I reach the base of the monument, the blue-veined white marble streaming rain. No Miss Tangerie. I do a circuit of the noble Doric column, and another. Half a dozen roads lead out from the little park, and she could have left by any of them.

I stand irresolute in the rain, feeling the gloom of the gathering dusk seep into my soul.

Sixteen

The realities of the world affected me as visions, and as visions only, while the wild ideas of the land of dreams became, in turn, not the material of my every-day existence, but in very deed that existence utterly and solely in itself.

—"Berenice"

It lacked half an hour of the time Edgar could expect the lamp-lighter to appear in the gathering dusk and ignite the four giant candelabra in the Place Vendôme.

Edgar found the great square as impressive as when he had earlier strolled through it with Alexandre—arcades on all four sides, steeply pitched roofs, massive paving stones underfoot. But the *pièce de résistance* was, of course, the lofty column rising from the center of the *place*, sheathed in bronze taken from twelve hundred enemy cannon captured at Austerlitz. Crowning it once more—it had been supplanted during the brief Restoration by a huge *fleur-de-lys*—stood a statue of Napoleon Bonaparte, now no longer in the imperial regalia of the original, but in an unheroic gray overcoat.

"A ridiculous statue from which one can read the recent history of my country," Alexandre had said with his usual ebullience. "Not that we Parisians have ever lacked an appreciation of the ridiculous. Consider this *hôtel particulier* here, my dear Poe. Once the home, the lair, of that mountebank Anton Mesmer, to whom all Europe came in hysterical homage."

"Numéro 16, Place Vendôme," said Edgar. "Of course."

Chagrined, Alexandre said, "How foolish of me to instruct you of all people on the subject of Mesmer. Nowadays the building is occupied by a personage no less singular. It happens I know him."

That Alexandre knew this singular personage, whoever he was, had not surprised Edgar. Alexandre knew everyone worth knowing in Paris, and not because he sought them out but rather the reverse. As for Edgar's interest in Anton Mesmer, born almost exactly a hundred years ago and notorious from Vienna to London, that was well known to any literate Frenchman. The translation of Edgar's long tale of horror "The Paradis Cure"* was, if not his most praised work, certainly his most discussed. Just as Mesmer was a pioneer of the sexual aspect of hysterical illness, so Edgar was a pioneer in writing of morbid mental states, and his fictional account of the lecherous charlatan's "treatment" of young women in his so-called Crisis Room, here at N° 16, Place Vendôme, had amused the French as much as it had shocked the American reading public.

---

* The Poe canon, unaccountably, contains no such tale, although in two of his lesser works he has written of Mesmerism, toward which he seems not unfavorably disposed. (Editor's note)

With a few minutes to spare, Edgar stood contemplating N° 16, wondering if he would feel some *rapport* with the setting of his celebrated story. He did not. He had used Mesmer's infamous history to pen a tale, that was all.

Entering the Rue de la Paix from the northern side of the square, Edgar saw a young woman in wide bonnet and shawl, carrying a large basket, walking toward him. He thought with a start that he knew her, only to conclude on closer inspection that she bore a superficial resemblance to his dear little cousin Virginia Clemm, who had been so kind to Henry when he was dangerously ill with consumption in Baltimore. Virginia was now living with their cousin Neilson, under whose auspices her introduction to society had been most successful.

Sipping a cup of black coffee at a small table outside the café where Henry was to meet him, Edgar experienced one of those peculiar, eerie, inexplicable . . . but let us be specific. It was then dusk and the street lamp made a loud popping sound as the lamp-lighter ignited the gas with his long torch. At that instant the extraordinary notion entered Edgar's mind that he had sat here before, on this very wicker chair, at this very marble-topped table, watching this very lamp-lighter (who dragged his left leg along like Frederick W. Thomas). With the glow of the gas, colors sprang into being in the black-and-white of dusk, and it became more than a notion: he was absolutely certain that all this was happening for the second time.

It was ten-thirty on his gold repeater when he became convinced Henry was not coming. He felt a distinct unease. He had written weeks earlier giving his estimated date of arrival. True, the ship had made superb time, and it was conceivable that he had arrived in Paris ahead of his letter. But even so, had not Alexandre sent a message to Henry earlier today, arranging the *rendez-vous* at this very café? Edgar now felt a fool for not getting Henry's address from Alexandre—for mail he had simply been using Poste Restante—when they dined together at Procope on the Left Bank near the theater where Alexandre's luridly melo-dramatic *La Tour de Nesle*, no less Gothic than Edgar's own tales, was playing.

Hurrying down to the river, Edgar paid his sou and crossed the iron walkway of the Pont des Arts, hoping to reach the theater before the final curtain and so find Alexandre there, as he was sure to be, at the end of the performance. Alexandre, no matter how many times he saw his play, would laugh and cry more enthusiastically than the most uninhibited members of the audience, since he enjoyed enormously "precisely the sort of plays I write, my dear Poe. That is why I write them."

Edgar found him, splendidly attired, surrounded by admirers, in the brilliantly lit foyer. Henry's friend Alexandre Dumas was then about thirty years old and at the height of his success as a playwright. He had literally to fend off importuners and hangers-on, and now used Edgar as a means of doing so:

"Ah, here is my American friend at last! You will excuse us, Macquet?"

He steered Edgar through the departing throng, murmuring, "Can you believe it? That tiresome little school teacher actually wants me to collaborate with him. On a long novel, if you please! I write for the theater, I told him."

"And superbly. Why should that dramatic flair not carry over to the printed page?"

"But the subject, my dear Poe—the memoirs of some Gascon called Charles de Baatz d'Artagnan. Hopelessly obscure. Yet Macquet keeps pestering. Well! And where is the flamboyant Henry?"

"I waited, but he did not come."

"Quite in character, I assure you. So! We shall go to his rooms and no doubt interrupt him in a delicate moment with someone's dissatisfied wife. For these, my dear Poe, your brother is lately considered the sovereign remedy, although he tells me such a role is more yours than his, in your country."

"He exaggerates."

"Always," said Alexandre Dumas dryly. "Cab!"

Alexandre and Edgar weren't the only ones waiting—but the playwright's commanding figure, his regal attire, his large head of frizzy hair and swarthy face were unmistakable, and they were soon in a hackney cabriolet on their way to Henry's rooms "in the Rue de la Gaîté, on the edge of the city, my dear Poe, but a stylishly *louche* street ideally suited—at least at night—to your brother's way of life."

The Rue de la Gaîté was chock-a-block with dance halls and restaurants. It was difficult to believe that by day the street was, as Alexandre said, hardly more than a country lane "too bucolic for Henry's tastes. But then, he sleeps by day, rather like the Chevalier C. Auguste Dupin. Here we are."

A crowd milled about the front of one of the larger restaurants. Three gendarmes stood sentinel before an adjacent narrow doorway, encouraging pedestrians to move along.

A worried little man with a completely bald head that looked yellow in the glow of the oil lamps that lit the street (gas not yet having reached the Rue de la Gaîté) was saying:

"A fortune! The apartment was worth a veritable fortune. The salon alone, a masterpiece, a scrupulous reproduction of the abode of the courtesan Madame de—"

One of the gendarmes recognized Alexandre. This was not surprising. His face was arguably the most recognizable in Paris.

"Monsieur Alexandre Dumas!" said the gendarme, and saluted.

Alexandre said, "I hope there is no trouble here?"

"Routine trouble only, Monsieur Dumas."

"Perhaps, but this gentleman is the brother of the occupant of the rooms upstairs."

The gendarme exchanged glances with his two colleagues, then addressed Edgar in rapid French. Edgar congratulated himself on his ability to understand. His self-satisfaction did not last long.

"You are the brother of Monsieur William Henry Leonard Poe, American, of Baltimore, Maryland, by occupation a merchant seaman?"

"I am."

"*Hélas,*" he heard one of the other gendarmes mutter.

The three conferred. The first gendarme grimly led the way upstairs.

————

The furniture—"priceless inlaid rosewood," the man with the completely bald yellow head had moaned—looked as if it had been attacked with ax and sledge-hammer. So did the white marble mantelpiece. Brocaded draperies lay heaped beneath denuded windows along with curtain rods and valances. Glittering shards of Murano glass and T'ang porcelain mingled with the shattered remnants of plain panes from two glass-fronted bookcases. Books were strewn about, splayed and broken-backed, the bookcases themselves reduced to so much kindling. The upholstery of the pair of matching sofas, of the *récamier*, of the occasional chairs was slashed and shredded. The *toile de Jouy* wall covering hung in strips. A section of the parquet floor had been prised up.

"In the bedroom," said the gendarme softly, showing the way with a ceramic lamp, miraculously undamaged.

In the bedroom, a corner cupboard was torn from its moorings, the canopy ripped from the four-poster bed, the wash stand broken—or broken into, as "in it was a small safe," said the gendarme. Chairs were dismembered, chair seats disemboweled, the mattress gutted, the pillows and eiderdown eviscerated. Feathers— bloody feathers—were everywhere. Blood was everywhere.

From the spattered carpet the gendarme picked up a rosewood footstool. In the light of the ceramic lamp, hair and gore could be seen clinging to it.

"The murder weapon," said the gendarme.

"Murder?" Edgar repeated.

"Whoever was beaten with that footstool could not possibly have survived, monsieur. That soft substance there? It is brain."

Alexandre and Edgar looked at each other.

"We know," said the gendarme, "that William Henry Leonard Poe was seen to return home at about seven-thirty this evening. Shortly thereafter—according to the testimony of patrons of the restaurant downstairs—a commotion could be heard coming from these premises. Alas, the customary noise from the dance halls on either side reduces the credibility of such testimony. No one was seen to leave, but there is a back entrance and a flight of stairs that egresses into an empty field. A trail of blood leads across the field, ending where the weeds have evidently been flattened by wagon wheels. It must be concluded, Monsieur Poe, that at or about seven-thirty an unknown assailant or assailants waiting here in the apartment beat to death and removed the body of William Henry Leonard Poe, or that, conversely, William Henry Leonard Poe beat to death and removed the body of an unknown visitor."

"That is ridiculous!" Edgar cried. "Do you seriously suggest that Henry searched his own apartment in the presence of a visitor and then killed that visitor?"

"Hardly, monsieur. But could it not be that William Henry Leonard Poe found the searcher here, and that they fought, and that your brother killed him?"

"No less ridiculous! Why try to conceal the slaying of an unlawful intruder?"

"Calmly, calmly. When murder has been committed in hot blood, any thing is possible. Not that I mean to imply that your brother . . . *donc*, monsieur, what can you tell me about him?"

Edgar wondered what he *could* tell the gendarme; it had been three years since he had last seen Henry.

Still, dawn was lighting the windows by the time he and Alexandre were downstairs and outside. Despite the hour, Alexandre had no trouble getting a cab. He never did.

"With luck, we may find Dupin still awake," he said, and told the driver, "Numéro 16, Place Vendôme, and hurry!"

Seventeen

"If it is any point requiring reflection," observed Dupin, . . . "we shall examine it to better purpose in the dark."
—"The Purloined Letter"

The Chevalier C. Auguste Dupin was living that year in one apartment of the *hôtel particulier* occupied in the last century by Anton Mesmer. Alexandre led the way into a vast room, its stained-glass windows casting a dim, religious glow reflected by mirror-covered walls. Incense wafted from an antique bowl upon the massive mantelpiece.

The Chevalier sat before a table in the exact center of the room bearing an oval vessel of majolica at least four feet long and one deep. In it were wine bottles "filled with magnetized water," said C. Auguste Dupin with a thin smile. "When 'receiving,' Mesmer would fill the vessel itself with water and toss in a handful of iron filings for effect."

There seemed an infinity of Dupins, for the mirrors on opposite walls reflected themselves back at each other in smaller and smaller versions of the room and its occupant. For a startling moment Edgar did not see himself or Alexandre reflected, but on looking again he did. It must have been some trick of the light.

After Alexandre presented the American, Dupin explained, "It amuses me to live here. Intrigues me, even. If a place can be 'haunted' by a former resident, if it can retain a residue of his personality, then perhaps I may learn the secret of that charlatan Mesmer's 'animal magnetism.' It certainly wasn't what he claimed it was." Again the thin smile. "Well—on what errand have you come, my dear Alexandre?"

While Alexandre told him their mission, Dupin stuffed and lit a meerschaum. Edgar could not see clearly the Chevalier's face, for he wore spectacles tinted dark green and sat in shadow cast by no discernible object. Perhaps it was just the dimness of the room.

Dupin asked Edgar a few questions, then said:

"*Bien*, I shall call today on my friend G——, the Prefect of Police, and with his permission—a matter of routine—visit the premises. Could you return at, say, eleven this evening?"

They left, Alexandre observing—to Edgar's surprise, after so short a meeting—that the case had manifestly piqued Dupin's curiosity. C. Auguste Dupin habitually slept by day, prowled the streets of Paris by night, and solved crimes, *if* they interested him, by ratiocination. "God knows when. He is like a vampire," said Alexandre, "in his aversion to daylight. This is the real reason he lives in Mesmer's old house; its past diverts him and its stained glass turns the day almost into night. If he could, the Chevalier would banish daylight."

"Why does he dislike it so?"

"Ah, why?" echoed Alexandre.

That evening at N° 16, Place Vendôme, C. Auguste Dupin was seated before the majolica vessel smoking his meerschaum as if he had not budged from the spot. He began speaking at once.

"First, one wishes to know what your brother was doing in Paris. He was a seaman, an inveterate wanderer, yet he had taken a lease on the apartment in the Rue de la Gaîté. Why?"

Edgar was unable to say why.

"Was he perhaps in hiding? No, for he lived openly under his own name. Was he waiting for something? What might it have been?"

Edgar said he did not know.

"No interruptions, if you please. The question was rhetorical," said C. Auguste Dupin with a touch of irritation. "Now then. Was he romantically entangled with a woman?"

Edgar said nothing.

"Was he, monsieur?" said Dupin with the same slight irritation. "*That* was no rhetorical question."

Edgar glanced at Alexandre, as if to ask, how can one tell the difference? Alexandre returned a cryptic smile.

"My brother," Edgar said candidly, "though a womanizer, avoided entanglements."

"I should not have said 'though a womanizer,'" said Dupin, "but rather '*because* a womanizer.' Never mind, we may let the subject of women pass, at least for now. In what is left of the apartment, there is no evidence of a woman's presence.

"There is, however, ample evidence of an intruder. Who might this intruder have been? A random burglar? I think not. The sneak thief, after all, sneaks. He does not, even in the throes of frustration, wreck the premises so very noisily.

"So, the intruder was drawn, *specifically*, either to the premises or to the tenant. Which is the more likely?"

Another rhetorical question? Edgar remained silent.

"We dismiss," Dupin went on, "the premises *per se*. Burglary cannot have been the object, for of the valuable furnishings, and they were all pricey if not tasteful"—the Chevalier smiled his thin smile—"none was taken away. *Au contraire*, most were utterly destroyed. Yet if destruction were the object—if the intruder wished, say, to avenge a grievance against the landlord—could he not have accomplished this more expeditiously, and with less risk of apprehension, simply with some volatile liquid and a phosphorus match?

"Thus, the tenancy of William Henry Leonard Poe appears the pivotal factor. Again, what was the intruder's aim? Theft? Destruction?"

This time Edgar hazarded an answer. "Not destruction. The furnishings belonged to the landlord rather than to Henry."

"Quite. So we postulate theft. The intruder sought an item *of which he had knowledge*. We may further assume, from the manner of the search, that the item was not large—and, from the wantonness of the destruction, that it was not frangible. Unless, that is, the destruction was all a blind.

"Now, was the mysterious item found? No, not unless it had been hidden in the last place searched—because every obvious place *was* searched. Probably, then, it is still there, whatever it is. If, of course, it ever was there at all."

Dupin sucked on his now dead meerschaum. "It remains to ask why the corpse was removed from the premises. Because the manner of death could yield a clue to the killer's identity? But the presumed murder weapon was a footstool which could have been wielded by anyone, man or woman, of reasonable strength. Perhaps, then, because the identity of the victim might point to the identity of his murderer?"

"The victim," Edgar said coldly, "was my brother."

"That is likely but not certain—as I believe the police, despite their shortcomings, have already recognized."

"Monsieur, I dislike the imputations of both the police and yourself." Edgar stood, trying to penetrate the opacity of Dupin's green spectacles. Alexandre placed a restraining hand upon his arm.

"A third possibility," Dupin said as Edgar sat again, "is that there was no corpse. The blood and the brain matter on the footstool could have been those of an animal."

"What!" Edgar cried.

"This would be the case if your brother, needing urgently to disappear, contrived the evidence of his own demise."

Again Edgar sprang to his feet.

"Please, monsieur," said Dupin. "I do not urge the thesis. I merely say it is not impossible. Are you a brave man?"

"If you are asking whether I place any limits on what I am prepared to do to find my brother's killer, I place none."

"*Bien*, for now we shall proceed on the assumption that, resisting the efforts of a visitor to search his premises, William Henry Leonard Poe was killed—and that the murderer failed to find the object of his search. Based on these assumptions, what course would you propose?"

Edgar said at once, "I should go and live there."

"Precisely, monsieur. You should," said the Chevalier C. Auguste Dupin, "occupy your brother's abode and await the return of the killer, who assuredly *will* return if what he sought is worth killing for."

Eighteen

Genius, as a general rule, is poor in worldly goods.

—*Marginalia*

Every morning just after dawn I would sit at my table, pen in hand, ink-well full, stack of cheap paper at the ready. Nights I slept little. I could not wait to attack my work—not that I knew what it would be. Inspiration would strike when I sat at my table. It had struck prodigiously for more than a year after I dragged myself back from Washington City, so why not now? Nothing had changed. It was the same small table, the same small room, the same small window facing the woods so that I could almost believe I was not in our part-of-a-house in Philadelphia but in some sylvan paradise that waited primordially to be filled by my imagination.

I had filled it. I had filled it with black cats and tell-tale hearts, with pit and pendulum, with the glory that was Greece and the grandeur that was Rome, with "The Gold Bug" (first prize of a hundred dollars in a story contest, and Henry said again in the awesome silences of memory that that would put a lot of roast beef on the table). I had transformed the shadowed paths of those woods into the streets of Paris, where, eyes inscrutable behind green spectacles, the Chevalier C. Auguste Dupin could walk all night, every night, ratiocinating. Editors clamored for more; readers liked the gifted French *amateur* of detection. Did I comply? No. I left the Chevalier in his unlit rooms in Paris, forever awaiting a new mystery to test his remarkable powers of deduction. Why? I cannot say why. I knew, and the critics said, that with Dupin I had created a new genre of fiction. Perhaps merely to have done so satisfied me. Perhaps I was glad to abandon the field to my imitators, of whom there soon were many, while I returned to those haunted haunts which, for whatever reason, attracted my pen and summoned my soul.

But I did not return. Like Dupin in the Paris of my imagination,

I waited. Soon every morning was the same. Inspiration would strike when I sat at my table? Inspiration did not strike. I looked at the gin bottle; touched it; shook it gently. Like a loved baby it gurgled at me. And of course I uncorked it. Every morning the same, starting with a single drink to prove I was no drunkard. I no longer frequented bar-rooms; no longer frequented anywhere; had not the money. Had, in fact, to trust that Muddy's piecework would keep us from starving. I wished she would remonstrate with me, but she did not. I wished Virginia would complain, but she remained unfailingly cheerful. The only one who despaired of me was myself.

Not writing, I lost the writer's one inestimable defense against despair. I could not lose myself in a world I was creating, a world virtually identical to the quotidian but with those small differences a writer will impose upon it to forward the tale he is telling, and in any event a better world because not exactly this world.

One day not long before noon, Rufus Griswold arrived unexpectedly, as he did every few months. Two years had passed since the fiasco at the President's House. It was early spring, as then; cold, as then. Rufus Griswold bowed over Virginia's hand, and Muddy's. He did not remove his box coat.

"Congratulate me," he said. "Third printing." He was referring to his anthology *The Poets and Poetry of America*.

I congratulated him.

"And your work, is it going well?" he asked.

The glances exchanged by Virginia and Muddy were answer enough.

He said, "Why do you remain in this stultifying town?" His brow was more furrowed than usual, but he was smiling his fleshy-lipped smile. Rufus Griswold seemed to wear the faces of two men at odds with each other, and I could not have said which, if either, was the licensed Baptist preacher.

"Why do *you?*" I asked.

"I? I am leaving." He unfolded a sheet torn from a newspaper. "As Horace Greeley says—"

"You are going west?" I asked in amazement. For Rufus Griswold maintained that the frontier was the refuge of scoundrels.

"Certainly not."

He handed me the tear sheet. It was an editorial by Greeley, editor of the *New York Daily Tribune*, extolling the virtues of his city. Manhattan Island (I read) was being developed far to the north. Along Fifth Avenue all the way to Forty-second Street the brown-stone mansions extended like Venetian *palazzi* along the banks of the Grand Canal. If you held on to property long enough you would become as rich as John Jacob Astor. Who was an immigrant. New York's population of almost half a million was almost half immigrant. Perhaps to distinguish themselves from these uncouth, illiterate foreigners, native New Yorkers *read*. The city abounded in poet-editors and fiction-writing editors, in publishing houses like Harper & Brothers, like Wiley & Putnam. Of magazines, fifty-four appeared in New York each month, with a combined circulation as large as the city's population. There were "literary soirées the equal of any thing Paris can offer," smile-frowned Rufus Griswold. "How right Greeley is, Poe! Sooner or later the ambitious, the gifted, man of letters must confront the challenge of the Empire City. I leave next week."

Again Muddy and Virginia exchanged glances.

"You are looking well, Mrs. Poe," Griswold said.

"Her bronchitis is much improved," said Muddy.

Virginia *was* looking well. She had spent her first easy winter since bursting a blood vessel while singing.

"I am happy to hear it," said Griswold. "Then, should the occasion arise, Mrs. Poe could travel?"

The thought of New York had always excited me; I needed no Horace Greeley or Rufus Griswold to remind me of its attractions.

"I haven't the money," I said frankly.

These words erased the moist smile from Rufus Griswold's fleshy lips. Left to itself, his furrowed forehead oddly seemed not a frown but rather a reluctant admission of happiness.

"What are friends for?" he said.

I did not reply.

"This is no place for you, Poe. Even those who once championed you say that you are finished. I have heard the words 'drunken sot' used."

Virginia came to my side.

Muddy said, "Please leave this house."

But I shook my head. "He came to talk. Let him."

Rufus Griswold bowed to Muddy. "I assure you, Mrs. Clemm, I mean Eddie no harm. I only wish him to recognize that his future is not here in Philadelphia."

Why? What difference did it make to Rufus Griswold if I had any future at all?

"I am prepared to lend you fifty dollars," he said, "to help you establish yourself in New York."

I was on the point of declining the offer with some minimal expression of gratitude when I saw that Muddy, with ill-concealed excitement, had begun to set the table. She produced tea, and bread toasted atop the stove, and, from God knows where, thin slices of ham, pink and succulent-looking. Rufus Griswold seated Muddy; I, Virginia. Upon the table was a dish bearing a slab, not small, of butter. Virginia and I stared at it, as if Muddy had duplicated the miracle of the loaves and fishes.

Tea was poured. There was little conversation. I watched Virginia eating. I imagined us seated *tête-à-tête* at a choice table, left of the door as you enter, at Delmonico's in New York. Virginia was wearing an emerald velvet gown, its deep neckline edged with a spill of frothy lace. Entering with his usual coterie, Horace Greeley bowed and kissed Virginia's cheek. We chatted. Virginia was witty and charming. Greeley and his party moved on reluctantly to their own table. A waiter appeared at my elbow with a bottle of champagne. "Compliments of Mr. Delmonico," he said, and poured bubbling wine into two flutes.

Muddy and Virginia cleared the table, Muddy brushing at a strand of her white hair, tucking it back into her widow's bonnet.

The other Virginia, the one at Delmonico's, laughed. The champagne bubbles tickled her nose, she said. Her eyes said we ought to hurry our meal and get home while we could still have the house to ourselves, before the children—twins; twin girls—came back from the park with their nanny.

"Then it is agreed?" Rufus Griswold asked. Muddy made some reply. I may have spoken.

A stage whisper at Delmonico's: "That is Edgar A. Poe. Author of — ——."

"His wife is so elegant. I would kill for an invitation to her soirées. Next week they say she is having the Hungarian pianist Franz Liszt."

"Some men have all the luck."

Everyone was standing except me, so I stood. Rufus Griswold was putting away his wallet, Muddy folding some bills. Virginia looked as if she were holding her breath.

"Eddie finds such details irksome," Muddy was saying.

"No more than I, my dear Mrs. Clemm. He is fortunate to have you to take them off his hands." Rufus Griswold, at the door, buttoned his box coat. He took a courtly leave of the ladies, and motioned for me to accompany him outside. The door shut behind us.

"There is," he said, "no urgency about the money. I am in funds. If you need more——"

"No. No, we will manage."

"I had in mind not a loan but a commission. Would it interest you to write a review for a Boston journal?"

"A review of what?"

But of course I knew.

"They wish to run a long piece on *The Poets and Poetry of America* to mark its third edition."

Had the fifty dollars been in my pocket, I would have returned it. But how could I demand of Muddy that she give it back? I had seen the look on her face, and Virginia's.

"I have always wondered," I said stiffly, "how one went about soliciting puffs."

Rufus Griswold's high forehead was now as unlined as a baby's. He smiled.

"Do you actually believe I require that you puff my book? My dear Poe! All I ask is that you review it, entirely as you see fit. They will pay you top rates. Thirty-five dollars, I should say."

I calculated swiftly. Added to his loan, thirty-five dollars would resettle us in New York with perhaps a fortnight's expenses in hand.

"Entirely as I see fit?"

"I never meant to imply otherwise."

Early in April of 1844 we arrived in New York.

Nineteen

And the silken sad uncertain rustling of each purple curtain
Thrilled me—filled me with fantastic terrors never felt before;
So that now, to still the beating of my heart, I stood repeating:
" 'Tis some visitor entreating entrance at my chamber door—
Some late visitor entreating entrance at my chamber door;
    This it is and nothing more."

—"The Raven"

"They won't collect it at the door, will they?" Virginia asked.

"No. Why should they?"

"I want to keep it always."

The invitation was engraved on heavy ivory stock.

Miss Anne Charlotte Lynch
requests the pleasure of the company
of
Edgar A. Poe, Esq., and Mrs. Poe
116 Waverly Place
Saturday, March 18
7 o'clock

"Now that your husband is a celebrity," said Muddy dryly, "you'll need a satchel to hold them all."

"Oh, Muddy, she should have invited you too!"

"Now hush, and let me help you into this."

"This" was an arcane contraption of plaited horsehair in the shape of a wheel. It disappeared from atop the screen which hid my wife and mother-in-law from view. Before the horsehair wheel, to begin at the beginning and proceed in order, had disappeared a flannel petticoat, and one of crinoline (more horsehair) with a braided straw hem, and one of simple calico. Remaining atop the screen now were a starched white muslin petticoat and Virginia's gown, pink and white and frothy as a summer cloud, in counterpoint to the blustery March evening and the rattle of sleet at the window.

Virginia squealed in what could have been delight or discomfort under Muddy's unseen ministrations. I myself was already attired in black frock coat, gray waistcoat with satin collar, black trousers. I stood before the small chipped mirror, adjusting my black silk cravat. Alongside my image appeared that frothy pink-and-white cloud above which floated Virginia's face.

"We look more like each other all the time, don't you think?" she said.

In the mirror the resemblance was indeed apparent. My eyes were gray, Virginia's deep blue; her features were delicate, although her mouth was fuller than mine; her face was round, mine triangular; hers wore an expression of tranquillity, mine seemed always on the verge of querulousness. And yet, somehow from these differences a strong likeness emerged.

"Well, you *are* first cousins," said Muddy.

"In addition to the fact," said Virginia, whirling about the room like pink smoke in her crinolined gown, "that Mr. Poe and I have been married for*ever*. Oh Eddie!" And for a fleeting instant she was in my arms.

Another whirl and she picked the invitation up again. " 'Miss Anne Charlotte Lynch,' " she recited, " 'requests the pleasure of the company of Edgar A. Poe. . . .' Can Mr. Poe dance the quadrille?"

"Not a single solitary step of it."

"Or the polka?"

"Not a hop or a skip or a jump of it."

"Hopeless. He may have to sing for his supper."

"It is entirely possible, but there won't be much supper. Tea and cookies, more likely, for such a crowd."

Virginia executed a graceful hop and three small steps. "Very swift, the polka. Swift as a swift. And not only do we look alike, my *cousin* and I, but observe this legerdemain."

She was leaning over the table. I heard the scratching of a pen, my pen, the pen that had written "The Raven" and made me famous overnight, if not precisely rich. If, in fact, no less poor than before. The poem, printed on the back page of the *New York Evening Mirror* of January 29 (how could I forget the date!), had already been re-printed a dozen times that I knew of. But the *Mirror*, not I, owned the rights, and while the Tree-Sparing Editor* was open-handed—his wife's seamstress had created the pink-and-white cloud worn by Virginia—there were limits to his generosity.

Poor or no, I had been transformed from a rather acerbic literary critic, one Poe, who also penned poems and tales, to Edgar A. Poe, Esq., author of "The Raven." Parodies of my black bird proliferated. I had seen copies of "The Corbie" and "The Craven" and "The Giant Squash." There was a Whippoorwill, a Turkey, a Temperance Owl. Even a medicated soap was advertised in rhyme poorly miming "The Raven." In short, on the wings of my black bird, I had arrived.

Virginia handed me what she had written: *Fame is the most famous of aphrodisiacs. Take heed, Sir Famous Raven. After the ball, I turn into an insatiable hetaera.*

She looked like a pixie in a pink cloud.

I desired her as I had not allowed myself to do in years.

Thus it was a moment before I understood: The handwriting could almost have been my own. I grinned at her, quite wolfishly, and thrust the paper into my pocket.

Muddy looked a question at her daughter.

---

* The editor and song writer George Pope Morris, author of "Woodman, Spare That Tree." (Editor's note)

"Gibberish," Virginia assured her. "The words are just words. It's the handwriting that— You tell her, Eddie."

"Your daughter is a master forger. I can hardly distinguish her hand from my own."

"Be warned," Virginia intoned darkly. "I can duplicate your signature as easily, Mr. Poe."

And she laughed. It was, over nothing, probably the gayest laughter I have ever heard, which, probably, was why I threw my head back and began to laugh too, which, probably, was why I did not notice Virginia's laughter breaking upon a cough until I saw her lovely face become mask-like, only the large eyes showing her terror as, standing motionless and rigid, she tried not to cough again. But she did. She coughed; she coughed. Muddy too stood frozen in place, both hands to her mouth. Virginia could not stop coughing. I gripped her shoulders tightly. She could not and could not stop coughing. Her face reddened, contorted. Her eyes shut; tears streamed from them. Her shoulders shook. Holding her, I felt each spasm as if something were tearing loose inside me.

"You will be late, Eddie."

She was in bed, her face as white as the paper on which she had duplicated my handwriting.

"I'm not going."

"Eddie, you must. *Please* go. I swallowed down the wrong pipe, and it made me cough. It's nothing to worry about."

I sat on the edge of the bed and reached for her cold hand, but she withdrew it.

"Eddie, go! You can tell me every thing later—every thing. It will be the same as if I went with you."

"There will be other *conversazioni*."

"But this is your first. And Miss Anne Charlotte Lynch, she's the *crème de la crème*. Oh, Eddie, if you don't go, I shall never forgive myself."

Miss Anne Charlotte Lynch was, if not beautiful, certainly an arrestingly pretty woman a few years younger than myself.

"Would it be a terrible imposition, Mr. Poe?"

"You catch me unprepared," I said, hoping my answer sounded unprepared as well.

"We would all be grateful. But you seem . . . preoccupied, Mr. Poe. I do hope it is not your wife's indisposition?"

"She has a touch of bronchitis, Miss Lynch," I said. "Nothing more."

"I am relieved, Mr. Poe." Miss Lynch smiled the social smile that is the product of the best schools for young ladies. " 'Nothing more,' " she went on. "Small wonder that you quote yourself. How . . . puissant 'The Raven' is! 'Nothing more'—and then the change to that remarkable, that haunting 'Nevermore' which becomes, if I may borrow a term from music, the *leitmotiv* for all that follows—that is little short of genius."

I replied with a few words of appreciation of her appreciation, all the while wishing I had not come. But I was here, and here was a *conversazione*, and as Miss Lynch seemed for the moment disinclined to seek hers elsewhere, I conversed.

"Are they Viennese?"

A plump woman in a tiered heliotrope gown was playing the piano, accompanying a tall man scraping a fiddle with swooping motions of its bow and his shoulders.

"She is. He is from Cracow. Jews, if the truth be known. But no one interprets the polka better. You do not dance it?"

"I never learned. If the truth be known."

"One day I shall shock my friends. A Viennese waltz, Mr. Poe. It is all the rage in London. But I fear that here in New York, some would find it . . . wicked."

A couple came polkaing energetically by. The man nodded to me. His partner's eyes sought mine. She was a sprite of a girl with alabaster skin and hair as black and glossy, I could not help thinking, as the wing of a raven.

"Rufus Griswold I believe you know," said Miss Lynch, following my gaze. The couple whirled, hopped, stepped, again whirled. The girl's eyes kept meeting mine until Griswold danced her away. "*She* is Fanny Osgood," Miss Lynch informed me.

"Frances Sargent Osgood?"

"The same. She is most eager to meet you."

"When I worked as an editor in Philadelphia, I published her poetry."

"They say she is a free spirit, a wood nymph. What are they called, mereids?"

"Dryads."

"Dryads, yes. She will not see thirty again," said Miss Lynch, "our delightful little wood nymph."

"Had you told me eighteen, I should not have doubted it."

Miss Lynch laughed a gossipy laugh. "She likes you too, Mr. Poe. My goodness, almost nine o'clock already! Time for your *Corvus corax*—you do understand Latin, Mr. Poe?—to appear at the window."

I surveyed the drawing room which Miss Lynch's guests, now executing a quadrille across the hall, soon would fill to hear me recite "The Raven." Chairs in rows faced a white marble fireplace. A fire of birch logs flamed brightly. On a dozen tables, as many lamps had been lit. I pictured myself, one elbow too self-consciously casual upon the mantelpiece as I recited, the lamps casting a pitiless glare on my face. "The Raven" required more intimacy; I, less light. I began moving chairs. Soon I had formed a small amphitheater facing away from the fire. At the center I placed a single table, on it an astral lamp, turned low. I looked about. Had I time to turn down all the lamps? Moving swiftly, I began to do so.

Our eyes met over a cut-glass shade near the fireplace as we both reached to turn the wick down. Our hands touched. I withdrew mine; she, hers. We both reached again, and again our hands touched. Her eyes were gray, the same gray as my own with flecks of hazel, and luminous in the astral lamp's glow. Her lips were trembling. The room was not cold. I realized with a start that she was frightened of me.

"You are most exigent in your arrangements, Mr. Poe."

" 'The Raven' needs a dim melancholy crepuscular light. Or even darkness. Have you read it, Mrs. Osgood?"

"I have read it a dozen times. And your tales hardly less often."

"What, only a dozen?" I could not have said whether my irony was intended to dispel or heighten her awe of me.

We were then standing over another lamp. She looked up, seemed on the verge of speaking but did not.

"Cat got your tongue?"

"More likely it was a raven."

I could hear footsteps in the hall, and voices.

She said, "I think they are wrong who say you are an unworldly man," and laughed a nervous little laugh.

"Is that what they say?"

"They find it charming, your unworldliness. Have I offended you?"

"No one who has read 'The Raven' twelve times can possibly offend me, Mrs. Osgood."

"Some even say unearthly, but that is mistaking the work for the man. Tell me, Mr. Poe, why does Rufus Griswold dislike you?"

The doors of the drawing room opened and the audience came in.

I found Virginia sitting up in bed, her knees making a tent of the blanket and the January 29 edition of the *Mirror*.

Lightly I kissed her dry lips. She felt feverish to my touch.

"Were you magnificent, darling?"

How to tell her I was rescued from a stuttering stage fright by the sprite who had sat, skirt tucked decorously about her legs, on the floor at my feet, rapt gray eyes looking up at me in the dim light, teeth a gleam of white, lips moving in unison with mine as, softly, she spoke the words I was reciting?

"They were still there when I finished."

"Is Miss Lynch as beautiful as they say?"

"Attractive. I would have said, rather, attractive."

"Tell me about the house."

I described the twin reception rooms flanking the entrance hall, the marble fireplaces, the rich crimson silk upholstery, the silver-gray wallpaper accented by heavy silver drapes, the ancestral portraits in frames with the luster of burnished gold, the gold-threaded marble table tops, the "astral lamps made gaudy, unfortunately, by cut-glass shades. But they could have been worse. They could have been gas jets."

"Was there dancing?"

"A few sets. Miss Lynch threatens to bring the Viennese waltz to New York."

"Oooh! Did you know anyone there?"

"Rufus Griswold. And, oh yes, a poet from Boston whose work I published last year in Philadelphia."

"Who is he?"

"She, actually. A Mrs. Osgood. Wife of the portrait painter Samuel Stillman Osgood."

"Oh yes, I have heard of him. What are they like?"

"He was not in attendance. Mrs. Osgood had Rufus for her escort."

It was five or six weeks before I saw her again, at the New York Society Library. It was a forenoon lecture, my audience mostly women. She arrived late and breathless, just as I had begun some observations, neither heated nor acerbic, on the unjustifiable ascendancy of New England poets. She slipped into a vacant chair toward the rear of the hall, and, looking at her, I began at once to extemporize with an unaccustomed glibness, to sharpen my attack with, as the newspapers would have it, a wit that fell just short of malice. "A champion of this gratuitous New England ascendancy is the anthologist Mr. Rufus Griswold, whose *Poets and Poetry in America* claims national scope but, as a perusal demonstrates, is quite depressingly provincial, placing at the center of the universe that city which its natives, should the rest of us harbor any doubts, style the Hub."

These remarks were greeted by smiles and a smattering of applause. *She* laughed and clapped her hands—not decorously like the others, but rather as a child might in response to a delightful if daring prank. This encouraged me to improvise further. I assailed Boston as "a city where, as any native will tell you unasked, the bricks are a brighter red than those in lesser metropolises. I am assured, by the same Mr. Griswold, that this is a consequence of the exemplary quality of New England clay. I am also assured that the clarity of Boston air, the only air fit for poets to breathe, imparts a corresponding clarity of thought, denied us unfortunates forced to dwell in such miasmic climes as Manhattan. The surpassing greenness of the grass on the Common—which I myself would describe as the surpassing commonness of the grass on the Green—"

The laughter mounted. When I concluded my remarks, I found myself surrounded by the usual seekers of autographs and askers of questions, mostly rhetorical. She, to my acute disappointment, was not among them; I saw her linger a moment at the edge of the crowd, then slip out through a side door. I wanted to follow, but it was half an hour before I decently could extricate myself.

As I descended the library steps, a large-wheeled tilbury pulled to the curb, and the straw-hatted Negro driver climbed down and walked off.

"Mr. Poe? If you will take the reins?"

I got into the tilbury. "What a glorious day for a drive!" Fanny Osgood said. "Fifth Avenue? The Bowery?"

I flicked the reins and hoped that the horse—skewbald, wearing a straw hat the twin of the vanished driver's—would not sense that I had no more expertise driving a tilbury than dancing a polka.

We moved in fits and starts through heavy traffic. When I approached a wagon too closely, the drayman shouted something at me in an impenetrable Irish dialect. I shouted back, "Go climb your *esprit d'escalier!*"

"His what? Is it naughty? French so often is," said Fanny Osgood.

"Not this time. It refers to the brilliant repartee that usually comes to one too late."

"I fear that is the story of *my* repartee. But obviously not of yours, Mr. Poe. I begin to see why Rufus Griswold does not like you, if not the reverse."

I had no wish to tell her that once, in exchange for money, I had written a favorable review of Rufus Griswold's anthology, a review he had considered fulsome.

"He is a New Englander," I said.

She laughed. She was wearing a shirred velvet bonnet with azure ribbons that fluttered in the light breeze.

"As am I, Mr. Poe."

"I know."

I drove south on Broadway to Battery Gardens, where I hitched the skewbald to a post and we went promenading past the bowsprits of great sailing ships. Fanny Osgood raised a parasol the same azure as the ribbons, flirtation ribbons they are called, that fluttered so gayly from her hat.

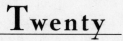

Twenty

> . . . I journeyed far down away into another country where it was all
> one dim and vague lake, with a boundary line of clouds.
> —"The Unparalleled Adventure of One Hans Pfaall"

The childhood toy I remember most fondly was a kaleidoscope given to me in London on my ninth birthday by my foster mother, Frances Allan. John Allan predictably objected to it as frivolous, but its novelty for a while fascinated even him, and I remember how he would guiltily put it down when I entered a room—as human a gesture as I ever saw my foster father make.

Alone, I would sit for hours by the window, every minute or so giving the kaleidoscope a little twist to make the shards of colored glass tumble apart and re-form in forever new patterns.

"Mirrors," John Allan would say in grumpy response to my never-answered question. "It is done with mirrors."

Which was how I would view my *amourette*, all these years later, with Fanny Osgood. But whether the mirrors were deployed by her or by me I could not have said.

A midday in late spring. Washington Square. We were promenading past the neo-Gothic building of the University.

"I'm famished, Edgar. Shall we try Delmonico's?"

"We would not get in."

"My name—or Samuel's—has always got a table. Your own, dear Edgar, will do likewise."

We had the table to the left as you enter. I have no recollection of what we ate but only of my shock at what it cost. But as I lectured frequently that year, I had the money.

Later that week. Wall Street. Another stroll.

"On this street more money is made and lost in a day than in all the rest of the country in a month. Or so Samuel says—and he has painted the portraits of half the people who made and lost it."

"*Two* exaggerations," I said, smiling.

She took my arm. "Life is more amusing if one exaggerates. Did you know that a billion dollars exchange hands every hour on this street?"

The spires of Trinity Church loomed.

"Which, no matter how you exaggerate, is why they need *that* here."

"You are a believer? I would not have thought so."

"A believer? In a wise and loving God who looks like Longfellow in a toga? Hardly. I believe there is, perhaps, a disinterested kind of a god who caused a . . . a primordial atom . . . to expand to fill space with an infinitude of worlds, more or less like this one, which some day will collapse in upon themselves to become again the primordial atom, which will then expand, and so on, indefinitely, so that every thing not only is repeated infinitely in space but comes around again in time.* You and I, for example."

"Then if the only God is a disinterested sort, one may feel quite free to do wicked things?"

"The history of the human race seems to confirm that."

"I meant you and I."

———

* Poe would elaborate upon these thoughts in *Eureka: A Prose Poem*, published the year after the death of his wife. (Editor's note)

Sunday morning. The reservoir on Forty-second Street. In the shade of the great granite wall, families strolled carrying picnic baskets. A little man wearing a feather in his hat and a long-tailed blue coat was grinding a mournful tune from a barrel organ. A monkey on a lead danced up to us holding a tin cup.

"What a melancholy tune," said Fanny.

"Irish. The Irish have a sad history." I dug into my pocket for a few pennies.

"Don't, Edgar. It only encourages them to spread the sadness."

The monkey danced before me with a scowl on his old man's face. I looked at the organ grinder; until then I had always felt too poor to toss a coin to a beggar, a street musician. I dropped my pennies into the cup.

"I told you not to!"

"He is poor. Poorer than I." I turned then to face her. "You *told* me not to?"

"Asked. I meant asked."

We stood staring at each other in stunned stubborn silence, and waited for the first omnibus back downtown.

Ten days later. Her first letter. My hand shook when I took the envelope—finest vellum, addressed in a feminine hand, franked at Boston—from the postman. I walked a short way from the house before opening it. There was no message, just the poem.

> *My leaves, instinct with glowing life,*
> *Were quivering to unclose;*
> *My happy heart with love was rife—*
> *I was almost a rose.*

Every few days another envelope would arrive. Each contained a poem; some contained short letters that spoke of friendship and, elliptically, of love. Our brief quarrel she never mentioned.

Soon I was answering letter for letter, poem for poem. All else became distraction barely to be tolerated.

One day Muddy asked me, "Who is she?"

"This? It's from a poetess seeking my advice."

"Under certain circumstances," said Muddy, "they are all poetesses."

Later that week, as I brought Virginia her evening tea, a sound made me stop outside her door, which stood ajar, a faint, elusive keening that I took at first for crying. She lay in her cotton nightdress prone upon her bed, rocking slowly from side to side, one hand outstretched upon the counterpane, where, scattered, I saw Fanny's letters, the other hidden under the curve of her hip.

I withdrew a few steps, rattled the tea tray, then advanced into the room. Virginia sat up swiftly and faced me. She was breathless. I was accustomed to how gaunt she had become, and to how her beautiful deep blue eyes looked out at me from shadowed sockets. But there was a wildness in those eyes now, as hectic as the spots of color in her cheeks.

I set the tray down. Her breathing slowed. Watching me all the while, she gathered the letters together, sheet by sheet.

"Is she very beautiful?" she asked. "Is she tall and blond and lithe and robust and unfailingly competent? All the things I'm not?"

"Your tea will get cold," I said.

"Eddie, oh Eddie, I'm sorry. I had no right to read these. But I simply couldn't bear not knowing."

I nodded and said, my voice almost steady, "And are you reassured now, knowing there is nothing to know?"

"Nothing? I know that Mrs. Osgood has a place in your life— from which I am shut out."

"My darling, I swear that you need not fear that your place in—"

"Please, Eddie, don't patronize me. We both know you need a woman to give you . . . what I cannot. Or you will grow to hate me. So there is no question of fear or—"

"I have said before, you are all the woman I—"

"—or jealousy. What I do feel, most acutely, is the *exclusion*. Eddie, I live my life through you. It is the only life I have. And now that too is being taken away from me."

Before I could reply, she sank onto her pillow and cried, "Eddie, I want something to *happen*! Any thing! I lie here all day, or sit at the window watching people walk by and wondering where they are going and if, perhaps today, their lives will change. I want . . . I want the roof to fall in or the street to flood or a comet to strike the earth like the one you wrote about, or a raven to fly in through the window this very minute, or, or," and she almost smiled, "or a peacock. I want us to come together again, for the first time. I want to walk into your life like . . . like one of those blond temptresses who stalk through life like a panther."

By then I was seated on the edge of the bed and stroking her hair.

"Tell me about her! Tell me! Tell me every thing you did together."

"Why, uh," I faltered, "we did what friends do. We met at *conversazioni*. We walked, drove, rode the omnibus. Oh, yes. We lunched once at Delmonico's."

"What did you eat?"

"I don't remember."

"Delmonico's and you don't remember? With a companion who was just a 'friend'? Tell me, Eddie, are her . . . caresses . . . more practiced than mine were?"

"My dear, you must curb your imagination. Mrs. Osgood and I have not so much as held hands."

Virginia stifled a cough. Her eyes fell to the sheets of vellum spread on the counterpane. She separated one from the rest and recited:

> " 'The fair, fond girl, who at your side,
>   Within your soul's dear light doth live,
>   Could hardly have the heart to chide
>   The ray that Friendship well might give.'

"It's lovely, Eddie, her poetry. Please tell her . . ."

"I'll tell her," I said, misunderstanding.

". . . that even if . . . even if you and she . . ."

I said stiffly, "I prefer to arrange my own life, Sis."

"*Won't* you understand? If you had a woman, if you had a woman, Eddie, it would thrill me as much as it did you."

A hot summer evening. The Bowery.

Gas jets lit the night and there were signs, signs everywhere, illuminated by candles within, balloon signs hanging from poles urging you to drink, to bowl tenpins, to visit Niblo's Theater Garden, to gorge yourself on " 'oysters in every style,' Edgar! Can you resist oysters?"

"You ask that of a man who lived for years on Chesapeake Bay?"

We descended stairs to a candle-lit room lined on three sides with curtained booths. Buxom sweating women hurried back and forth with pots, with crocks, with platters, with fistfuls of pewter mugs.

A man dressed as a steamboat steward led us to a booth in which were a small round table and a curved bench upholstered in the same deep red plush as the curtains. We sat, decorously facing each other, at opposite ends of the bench, and ordered our oysters—raw, three dozen of them.

"Edgar, how I've missed you!"

"And I. I miss you always, even when we are together."

She unfolded her napkin. "Samuel has seen your letters."

"Fanny!"

"No, don't be concerned. He can hardly object. He has his life. He is in demand as a portrait painter from Portland to Charleston. And."

"And?"

"And he has had other women for years."

A waitress brought our oysters on the half shell on a bed of ice on a pewter platter.

I watched Fanny loosen one from its shell with a tiny pewter fork, then bring shell to mouth, then tip head and shell so that the pale pink-gray flesh of the oyster slid into her mouth and down the alabaster column of her throat in a single sensuous ripple.

After I ate an oyster, with rather less flair, we drank beer from huge pewter mugs, and I waited for her to repeat her performance.

But this time, loosening an oyster in its shell, she raised it not to her mouth but to mine. I felt the soft slippery succulence slide down my throat. I fed her an oyster in turn.

The bench, as I said, curved around the table. We started feeding each other at arm's length. With every offered oyster we were closer. Did she move? Did I? Her hair, dark as the wing of a raven, tickled my cheek. Once I failed to tilt the shell enough, and her tongue darted out to lick the sea water remaining in it.

A single oyster survived, an island on an ice-and-pewter sea. I raised it to her mouth and she diverted it with a fingertip toward mine. I could have counted the flecks of hazel, like minute shards of amber, in the gray mirrors of her eyes, from which two tiny images of myself looked back, watching me, judging.

When there was no longer room between our mouths for the oyster shell, I let it drop. She tasted of the sea.

Some days later. The Washington Square townhouse of the publisher John Russell Bartlett and his wife, with whom Fanny stayed when in New York.

We had dined with Fanny's hosts and taken our leave, bound for a lecture on Grecian antiquities. But Fanny, on seeing the sky, had run upstairs for a cloak. Waiting in the entrance hall, I overheard these words exchanged by the Bartletts.

"Handsome enough devil, isn't he? And clearly smitten with our Fanny."

"It seems mutual, and who can blame her? He's a fascinating conversationalist, with the manners—don't laugh, John; these things matter to a woman—of a Castilian grandee."

"But with a grandee's temper to match—especially when he indulges."

"Drink?"

"So they say. So even his closest friends say. Rufus Griswold was there in Washington City, you know, the day Poe became disgracefully inebriated at the President's House."

"The President's House? I never heard *that*."

"I don't know the details. After all, as a friend Griswold is reluctant to discuss it," John Russell Bartlett said. "A drinker *and* a literary lion, hence doubly dangerous to a woman, as he excites both her maternal and her aesthetic sensibilities."

"And his wife? Is she utterly complaisant? *I* wouldn't be."

I heard Fanny's footsteps coming downstairs.

"Mrs. Poe is dying of consumption," John Russell Bartlett said, and I burst in upon them.

"Mrs. Poe is recovering from a touch of bronchitis," I shouted. "And you are a pair of malicious gossips."

Outside, rain that bounced off the pavement almost like hailstones had cleared the streets of people.

I held my umbrella, and Fanny my elbow.

"Oh Edgar, the looks on their faces." She giggled. "Well, we can't go on meeting *there* any more. No matter. I must go back to Boston soon."

"Already? But you just got here."

A wind sprang up, almost yanking the umbrella from my grasp. With a loud report it burst inside out. Fanny and I ran through the downpour, found a cabman's shelter, and ducked in. A man sat on the bench with his hat over his face, snoring.

Fanny and I clung, kissed.

"That did you no good," she said.

"Kissing you? Are you mad?" And I kissed her again.

"I mean at the Bartletts'. Because you were right. They *are* malicious gossips."

I said, "In your set, isn't everybody?"

"My, we are angry tonight, aren't we? Is it about Rufus's talebearing?"

"You heard?"

"From Rufus himself. The night you and I met."

"And? Does it trouble you?"

"It troubles me that Rufus maligns you with such obvious pleasure. Whatever John Bartlett may say, he spares no detail. Which makes me wonder how true it is."

"Shall I tell you?"

"No. I don't want to know." Fanny averted her face. I lifted her raven's-wing hair and kissed the nape of her neck. She shuddered and turned hard back into my arms.

"Oh God, Edgar, how I want more than a few moments stolen in a cabman's shelter with you!"

"When things have settled in Boston, write to me."

"Write!"

"There is a steamboat from New York to Providence every day."

"Yes. But isn't the boat to Boston direct?"

"You mentioned friends in Providence whom you sometimes visit."

"Yes."

"Write to me. When you can get away, we shall meet in Providence."

She gasped. She smiled. She looked like a little girl.

Twenty-one

It was immediately seen, however, that *this* would not do.
                                    —"The Rationale of Verse"

Excerpts from correspondence, autumn-winter 1845–46:

. . . seems La Quotidienne published my "Murders in the Rue Morgue," calling it "Histoire trouvée dans les papiers d'un Améri-cain." A while later a rival paper, Le Commerce, printed a differ-ent translation under the title "Une sanglante énigme." Neither credited me as author. There followed an accusation of plagiarism, a law suit—and a counter-suit for libel. And, as everyone loves a juicy legal battle, all the other dailies took it up. In consequence, both parties acknowledged the tale as mine and, I am told, I have become more famous in the City of Light than here in New York! Perhaps, my dearest Fanny, if we could contrive to cause a scandal, it would enhance my fame on this side of the ocean?

A propos, the train from Boston reaches Providence a mere quarter-hour before the boat from New York, so you would scarcely be "cast adrift" until my arrival. But I appreciate your hesitation, my dearest one, and if your fears outweigh what you have called your heart's passionate desire, I shall understand. . . .

. . . to be expected after a long absence. But eventually he will lose interest in my comings and goings. Sooner or later, he always does.

Believe me, dearest one, it is not my design to make you wait. I can tolerate the delay no better than you.

I not only dream of you, my love, I day-dream of you. Recently Samuel and I shared a platter of oysters, and I could not meet his eyes. . . .

. . . would be untrue to say I also dream of you. I do not, for the simple reason that I have lost the ability to sleep. That balm denied me, I lie all night seeing your dear face in the darkness.

In respect of my work, it is no exaggeration that the French tail seems to be wagging the American dog. Mr. George Palmer Putnam recently returned from his London offices where, apparently, he heard of the flamboyant litigation in Paris, with the result that Wiley & Putnam will soon issue a collection of my tales here. Vive la France!

Sometimes, in the sleepless silence of the night, I imagine us there in Paris—perhaps strolling arm in arm through the Place Vendôme, past the bronze-clad column with its statue of the Emperor Napoleon. Did you know that Anton Mesmer once lived in the Place Vendôme? And no, to answer the question you now ask yourself—how much we still have to learn of each other, my darling, you and I!—no, I most decidedly am not a disciple of Mesmer, who was a fraud. But I do, also most decidedly, believe in animal magnetism in a special sense, that is, the attraction be-

tween the sexes, if I may make so bold, with the observation that
you are the lodestone and I but a congeries of iron filings completely at your mercy.

If it cannot be Paris yet for us, my pole star, please make it
Providence—and please make it soon!

Ever thine
Edgar

. . . I am drawn, like those iron filings of yours, every afternoon
to the lodestone of the railroad station, to watch those loveliest of
cars follow their plume of smoke south. . . .

. . . For one who allows his past a greater hold over him than
all his possible futures, memory becomes a prison. Certainly I remember our all too few hours together, love. But I live not each
one again, detail by detail, as you do. Instead, I see the Providence
dock, ablaze with light, approaching; I see, standing at its end
and waving, a tiny figure wearing a straw hat whose ribbons flutter gayly in the wind.

I shall arrive aboard the "Woonsocket" on . . .

. . . railroad tickets under my pillow. Have ever simple strips of
paper been so gloriously beautiful? But they are sodden with my
tears of joy. Until next Tuesday in Providence, heart of my secret
heart. How aptly that city is named!

Your enslaved
Fanny

. . . I send this franked urgent, trusting that it will reach you
in time. What ever made you write "Tuesday"? Thursday, darling.
I shall come to Providence on Thursday aboard the steamboat
"Woonsocket." I could not have written that I would come on
Tuesday. Tuesday would have been impossible, since she whom
you call the "fair, fond girl at your side" will be visited on Tuesday by a specialist, and I must be present. . . .

. . . I died, Edgar. I stood at the end of the dock watching the passengers disembark, and when they removed the gangway, I died.

I will not burden you with the night I spent in Providence (so ironically named!). I could only conclude that some awful calamity had befallen you—and pass the sleepless hours conjuring the possibilities, each more horrifying than the last—while never suspecting that calamity had already befallen me. For, when I returned to Boston, Samuel gave me your letter—opened! ("Urgent, my dear, means urgent, and as you were absent—") Oh, how I hate him!

Must I hate you as well? Thursday, you wrote in your urgent letter, insisting that you could not have written Tuesday in your previous letter, as Tuesday would have been impossible for you. Edgar, can you be insensitive enough to think I have not kept all your letters? I looked at once at the earlier one. This is what you wrote. "I shall arrive aboard the 'Woonsocket' on the evening of Tuesday next. Tuesday next! I count the seconds. Tuesday night! How precious shall all the Tuesdays of my life ever after be!"

Tuesday, Edgar. That is what you wrote four times. That is when I went to Providence. And you were not there.

Edgar, why!!

Your heartsick
Fanny

. . . naught of the night I spent alone in Providence, like you wakeful and despairing. There was this one difference: I knew what must have happened—you remained fastened upon the wrong day—though I knew not why. How much less can I now fathom your bizarre misapprehension?

I know which day my pen appointed (four times, just as you quote them except for the day). I wrote with the steamboat tickets before me; I wrote that I should come on the Thursday; and so I did.

You temporized before, my Fanny, but when you gave your word, I trusted. What shall I now? . . .

. . . find most disturbing your refusal to admit even a <u>possibility</u> of having been at fault. When I quote your words exactly, you do not believe me. But you cannot, I think, dismiss the letter itself. I return it herewith, that you may see that the "bizarre misapprehension" is not mine.

Oh Edgar, Edgar! What are you trying to do to us? . . .

. . . you wrote that you stood on the dock watching the passengers disembark, and you died. What can I write now but that, since seeing the evidence of my own words, I have died a thousand deaths? I simply do not comprehend how I can have made such a mistake in a matter that has consumed all my hopes and dreams for so long. . . .

. . . dare not suggest, and yet I must. You recently published a tale, Edgar, about a man who, driven by an ungovernable impulse at odds with his best interests . . .

. . . I find your implication, Fanny, deeply hurtful. For me to write of a fictional character, compelled to act contrarily, for the very reason that he should <u>not</u>, in no way signifies that such perverseness is any part of my own character. . . .

. . . That is what you wrote, Edgar. And <u>that is what you did</u>. . . .

Dear Miss Lynch,

I enclose several letters which you may consider suitable for reading at your Valentine's Day party, to which, I trust, I shall in due course receive invitation.

Yours sincerely,
Edgar Poe

Dear Mr. Poe,

I have forwarded to their author the letters you sent for reading at my Valentine's Day party. You leave me no choice but to say, sir, that, with all your genius, you have no moral sense. You were not invited to my Valentine's Day party because, should I receive you, I should lose the company of others whom I value more.

Yours truly,
Anne Charlotte Lynch

My dear Greeley,

Do not, pray, so hastily condemn Edgar Poe. He has, as you say, "defamed an eminent literary lady." But horsewhipping? Consider that Poe has not had certain social advantages that convey the—the code of conduct, shall I say?—by which gentlemen live. Thus, for example, he sees no harm in accepting payment—as I have on good authority heard he has done—to write a favorable book review. My point, however, is that we should suspend judgment on his actions, as they stem less probably from a culpable lack of scruple than from a pitiable obtuseness. . . .

Yours,
Griswold

Twenty-two

Examine these and similar actions as we will, we shall find them resulting solely from the spirit of the *Perverse*. We perpetrate them merely because we feel that we should *not*.
—"The Imp of the Perverse"

Virginia sat at the window looking down through the leafy branches of the elm in the front yard. On her face, even in profile, I could see such intense yearning that I paused a long moment in the doorway, the incriminating letter in my hand, before coming to her side. Below through the branches I saw a young couple strolling arm in arm.

I said, "I would like you to look at this. You wrote it, did you not?"

Virginia started. She stared at the letter I held, then slowly shook her head. "Wrote it?" she repeated. "Why, no, Eddie. I merely copied it."

"Why?"

My voice was not angry. I was not angry. What I had seen on her face had moved me.

"I—I spilled some tea on it."

"What were you doing with it?"

"Doing? Why, I was reading it, Eddie."

"By what right did you read my private correspondence?"

"Eddie, you left *her* letters for me to find, so naturally I assumed—"

"That you might read mine to her? I cannot believe I left this, this particular letter, lying on my writing table."

"No." Her eyes would not meet mine. "I found it in the basket at the front door."

"You would have had to unseal it to read it."

"I steamed it open. Just like a character in a book. The tea I spilled on it left a big stain in the shape of a trefoil, so I copied it in your handwriting. What harm was there in that?"

"Had it been a true copy, none."

"It was! Oh, it was, Eddie. A faithful copy."

"In the letter I named a day of the week. Four times. The day was Thursday. But you wrote Tuesday. Four times."

"If I wrote Tuesday, it was what *you* wrote. I wrote what you did, word for word—copied it exactly," she said. "There was a tiny blot above the 'u' of the first Tuesday, Eddie. I even copied that."

"You're lying." I spoke calmly but in a flat voice that brooked no denial. "Your intention—and it worked—was to keep us from meeting in Providence."

"But I *wanted* you to meet. I dreamed of your meeting." Tears shimmered in her eyes. "Oh Eddie, it thrilled me so! I wanted you and Mrs. Osgood to . . . to . . ."

The hectic spots of color on her cheeks were lost in the flush that suffused her face. She smiled a hopeful smile, guileless, like a child who, having done something slightly naughty, awaited forgiveness.

But I did not forgive. I said, "You changed Thursday to Tuesday."

Looking out the window, she nodded almost imperceptibly and spoke in a soft, wondering voice. "I cannot tell you why, Eddie. Because I do not know why. Did not then and do not now. I was unable to stop myself."

And I, with whatever dismay, with whatever bottled-up fury, I understood her jealousy, even if she did not, and might have let the matter drop—had there not been more.

"You wrote in my hand one other letter that I know of," I said. "That letter was no copy. You composed it yourself and sent it along with Fanny's letters—"

"Not all of them. I kept some. I re-read them all the time."

"—sent them to Miss Lynch as if *I* wanted them read publicly."

"Why not? Your lovely little poetess writes lovely little love letters."

"You know perfectly well why not. Sending those letters was the same as announcing to the world that Fanny Osgood and I were—"

Virginia laughed, a cruel sound, brittle, perfunctory. "The *world*? As if Miss Anne Charlotte Lynch and her parlor literati, who pass their time telling tales about one another instead of writing, are the *world*!"

And Virginia lowered her head and covered her face with her hands and wept.

Awkwardly I patted her shoulder. She stifled a cough; brushed tears from her cheeks; gazed directly at me. "Oh, Eddie, why *won't* you see? You know the doctor says I need clear air, country air. How right he is. The city, Eddie—I am no part of it, and still it overwhelms me. Take me from here, Eddie. Please. I'm begging you."

How I might have replied I cannot say, for just then the door knocker sounded. I hurried downstairs.

Miss Anne Charlotte Lynch stood before the door with a female companion.

"Good day," I said, and stepped to one side with a small bow. "Pray come in."

But they did not. "I have come," said Miss Lynch, "on behalf of Mrs. Osgood, to retrieve the rest of her letters."

I was not surprised. Again I motioned them inside.

"We will wait here."

I went upstairs.

"You heard?"

Virginia's answer was to hand me the letters. Then she said, "I'm sorry, Eddie. Truly I am."

"We will talk later."

I could not help thinking as I descended the stair that, were we to leave New York now, it would appear that I had fled the censure I had brought upon myself—not just a cad but a coward.

At the door I handed the packet of letters to Miss Lynch.

"These are all?"

"Yes."

"Then I bid you good day, Mr. Poe."

An hour and a half later, Samuel Stillman Osgood arrived.

He was a large man. Six feet tall and almost half that wide across the shoulders, with a craggy handsome face and long dark hair.

"Poe? Are you Poe?"

"I am."

"A little runt like you? I am Samuel Osgood. I want my wife's letters."

"I no longer have—"

He bunched my lapels in a fist as big as a paddle wheel and raised me on tiptoe. "God damn it when I say I want them I mean *now*!"

Trying to free myself, I found that, with both hands, I could barely encircle his wrist. My coat ripped at the shoulder as, twisting one arm behind my back, he turned me and marched me, bent over, inside. A shove sent me falling across the fire grate, where, had I any sense, I would have remained. But, gathering the remnants of my dignity, I emerged covered with soot.

"Eddie, what is happening?" Virginia called from upstairs, and

Samuel Osgood said, "Your last chance, you little bastard," and I said, or began to say, "I do not have—" and he hit me on the side of the jaw. I fell down. He kicked me. I tried to hold on to his boot. He kicked me again. I crawled toward the poker. He kicked it across the room. I went scuttling after it and rolled over with it in my hand. I swung it. I saw Virginia at the bottom of the stair and Muddy in the kitchen doorway. The poker took Samuel Osgood's legs out from under him. He dropped to his knees, I rose to mine; he with his fists raised, I brandishing the poker. There was a swish of petticoats. Muddy in widow's black—all I could see were her skirt and a glimpse of her black shoes—entered the gap between Samuel Osgood and me. She did not shout. Did not scream. Spoke in, indeed, a notably restrained voice. "Miss Lynch has your wife's letters," she told Samuel Osgood. "You may leave this house."

Still holding the poker, I watched his broad back retreating. I raised the poker—could feel the muscles in my arm bunching, preparatory to hurling it at him—could see it striking his head, dropping him where he stood—could see a dark stain spreading on the floor under his head—could see the look of horror on Virginia's face, on Muddy's. By the time I saw all this he was gone. Muddy shut the door. I looked at her. I looked at Virginia. Still holding the poker. Wanting to hurt someone, as I had been hurt. When the terrible realization came to me that it mattered not who, I hurled the poker against the wall.

I was eleven when John Allan's business in London failed and the family returned to Richmond. Soon afterwards I came down with measles. Bed rest was prescribed, and darkness. My head hurt. My eyes hurt. I had fever and a hacking cough and "one big rash all over, Eddie, poor Eddie," said my foster mother, Frances Allan, bathing my head with a cool cloth as, now, in the parlor of our house near Washington Square in New York, Virginia was doing.

A boy not twelve years old, forced to lie in darkness all day, feels he is being punished. He must stave off not only boredom but resentment. Frances Allan read to me. I remember *The Heart of Midlothian* by Walter Scott; or part of it. Perhaps it was not suitable, but, lying with my eyes covered and hearing Frances Allan's breathless disembodied voice, I was thrilled. She got no further than the part where Jeanie began her dangerous walk to London to seek King George's pardon for her half sister for "murdering her own misbegotten child!" John Allan shouted as in three strides he covered the distance from the doorway to the bed and tore the book from his wife's hands. "This you consider appropriate to read to a boy of eleven?"

As it was John Allan, not Frances, who had enjoined me to keep the window shades drawn lest the sunlight damage my eyes, I rebelled. Surely sunlight would be no more harmful than the now forbidden Walter Scott—and it would let me use my kaleidoscope. That same afternoon I stole silently across the floor and rolled the window shade up a hand-span. I returned to bed, took the kaleidoscope from under my pillow—and waited.

For I had become convinced that with a single slight twist of the tube, just one, I would see something so strange and wonderful as to transcend any thing that could be expected of shards of glass reflected in mirrors. Awaiting, postponing, this vision—no less fraught a word would do—I felt giddy with excitement.

When finally I twisted the tube and saw the shards begin to tumble, John Allan shouted, "Give that to me!" and made to snatch the kaleidoscope from my hand, but I hurled it as hard as I could against the wall.

Later, Frances Allan found me seated cross-legged on the floor, shards of glass scattered on the parquetry and more on my lap. I held in my hand a single shard of a brilliant golden color. I could feel its sharp edges. I could also feel its golden warmth, like the warmth of a living thing, as I clutched it. That the warmth was imparted by my own fevered body did not even suggest itself to me.

"You will cut yourself."

I clutched the shard more tightly. I wanted to cut myself.

Suddenly I was crying. I cried like a baby. From downstairs John Allan bellowed, "*Will* you make that brat stop screaming!"

"I shall get you another," Frances Allan told me. "With a brass tube, like a spy-glass."

"I don't want another."

And with all my strength I closed my fist on the golden shard and watched blood seep between my fingers.

I never saw Fanny Osgood again.

And for the first time I was almost able to accept that one day soon Virginia would die.

Twenty-three

"Listen to *me*," said the Demon.
—"Silence—A Fable"

My name is Thomas W. Frederick—a chance inversion, as more than one acquaintance has remarked, of the name of a writer of popular songs and stories. Panchatan, our plantation across the Chickahominy River from Hopewell, provided the family with social standing and a comfortable income until its sale following the tragic deaths of my widowed father, my older brother, and both my sisters, murdered in their beds during the hot summer of 18—, when refugees from the cholera-ridden cities infested the countryside.

Only my residence at the College of William & Mary, where I was preparing for a career in the law, saved me from sharing my family's fate. My cousin Nola, who had lived at Panchatan since she was orphaned, also escaped with her life, as she had gone for one of her solitary moonlit gallops on that terrible night.

On receiving news of the murders, I returned in all haste to Panchatan, to be informed by the sheriff that the intruder or intruders had vanished with the night. Our slaves had heard no untoward sound. Nothing in the house, not even my sisters' jewelry, had been disturbed—nothing but the bodies, each with a single knife-thrust piercing the heart.

After burying my kin in the family plot by the riverside, where our best blond tobacco grew, I methodically searched the main house and dependencies. I could not have said what I was looking for. But I learned that something *had* been taken, or, at least, was missing. Our late uncle Thaddeus had left a small sea chest containing some terra-cotta potsherds incised with obscure symbols. These he had brought back from his last voyage to the Orient.

Uncle Thaddeus told us children he had found the potsherds in the interior of the island of Panchatan, whose dense jungle few white men had penetrated (and whose name he had bestowed upon the plantation he purchased with profits from a trading venture in the Malay Archipelago). The fragments of terra cotta were said to hold the key to a source of magical power—*if* these were the right potsherds and *if* one knew what to make of them. Uncle Thaddeus seemed to believe all this, which was surprising, for he had not been a credulous man.

I pondered for days the significance of the theft.

If the potsherds were worth killing for—and someone clearly thought they were, for my family *had* been killed—how had the murderer learned of them? When? Where? Not from the family. Uncle Thaddeus had solemnly sworn us children to secrecy, and he himself was not given to loose talk with chance acquaintances. Also, it was some time since his death. It was even longer since his last voyage to the Orient, when, most probably, the thief had come to know—or to know of—Uncle Thaddeus and/or the chestful of potsherds. But if so, why had the thief waited so long?

These questions haunted all my waking hours. Soon they invaded my sleep, for I dreamed a strange dream in which I was a *détective* from Paris who came to the plantation to solve the diabolical crime. My dream-self wore green-tinted spectacles, even at night. Or, for all I knew, *only* at night. For in my dreams there was no daylight. Was he, I would wonder, trying to mask his identity? He, in turn, began to wonder about me. Where had I heard of him? Even the word *détective* did not exist in the English language. Why did I dream of him every night, giving him no peace? We began to dislike each other. Presently he balked at being the dream-self. On waking,

I would suffer a profound disorientation in which I believed I was not waking at all but only dreaming I was, in a dream dreamed by my dream-self. One day I found myself in a shop purchasing a pair of green-tinted spectacles. I hurled them to the floor, crushed them underfoot, and fled.

To escape these demons, I avoided sleep and commenced a dissolute life. I drank, I gambled, I brawled, I galloped my skittish mare Jewelweed* recklessly. One windswept night, shying at a moon-cast shadow, she threw me, breaking my right leg in two places.

Convalescing, I was relieved to find that I dreamed no more dreams of another self. Calmer than I had been since the murders, I took stock of my life, with the result that, shortly before selling Panchatan to a wealthy Richmonder, one John Allan, I manumitted our slaves. I contemplated a return to the College, but musty books and dry-as-dust courtrooms were no longer for me. A banker of my acquaintance assured me that, investing conservatively the proceeds of selling Panchatan, I would have enough to live a life of gentlemanly leisure. But that held even less appeal.

I resolved to sail to the Orient and find the island of Panchatan.

Determining to work my passage, as Uncle Thaddeus in his youth had done, I came to Baltimore and took a room in a boarding house in Amity Street and set about securing a seaman's berth on a Baltimore clipper—an enterprise that, because of my limp, has proved more difficult than I anticipated.

It is the limp that makes Obadiah, once the chief field hand at Panchatan, almost fail to recognize me. Moreover, in an attempt to add years to my boyish face, I have grown a mustache.

When we meet, I am dejectedly limping along Orleans Street, having just come from my latest fruitless interview with a clipper captain.

"Mister Thomas?"

---

* A local name for *noli me tangere* or touch-me-not, a weed of the balsam family (genus *Impatiens*) bearing seed pods which, when ripe, split to the touch. (Editor's note)

Obadiah does not talk like a darkie. He was still a child when Panchatan was bought by Uncle Thaddeus, who was both fair-minded and practical. So he gave Obadiah some education.

"Good day to you, Obadiah."

"It *is* you, Mister Thomas."

Obadiah, even when expressing surprise, speaks in a deep soft gentle voice. He is a very large, very black man. His face, in repose, seems on the verge always of a smile—a sad smile, I should say.

We fall into step. With the aid of my malacca stick I have developed a rapid, lunging gait.

"Have you found work?" I ask him.

"Yes, Mister Thomas, I have. I clean up nights at a tavern."

"But you're a literate man. You could—"

Slowing his step, Obadiah faces me, fists on hips, not quite smiling his melancholy smile. "I worked in the fields at Panchatan, Mister Thomas. I don't mind physical labor. Yes, I can read, I can do sums. But you won't find me bent over a desk," he says. "Anyway, I aim to leave Baltimore, Mister Thomas. This is no place for a Negro, not if he is free."

"Where will you go?"

"North. When I manage to save a few dollars. I hear a Negro can go into business for himself, in Philadelphia."

How many times have I heard supposedly educated whites pronounce it Philuffya?

Impulsively I take some bills from my pocket.

"I can't, Mister Thomas. You've done enough for me."

But I thrust the money into his large hand.

Obadiah, holding it, looks uneasy. He does not speak, not even to thank me. It is clear the gift has embarrassed him.

"You may consider it a loan," I say.

"It ain't that, Mistuh Tom."

I have heard Obadiah use the word "ain't" only once before, when he was unjustly accused of theft. To play the abject, stupid nigger is the intelligent Negro's final defense.

We have resumed walking. I hold my silence. Obadiah will talk when he is ready.

"I seed him, Mistuh Tom," he says, the darkie dialect more pronounced, almost a parody of itself.

"Saw him? Who?"

"You knows who, Mistuh Tom," says Obadiah.

"Obadiah," I tell him impatiently, "pray credit me with an intelligence the equal of your own. I can hardly understand what you are saying."

Obadiah takes enormous, ground-consuming strides. Despite the rapidity of my lunging limp, I find it difficult to keep up. When he stops again, abruptly, I stumble. Gently, with his big hands, Obadiah prevents me from falling.

"I suppose you knew," he says, "that I used to work a plot beyond the kitchen garden on my own time. Collard greens, black-eyed peas, some 'taters." He almost smiles his sad smile. "*Po*tatoes. I used to sell my crop to a freedman from Petersburg."

"I knew," I say. "Father told me. But he never told Thad."

"I can understand that," says Obadiah. "Your brother had a different attitude toward niggers than you and your papa did."

It seems an odd conversation for us to be having now, on a busy street in Baltimore, after Obadiah has been freed, until he says: "Mister Thomas, the night your family was killed?"

He has begun to sweat. I find that I am holding my breath, actually holding my breath as characters in melo-dramatic tales do.

"I had just finished working my plot and was standing under that big tulip tree on the south side of the house. In the moonlight I saw a man come out. White man. He was carrying a crocus sack over his shoulder. He had a scar running clear down one side of his face, Mister Thomas, shaped like the blade of a scythe."

Orleans Street is crowded, festive, rowdy. It is not yet noon but many drunks are about. A brass band plays on a nearby street. A half-dozen disreputable youths race past yelping like Indians. A fat man with red side-whiskers comes lumbering after them, discharging a revolver into the air. An old man is making steady progress along the street using a paint brush to paste posters on shop-fronts urging you to vote Democrat. He is followed by three boys who tear the posters down as quickly as he can put them up. This does not deter him. The band rounds a corner into view, instruments silent except for the boom of the bass drum. To its beat the bandsmen chant, "A dollar a day is a white man's pay! A dollar a day is a white man's pay!"

"It is indeed," says Obadiah just as a phalanx of men, all young, many of them freckle-faced, come charging after the band. Instruments are torn from the bandsmen's hands.

Obadiah and I draw a few curious looks—a white man and a nigger standing face to face in conversation on the Orleans Street sidewalk in the Election Day crowds.

Obadiah, with reluctance, resumes his story. "He walked down to the riverbank, carrying his sack."

"And you? Did you not try to stop him?"

"I just watched him go, Mister Thomas. And then in the morning old Isaac found the bodies."

"And you held your tongue until now? Why?"

At that moment a man comes swaggering toward us. You can see in the narrowing of his eyes how he appraises the big nigger's size before walking straight at him, shoving him out of the way. Although tall and brawny, the man would be no match for Obadiah. But Obadiah allows himself to be shoved.

"That's why," he tells me.

"How did he leave the plantation? Did he have a horse?"

"Boat. He had a boat."

"Was anyone waiting in it?"

"No. He was alone."

"Had you ever seen him before?"

"No."

"Not around Panchatan? A peddler, perhaps?"

"No."

"Could you have seen him in Hopewell?"

The brass band has been dispersed. One of its freckled attackers blows a squawking sound on a dented trumpet. A small towheaded boy jumps up and down on the tympanum of the bass drum until it gives and he all but disappears inside. There is applause. A tall woman, as tall as my cousin Nola and as blond, but lither in a stylish riding costume and with a more aristocratically fine-boned face, comes purposefully along the street. The sound of the tympanum bursting seems to startle her, for she claps a hand to the black silk hat that makes her look still taller, and lengthens her stride.

"I could have," says Obadiah in a dry voice, "but I did not. I never saw him before, anywhere. I told you, Mister Thomas." Obadiah pauses. He looks at me with that way he has, ready to break into his familiar smile that is, somehow, the negation of mirth. "But I did see him after."

"Where? When?"

"Last night. The tavern where I work. He's a big man, almost as big as me. He was still there when they closed for the night, drinking with the proprietor. That's Mr. Ryan. Monk, he said to the man, if we had a few more like you, there wouldn't be a Whig coop left in the state of Maryland."

My first impulse, to go to the militia, I swiftly reject. I have studied the law. I know how stringent are the criteria for arresting a man, extraditing him, convicting him of murder. Even assuming I can find this Monk, what proof can I offer? Only the word of an ex-slave that he saw the accused man near the scene of the crime.

The alternative, the sole alternative I see, is to take justice into my own two hands. And if I do? If I do what a voice inside my head clamors for me to do? Then I will become a fugitive, forever outside the law—if I am not caught in the act.

It is also possible that Obadiah has identified an innocent man. What, after all, did he see but a sickle-shaped scar? It could have been no more than a moon-cast shadow.

Damnation! "It is also possible!" I have always seen two sides— at least—to every thing. The plight of the intellectual.

I ask Obadiah, "Where can I buy a gun?"

He looks at me. He shakes his head in dismay.

"Where?" I say.

Ten minutes later, I am the owner of a Colt .22 pocket revolver.

Twenty-four

The night having arrived . . . the lady Scheherazade not only put
the finishing stroke to the black cat and the rat (the rat was blue)
but before she well knew what she was about, found herself deep
in the intricacies of a narration, having reference (if I am not altogether mistaken) to a pink horse (with green wings) that went, in
a violent manner, by clockwork, and was wound up with an indigo
key.

—"The Thousand-and-Second Tale of Scheherazade"

On a sign swinging over the tavern door in the wind is the name
Gunner's Hall. Another sign, pasted to the door itself, informs the
public that these are the Fourth Ward Polls. Outside, men mill
about. By law, Gunner's Hall may serve no alcoholic beverages until
the polls close, but red faces and loud voices bear witness that the
law is honored in the breach.

Perhaps half the men wear the bright-buttoned, long-tailed blue
coats that, along with their workday trousers, are the holiday attire
of the Irish. They carry cudgels, billy clubs, a few marlin spikes;
some, I suspect, are armed with revolvers. Mine makes a discernible
bulge in my coat pocket. They anticipate trouble, Obadiah tells me,
from a violent group of native-born workies calling themselves the
"American Republicans," who five years ago in Philadelphia torched
dozens of houses and two Irish churches. In the aftermath, mobs
roved the streets and thirty people died.

Obadiah is not making idle chatter. "With luck they'll give us a
good riot," he says outside Gunner's Hall. "And there is nothing
better than a riot to hide a homicide."

It occurs to me, for the first time, that Obadiah feels no moral
objection to what I intend. He confirms this by saying, "I loved
your papa. Nobody ever treated a Negro better."

We stand a moment surveying the scene. Most of the blue tail-
coats are congregated on the near side of the street. Across from
them are what I take to be workies, many carrying two-by-fours. In

the middle, impeding traffic, is a faceless, changing crowd of voters who enter and leave the Fourth Ward Polls under the scrutiny of the blue tail-coats. A few militiamen, recognizable by their brassards (show me an American who will wear a uniform unless compelled!), stand anxiously at the corner. There are no Negroes except Obadiah.

It is clear that the watchful confrontation of armed workies and Irish must sooner or later erupt into violence. When it comes, I will not be found wanting.

"I could go inside," Obadiah suggests, "see if he's there."

"A Negro? Would they let you in?"

From under raised eyebrows he gives me a tolerant look. "I work here."

Even so, one of the Irishmen blocks his way until a bar-tender comes out and nods in recognition.

Waiting alone, I feel no disquietude, only a sense of inevitability. From where I stand at the corner near the militiamen, I can see the Gunner's Hall doorway and also the main entrance to the hotel, called Coath & Sargent's, of which the tavern is a part. From this entrance two well-dressed men come out supporting a third, any thing but well dressed, his arms hauled over their shoulders, his boots scraping the ground. I cannot see his face because of the dirty palm-leaf hat he wears, a Tidewater planter's sort of a hat, not for town use. With the aid of the driver, the two men bundle him into a waiting hackney cabriolet. I start forward. I know the man. I am certain of it. He is slender, and not tall, and I am convinced that his face, if I could see it, would be familiar.

"Hamstead and Broadway," one of the well-dressed men tells the hackie.

"The hospital?"

"You saw him, did you not?"

The driver flicks the reins and the cab begins to move. The two well-dressed men turn the corner.

"I need a drink," says one.

"*His* drinking days," says the other, "are over. Damned waste of a talent."

"Of a life. Poor devil."

I cannot prevent myself from asking, rather rudely I fear, "Who is he?"

They ignore me. Look right through me as if I do not exist.

"You see," I persist, "I believe that I know him, know him well."

Does one of them begin to turn in my direction? If so, he is immediately distracted by what now takes place outside Gunner's Hall.

A workie, refused admittance, shouts—is shouted at in return— is surrounded by half a dozen of the blue tail-coats—is hidden from view. The handful of militiamen, carbines held uneasily at port arms, remain at the corner. A savage cry comes from those surrounding the hapless workie. They begin to leap about, as if performing a wild jig. The workie, I realize with horror, is down, and they are stomping him. Across the street, a whistle shrills. By then the two well-dressed men have disappeared into the crowd. In their place stands a woman. I stare at her, mouth agape. She is the tall woman in the riding costume whom earlier I saw hurrying along Orleans Street. Her resemblance to my cousin Nola is more striking than I had thought.

Workies wielding two-by-fours dash across the street. Militia carbines, discharged skyward in nervous warning, seem—as if enwrapped in the vagrant logic of a dream—to cause the rain that immediately follows. I welcome this dream-like release from the constraints of normal logic, for it insulates me from my own perturbations as I see a man almost Obadiah's size appear in the doorway of Gunner's Hall, followed by Obadiah himself. The man, of course, has a sickle-shaped scar—why do I think of it then as *parang*-shaped?—on his face.

The woman who so reminds me of Cousin Nola gasps. She too is looking at the scar-faced man. She tugs at my left arm. "What are you doing here?" she asks, and calls me by an unfamiliar name that might be Phineas, as in Phineas T. Barnum. But no—it is Phidias, like the sculptor of Greek antiquity. By then, hardly aware of what I am doing, I have pointed my Colt .22 pocket revolver at the man called Monk, who has lifted from the doorsill of the tavern an inert body, likely the stomped-on voter, to hurl it into the crowd. As he does so, Obadiah seems to be shoved—*pretends* to be shoved?—from the side and, reaching out to recover his balance, himself shoves Monk against the door frame, pinning him there, a stationary target. "Mister Thomas, now!" shouts Obadiah just as the woman cries, "Phidias, no!"

And, upon hearing her—there is no other way to describe the experience, though it be so outside the ordinary that the reader may doubt my sanity—upon hearing her, I *become* Phidias. I cease—in the beat of a heart—in the blink of an eye—in the cry from her lips—I cease to be Thomas W. Frederick. I am someone named Phidias, Phidias Peacock. In my hand, in my raised hand, I am clutching a small revolver. In bewilderment I let my arm fall to my side. A huge Negro standing in the doorway looks at me with a melancholy smile that gives way to one of groveling subservience when a scar-faced white man at his side looses upon him a stream of pungent vituperation.

The rain beats down harder; the wind rises. The mob breaks for cover. The woman, whom I know to be the enigmatic Miss Tangerie, is running at my side, one hand clutching her black silk hat to her head. Why do we run? Phidias Peacock, his memory riddled with lacunae, cannot say. He runs because she does. If he asks, will she say she runs because he is running? He does not ask.

"I must talk to you," she says. And gives me a doubtful look. "I must talk to *someone*." Her voice is small, anxious, all but swept away by the wind.

An omnibus, its two bay horses sleekly wet, rumbles toward the curb ahead of us where a few men wait under umbrellas.

"Watch out!" Nolie Mae Tangerie screams, backing away. "It's jumping the tramway!"

I grasp her arm and say, "Jumping the tramway? But there is no tramway."

Baltimore, I need not say, has no trams. Since 1844—or was it '45?—omnibuses have been running from one end of the city to the other. But not on tracks. And quite right, too. Those iron rails on which omnibuses run in, for example, New York City, only make them the less maneuverable.

The waiting men furl their umbrellas and board the omnibus. Still grasping Miss Tangerie's arm, I try to propel her forward. But she resists me.

"It has jumped the tracks, I tell you!"

I make no reply. How shall I, with my tenuous hold on reality, persuade her that she suffers from the same?

The omnibus, its wheels skidding over wet paving blocks, resumes its eastward journey.

Miss Tangerie watches it go, then turns her doubtful look on me. "No . . . tracks," she says.

"No," I agree, trying for a cheery tone. "Not a one."

She glances down at my hand on her arm. I think at first that she objects to the liberty, but she slips her hand inside my own. I feel crumpled paper.

"I would like you to look at this."

I take the ball of paper from her and smooth it, to see a handbill, floridly printed. The ink has run but the words are still legible.

SUPPORT PRESIDENT TAYLOR

→   *Elect WHIGS to Congress*   ←

"What is it?" Miss Tangerie asks.

"Why, you know what it is."

"Yes, yes, it is a political handbill," she acknowledges impatiently. "But what does it *mean*?"

"Mean? It means exactly what it says."

Miss Tangerie nods. She sighs. And, in the smallest and most insecure of voices, she asks:

"Phidias, tell me, please—who is President of the United States?"

Assuming her question to be a joke, a riddle perhaps, I smile. "Taylor, of course. As it says right here. Not to be confused with *Tyler*, the last President but one—whom, it so happens, I have met."

On hearing my answer, I feel as startled as she looks. How, I wonder—how, when, where, why—would I, Phidias Peacock, have met John Tyler or any other President?

She gasps. "Why do you say that? Henry Clay became President just this year."

"My dear Miss Tangerie," I say, "Zachary Taylor has been in office since March. And before him, Polk. Senator Clay was never President and, at his age, never will be."

"But—but I never even heard of Zacharias Taylor."

Can she be serious?

"Zachary," I correct her. "General Zachary Taylor. Hero of the Mexican War."

"You would have me believe we fought a war with Mexico? Come now! It is just three years since the perpetual peace treaty was signed, the Pact of Matamoros—the crowning achievement of our beloved President Harrison's second term."

"Harrison? Old Tippecanoe? He caught a chill on Inauguration Day 1841 and died a month later." I do not allude again to John Tyler's succession as President. I wish not to think of President Tyler. I force a smile and say, "You are having me on, Miss Tangerie."

During the course of this bizarre conversation we have been walking aimlessly, quite oblivious to the downpour, caught up as we are in her mad joke and my own mystification. We are drenched, sodden, in need of shelter. In a warm and dry room, I try to persuade myself, I shall be able to make sense of what I have heard—what I have said—these past few minutes.

Shelter of a sort is available, for I see that we are standing at the foot of Federal Hill, close to the gangway of the seamen's bethel *William Penn*, once the ship *William Penn*, a veteran of the South America trade, fitted these many years with pulpit and pews and a red roof over its deck.

"We can wait out the storm here," I tell her just as a sudden gust of wind makes her reach frantically for her hat, catching it in mid-air and jamming it back on her blond head. Then she gives me a lost, bewildered look and begins to cry.

"Oh, Phidias, help me! I think I am losing my mind."

Twenty-five

It is, above all, a legend in which shape-shifting characters are whelmed by the unpredictable tides of time and circumstance.
—"How the Yaanek Found Their God"

We slide into the last row on the left. Before us isolated figures slouch in the dim pews, whether to escape the rain as we are doing or to seek communion with the Deity I can only guess. There is the smell of wet wool, of stale bodies, of prayers too long unanswered. From the pulpit comes a droning voice. I distinguish the words "Jonah" and "Nineveh."

"You would have shot him," says Miss Tangerie. "You would have shot Monk."

More madness from the mad Miss Tangerie?

But I feel the weight of the revolver in my pocket.

"And if you had, who could lead us to the Shard?"

I say nothing.

"For the first time I am able to believe that you *are* Will Henry's brother."

"I told you I was."

When? When have I told her that?

"The Negro called you—was it Mr. Thompson?"

"Thomas."

"A *nom de guerre*," says Miss Tangerie, pleased. "Such as your brother always used."

"Thomas W. Frederick," I say.

"The song writer? You used his name? How droll."

"Isn't his the reverse? Frederick W. Thomas?"

And I sit bemused, struggling with the possession of two identities somehow connected by this enigmatic young woman beside me.

The preacher lifts his voice. "And did not Leviathan flee before the sign upon Jonah, and was not Jonah borne in gratitude to the ends of the earth by the great fish he had saved, to see all those things he wished to see, not least the very source of the earth-girdling river called Ocean and the pitiful remnants of a god with no worshipers, smashed, broken, its fragments scattered like infertile seeds broadcast into a gale of wind?"

Miss Tangerie says, "I lied when I told you at your house on Mechanics Row that I came seeking employment."

As she speaks, I remember.

Smiling, I admit, "It is as well. I was offering none."

"The truth is, I am unable to say why I went there. I was dazed, you see. I had suffered an accident. My mare stepped into a hole, throwing me." Miss Tangerie's eyes squeeze shut; her voice falters. "I—I seemed to fall such a long way. Into a hedge, fortunately." Then, spoken more crisply: "But my mare broke her leg. Poor Jewel-weed, they had to shoot her."

"Jewelweed? Your mare was named Jewelweed?"

"Yes."

I marvel at the extraordinary coincidence. "But *I* had a mare named Jewelweed, who threw *me*. In this case the broken leg was mine. It is why I limp."

"But you do not limp, Phidias."

"If you mean you find it not terribly noticeable, it is kind of you to—"

"You do not limp at all."

I recall coming the considerable distance with her from Gunner's Hall in the Fourth Ward to the foot of Federal Hill, first running, then striding out easily, my malacca stick no more than a stylish accessory.

"But I did limp," I insist. "This very morning I—"

"Oh God," she moans. "How can you help me if . . . if your world is changing too?"

My world? Well, something, I am not certain what, has changed.

"Ever since my accident," she says, "things I always took for granted have become—unpredictable. I hesitate almost to inquire whether two plus two still makes four."

"My dear Miss Tangerie," I say, groping for words to reassure myself as much as her, "don't you see, the shock of a bad fall or, or a blow to the head . . . the human brain is a delicate mechanism in which, or so I have read,* memory and the ratiocinative functions . . . rather like a galvanic current when the battery has been disconnected . . . may cause the victim of a trauma to experience an abrupt—but reversible, I assure you, my dear Miss—"

"Words!" shouts Miss Tangerie, and the preacher gives her a look of sad disapprobation. "Those are just words! *Won't* you try to understand? I'm here, in a seamen's bethel at the foot of Federal Hill, even though I know there is no such place."

"As Federal Hill?" I ask in wonderment.

"As a seamen's bethel docked at its foot."

"But the *William Penn* has been a bethel for years."

"Not here! It is moored permanently at Fells Point!" she cries. "It was never here, just as President Harrison did *not* die a month after his inauguration, and just as there *are* tram lines here in Baltimore and—and explain to me, you who know so much, explain what happened at the library. *That* was where I went, the Free Library on Cathedral Street, seeking work."

"You are a librarian?"

"I no longer know what I am! But I do know, as I told you, that I received a most liberal education. The head librarian seemed favorably disposed toward me. His filing system may have been eccentric but nothing I could not master. A wide-ranging conversation established my familiarity with contemporary American letters. The Deerslayer novels of Cooper, Irving's *History of the Life and Voyages of Columbus*, Longfellow. I was able to discuss intelligently *A Pilgrimage Beyond the Sea*, quote from *Voices of the Night*. All went well until the librarian mentioned a writer named Edgar Pope."

"Do you not mean Poe?" I suggested. "Edgar Poe?"

"Poe, yes, that was the name. But I never heard of any Edgar Poe. Have you?"

---

* Poe probably refers here to *Galvanism and the Human Brain* by Sir David Humphries (London, 1841), one of the pitifully few volumes found in his last home at Fordham, New York. (Editor's note)

"I have. He is known for tales of terror, and of scientific phenomena like airships that can cross the ocean—and for poetry with the power to mesmerize. But they say his longer tales end poorly, that he has not the perseverance to finish them. They say he drinks. Perhaps that is the difficulty."

"But he is famous? I ought to have heard of him?"

" 'Infamous' might better describe him. There was a scandal in New York with a literary lady. It seems that—"

"Infamous, and I do not even know his name? No more than of this President Zacharias Taylor of yours? Either I *am* losing my mind—"

"Now, now, Miss—"

"—or the world has *changed*. It is as if, as if I have gone into some other place, alien and frightening, and *I am trapped there unable to get out*."

I sit for a time wrapped in my own silence, fearful of emerging. I have had, after all, no experience dealing with the deranged. But finally pity makes me speak. "You did, though. You did, my dear Miss Tangerie, so it cannot be as bad as all that."

"I did what?"

"Get back out. Clearly you managed to do so."

"Why can't you understand?" she cries. "I did *not* get out. I am still trapped here."

Twenty-six

Carefully locking the door on the inside, I commenced a vigorous search. It was possible, I thought, that, concealed in some obscure corner, or lurking in some closet or drawer, might be found the lost object of my inquiry.

—"Loss of Breath"

Except that she smoked cigars, the Brazilian bareback rider would have been adequate diversion for Edgar while he awaited the return of his brother's murderer. Her big eyes flashed boldly, her mane of hair was the color of mahogany, she had a rollicking laugh, she was tireless in the bed of her exotic American. But by the time the apartment at 15-*bis* Rue de la Gaîté reeked of tobacco, both knew the affair had run its course.

Edgar next acquired, in a narrow street in the huddle of old buildings in the Cité, not five minutes' walk from the cathedral (Edgar was then reading, in French, Victor Hugo's *Hunchback of Notre Dame*), a jet-haired, *café-au-lait*-skinned girl with smoldering eyes whose name was not Esmeralda, though she said it was. She remained installed in the Rue de la Gaîté until Edgar discovered that a diamond stickpin was missing.

This did not make Edgar desist. He was of a restless nature and even in the best of circumstances disliked living in one place for long; women were a substitute for moving. There was the self-styled Polish countess, Rubenesque but lugubrious. There was the *midinette* from La Fille Mal Gardée whom he met through Alexandre Dumas's wife, Catherine, but Edgar soon found that they had no common interests except "each other's bodies, what else is there?" asked Alexandre in surprise, the night Edgar had given the *midinette* a pearl necklace and bid her farewell. There was the statuesque if self-absorbed redhead who modeled for the *couturier* Leroy. There was the bored young matron Edgar met in the conservatory on the Pont des Arts when both took shelter from a sudden thunderstorm. There were "*mon Dieu*, my dear Poe, every thing but nuns," said Alexandre. "Your reputation here in Paris almost puts me to shame."

"They help while away the time," said Edgar.

He walked. He walked everywhere, from dawn to dusk, every day. He knew each of the eighteen belltowers of the Cité, and every suburban parish church (from the outside, that is; Edgar was no believer). He knew all the shops in all the new covered *passages* and under the arcades of the old Palais Royal. He went Sundays to the country taverns of la Courtille to drink the wines of Suresnes and Argenteuil and dance under the arbors with the saucy, uncomplicated girls of the *faubourg*. He walked the length of the Boulevard du Temple, called Boulevard du Crime, and sometimes managed to sit through an entire melo-drama in one of its theaters. He paid to see packs of dogs fight bulls in the pits in the Rue de la Grange-aux-Belles at the Barrière du Combat. He even climbed to the former chalk quarries, now garbage dumps, of the Buttes Chaumont, from whose highest point he could look down over the teeming city and ask himself, "Where is he? Why hasn't he come? What is he waiting for?" Frequently he followed the remains of the wall of the Fermiers-Généraux, intending to circumambulate the city, a distance of twenty-four kilometers, but with random impatience he would abruptly plunge down this narrow lane or that.

When some weeks had passed, he went again one evening to see the Chevalier C. Auguste Dupin. Dupin by then had given up his quarters where Anton Mesmer had lived in the Place Vendôme for an undistinguished apartment *au troisième*, N° 33, Rue Dunôt, in the Faubourg St-Germain.

"Of course I remember you, my dear Poe. Pray be seated."

Dupin was smoking his ever-present meerschaum. His green-tinted spectacles looked black in the murky light. Edgar groped his way to a chair, declined a pipe. The two men sat in silence for some time. Dupin seemed to encourage such silences, as if, like darkness, they helped him think.

"You wish," he said at length, "to search minutely the premises you occupy in the Rue de la Gaîté."

This was no question.

"Indeed. But how did you know?"

"How could I *not*? You come here either because you think your brother's murderer—*presumed* murderer—has returned, or because you now incline to the view that he never will. If the first, you would have blurted your suspicions at once. So, the second."

Edgar was about to speak, but Dupin blew a cloud of smoke, waved a hand through it, and continued. "This new conviction may stem as much from restlessness as from reasoning. You Americans are so impatient. Clearly you have not sat waiting at home for the murderer to reappear. You have, have you not, been walking the streets of Paris by day?" Dupin spoke the last word with distaste.

"I have. But—"

"Your boots proclaim as much. Though they are not old, the heels are worn down markedly on the outsides. Only rapid striding over long distances would account for that, and one steps out more smartly when he has no difficulty in seeing, does he not? Moreover, had you done your restless wandering by night, my dear Poe, you would have visited me sooner. Well! Exactly what is it you wish of me?"

"I wish to make a far more thorough search of the premises than the Prefect G—— did. I wish to find whatever the murderer sought—or satisfy myself it is no longer there."

"And you believe there is a method to searching, some logical approach, which I possess and the Prefect G—— does not?"

"I believe you can advise me how to be most thorough."

"So I can. But I must warn you that a methodical search of the premises will take weeks. Moreover, one may fail to uncover the hidden object precisely because one *is* so methodical."

"Explain," said Edgar, not without impatience.

"The methodical leaves no room for the intuitive. Consider: You know nothing whatever about what you seek. Not even its size. Would a scientist dream of beginning an empirical investigation when he does not know whether he will need a microscope or a telescope?"

"There are only so many square meters in the apartment."

"There is also the cellar. The roof. Not to mention the staircases. You will need certain tools."

"Tell me what they are."

C. Auguste Dupin did. Then he said, "Most important, my young friend, while you are searching you must endeavor to think of nothing."

"To think of nothing?"

"Nothing." Dupin removed his green-tinted spectacles. In the dimness, through the layers of blue smoke, Edgar could not see his eyes. "What you do must become as automatic as breathing. When that happens, your mind will become . . . receptive."

"To what?"

"*Eh bien,*" said the Chevalier C. Auguste Dupin, "who can say?"

The search lasted three days into its second week.

To catalogue methodically all that Edgar methodically did would serve no purpose. Let it merely be said that among other activities he: tapped, with appropriately sized mallets, all paneling, moldings, marquetry, and wooden furniture elements; scrutinized with a powerful magnifying glass the fitting of chair rungs to legs, legs to seats, and the like; plunged long fine needles into upholstery; probed with still finer needles the binding of every book in Henry's library (surprisingly large for a transient's) and then turned over every page; ascertained with his magnifying glass that the silk wall coverings—except where he himself had had them repaired—had been neither pasted over nor otherwise disturbed; lifted the carpets and, on hands and knees, swept up with small camel-hair brushes the dust, which later he examined under a microscope for metal or wood shavings that would have betrayed the use of a gimlet upon the floorboards; and in all conducted, in ten days, no fewer than three thousand separate operations, their repetitiveness so numbing that on the eleventh morning he found himself beginning again, where he had started, in the bedroom.

First he congratulated himself on how automatic the activity of searching had become. Then he realized that his mind, although rendered "receptive" enough to satisfy even Dupin, had received nothing.

The cellar was next. He lit his way down steep stone stairs with the same ceramic lamp the gendarme had used the night of the murder. The ceiling was low and vaulted and, like the rough stone walls, so encrusted with saltpetre that, in the light cast by the lamp, the surfaces glittered wetly, as if composed of millions of shards of glass. The glitter was everywhere untouched: Edgar would not have to sound the walls or ceiling. Likewise, the floor needed no scrutiny. It was, in effect, the seamless bottom of an excavation pit or quarry.

The cellar was no single room but three small connecting chambers, each crowded with wine casks. Edgar struck the nearest hogshead. There was a scrabbling sound. A large rat scurried across the floor. Edgar recoiled. A moment passed before he returned his attention to the hogshead, which indeed contained liquid. So did a second, and one of the double-sized pipes. But the next pipe he thumped responded hollowly. In the dim light Edgar could not tell if the barrel heads had been disturbed. He returned upstairs for tools and his magnifying glass. Seeing in a corner of the hall his malacca stick, he took that too. The size of the rat had unnerved him. Like not a few stout-hearted men, Edgar harbored a squeamish dislike of rodents.

There were, in all, sixty-two casks of varying sizes. With the magnifying glass Edgar could discern minute gouges in a dozen heads where nails had been prised out and driven back into the wood. He concluded that the Prefect of Police G—— had been less than thorough. Edgar himself would open the untouched barrels first, then re-open those examined by the Prefect.

Setting tools and lamp upon an up-ended barrel and leaning his stick against it, he seized the first cask.

Instantly he was assailed by a red gleam of rodent eyes and a furor of squeals and scurryings and, before he could release the cask, by a spine-chilling sensation of fur brushing against his bare hands and of bestial bodies wriggling upon his own, as several of the horrid creatures used him as an avenue of escape. In a paroxysm of revulsion, Edgar grabbed up his malacca stick and laid about him with a flurry of blows.

The ceramic lamp spun toward the floor, where, with a reverberating crash, it shattered. Spermaceti oil, catching fire from the still-burning wick, ignited a trail that Edgar quickly trod upon and extinguished, leaving himself in utter darkness. He fumbled in his pocket for a phosphorus match and struck it. It flared briefly and was extinguished by a cold draft—from where? Yet Edgar was sure he had felt it. He struck another match, and a third. Each was extinguished almost at once. Edgar stood without moving. He thought he heard the sound of water dripping. He had an eerie sense of not being alone in the cellar. He lit another match, and another. They flared and flung shadows and died. He began to feel foolish.

A grown man, to allow himself to be so unnerved by a nest of rats!

He groped his way to the steps—foolish or no, holding his malacca stick at the ready—and went upstairs to fetch another lamp, a sturdy brass one with a tall glass chimney. Returning to the cellar, he saw on the upended barrel what he took at first for a single shard of pottery. This puzzled him, for he was certain that the lamp had not smashed until it struck the floor.

Edgar stared at the shard. Perhaps three inches across, it was hexagonal in shape, with cleanly sheared facets that caught the lamplight. He picked it up and was surprised by its weight. Too heavy to be ceramic, it seemed rather a shard of some dense, dark stone. But then where had it come from? Surely not from the broken lamp.

He felt a tingling in his fingers, as if a galvanic current were passing from the stone into his hand. There followed this sequence, each part of which Edgar would later recall as a discrete event:

An icy draft, like those that had extinguished the matches, blew across the back of his neck. Next, instead of the dankness of the cellar and the acrid tang of phosphorus matches, he smelled the sea, or rather the edge of the sea. Next (he would tell Dupin later), the walls aglitter with saltpetre began to fade and, fading, parted like the curtains in a theater, leaving only (he would tell Count Dionisio di Tangeri later still) the glitter of the saltpetre itself. Next, the glitter fell like snow, and he heard a sibilant sound as of the sea racing as fast as a galloping horse across a black sand beach below a cliff on which stood a turreted castle, its windows like eyes, blank eyes with their pupils rolled back, its battlements and crenellations redly glowing as if a fire raged within. Edgar fled the raging phosphorescent surf, fled for his life, but the sea was swift.

Had this not happened before? But when? How?

His nerveless fingers dropped the stone shard. He was instantly back in the sepulchral silence of the vaulted cellar.

For fully five minutes he stood absolutely still. But when curiosity and fear waged their immemorial battle, for Edgar there could be but one outcome.

His hand crept toward the shard, and closed about it.

An hour later, he was tugging at the bell-pull outside Dupin's door.

Twenty-seven

I now feel that I have reached a point of this narrative at which every reader will be startled into positive disbelief. It is my business, however, simply to proceed.
—"The Facts in the Case of M. Valdemar"

When Edgar had finished his story, Dupin sat inscrutably behind smoke from his meerschaum, behind green-tinted spectacles. He extended his hand.

Edgar took the stone shard from his pocket and passed it to Dupin.

"I feel no tingling," said the Chevalier, "galvanic or otherwise."

"Nor do I—now."

"I see nothing out of the ordinary," said Dupin, turning the shard this way and that under a large magnifying glass, green-tinted like his spectacles.

"You were, however," Dupin pointed out, "in a state not only of receptivity but of high excitement. And, further, the fertile imagination of Mr. Edgar Poe is a given. This combination, my friend, could easily lead to—forgive me if the suggestion offends you—hallucination."

"It doesn't offend me. I want to get to the bottom of whatever happened."

"Would you accept that this small stone—which seems, from its facets, broken from a larger one—is no more than it appears to be, a coarse-grained Plutonic rock?"

Wordlessly Edgar removed his boot. Turning it sole up, he let something trickle into his cupped hand, and from his hand into Dupin's.

"Sand," said Dupin.

"Black sand," said Edgar.

"I can see that the sand is black," said Dupin. "It is not unusual, black sand. It is of volcanic origin. On the island of Tenerife in the Canaries, for instance, the beaches are black."

"How did it get into my boot if what I experienced was a hallucination?"

Dupin tapped the dottle from his meerschaum and stood. He was as slender as Edgar, and no taller.

"When a man is gifted with certain talents," he said slowly, "you with your fecund imagination, for example, or I with my modest ratiocinative skills, he is wise to limit himself to what he does best."

"Meaning?"

"Meaning that you appear to have experienced something decidedly *outré* and I am not the one to, as you say, get to the bottom of it. But, fortunately, I number among my acquaintances one who might . . . plumb those depths for you. Are you averse to being hypnotized?"

"Hypno—put to sleep, do you mean? Mesmerized?"

"Yes and no. Mesmer was a fraud. His disciple the Marquis de Puységur was not. Be assured, the hypnotism practiced by de Puységur and his followers has nothing to do with Mesmer's quackery. No, it is a science, and its most skilled practitioner here in Paris if not in all Europe is the Neapolitan Count Dionisio di Tangeri. I shall write you an introduction to him."

Dupin scrawled a few lines on a card. "Wait for dawn. Unlike me, the Count sleeps nights. And, Poe?"

Edgar, clutching the card, already was at the door.

"Take your sand with you. And your boot."

The door was opened by a tall young woman most fetchingly attired in a trim riding habit of that gray cloth the French call London smoke. Her eyes were of the same smoky color, her cheek-bones high and pronounced, her generous lips so red as to have, almost, a bruised look. Her blond hair peeked out from under the brim of a black silk hat. She was quite the most attractive girl Edgar had encountered during his sojourn in Paris, which, given his appreciative eye and that city's great beauties, says much.

"Oh!" she cried.

"I have startled you, mademoiselle?"

"No, it is just that I . . . have we met before, monsieur?"

Edgar, on first seeing her, had for a moment the same impression. But he rejected it at once, and now did so aloud.

"It is not possible, mademoiselle. Had we met, I could never have forgotten you." He bowed over her hand. "I am Edgar Poe, Mademoiselle—?"

"Tangeri. Maia Tangeri. You have come to consult my father, the Count?"

Edgar gave her Dupin's card. She read and returned it. "You are the writer?"

"I am afraid so," said Edgar with his most charming smile.

"I have read your tale 'How the Yaanek Found Their God'* with enormous interest, and so has my father. His greatest diversion is to read whatever he can find about the fabled land of Atlantis that sank beneath the seas nine thousand years ago."

"Not Atlantis, actually," Edgar said. "I set my tale on the island of Panchatan because I had in mind the lost Lemuria."

"Lemuria?"

"You see, I believe that when Plato coined the name 'Atlantis' in his *Timaeus*, he was recounting what he had heard of an ancient— an immemorial—myth of a lost continent *not* in the Atlantic but on the other side of the world in the South China Sea. In short, of Lemuria.† As for *its* name, it has, at best, an uncertain provenance."

---

* Not in the Poe canon. (Editor's note)

† Those conversant with the myths surrounding the lost continent of Lemuria know that if it existed, it lay far to the west of the island of Panchatan, the setting for Poe's tale. Thus it is tempting to conclude that the narrator had knowledge of a third, unnamed lost continent which he conflated with Lemuria. (Editor's note)

"Yet you have written of it so enthrallingly, monsieur. My father says that your slim tale is worth a dozen so-called factual volumes. He conjectures that you must be the possessor of some *recherché* work upon the subject, whose very existence you keep to yourself."

"Hardly," said Edgar with a smile. "I fear that this secret source is but my own meager imagination."

"Meager! I would have said magnificent. Especially in one so young."

Their eyes met and held. A delicate blush suffused her face. He was sure that his heart skipped a beat. Each was on the point of speaking, each waited for the other to do so. Both laughed nervously.

She said, "I really must go. I—"

He said, "I very much hope—"

She said, "—am already late."

He said, "—we may meet again."

She laughed again. "One cannot keep the army waiting."

"The army?"

"The friend with whom I ride is a cavalry officer."

Sideways, careful not to touch, they passed through the doorway, she out, he in.

"I would," she said, "be very glad if we were to meet again," and fled down the stairs.

He stood looking through the empty doorway, for how long he could not have said, until the card in his hand recalled to him Count Dionisio di Tangeri, and Dupin, and the shard.

Count Tangeri wrote that afternoon, in a hand that bespoke great emotional distress:

My dear Dupin,

I set this upon paper as soon as I may, lest I forget some aspects of the most unwonted, the most unparalleled, the most bizarre session I or any hypnotist has ever conducted. I send this letter by courier, in the fervent hope that you can suggest some course of action that, under these extraordinary circumstances, might be at all availing.

I had no difficulty in lulling Monsieur Poe into a deep hypnotic sleep—the subject's imagination and intelligence rather aiding than impeding the process.

There followed this dialogue:

TANGERI: You are comfortable?

POE: Yes.

T: Raise your left arm level with the table. Good. You could maintain it there for hours, without strain?

P: I could, yes.

T: You may now relax it. Relax your whole being. But—you are distracted?

P: Yes.

T: By what?

P: (*smiling*) By a beautiful woman—who is your daughter.

T: Maia? Shall I make you forget her?

P: No!

T: Temporarily, monsieur, so that you may concentrate on the matter at hand.

P: Yes, I understand. All right.

T: Now, who is Maia Tangeri?

P: I do not know the name.

T: Very good. I should like you to tell me all that occurred when you explored the cellar of the premises at 15-*bis* Rue de la Gaîté.

(*P then repeated—or, from the expression on his face, relived—the events that he had already, waking, related to you, my dear Dupin, and to myself.*)

T: This shard—kindly place it upon the table. You felt nothing untoward?

P: No.

T: I am going to put you into a still deeper sleep. You are now sleeping very deeply. Take the shard in your hand. What do you see? No, let me re-phrase that. Where *are* you?

P: I stand on the edge of a shoreless sea.

T: Shoreless? But where you stand—is that not a shore?

P: I mean perhaps to suggest endlessness at the *other* end.

T: Tell me, is this the same sea, the same beach of black sand, that you . . . experienced earlier? Does a tide threaten to engulf you?

P: No—yes—I can't tell. There are mountains, great mountains, craggy, toppling, plunging into the sea, which surges, boils, under a flaming sky.

T: You mean sunset? Or sunrise?

P: No. The sky is burning!

T: Are you in danger?

P: Everyone is in danger!

T: Calmly, monsieur. Replace the shard upon the table. Good. You are again sleeping less deeply. Where are you?

P: In Paris.

T: You may wipe the sweat from your face. Now, monsieur, from your writings, it seems you are conversant with accepted theory regarding the destruction—was it nine thousand years ago?—of the continent of Atlantis.

P: Nine thousand, yes. But Atlantis is a myth. It was Lemuria I wrote of, Lemuria that was destroyed.

T: How? How was it destroyed?

P: The *accepted* theory is that an earthquake ripped the continent apart.

T: But?

P: The theory is incorrect. Lemuria was destroyed by a comet that entered the solar system from the depths of the unknown.

T: As in your tale "The Conversation of Eiros and Charmion"?

P: Yes, but *that* comet destroyed not a continent but all living things, when the earth passed through its tail.

T: And this comet, the comet of your story "How the Yaanek Found Their God"?

P: It struck the continent of Lemuria, which, upon the explosion of the comet, sank—partially sank—under the South China Sea.

T: Partially?

P: What remains of it is the Malay Archipelago. There, on an island called Panchatan, it is written—

T: Written where?

P: (*smiling*) In "How the Yaanek Found Their God." And in notes for another story I hope one day to write. You see, the Yaanek people found a considerable mass of cometary matter—

T: Cometary matter?

P: Residue of the explosion of the comet. From this stone they carved an idol said to be possessed of magical powers.

T: What magical powers?

P: The power to suspend certain natural laws.

T: I do not understand.

P: (*wryly*) Nor do I.

T: But you intend writing a tale in which this idol plays a part.

P: One day. If I can determine the ending.

T: The shard, has it some connection with the idol?

P: I should like to hold it again.

T: By all means. What do you see?

P: (*in a tense whisper*) I see a horseman racing up a steep trail. No—a horse*woman*! (*Poe rose from his chair, gripping the shard in his right hand.*) She is Maia, your daughter Maia! She flees—is fleeing a very great danger. (*Poe rushed to the door.*)

T: You will return to your chair and sit when I say now. Now.

P: (*sitting*) But don't you see, I must help her!

T: Tell me, what is the danger she faces?

P: It cannot be described. I only know that I must rescue her . . . and save the Yaanek. . . .

Whereupon, my dear Dupin, Monsieur Poe fell silent. He became deathly pale, literally taking on the dead white hue of a cadaver. I bade him wake. I used all my skills as a hypnotist, to no avail. I could not wake him. His color so alarmed me that I feared for his life. Yet when I felt his pulse, it was strong, steady, one hundred forty beats to the minute, as if he were engaged in violent exercise. Even as I counted his pulse, his arm—how can I write this so that you will believe?—his arm began to feel lighter. Soon it was quite weightless. By then the skin of his face had assumed the translucent look of a very old man's. Would that that had been all! But before my horrified eyes Monsieur Poe began to fade. Through him I could see the wall, and the Ingres portrait of my beloved Maia. And then only the wall and the Ingres. Monsieur Poe was no longer here.

Maia too is not here. She went this morning to ride in the Bois with her cavalry officer. She ought to have returned five hours ago.

Twenty-eight

An infinity of errors makes its way into our philosophy, through man's habit of considering himself a denizen of the world solely—of an individual planet—instead of at least occasionally as a denizen of the universe.

—Marginalia

A thin snow had been falling all day and, shortly before dusk, was falling still. I could just descry a figure trudging uphill from the direction of the railroad station of the village of Fordham, thirteen miles north of New York City. He was so laden with packages that I at first took him for a peddler. But when he was close enough for me to make out his familiar lunging gait, I quickly gathered the untidy papers on my work table, put them in the box beneath, and hurried to the door.

"What a splendid surprise," I said.

"Rather it is I who should be surprised," he told me, "not to find you dangling by your arms from the lintel and gibbering like an ourang-outang."

"Oh, I only do that in the dark of the moon when no one is about. I have my reputation to think of."

"You would do well to think of it more, from what I hear."

Stamping snow from his heavy boots, he entered the cottage and deposited boxes and twine-fastened bundles on the table.

"Who is there?" Muddy called from Virginia's room.

"It is my old friend Frederick Thomas," I replied, "up from Washington City." By then we were gripping hands and thumping shoulders.

I heard a grunt, and the bedroom door shut. Muddy inclined to the view that all my old friends were drinking friends and that I would do well to make new friends or, better, have no friends at all. Which was nearly the situation these days.

I helped Frederick W. Thomas off with his coat. From its pocket he produced a folded newspaper; no, two of them.

"Why did you not let me know?"

The December 15 edition of the *New York Morning Express* was folded open to this:

ILLNESS OF EDGAR A. POE

We regret to learn that this gentleman and his wife are both dangerously ill with the consumption, and that the hand of misfortune lies heavy upon their temporal affairs. —We are sorry to mention the fact that they are so far reduced as to be barely able to obtain the necessaries of life.

The writer went on to urge that, in this holiday season, Poe's friends and readers rally to his support.

"At least," I said, "they call me a gentleman."

Frederick W. Thomas studied me. In a low voice he asked: "Is it true you have the consumption?"

I shook my head. "Perhaps I have been consuming too much gin," I said, and heard from the back of the cottage a muffled cough, and wished I had not spoken so frivolously.

"How is she?"

"She will get no better."

Frederick W. Thomas opened his packages. There were two plucked chickens, a tin of China tea, oranges, butter, a wheel of cheese, wine, manzanilla. There was a down comforter for Virginia and a dressing gown in a gay flowered print, a black woolen shawl for Muddy, a warm hat for me.

"Wear it low over that broad Poe brow," Thomas suggested chaffingly, "and people will be less likely to recognize Marmaduke Hammerhead." Then, in earnest, "What ever got into you? What made you sue?"

"There are limits to what a man can take. The piece was scurrilous."

"Of course it was. But that doesn't alter Thomas's First Rule: Those who write must never sue those who publish. Even when the writer wins, he loses—for he will find himself with no publishers at all. Besides, if there are limits, it can be argued that you exceeded them yourself."

"My 'Literati of New York City,' " I said, "was an accurate portrait of the most intellectually incestuous group of second-raters that ever filled a city's journals with mutual back-scratching."

Thomas sighed. "Even granting it *was* accurate, how did you think you could loose such a volley of criticism without taking some shots in return? Damn it, Poe, you managed to revile or ridicule nearly every literary eminence not just in New York but in the country! Not to mention what you did to the wealthy hangers-on who make a hobby of collecting writers."

Here Thomas threw back his head and laughed. Then he sobered and said, "Still, you should not have sued the *Mirror*. Even if what they wrote would give any man apoplexy."

He opened the second newspaper and read:

" 'A poor creature called at our office the other day, in a condition of sad, wretched imbecility, bearing in his feeble body the evidences of evil living, and betraying by his talk such radical obliquity of sense that every spark of harsh feeling toward him was extinguished, and we could not even entertain a feeling of contempt for one who was evidently committing a suicide upon his body, as he had already done upon his character.' " Thomas rolled his eyes.

"That wasn't what made me sue. It was Marmaduke Hammerhead."

Thomas gave me a curious look. "But that was ham-handed Tom-Foolery, beyond the point of burlesque. 'Marmaduke Hammerhead, hack journalist'! With, was it, 'a broad, low, receding forehead'?"

" 'Receding and deformed.' You left out 'deformed.' "

"Author of 'The Black Crow.' Marmaduke Hammerhead who is, if I recall, a faller from the salons of New York to the saloons of New York, an imputer of plagiarism because so prone to commit it himself, a philanderer with an ungovernable impulse to assault portrait painters and others, invariably ending on his back on the sidewalk, from which position he will offer to take on six at one time, meaning, no doubt, bottles of gin. Hammerhead who, believing himself the object of persecution by the leagued literati of the Republic, can now be found in a cell for the dangerously deranged, babbling criticism of his betters." Thomas paused for breath. "Such un-subtle drivel. Why should it have exercised you so?"

"Someone sent it to Virginia inside a copy of *Godey's Lady's Book.** She took it badly. Worse than you can imagine. Rather as if she considered it her fault."

He gave me another curious look. I wished I could call back my words. I said hastily, "I shall win the suit."

"It is not likely," said Frederick W. Thomas. "The consensus is that, since 'The Literati,' you are fair game. But whether or no— Poe, listen to me. The *Express* wrote of consumption. Another paper said you had exiled yourself to Fordham with brain fever. I have seen worse. In Washington I read that your friends are soon to place you under the charge of a Dr. Bingham at the Insane Retreat at Utica. The *Baltimore Saturday Visiter* has it that your 'mental derangement will be a painful piece of intelligence to thousands.'"

"I read the papers too," I said.

"Don't you see? By suing over a trifle, you feed the speculation. More grist for Rufus Griswold's rumor mill."

"It is Griswold spreading the rumors?"

"Repeating them, at the least—assiduously. But what can you expect, given his lack of character? You threaten his standing as a critic. Further, Poe, you were not exactly discreet in your . . . friendship with Fanny Osgood. And now that she is separated from her husband, Griswold again is squiring her everywhere."

I nodded, unsurprised. "Also," I said, "Griswold was witness to certain . . . aberrant behavior on my part."

"You mean at the President's House? You were drunk, not de-

---

* The Philadelphia magazine which, in thirty-eight installments, published "The Literati of New York City." (Editor's note)

ranged. For God's sake, Poe, you can fight this thing. Everyone knows Rufus Griswold for a malicious gossip. You need only show your face, emerge from your hibernation. It so happens I have a good friend who is president of a literary society at the University of Vermont. They would like you to give a reading."

"Vermont?"

"It is a place to start. The lecture circuit is remunerative."

"I can go nowhere."

We both looked at the bedroom door.

He said, "How long do they give her?"

"How many weeks or months is not important, but how she spends them. I must bring what solace I can to her dying. God knows I brought to her life only deprivation and misery. It could have been so different. With our cousin Neilson she would have had all the advantages. She would have been a healthy young woman! Would be one today!"

"Easy, my friend. She knew the uncertainties of your profession when she married you."

"A thirteen-year-old child?"

"Then her mother did. Virginia may have been young, but Maria was not—nor yet was she old." Frederick W. Thomas limped across the room and back. He said softly, "And that raises more speculation. How do you answer it?"

"What? What speculation?"

"That if the daughter was first too young and then too ill, did you sleep with the mother?"

His head jerked back and blood spurted from his nose. My hand throbbed; I could feel the knuckles swelling. He stanched the blood with a handkerchief.

"Get out," I said.

"You don't think *I* believe that? But I have heard it. Make no mistake, Poe. They are returning the favor of 'The Literati.' They are raking up every last thing, real or imagined, to your discredit. They will destroy you, if you let them. You must go about in public. Attend readings and lectures. Give some yourself. Be as contentious

as you wish; that is expected of you. Flirt outrageously with some
new Fanny Osgood. But go."

"Not as long as Virginia needs me."

"That may be too long to save yourself."

I said nothing, just reached below the table for the gin bottle
behind the box of manuscript. My hand closed upon it. Then I
hesitated, released the bottle, picked up the box instead, and set it
on the table.

I sensed that I was acting unwisely even as I felt the weight of
the box, even as I aligned its edges with those of the table top, even
as I said, could not stop myself from saying:

"Thomas, what you see before you could be the most important
scientific work ever penned. I say this with humility, but I say it."

Frederick W. Thomas smiled, quizzically, waiting for the joke.
After an uneasy silence he said, "Scientific?"

"Yes."

"Why then, you have hidden depths." His smile had not quite
faded. He still expected to hear the self-deflating line, to smile
whole-heartedly, to laugh with me.

But I waited. I would wait him out.

"Has the masterpiece as yet a title?"

"*Eureka*," I said.

"Eureka?"

"*Eureka*. As Archimedes said. 'I have found.' "

"Archimedes exclaimed this, I believe, upon finding a way to assay
gold," said Frederick W. Thomas, still with that hopeful half-smile.
"What have you found?"

"Ahh," I said.

Some small, commonsensical part of me still wanted to remove
the manuscript from the table, to shove it out of sight, to pretend
I had not mentioned it. But the rest of me stood looking at Thomas
with amused condescension and thinking:

He does not know, poor benighted devil. No one knows. But they
will, when I finish it, when I publish it. George Putnam, I shall get
George Putnam to publish it. George Putnam, who was so impressed

by my notoriety, my overnight fame, in France. France . . . they will appreciate *Eureka*, the French. It will appeal to their self-contained logic, and to that uniquely French ability to step back and leap boldly into a new paradigm. The French, ah yes, if no one else, the French will understand *Eureka. Vive la France!*

I was calm. Calm. So utterly calm and sure of myself, sure of what I had been writing—not at all uncertain or insecure, as so often when penning a tale, a poem. Would this tranquillity, this almost preternatural tranquillity, help Thomas W. Frederick—that is, Frederick W. Thomas—to step back and leap into this new—*my* new—paradigm?

I began in a clarion voice to expound on things hypothetical—*for now* hypothetical but one day soon to become an elaboration upon—a crowning of—a level beyond—the work of Newton, of von Humboldt, of Laplace. As once disease had sharpened the senses of a character of my creation,* so now—would Thomas be able to grasp this?—disease, not my disease but Virginia's, had made my intellect more acute. How could it not? We were close, Virginia and I, some would say morbidly so. I heard, felt, suffered her every cough, her struggle for breath, for one more breath, for one more hour, one more day; I endured the agonies of her death to help her *not die.* How? Oh, the power, the death-revoking, immortalizing power of the pen; not a nib of steel, not now, no; a quill, a feather, a *raven's* feather, sharpened every day, reborn, do you not see? I wrote. I wrote, to make my discovery the new, the accepted, the *only* paradigm of the uncaring, fluctuating, no longer inexplicable universe. I wrote, to master time and space and change and change-lessness. Writing, could I not dispatch death, wipe out anni-hilation?

I admonished myself, even as I spoke, not to reveal all of this to Frederick W. Thomas. For was *he*—a writer of popular songs and trashy novels; worse, a lawyer; worse, a politician—was he one who could, when confronted with a whole new cosmos, distinguish genius from madness?

---

* The reader is referred to "The Tell-Tale Heart." (Editor's note)

But I spoke. I spoke. I spread upon the table the pages of my manuscript and I talked him through it, wishing again that I could stop, wishing I had not begun. But I had begun, and I could not stop. Even though I knew I had yet to work the whole thing out. (Knew I never could.) Knew it would be published never the less. Could see it (yes!) as I discoursed upon the creation and essence and destiny of the universe (annihilating annihilation!), as I predicted how I would revolutionize physical science (all in due time!), as I explained with unassailable logic that because Nothing Was, therefore All Things Are (and vice versa!), as I let roll from my tongue spiral nebulae and transcendental unity and absorption of the universe (nothing and every thing!) into itself, as I raised and lowered my voice (analogy, analogy is all!) with the expanding and contracting of the infinite plenum, which pulsated in accordance with the vacillating energies of the imagination (God's imagination, if there was a God!), as I whispered (it was, after all, still a secret!) that no one who died could fail to come back, that return was eternal if life was not, that he, Frederick W. Thomas, would again stand here (and *again* again!) absorbing this new paradigm which he had absorbed before (and *before* before!), listening to these truths, listening and wishing desperately that he had not come. For I could see the glaze in his eyes, making them at once brighter and duller. But on I went, even as I willed myself to stop, even as I saw how his bright dull eyes were staring, staring at me. And I revealed that, out of the terrifying concept of a universe disappearing into itself, is born hope, for the universe will come back, all will come back, all, you, I, everyone living and dead, everyone that has yet to live, Virginia. . . .

Suddenly I began to weep. Just sat there and wept while the universe contracted. Spoke no more; wept. I think he placed his arm about my shoulder. I think Muddy came into the room. Did I hear a crackling sound? Smell chicken roasting? Did we eat? After a long time I saw that Frederick W. Thomas was no longer there. Did I hear a railroad whistle, mournful in the tenebrous night? I went into the bedroom. Virginia lay sleeping upon the straw mattress, between soft flannel sheets, under my old army greatcoat. I replaced it with the down comforter. She made a small sound, less than a sigh. Perhaps it was only the rustling of the straw as her hand moved, to close upon the hem of the comforter. She may almost have smiled. Her complexion was beautiful with a deadly beauty, as white as pearl and with the same soft luster. I leaned down and kissed the deep hollows of her eye sockets and her dry hot lips, and I put on the greatcoat and gently closed the door, and I got the gin bottle from its place under the table behind the manuscript of *Eureka* and took it outside with me to the darkness and the falling snow, falling still, that had already covered the footprints, coming and going, of my visitor. It was cold. It had grown so much colder that by the time I hurled the empty gin bottle away I could feel the tears frozen on my cheeks.

Twenty-nine

The only thing well said of Purgatory is that a man may go farther and fare worse.

—*Marginalia*

One Monday early in the new year, I rode the railroad cars to New York City. I had a lingering fever and a cough, a deep cough in my chest, tight and painful, that seemed the echo of Virginia's.

To ride the railroad was to enter a fantasy where you sat motionless and the world, the gloomy world of winter, came at you in layers—the closer objects racing by: a tree, or a farmhouse with its tendril of gray smoke rising, or a man in black in a black buggy pulled by a black horse; farther objects coming at you more slowly; those still farther at a crawl—all the world passing you at varying speeds even as you yourself sat without moving, even as you listened to the iron wheels sending their message along the iron rails—the rails that every day encompassed more of America, the boundless land of boundless opportunity—sending their quintessentially American message beat out in merciless mesmerizing meter, over and over, penury-is-a-crime-a-crime-a-crime-penury-is-a-crime— even as you sat listening while the world came at you and at you on the stationary speeding cars, with a lurch they stopped (or the world did) and you were in New York.

I did, despite what Frederick W. Thomas thought, go in to the city with fair frequency. But I did not go for glittering literary soirées. I went for day labor. How could I tell Thomas that I performed, for any magazine that would have me, the same humble tasks I had performed as an unknown in Richmond and Philadelphia, and for the same pittance? If that. Too often, as I took my anonymous place in an inconspicuous corner to produce innocuous blurbs and fillers, a ripple would pass through the editorial room and I would feel eyes staring at my back, staring, staring; would hear voices murmuring, "It's Poe, Edgar Poe, *Edgar Poe*!"; would sense the exchanges of smirks. It was not easy to catch them out, while pretending to do—while doing—what I was hired to do. But soon or late I would intercept a stare or a smirk, and march out to seek the man who had hired me for the day, and sometimes he paid me for the hours worked and sometimes not.

On the street that Monday afternoon, having just departed the *Town*, unless it was the *Lady's Companion* or some other magazine, I found that I suffered difficulty in breathing, as if I had not merely walked a block or so in the direction of the station but had run up five flights of stairs with a trunk on my back. Soon I began to sway, to sway and tremble, rather like a small boat sailing too close to the wind, and I became aware that people in the crowded street were avoiding me as they would a drunk—all but one man who walked straight at me and grasped my arm. He was carrying a large portfolio. "Are you ill, Edgar?" he asked. "Do you need a doctor?"

It was the Philadelphia illustrator John Sartain.

I shook my head, no, but if Sartain had not been supporting me I would have fallen.

"Can you walk?"

My breathing had become less labored, but my heart was beating in my throat, in my ears, in the top of my head. I took a few steps, my weight on John Sartain's shoulder now. My vision blurred and then darkened. I could see nothing. I did not mention this to Sartain. I heard the sound of voices in an enclosed place and felt warmth and smelled smoke and beer and stale clothing. My vision returned from dark to blur to normal. Sartain found a table and helped me to sit.

"How do you feel?"

"Faint."

"When did you last eat?"

"When did I—last night. No, yesterday afternoon."

John Sartain ordered biscuits and a carafe of red wine. A sip of the wine was tonic. A second was nectar.

"Have you no money for food?" he asked in so kindly a voice that I could not resent the question.

I drank more wine. Nibbled at a biscuit. Wondered how I could have felt so ill but moments before. "It seems," I said, "that I spend about as much on the train to and from New York as I earn as a mechanical paragraphist."

He refilled my glass. I drank it off at one swallow. It made me light-headed.

"John," I said, "John, do you remember back when I was in Philadelphia you did an illustration for a tale I wrote called 'The Oval Portrait'?"

"It is one of my favorite tales."

"I was wondering, John—when you illustrated it, had you anyone in mind?"

"More than in mind, in view. One of my favorite models. She had a most . . . ethereal look."

After a while I said, "A model, eh? You know, John, there was a time when I believed it was my wife's face you drew."

He looked at me. To make light of what I had just said, I laughed—a thin sound swallowed by more virile laughter at a nearby table, where three men with red faces were swilling beer from large pewter mugs.

One of the red-faced men looked directly at me and laughed

again. I waited until I was absolutely certain. The laughter grew louder, a phlegmy *mocking* roll of a laugh. I got up without a word. A waiter stood at their table with a tray of full mugs. As he set it down I saw three tiny reflections of myself in pewter, then beer sloshed over the tops of the mugs, obliterating them. I snatched up a mug and poured beer over the laughing man's head.

The next thing I knew, I was on the floor. My face felt numb. I heard John Sartain's voice, as if from a great, and increasing, distance. Then I blacked out. Then I was riding in a cab.

"What if you had been alone? You must get a grip on yourself."

"She is dying, John."

Awkwardly he patted my knee.

"Do you not see that I have been killing her for years?"

"You must not talk like that," he said.

At the station he walked with me to my track.

Thirty

> Ah, broken is the golden bowl! the spirit flown forever!
> —"Lenore"

One morning a few weeks later I heard the jingle of harness bells on the hill below the cottage. Expecting Muddy to answer the door, I continued to write. But when the knocker sounded, she called out that she was sponge-bathing Virginia. I stuck my raven quill behind my ear and went to the door—or, rather, to the window to the left of the door. Lifting a corner of the shade, I peered out to see a tall, rather plain-looking woman of twenty-five or so, wisps of her hair escaping from a felt bonnet, ample bosom rising and falling rapidly under a fur-trimmed cloak, cheeks rosy—all giving the impression that she had walked here from the station carrying the carpet-bag which I saw on the porch at her feet. But I had heard harness bells and, I was almost certain, the creaking of a hackney's springs. If so, horse and two-wheeler had already returned down the lane that curved out of sight past the cherry orchard. But could so much time have passed? Had I been so engrossed in *Eureka*?

When I opened the door, the woman picked up the carpet-bag.

"May I help you?" I said.

"Thank you, but a nurse is accustomed to doing her own fetching and carrying, Mr. Poe."

"Nurse?"

"I am here to care for Mrs. Poe." Her voice was soft, breathy.

"We can afford no nurse," I told her.

Undeterred, she swept past me and inside. Before following her, I looked downhill to make absolutely sure: no cab.

"Where is my patient?"

"I fear there has been some mistake."

"You *are* Mr. Poe? Yes, certainly you are. I have seen your likeness in *The Tales of*."

"Of . . . ?"

"Of Edgar A. Poe, of course. I am an admirer of your work, sir. And a sympathizer in your woes." She set the carpet-bag down. "I am Marie Louise Shew. My friends call me Loui. I am married to a doctor. My late father was one as well, a country doctor in Greenwich Village. I have experience as a nurse, particularly"—here her breathy voice dropped a trifle—"to the terminally ill. In addition, I am a water-colorist of middling skill. And that, Mr. Poe, about sums up my modest talents."

"Yes, well, we—aside from being in straitened circumstances, we are very private people. So you see—"

"I shall come each day by the first train and leave by the last. You will kindly not mention money again. Now, where is my patient?"

"This way," I said, and she hefted the carpet-bag and followed me. The bag made a clinking sound.

I looked at her; she, at me.

"Wine," she said.

"Wine?"

"Elderflower wine. Do you suppose that dying is easy? Wine is balm."

"Not to me."

"It is not *for* you, Mr. Poe."

"Mrs. Shew, I really must—"

"You do not speak as you write," she pronounced—a surprising judgment in that she had hardly given me the opportunity to speak. "And I sense that you do not *think* as you write, which is a relief to me, sir, for if you did, I should be terrified in your presence. But I am saying more than is polite." And she purposefully opened the sick-room door.

A murmur of voices followed, and footsteps and a bang which had to be the window sash—shut since the onset of winter—slamming open. Then came more footsteps and a rustling, sliding sound and the murmur of voices again and laughter, tentative laughter from Virginia.

I crept to the doorway. The room had been gloomy, the dark shade drawn over the closed window, the air heavy and redolent of illness. Now sun streamed in. Virginia's mattress was propped into an L-shape; she sat up on it, wearing the dressing gown Frederick W. Thomas had brought, the down comforter surrounding her like a fluffy cocoon. Marie Louise Shew sat beside her, combing her long dark hair. On the window sill stood a green bottle. Virginia and Muddy each held a glass. I had not seen the glasses before. Mrs. Shew was saying, ". . . so *then* Papa told him, 'Do not worry, young fellow, your condition is no impediment to matrimony. On the contrary, after your wedding I am confident that what you call your, uh, swelling will quite cease to be a source of concern.' " And I heard Virginia's laughter, unrestrained this time, and Muddy's chortle, and Loui Shew poured more wine and commenced another story featuring her father the Greenwich Village country doctor, and, realizing that my presence was quite redundant, I went back to my writing table.

Late that afternoon Loui Shew emerged from the sick-room bearing her empty carpet-bag. As she reached the door I heard the sound of horses' hooves and the rattle of the hackney's wheels. "I shall return first thing tomorrow," she told me.

And she did, her carpet-bag full again, and she spent the morning and afternoon of a second day with Virginia. But not just with Virginia. She was everywhere at once. Pies were baked, deep-dish apple pies, two of them; and a savory stew of venison made its appearance on the table. The small sitting room, where in winter I also worked and slept, was aired. The little cottage gleamed. Make no mistake; Muddy was a fine housekeeper. But Loui Shew seemed by her mere presence to make every thing sparkle. I suppose that, if I watched, I would have seen her at work, but whenever I looked up from *my* work she was closeted with Virginia.

Before dinner on the third afternoon, Loui called my name, and this was so unusual that I raced into Virginia's room. Virginia was on her feet in her gay flowered dressing gown. She smiled at me, the smile of a mischievous little girl.

"Loui says I can come out."

Virginia took a step in my direction and swayed. At first I attributed this to her weakness. Then I realized she was tipsy. I caught her. She clung.

"To eat with you all," she said.

She would not let Loui help her, or Muddy. "Only you, Eddie." At the doorway she stumbled, and I caught her up in my arms. She weighed almost nothing. She made a cooing sound against my ear. Then blew in it soft little puffs. Then tickled it with her tongue. When I turned to smile at her, she kissed my lips.

In her carpet-bag Loui Shew had brought four plump squab, now braised to perfection. There was apple sauce, and mashed potatoes drowning in rich brown gravy, and cranberries as red as asphodel. Loui Shew surprised me when, ignoring knife and fork, she dismembered her squab with clever, precise movements of her long fingers. Muddy, plying her own utensils fastidiously, even more fastidiously than usual, looked everywhere but at what was taking place on Loui's plate. Virginia began to imitate her nurse. With great forbearance Muddy said nothing. Virginia licked greasy fingers and grinned.

On Loui Shew's fourth day with us, it rained. She had a novel in her carpet-bag, one of Jane Austen's. She read all day to Virginia in her room. Muddy brought them their dinner. As Loui Shew carried no timepiece ("It takes the pleasure from living, Mr. Poe, to monitor the passage of the hours"), I went to tell her it would soon be time to return to Fordham for the last train to New York. Through the closed door I heard them talking.

"Then I won't know how it ends until tomorrow."

"I can leave it with you, if you like."

"It wouldn't be the same as you reading it. At least tell me now if the ending is happy."

"With Miss Austen that is a given, because her novels invariably end on the verge of marriage."

In the ensuing silence I almost opened the door. But Virginia's voice stayed me. "For Eddie it was no happy ending."

"Nonsense. Anyone can see he is devoted to you."

"There was someone else he might have married."

"He is enough older than you that there must have been several someone elses."

"He truly loved her. Henry told me about it when I was a little girl. She was every thing that I am not."

"Did Henry tell you *that*?"

"They were engaged when Eddie went to study at Charlottesville."

"Now really, Virginia. Before he went to university? How old was he, sixteen, seventeen?"

"Henry said they were engaged. But Elmira's father—that was her name, Elmira Royster—her father destroyed Eddie's letters when they came, and she thought he had forgotten her. Then, when Eddie returned from Charlottesville, he was invited to a party at the Royster house. He did not know it was an engagement party—Elmira's engagement to Alexander Shelton. But she should have married Eddie. *Would* have."

"According to whom?"

"According to his friend Eb Burling. After Elmira married, Eddie was very lonely. He went into the army and then to West Point, and he became a cavalry officer in Iowa or somewhere out West, and was almost killed by savage Indians. Then he came to Baltimore. He felt sorry for us. We needed someone to care for us."

"Who told you that?"

"Muddy. She said that we would place ourselves under the protection of her nephew, Edgar Poe."

"Perhaps," said Loui Shew, "*he* needed someone to care for *him*?"

Once more I almost opened the door on silence. But Virginia said, "If so, I was hardly that person. He should never have married me." And she began to cough. I waited until it subsided before rapping softly upon the door.

On the fifth day the air had that crystalline quality that sometimes follows a winter rain. A smoky haze lay in the dales, but from our hilltop cottage you could see a long way. You could see other hills and other cottages rising from the haze like islands from the sea. You could not see the toy railroad cars on their toy tracks coming from New York City, but you could hear the whistle. I stood on the porch. I wanted to see Loui Shew riding up from the village in the hackney. Ten minutes passed, and fifteen. I could see the lane rising from the haze below the orchard toward our cottage. The lane was empty. Virginia would be disappointed. I went around to the shed for an armload of firewood, and as I brought it in through the back door I heard the sound of horses' hooves. I put the wood down quickly alongside the hearth and hurried out front. Loui Shew was crossing the porch, carpet-bag in hand.

"*Good* morning, Mr. Poe. What a lovely day. And how is Virginia?"

"Still asleep."

"She will want an adventure today."

"An adventure?"

"An outing."

"But . . . should she?"

Loui looked at me. "Does it matter, Mr. Poe?"

Before dinner I carried Virginia, bundled in my army greatcoat, out to the orchard. Through the winter-bare trees we caught glimpses of the Bronx River.

"Remember the peacock, Eddie?"

I said I remembered.

"Which you refused to believe was there?"

"I believed," I said. "You made me a believer."

A few steps at a time, we started to skirt the hill above the orchard.

"What are those buildings down there?"

"St. John's College. Jesuits."

"Henry had a friend in Baltimore who was a Jesuit. I heard them talking one night. Drinking and talking. I was too young to understand then, but now I do. He said, the Jesuit said, a man wants three things in life. Security and love and—and, you know. He said his faith guaranteed the first two, which was more than most men could count on. So he was willing to forgo the third."

She touched my cheek. Her eyes were brimming. "One. Just one. Love is all we could give each other. It was the most important one, I know—but was it ever enough? I didn't care about the security, truly; that was not your fault. You tried. But the third one—oh, Eddie, I did mind about that, so very much! I kept thinking, if I only willed it hard enough, I could be better and we could—could— Eddie, do you know what I wish? I wish we could go back and find that peacock feather again."

She clung with her frail arms around my neck. I could feel the rapid flutter of her heart. "Find it again and it would be like the first time and while it was happening I would die, just die of happiness. . . ."

Backing away, she flung herself upon the ground, and I saw in the pitiless sunlight a little girl with the gaunt, ravaged face of an old woman. She was twenty-four. My mother had died at twenty-four. So had my brother Henry. Of the same disease. She had shed my greatcoat and was undoing her dressing gown with its gay floral print, tiny roses repeated, as red as blood, and I felt the forbidden excitement building in me. Something of this must have communicated itself to her, for when I reached down, meaning only to help her to her feet, she misunderstood. "No," she cried, "no, it's not true, what I said was just words, I don't want to die, Eddie, Eddie, I don't want to die!''

She swooned. I carried her back to the cottage. She slept an hour near the fire, and when she awoke, Loui Shew gave her wine to drink and read to her from the novel with the happy ending.

During the night I could hear the wind blowing. A window rattled in its frame. The rafters creaked. In one enormous gust I could feel the house shake. I lit my bedside taper and tiptoed to Virginia's room. The door was open and in the light of the taper I saw her eyes staring at the ceiling, and silver tracks of tears upon her cheeks. I blew out the taper and slipped in under her down comforter. She was shaking. "It's so cold," she said. I drew her close, her head nestled under my chin, and held her in my arms all night.

She awoke before I did. Dawn was just breaking. I sat up and saw her standing in her shift before the small mirror on the wall. Her face, I cannot say why, looked less gaunt than it was. Perhaps the half-light in the room hid the ravages of her disease. She drew the shift over her head and let it drop to the floor. She turned a little to the right, to the left—struck a saucy pose with hands on hips and head canted to the side. She did not look wasted by the disease but rather, I could not help thinking, as she had looked in Hopewell on our honeymoon, a gawky child of thirteen. She smiled. She liked what she saw. Or thought she saw. I must have made a sound, for she whirled to face me. There was on her drawn face, in her sunken eyes, a look of intense sexuality. She drifted to the mattress in a graceful pirouette and let herself go all loose, falling across the comforter with her long dark hair fanning over my lap. I dared not move. She was making a sound, a humming sound, her mouth against the comforter. Then I heard her sing-song words, and saw her outside the schoolyard in Hopewell. *When the girls came out to play, Eddie Beddie ran away.* Just when I despaired of being able to stop her, or myself, she raised her head, she laughed, she said, "I haven't felt this well in years, Eddie. Something changed in the night, Eddie, something happened, I don't know what or how, all I know is that I am not ill any longer, I am not dying, don't you see, Eddie," and with a startled look on her face she began to cough.

I wrapped her in the comforter. She was cold, she coughed, she shook, she became drenched in sweat, she coughed, she was hot, she coughed, she was burning up, I held her, she coughed. From the kitchen I heard the clank of the stove lid as Muddy built up the fire. Soon the black stovepipe that ran through Virginia's room began to make ticking noises. I heard the sound of harness bells on the hill. The room grew warm. But Virginia was cold again. "So cold," she said, and she shook.

I drew her head against my chest. "Next winter we'll go south."

"South, Eddie? Baltimore?"

"Farther."

"Richmond, Eddie?"

"South to a place where it is never cold."

"New Orleans, Eddie?"

She rocked forward then, the comforter cloaking her shoulders. She looked like the little girl in the attic watching me write, saying she could hear the words in the scratching of my pen.

"An island," I improvised. "There is an island in a warm azure sea—"

"Where it's never cold?"

"Where brilliant star-shaped flowers burst every day into bloom like the ruby asphodel beside a swift river that flows without a sound from sunset fountains in the sky into an emerald lagoon."

"Is it Henry's secret island, then? Is it to Panchatan that you will take me?"

Henry had mentioned no secret island to me, but I said, "Yes, it is," and spoke the name I had never heard before. "To Panchatan."

And Virginia smiled, and then she coughed a little cough which hardly seemed more than a tiny voice saying forgive me, but her face, pale as the color of pearl and of the same soft luster, blossomed red, as red as the ruby asphodel, and I held her, I held her tight against me, and then Muddy came into the room with Loui Shew, who gently took the body from me and laid it upon its back.

Thirty-one

And all my days are trances,
    And all my nightly dreams
Are where thy dark eye glances,
    And where thy footstep gleams—
In what ethereal dances,
    By what eternal streams.

—"To One in Paradise"

Time ceased. I walked every day until exhaustion halted my steps. I walked along the bank of the Bronx River and to a rocky escarpment east of the cottage to gaze upon the blue haze of Long Island. I walked on the narrow way atop Croton Aqueduct to High Bridge. I walked upon the roadway of the bridge from where I could gaze south to New York City, and I saw pinnacles and spires, turrets and shrines and kingly halls and immemorial fanes and a burial vault guarded by an idol with a diamond eye. I saw her. I saw Virginia. I saw her. I saw her.

I worked. I must have worked, because I have the memory of riding the railroad cars to the city; I have the memory of sitting, nervous, over-excited, across a desk from Mr. George Putnam, my publisher, whom I had never met. When I said I was Edgar Poe, my own name sounded strange to my ears, as if I were impersonating myself. Fingering the package on my lap, I searched for the right words to introduce my complex cosmogony, an exegesis at once on the universe and on art, born of the endless struggle between the poet and the bedeviling world. But I was too anxious, too eager, and I blurted that I had written a complete explanation of the physical and spiritual universe in a single book-length prose poem. Mr. Putnam's firm, I said, could with confidence drop every thing else, perhaps permanently, and make it their business to publish *Eureka*, to purvey *Eureka*, to promulgate *Eureka* so that every educated reader in the Republic might have his own copy, rather like a Bible for those of intellectual bent, you see? Mr. George Putnam smiled a publisher's non-committal smile, respectful perhaps because I was the author of "The Raven" and "The Fall of the House of Usher." A first printing of fifty thousand copies, I said, would be appropriate. Well, of course he would have to read the manuscript, Mr. Putnam said.

I must have asked if I might meanwhile have a loan, a small advance against the price he would pay for the rights to the book, for Mr. George Putnam gave me ten dollars in folding money. I took it to a florist nearby, Pfaall's, the finest in the city, where I bought orchids, all the orchids that ten dollars could buy, white and faintly purple with their look of predatory decay, and I took the box to the station and rode the cars to Fordham, where I engaged a hackney and directed the driver to the cemetery of the Dutch Reformed Church, where, in the vault of the family who owned our cottage, Virginia lay interred.

I have said that time ceased. But it was still winter. Or the seasons had turned and it was winter again. Or perhaps it was always winter. I knew it was winter because it was cold, very cold that late afternoon, and colder that night. A wind tormented the bare oaks and elms, clouds raced past the high moon, I thought the orchids would freeze. But if so, they would come back. Because every thing did. As I had written in *Eureka*.

I went into the vault. I lit a taper in the deepest corner, where I hoped the wind would not extinguish it. In the fluttering light I could not make out the friezes upon the marble walls. There were four sarcophagi, and as many gravestones in the floor, one uncarved. This was Virginia's. This was Virginia. I opened my box from Pfaall's and scattered my orchids over the virgin stone. Then, huddled in the army greatcoat that so often had warmed her, I determined to wait through the night. The wind moaned softly, then rose to a howl. The taper cast three uncertain shadows, like puffs of black smoke, and went out. It did not matter. It would come back. Every thing came back.

Later, when moonlight entered the vault, the friezes upon the walls were a phantom city tenanted by all those who had gone. And would return. The city teemed with invisible death and life. I could almost see my brother Henry, but I saw Virginia nowhere. I could almost see a door open, paler than the moonlight. Through it like some ghastly river running silent, so silent, streamed people, a horde of people, everyone I had known and not known, and all were laughing, soundlessly laughing as hard as they could, but not smiling, they could not smile, the more they laughed the more certain it was that they never would smile. Why should this be so? I did not know. But I knew this: I knew I had failed Virginia by failing myself. Virginia had not complained. Had never complained. Which only made it worse. Which had brought me here so I could tell her. I told her. I told her she was innocent of any thing but living, and precious little of that.

In the morning I did not leave. I needed to tell her more. I needed to tell her every thing—even those things, all those things, I would never know. I stayed. I stayed in the vault. Hid in the corner where the taper had gone out.

After a while I heard footsteps. I saw through the grille two men carrying spades and pickaxes. I heard the pickaxes ringing against the frozen earth and I thought, sometimes it is more difficult to be buried than to die. Was it my grave they were digging? No—I would stay here in the vault with Virginia. The ringing of the pickaxes gave way to the scrape and thud of the spades, and later a crowd of people filed slowly by, following pall-bearers carrying the coffin of someone who had died, and who would come back. After a while the mourners filed by again without the coffin. Gradually darkness seeped into the vault. Why was Virginia here instead of me? But I was here. I was here too. There was no moon. Fitfully it began to snow. I dozed. I must have dozed, because otherwise how could something have awakened me? What awakened me was a voice calling my name. At first I thought it was Virginia's voice, but it was not. A figure stood outside the grille, stood waiting in the snow, snow falling on its hooded cloak. I did not know who it was, nor even if it was man or woman. No, that is not true. I did know. Yet, knowing, I did not know, did not know why she had come, or from where, to do what needed to be done. She offered her hand, but I did not touch it. I did, however, open the iron grille of the vault and follow her home through the snow—home to the cottage where Virginia had lived with me and died—and with every step I was careful to avoid treading in the blurry footprints left by Loui Shew.

Thirty-two

It was night in the lonesome October
Of my most immemorial year.

—"Ulalume"

Often I took the railroad cars to New York, with no other purpose than to select at random a man in the crowd, and follow him, and try to imagine his life. Who was this one who stood a silent hour at Battery Gardens staring at ships anchored in the bay? What crucial appointment, what dramatic *rendez-vous*—see him look at his pocket watch every few minutes?—brought that one to the steps of the Carlton House Hotel on Broadway? Or that one, for what illicit purpose was he walking into the unutterable squalor of the Five Points? Why did he not see me behind him as he penetrated the warren of narrow and yet narrower lanes, muddy now with the rains of spring (dusty now with the drought of summer, frozen now with the chill of winter), past houses crumbling to ruin, beams fallen, broken windows peering sightlessly at the late afternoon like the eyes of a blind man? Or that one, why did he stand long minutes outside a bar-room, why but to contemplate his own weakness before squaring his shoulders and going in?

I remained outside. It was my rule not to follow them indoors. Indoors, I might learn more about them than I wished to know. Indoors, it would be difficult to imagine lives for them, for they would be engaged in the lives they imagined for themselves. (Did God experience the same difficulty—God who, if He did any thing, imagined our lives for us all? How much simpler to detach another face from the crowd and follow it!)

Indoors, in the autumn of some year, I saw that a new rag carpet covered the floor of the small front room in Fordham. Indoors, that autumn, Muddy served coffee from a gleaming silver-plated urn. We had visitors. Frederick W. Thomas came when business brought him to New York; so did John Sartain. Loui Shew came with a water-color of Virginia. The day she delivered it, I was shoveling snow from the path out back and did not even hear the hackney. I found Muddy and Loui leaning over the table in the kitchen, leaning over the portrait, when I came in. I saw Virginia's eyes, more violet than blue in this, the only portrait of her. We hung it in the room that had been her room.

While Loui was out in the garden throwing crumbs to the birds, I asked Muddy, "Did you see her come?"

"Loui? Of course I saw her come. Not an hour ago."

"It was—an ordinary cab she came in?"

"Land sakes, Eddie, it was that pleasant Mr. Whelan's cab, with him on the box. Why?"

"And you have seen her come before?"

"Of course I have."

"And seen her leave? In Mr. Whelan's hackney?"

"Or that grumpy Mr. Phelps's. Why do you ask, Eddie?"

"No reason. Where does she come from?"

"Greenwich Village. You know that. She lives cater-corner across Washington Square from the University."

"She says. Have you been there?"

"What would I have been doing, going there? *She* comes *here* all the time, she is here now. What strange questions you ask, Eddie, a person has no way of . . . I know!" said Muddy, suddenly pleased with herself. "You are thinking of writing a tale, one of your fan-tastical tales, and in it will be a woman like Mrs. Shew only she doesn't come from anywhere, she just . . . uh, well, it is beyond *my* imagination. A tale," said Muddy, closing the discussion. "You are going to write a tale."

Even as I nodded, I wondered whether I would ever write a tale again.

Indoors, I had letters to answer that I had not read during the time when time ceased. But now that time was moving again, things began to happen.

What happened was, I saw that one letter of condolence came from Richmond, from Elmira Shelton of Richmond, the widow Shelton, and I answered it at length. What happened was, she wrote again, as did I.

What happened was, one day in late winter or early spring I looked into the mirror, the new mirror with the gilt frame that made the sitting room seem larger—another transformation my libel-suit money* had wrought upon the cottage—and I saw a stranger. The stranger was dressed elegantly in black (of course) with a white stock. His hair was black, curly black, and he wore it long, all but hiding his ears; what had he no wish to hear? His lips were thin, thinner than my own, under a small mustache with waxed ends—or did he twirl them into points? He seemed, to judge by the waxed (twirled?) mustache and the sparkle in his eyes, a debonair sort of fellow with, even, a touch of deviltry in him. I was eager to follow him and, from what clues he supplied, imagine his life.

What happened was, George Putnam brought out an edition of *Eureka* of five hundred copies, one per cent of what I had envisioned, a mingy first printing for a book that explained the universe.

What happened was, I wrote a ballad which in its elliptical way contradicted every thing I had propounded in *Eureka*. In the ballad, all things died, even moons and planets. There was not a single mention of rebirth. Dead was dead. Many people failed to understand my ballad. In a critique, I tried to explain that cosmic doom had its place in the scheme of things, if there was a scheme of things. I could review my own ballad because at first it was published

* Poe was awarded $225.06 in damages and $101.42 in court costs. (Editor's note)

anonymously*——my only way back into magazines at the time, or so I believed. I also believed that anonymity would generate curiosity; and curiosity, interest. By and by, all the other critics, Rufus Griswold among the first, said that the author of the ballad had to be Edgar Poe. Elmira Shelton wrote from Richmond to say that the ballad troubled her. I wrote back to tell her it troubled me too, and went in to New York to go about the business of following myself.

Thirty-three

> Then came a craving desire to keep the man in view——to know more of him.
>
> ——"The Man of the Crowd"

To know that you are pursued lends wings to your feet.

My pursuer was a slender man no taller than I. He wore black, which struck me as ominous, though I could not have said why. Others in the streets of New York wore black too, myself included. His hair was dark and he wore a mustache rather like my own. He carried a malacca stick. The knob was suspicious: might it have been filled with lead? I would be wary of that stick, should he overtake me. He was as fast a walker as I and, it soon became evident, as indefatigable. He was always there, behind me, varying the distance between us according to circumstances, approaching closer in a thronged thoroughfare, dropping back in a by-street.

Once I stood half an hour or more at Battery Gardens gazing across the bay to Staten Island while he waited stoically in the cold.

---

* "Ulalume——A Ballad" was published in the *American Review*, then reprinted in the *Home Journal* in 1848, when the author's identity was revealed. It is interesting to note that in this ballad the word "Yaanek" appears for the only time in the Poe canon——as the name of a volcanic mountain. (Editor's note)

Another time, outside one of the city's finest hotels, the Astor House in City Hall Square—or was it the Carlton House on Broadway?—I waited with feigned impatience, pretending every few minutes to look at my watch (I had none), while he loitered on the far side of the square keeping me in sight. One morning I plunged into the wretched warren of the Five Points and saw, through the fire-gutted ruins of one building, those of another, from which vantage he was observing me.

Finally on a day in early spring I tested him by walking at full stride the length of Broadway from where it began at Battery Gardens to where it petered out in a country lane four miles to the north. He maintained the pace, swinging out jauntily with his malacca stick that might have been a weapon. That I could not outdistance him began to infuriate me. My feet were blistered by the time I reached what might have been the city's northernmost barroom. I stood outside in the heat of the day listening to the beckoning, mesmerizing clink of a hammer breaking ice. I went in.

To my great pleasure he did not follow. I had a whiskey; another. After that it became an easy matter to lose him, for like a vampire fearful of the crucifix he would not follow me indoors. Soon there seemed little point in returning to Fordham. The weather was warm for May. Or was it already June? I slept wherever I could find shelter.

One afternoon I was asked by the doorman of an accommodations house in Clinton Place to deliver a letter uptown. He was a huge Negro with the most melancholy of smiles. He found other errands for me to run and, in the cellar of the accommodations house, a cot on which I could sleep among the barrels and casks. In the darkness I heard the scurry of rats. No matter; I have always had a fondness for rodents.

Evenings, I liked to watch the women taking their customers into the house, how they made it seem their customers were taking them. Men who did not care to stay the night would emerge presently to reclaim their cabs, and the women would soon be on the street again. Most of the women were tired-looking, the paint on their faces crazed like old pottery, their smiles stiff like *papier-mâché* masks.

The manageress of the accommodations house had a round, chin-less head like a turtle's. She did not like me, did not like how whiskey made me first self-confident, then assertive, then "ugly, he is a bad drinker, Obadiah," she told the big doorman, "you should not permit him one drop." But I did my work, and most days I shared an afternoon whiskey with Obadiah, and she did not turn me out.

One night a gleaming four-wheeler pulled to the curb, and out stepped the man who had been following me. I had not seen him for weeks. He wore a red-lined cape over his customary black frock coat and, on the satin facing of his lapel, a pin in the shape of a tiny dagger with a diamond in the hilt. The dagger was silver; the diamond, real. He handed down a girl who surely was too young. She looked frightened. She had dark hair and a Grecian profile and a plump, pretty figure that was still childlike. I followed them in-side. The bar-tender was removing the wire from a bottle of Dom Pérignon champagne. "Is it the '37?" the man demanded. "I only drink the '37." Apparently it was, for, seated on a sofa, they drank. He twirled his mustache ends, all the while speaking sophisticated inanities that only frightened the girl more. When he began to fondle her, a blush hid the hectic spots of color on her cheeks. Her eyes widened—in the light of the gas lamps, they were the blue of gentians, almost violet—and they looked at him with such terror that it amazed me he failed to notice. But perhaps he did. Perhaps her terror enhanced, would enhance, his pleasure. When his mouth fastened on hers, I could not bear to watch but neither could I tear my eyes away. His fingers explored under the sheer fabric of her white organdie bodice like five hairy serpents. She lay back inert, eyes shut, lips parted in a swoon of dread so utter that no man of any sensibility could still have desired her.

He rose with her cradled in his arms. "Which room?" he demanded.

The bar-tender, finding the manageress absent, consulted the doorman. "Second floor, number three, it is not locked," said he, and smiled his melancholy smile.

Leaving the red-lined cape and malacca stick behind, the man who had been pursuing me (and whose resemblance to me, I had to admit, was striking) carried his burden from the bar-room, her arms dangling. I heard his footsteps on the stairs, then overhead.

"Let me have an ale," Obadiah told the bar-tender. "Yours, Eddie?"

"Whiskey," I said.

The bar-tender poured. I stayed his hand before he could take the bottle away. I drank a second whiskey, a third.

"Now, Eddie," said Obadiah.

I poured and drank.

"Put his cape and stick in the cloak-room," Obadiah told me.

I picked up the malacca stick and the cape. I had been right about the stick. Its knob was weighted.

Obadiah asked me, "Where do you think you're going?"

The bar-room occupied the entire width of the downstairs. There were two ways out—the front door, with the cloak-room beside it, and an archway giving on the staircase to the upper floors. I stood in the archway with the stick and cape.

"I'll leave them outside their room," I said.

"The cloak-room, Eddie. You will put them in the cloak-room," said Obadiah with his melancholy smile.

But I turned and hurried up the stairs.

The passage was narrow and dimly lit. I made my way to their room. No sound came through the door. I crouched to look through the keyhole but could see nothing. The key had been left in the lock. I tried the knob. It turned and the door opened.

I saw mirrors everywhere—on the walls, covering all four walls; on the ceiling, covering the ceiling; on the inside of the door.

Which was the real bed? I saw multitudes of myself gazing this way and that in confusion. All the beds, reflected ever smaller between facing walls, receding endlessly in intersecting glass-lined tunnels—beds of brass, beds with rosewood headboards, with mahogany, with sky-blue quilted headboards, four-poster beds whose curtains were held open by receding replicas of me—all the beds and reflections-of-beds and reflections-of-reflections-of-beds were empty.

Then I saw them.

I saw them from behind and from all four sides, I saw them from above, I saw them in smaller and smaller repetitions of the room, multiplied and interlocking as if refracted by the facets of a diamond, saw them in such a complexity of images that I could not have said what he was doing to her while she bent over the backs of an infinitude of chairs, could not have said what obscene act he was committing upon her, repeated, repeated at every possible angle in all the mirrors and not the same in any two of them, never the same. Nor was her face, for the dread I had seen downstairs was intensified in some reflections, while in others she glared a fierce virago glare and in still others her head was tilted provocatively as she smiled over her bare shoulder up at him, down at him, sideways at him, at his face—his face that unlike hers was always the same, the face of a very old man with curly white hair falling over his broad forehead and ears and the wax-yellowed ends of his mustache curling upwards upon his cheeks almost to his crafty yellowed bloodshot degenerate's eyes, his face that lived as yet in the future, his face and mine, the face we would have if we were to survive another thirty years, and I hated it, I hated that face, I could not abide it.

Holding the malacca stick by its tip, I swung the lead-weighted knob at the image in the mirror, the single mirror in the now unremarkable room in which a young girl, nondescript and a stranger to me, naked except for a sleazy shift, a girl as unremarkable as the room itself, stood facing me, the two of us alone, alone, the back view of her bursting into shards of quicksilvered glass as the mirror shattered, the front view crossing arms over breasts and the mouth forming an O of fright just as Obadiah rushed in and took the stick from me.

I was walking. Seemed to be walking on Wall Street, the loneliest place in the world, it has been said, in the small hours of the morning. A soft rain began to fall. My legs felt strange. I was drunk no longer, but I staggered. My knees would not lock properly. I lurched against a lamp post and clung. A bubble of pain stuck in my throat.

I waited for it to break, but it did not break. I waited for strength to return to my legs, but it did not return.

I heard heavy footfalls and told myself that a man clinging to a lamp post is the universal image of the drunk ever since there have been lamp posts and that, with those heavy footfalls approaching, I would do myself a service to part company with this particular lamp post. So I slid to a sitting position on the curb. The bubble of pain in my throat expanded. I groaned; tried to get to my feet. The bubble dropped down to my chest. I thought that, knew that, if it were to burst in my chest it would kill me. I sat absolutely still, leaning forward, head down, not daring to move.

Something hard prodded my shoulder.

"Have a bit too much, sir?"

It was, of course, a policeman. He said "sir" only once.

"Need some help getting home, do you?"

His billy club tapped my shoulder again.

"And where *is* home?"

His boots were highly polished.

"Some identification? No? A letter someone wrote you? Have you money? With money you are no vagrant. Have you two dollars? No?"

I sat while the bubble of pain contracted. Soon it was a point, a single point of pain in the exact center of my chest burning like a gas jet.

I heard the sound a billy club will make if it is run swiftly along the iron bars of a fence. Then nothing for what seemed a long time. Then the clop-clop of horses' hooves.

Dawn found me standing at the window of my cell gripping the bars. The pain had gone. I saw, at a considerable distance, a tower of Egyptian granite and in its single high window a woman, young and radiant. She looked like silver dipped in the lambent light of the new day. She looked like the light itself. On her blond head she wore a black silk hat. She called across the gulf separating us, called questions I could not hear. They were a test. To answer incorrectly

would have terrible consequences. I flung random yesses and noes at
her, hoping for the best. The yesses sounded like cell doors opening,
the noes like cell doors slamming shut. A wind howled through the
gulf and the radiant woman clapped a hand to her hat, then
disappeared.

I heard slow, sinister footsteps. My cell door opened.

A guard with no face led me from the cell out to a gallery and
down iron stairs that rang underfoot. At the bottom stood a gibbet.
There was a rope with a heavy weight at its end. The condemned
would be the counterweight. The guard stopped. For a moment my
heart stopped too. Then he led me past a boiling cauldron (offering
me a drink, which I cannily declined) to a large butcher's block
where Muddy lay spread-eagled. Two men in leather with a two-
handled saw sawed off her feet at the ankles, then her legs at the
knees and again at the hips.

I screamed and came out of wherever I had been, and the cell
door opened again, for the first time.

A cheerful Irishman looked in.

"Three-toed sloths, *albino* sloths, hanging from the ceiling?" he
inquired. "Boa constrictors slithering down the walls? Scorpions
under the bunk? All gone now, there's a good lad. If it's your
first visit you'll be on your way before noon. Bit of a fine. You
can pay?"

"I'm afraid not."

"Judge will give you time then. Careful there, lad! You almost
fell."

Police Court was crowded. Last night's drunks shuffled up in
batches to be scrutinized by the judge. "Hello there, you again,
O'Malley, thirty days," and bang went the judge's gavel. Most of
us, however, were unfamiliar, nameless faces. "Two dollars or two
weeks," bang went the gavel, and those with two dollars shuffled
toward the cashier, and the others shuffled to where the guards
waited, and another batch shuffled up to face the bench.

"Don't I know you?" demanded the judge.

My five companions were looking floorward. No one spoke.

"Well, don't I?" demanded the judge; he meant me.

Off to one side behind a railing a few men sat, and one of them said in a surprised voice, "Bless me, isn't that Edgar Poe?"

"Oh? The writer?" said the judge.

"It is," said the man. "I'm sure of it."

The judge narrowed one eye. "So it is," he said, and nodded. "You have given me pleasure, sir." Down banged the gavel. "Dismissed."

Outside I stood blinking in the morning sunlight.

"Mr. Poe, are you writing?"

I walked away from the voice.

"Are you, sir?"

I walked faster.

There were three of them, two mere boys and the third a middle-aged man with a swollen red nose. All had been waiting for something to happen in Police Court, something that would make a paragraph or, if they were lucky, a feature story.

"Mr. Poe, if you had it to do over again, would you write 'The Literati of New York City'?"

"Mr. Poe, is it true you said *Eureka* is an advance upon the work of Sir Isaac Newton?"

"Mr. Poe, will you deny that you have been a patient at the Insane Retreat in Utica?"

"Mr. Poe . . ."

"Mr. Poe . . ."

"Mr. Poe . . ."

I ran. The two younger ones followed in half-hearted pursuit, flinging questions in my wake. Soon I was running alone. I slowed to a walk but did not stop, fearing that if I stopped I should be unable to get underway again. I walked; destination, nowhere. The best of all possible destinations. The sidewalks were narrow, unfamiliar. I was cold and clammy. I lurched this way and that. Pedestrians got out of my way. I crossed streets recklessly. Draymen shouted. After a while the sidewalks were wider, the streets less clogged with traffic. I saw a park. I waded like a child through brilliant autumn leaves to my knees, scattering them, laughing. I felt, all at once I felt, young and full of wonder and of life. Every thing was as splendid as the brisk autumn day.

I saw a huge gray building, high steep roofs, pointed arches, ribbed vaulting, flying buttresses—the University.

She lives cater-corner across Washington Square from the University.

I climbed the stoop, stood in front of the door, swayed forward, grasped the heavy wrought-iron knocker. After too much time the door opened. Every thing began to slip away. Someone may have spoken my name. I lay back against soft leather and smelled ammonia.

Dr. John Francis waited until I had dressed. Chin supported on interlaced fingers, he stared across a large desk at me. The desk, and the consulting room, belonged to Loui Shew's husband. Dr. John Francis sat in one of those chairs which swivel upon the base. He swiveled toward the window and back.

"As Loui suspected—heart disease."

Faceless with the light streaming in through the slats of the Venetian blinds behind him, he leaned back, then forward. The chair creaked. It was an irritating sound.

"I can have you admitted to hospital, or you can spend a few days here with the Shews before returning home. Hospitals are for the poor. They are overcrowded, filthy. Stay here."

I asked a question.

"With some patients," he replied, "it is wise to beat about the bush. Whereas with others, mature individuals . . ." He unlaced his hands and his chin dropped noticeably. I realized that he was very tired. "Some time recently you suffered a seizure. You must rest for several weeks, months if possible. Loui tells me you live in the country. That is fortunate. You will benefit from country air. And, after a few months, from exercise, in moderation. I recommend no foot races. I should, if I were you, chew no tobacco, nor smoke it. I should drink but little alcohol."

"And?"

"You are asking for a prognosis?"

I think I smiled. "I assume there is one," I said.

"Follow the regimen I have outlined and you have every expectation of leading a productive life."

"And if I do not follow it?"

"You will die. Rather sooner than later."

"Whereas, if I do follow this regimen—"

"As I said. A productive life."

"How long?"

"I am no fortune-teller, Mr. Poe."

"Ten years? Fifteen?"

"The human body is unpredictable."

"Five?"

"I am not God, Mr. Poe."

"You are saying I will not live to see fifty?"

"I should not count on it."

"Then, forty-five? Will I live to be forty-five?"

"There again—"

"Three years then. Have I three years?"

Three years, I told myself. That is a long time, three years. In three years there are more than a thousand days, a thousand nights. How many dreams are there, in three years?

The chair swiveled, creaked. Dr. John Francis said, "I should cut that figure by half."

Thirty-four

Mimes, in the form of God on high,
  Mutter and mumble low,
And hither and thither fly—
  Mere puppets they, who come and go
At bidding of vast formless things
  That shift the scenery to and fro.
                    —"The Conqueror Worm"

During my convalescence, Loui Shew told me she had read *Eureka*. What was worse, so had her religious mentor, a young divinity student named Hopkins.

"He says that in writing of a primary particle which expands—explodes?—to become the Universe, you belittle God."

"How?—if God causes the explosion, and if the expansion and contraction of the Universe is but a single beat of His heart."

I ought to say that I was far from committed to this argument. But it seemed a good one to use against a theologian.

"This primary particle of yours, Mr. Hopkins says, is not infinite, and God is. Therefore you belittle Him."

"Loui," I said, "has Hopkins managed to persuade you with any of this nit-picking nonsense?"

"He has urged me to—protect myself against your influence."

"That will be no problem," I said coolly, "as I leave for Fordham at week's end."

"Eddie, I do not mean to suggest that *I* believe you are either a heretic or insane, but—"

"Is that what he said, the brilliant Student of Divinity?"

"It is what *I* say."

This voice, smug, deep, authoritative, belonged to Loui's husband. Dr. Shew was, as nearly as I had been able to make out, a water-cure therapist. A man of florid face and considerable girth, he stood in the doorway. In his hand, one finger parting the pages, he held a slender book—a copy of *Eureka*.

"Shall we let Mr. Poe speak for himself? Here, for example. 'No thinking being—' "

"Dr. Shew, please," said Loui. She sometimes called her husband that, sometimes just Doctor, always with an edge to her voice.

" 'No thinking being lives who, at some luminous point of his life of thought, has not felt himself lost amid the surges of futile efforts at understanding, at believing, that any thing exists *greater than his own soul*.' If that is not sacrilege or insanity—what, pray tell, is it?"

Loui ranged herself alongside the bed where I sat propped against the pillows. "But Eddie did not claim he believed that. Rather that he felt lost in an effort to understand it."

"He *is* lost—utterly and eternally lost," said the water-cure therapist Dr. Shew so smugly that I threw back the covers and rose—rather shakily—to my feet, wearing nothing but my night-shirt. It was, in fact, a new nightshirt, no doubt paid for by my host.

"You would," he demanded, "parade before another man's wife in only your nightshirt?"

It was ridiculous. Loui was a nurse. During my first few days with them she had changed the bedclothes with me in the bed, expertly rolling me over, rather like a log; she had shaved me and brushed my hair, had sponge-bathed me; she had brought and removed the bedpan.

"You will go from here at once, sir!"

"That is my intention."

"Eddie! Doctor! Please!"

I went to the wardrobe, where my clothes, sponged and pressed, hung.

Five minutes later I stood with Loui at the door.

"How do you feel?"

"Splendid. Actually quite splendid." And, strange to say, I did.

Outside, Dr. Shew went to look for a cab.

"I'll walk," I told Loui. "It's a fine day for a walk."

"You must not strain yourself."

"I could walk from here to Philadelphia, on such a day as this."

I felt capable of meeting every possible eventuality, even dying. I wanted to be on my way back to Fordham; wanted to be on my way to somewhere, to anywhere. My moral superiority to the Dr. Shews of this world I wore like a suit of armor.

An open cab entered the square with Dr. Shew in it. He got out and waited for me. The horse exhaled two jets of vapor in the cold, clear morning air.

"We have decided to walk to the station," Loui said.

"He, perhaps. Not you."

Loui took my arm. "He may need my help."

"He can ride."

"He wishes not to."

"Go inside," Dr. Shew the water-cure therapist ordered his wife. Staring coolly at him, Loui kissed me. It was an awkward kiss, half upon the lips, half the cheek. Startled, I hurried down the steps.

I walked up Fifth Avenue and, from a by-street, heard the piping of young voices chanting sing-song verses. In sunlight and shadow, the bright plumage of their skirts fluttering, several girls were skipping rope. Every so often they would scatter before the passage of a coach or a cart, then re-group. The rope would swing slowly, then faster and still faster, so that, despite the coolness of the day, the young faces were flushed and damp with perspiration.

> *"Mother, mother, I am sick;*
> *Send for the doctor,* quick, quick, quick!"

In sunlight and shadow the rope swung faster and faster, the young legs skipped faster and faster, my heart raced faster and faster—

> *"Charley Barley, pudding and pie,*
> *Kissed the girls and made them cry;*
> *When the girls came out to play,*
> *Charley Barley ran away."*

One girl a year or so older than the rest skipped away from the blurring arc of rope and stumbled so close past me I could have reached out and caught her. She was breathless, as breathless as I. I *wanted* to reach out and catch her. Her eyes met mine—merry youthful eyes into which for an instant something old and wise came, only to flee as she skipped by, only to flee as I fled, only to flee as I almost persuaded myself that my wish to touch her merely meant she reminded me of Virginia, of Virginia long ago in Hopewell.

I fled the sound of their voices, fled until I saw—on the same by-street, on another?—a horse, a venerable nag down in the shafts of a hackney. Four men hovered about. Was the one with the coat and glazed cap of striped jean the cabman? All had grabbed the harness in various places, a hip strap, a trace, the throat latch, the belly band. They tugged, their efforts unavailing. The nag kicked out with a rear leg at the hip-strap man, who skittered back. I approached, I who know next to nothing about horses, and reached between the thrashing forelegs to grasp the martingale and give it a mighty pull. In an instant, with a clatter of shafts and hooves, the horse was upright.

The cabman removed his glazed cap and thanked me.

Another man said, "What do you think, sir? Twenty-five, sir, is very old for a horse that has worked all his life. Look at that hock there, that knee. Don't you think, sir, that Frank should put him down?"

I admitted my ignorance of matters equine.

"I would shoot him, Frank. If I were you," the man said.

"Well, you ain't," said Frank. "You ain't me."

I am no fortune-teller, Mr. Poe.

I admire your honesty, Dr. Francis.

I am not God, Mr. Poe.

I salute your humility, Dr. Francis.

Three years? I should cut that figure by half.

But there, Dr. Francis, don't you see, there you speak with the voice of the God you are not, the voice of that God who created—dreamed?—a man named Edgar Poe who will live in God's teeming—cluttered?—Creation (or dream) no more than forty years. *Unless.* Unless this God is not all-powerful by His own standards but only by the less exigent ones of the creatures he has dreamed. If so, should it not be possible occasionally for one of the dreamed to outwit the Dreamer?

I, for example. I shall outwit Him by living to be, say, fifty. Fifty-five even. Why not? Why should God be able—be *permitted*—to snuff my life at His will by dreaming my death?

Have we always been enemies, God and I? It has been said that, *Eureka* excepted, I always wrote as if the world of my imagination included no place for God.

Approaching the station, I heard the chuffing of steam. It was not the Fordham train. I still had fifteen minutes. Plunging down a nearby street, I saw an ironmonger, a greengrocer, a baker. An apothecary shop. I entered, and smiled, and stated my business.

"How much is it you want?" the proprietor asked.

"Two ounces."

"It is no nostrum, you know."

"My brother is deranged. It is for his hallucinations."

"You have cotton for ear plugs? Keep them wet with it. And keep the flask away from him."

"I shall."

At the station I told the ticket agent, "Fordham, one way," and found a seat in the next-to-last car.

The train began to move, gathered speed. Black smoke roiled past the windows. At full throttle the wheels on the iron rails spoke in a mesmerizing meter—her voice, her voice of a child, chanting *do Eddie do Eddie do Eddie* . . .

I pulled the cork and tilted the flask and drank off half the laudanum.

Thirty-five

And the man sat upon the rock, and leaned his head upon his hand, and looked out upon the desolation.
              —"Silence—A Fable"

As they approached, Edgar could hear nothing above the surf smashing against the lighthouse. Waves exploded to hurl great fans of spray, silver in the tropical sunlight, almost to the top of the shaft, which, he estimated, rose a full 180 feet from the sea.

At a signal from Lieutenant De Grät, who sat at the tiller, the seaman put the boom over. The pinnace on its new tack plunged into a trough and the lighthouse sank from view, only to loom again moments later as they crested the next wave. Edgar, expecting the worst, looked longingly back at the brigantine, bobbing like a cork at her anchorage not a mile away. Yet until half an hour ago, when he had boarded the pinnace, the voyage on the brigantine herself had seemed a trial, perhaps terminally perilous.

Edgar was most dreadfully nervous, his every sense agonizingly alive as the pinnace surged toward the lighthouse, heeling so steeply to starboard that De Grät signaled him to throw his weight against (sit upon, did he mean?) the port gunwale.

His unstrung nerves were, of course, what had brought Edgar here, two hundred miles from the nearest land, which, the Director of the Compagnie Générale des Phares d'Outre-Mer in Paris had told him, was the island of Panchatan. His unstrung nerves were why he had been unable to finish the most ambitious work he had ever undertaken, a novel, as yet untitled, about the end of the world. Although the last few chapters remained to be written, he had not set pen to paper for months. In that time the insidious idea grew that, possibly, the story *had* no ending. Was it too apocalyptic? Or too far beyond his imaginative powers? It had come to obsess him, to consume his every thought, his every waking hour. He drank little, ate less. He avoided social contact, persuading himself that *that* was the real problem, that people insisted on bedeviling him with talk, talk and more talk, when he craved the silence to immerse himself in the ending of the work he could not finish. Soon he began to dream of a writer, rather like himself, who was obsessed by a story he was struggling—with what desperation Edgar well knew —to finish; a story about the end of the world. His dream-self, deciding that isolation was the answer, sought employment as a lighthouse keeper.

To abandon the familiar world for utter solitude was a romantic gesture that appealed to Edgar. Moreover, such a dramatic change of scene—literally a sea change—might, he dared hope, bring him to his senses. His belief that a shard of stone he carried on his person could suspend the laws of nature was not normal. Even less so was his unshakable impression that in an instant he had gone—had somehow been *translated*—from the sanctum of a hypnotist who called himself Count Dionisio di Tangeri to the offices of the Compagnie Générale des Phares d'Outre-Mer.

He feared, in short, for his sanity.

And so now, many weeks later—still nervous, still most dreadfully nervous—here he was, halfway around the world, fast approaching the lighthouse that would be his home for the next six months.

The pinnace sailed past a breakwater into a protected anchorage in the rocky islet, barely larger than the base of the lighthouse. Here in the lee of the great stone shaft, the roar of the surf was muted and the sail hung limp. The seaman tossed a line about a bollard and the pinnace bumped against a small landing stage. In the calm water nearby Edgar saw a row-boat, half sunk, or half afloat.

"Your means of escape," smiled Lieutenant De Grät, "should the lighthouse sink beneath the waves."

"Escape in that?" said Edgar. "With the nearest land two hundred miles distant?"

"A *plaisanterie*," De Grät assured him. "You have no need to worry, monsieur. Those walls are almost two meters thick at the base, and you can see the size of the rivets."

De Grät stepped ashore while the seaman began unloading Edgar's provisions. Going in an instant from gloom to the absolute conviction that this was the place he would finish his novel, Edgar sprang eagerly after the lieutenant. De Grät, for his part, was now frowning.

"Odd," he said. "Most odd. Surely after six months of solitude your predecessor should be eager to greet us."

De Grät craned his neck to look up the length of the shaft, broken only by narrow embrasures and, high up, a ring of windows beneath the great lamp itself.

He strode to the heavy iron door in the base of the lighthouse and pulled. The door swung outward. Cold dank air like the hand of a corpse (why did he think such things?) brushed Edgar's face. De Grät shouted:

"Monsieur Henry!"

No answer.

"William Henry!"

Edgar literally felt his heart skip a beat. He waited speechless while De Grät returned to the pinnace for a small lantern and lit it with a match he took from an oilskin pouch. At last Edgar found his voice:

"William Henry—was that who you called?"

"I did. That is his name."

"My brother."

"Your brother?"

"My brother sometimes used that name—Will Henry. He was murdered in Paris."

"Then *this* William Henry," said De Grät, "cannot be your brother, can he?"

Edgar snatched the lantern from the surprised lieutenant and rushed inside. The light revealed rough-hewn stone walls with crates and casks stacked at the base, and a tight spiral staircase of iron. Edgar raced up, De Grät behind him. "Henry!" Edgar shouted, irrationally certain that he would soon hear his brother's voice. "Henry!"

Through the cold dank void, up and ever up the steeply spiraling stairs, Edgar climbed. At the top he encountered a trap door. Heaving it open, he called again, "Henry!"

He found himself in the living quarters—comfortable sitting room, tiny kitchen, small bedroom. Beside the neatly made bed stood a bookcase. There were volumes in French and Italian. The word "Mohicans" caught Edgar's eye. He saw the three volumes of James Fenimore Cooper's *Leatherstocking Tales*. More than once Henry had said (to Edgar's mock horror) that those were the books he would wish to have were he exiled to a desert island. Edgar knew he always made room for them in his seabag.

He had not died in Paris, he had preceded his brother here—of that Edgar was now certain.

Edgar ran up more spiral stairs, his footsteps clanging. Now he was in a room cluttered with pendular iron weights, with chains, with pulleys and ropes. A catwalk at eye level crossed the room to yet more stairs. Against one curving wall stood a table; on it lay open a logbook. Edgar heard De Grät mutter a surprised "Empty!"

then made his way along the catwalk and up the final short flight of stairs to the lamp.

There was too much to take in at once: the great lamp itself, with its six rows of wicks, like votive candles in a church, waiting to be lit; the ring of huge convex lenses, faintly blue, and mirrors of some gleaming white metal that walled the lamp and, Edgar had been told, would be rotated by the clockworks in the room below—the whole girdled by a narrow balcony. Edgar stepped out upon it into the wind. White water foamed over shoals to the north, in the direction of Panchatan, as far as the eye could see.

De Grät came up behind him. "Monsieur Poe," he said deliberately, "it may well be that the lighthouse keeper you are here to replace was your brother, but, whether your brother or not, the man who called himself William Henry is no more." De Grät stood for a time silently, surrounded by nothing but sky. Then softly he spoke. "When such . . . losses occur, Phares d'Outre-Mer attributes them to mischance. But, between us, Monsieur Poe, the loneliness, the desperate loneliness of the most isolated spot on the face of the earth, sometimes proves too much. . . ."

Edgar felt twice bereft, suffering anew the loss of his brother. With an effort of will he reminded himself why he was here. He had six months in which to finish his novel about the end of the world. They seemed to stretch in his imagination, those six months, like the gulf between now and eternity. And yet he knew the time would pass swiftly.

He followed De Grät down the spiraling stairs. Three hours later he stood on the breakwater and watched the brigantine drop below the horizon along with the setting sun.

He had to light the six rows of wicks every night at dusk, had to set in motion the pendulums and chains and pulleys which, with a rattling that reverberated through the lighthouse, turned the wall of lenses and mirrors that protected the flames from the wind and concentrated their light into a great blue beam that rotated through the night. At dawn he had to stop the clockworks and extinguish the flames. The only danger he faced was when cleaning the lenses.

Then, venturing onto the narrow balcony to scour off the salt spray accumulated on the glass, he was at the mercy of the wind. The first time, it almost blew him into space before, on hands and knees, he was able to make his slow way inside. He told himself that in future he would wait for a windless day, but such were few, and before long he could stand straddle-legged upon the narrow balcony, exhilarated by the shriek of the wind and the smashing, so far below, of white water against the base of the lighthouse.

He did not think at such times of the risk to his life—except once, when to his horror he imagined he saw his brother Henry falling.

A scant three hours a day Edgar gave to his duties, but for weeks paper and ink remained untouched. He whiled away the time reading and re-reading the three volumes of *The Leatherstocking Tales*—communing, he told himself, with his dead brother.

He sought excuses to postpone writing. There was the row-boat, for example, half sunk, or half afloat. He wondered if he could find some way to caulk it. He found pitch among the stores, but how could he drag the boat from the water to the landing stage, to work upon it?

One morning he swam the few yards to the row-boat. Boarding it, he expected—half expected—his weight to sink it. But to the contrary, it felt marvelously buoyant. Curious, he bailed with his cupped hands, but, try as he might, he could not lower the level of the water in the boat.

Afternoons, if reading wearied him, Edgar would sit for long hours contemplating the hexagonal fragment of stone. To suspend natural laws, what did that mean? What laws? And suspend how?

Edgar stared at the shard—or the Shard, as he now thought of it. He stroked it. He enclosed it in his hand. Was one supposed to wish? He wished that Henry be still alive. Wished to encounter again the captivating daughter of the hypnotist Count Tangeri. Wished that he would remain eternally young. Wished for everlasting fame.

Wished that he could complete his tale about the end of the world.

The elemental fury of the first storm shocked him. Waves broke like thunder against the lighthouse, which seemed—was it possible?—to sway. To light the huge lamp and set it in motion seemed pointless, for no ship could survive such a storm. Still, Edgar carried out his duties.

The second storm was, if any thing, worse. The wind rose to a high steady howl. White water surged from all sides, submerging the base of the tower. The lenses of the lamp, opaque with streaming water, stared sightlessly out at the raging sea. For forty-eight hours, except for the wind and the surf, a world outside the walls of the lighthouse ceased to exist.

And then it was over and nothing, not even the row-boat, had changed.

Edgar had expected to find the boat smashed to kindling, but when he ventured out upon the landing stage, there it was, as usual, partially submerged, the oars still in the oarlocks, angled in so that their blades rested on the transom. That the row-boat had survived was outside the realm of the possible. Yet could Edgar doubt the evidence of his own eyes?

He swam out to the boat again. As before, his weight had no effect upon its buoyancy. As before, it was unavailing to bail. He was on the point of swimming back to the landing stage when something under the thwart caught his eye. He reached down and fished it out.

It was the Shard, or one just like it.

With it gripped between his teeth, Edgar swam back. He climbed the spiral staircase directly to the clockworks room, where he had left the Shard on the table alongside the logbook. It was not there. He spent the rest of the day searching everywhere. There was only one shard, the one he had brought back from the row-boat.

But how had it come to be there?

Edgar prowled the living quarters until dusk. Then, after lighting the lamp and starting its clockworks, he placed a stack of paper on the logbook table. The wind had dropped. There was no surf. It was so silent that Edgar could hear the beating of his own heart. He remembered writing once* that the road to fame and immortal renown lay straight open and unencumbered before any writer bold enough to publish a book—it had not necessarily to be a large one—entitled *My Heart Laid Bare*. But—the book must be true to its title.

Edgar, dipping a pen, was about to write that title on the first page of his long-neglected manuscript. But something stayed his hand. *My Heart Laid Bare*—what, for Edgar, must that mean? He rose from the table and descended to the living quarters. The reflection that from the small mirror in the bedroom stared at him with troubled eyes, what had it to do with the self he sought? He climbed again, the iron stairs ringing underfoot, and stood on the balcony that girdled the lamp, stood still as a statue, silent as his own waiting tomb, gazing out at the limitless sky, at the shoreless sea. It was in those, in the eternal ever-changing blue of sky and sea, that he saw himself—*almost* saw himself. The way to truth lay out there, along a distant shimmering path, at once familiar and unknown, that penetrated—*seemed* to penetrate—those vast mutable improbabilities (why, thinking that, did he see a peacock feather in a Pennsylvania wood?) which, for all their fantastical nature, were no less real than the workaday world and which led, by twilit lonesome routes, back to it, always back to the world, always back to it but away again.

In the clockworks room once more, Edgar swiftly wrote *"The Lighthouse at the End of the World,"* and in the solitude resumed at last to write.

* In *Marginalia*. (Editor's note)

Thirty-six

I slept. I slept in darkness, I slept in daylight, I slept the clock
around. I slept sleeping and slept awake. I slept reading and slept
walking in the orchard below the cottage or along the Bronx River.
I slept on the high overlook from which I could see the spires and
domes and minarets of a city that might have been New York or
Benares. I slept painting the window sashes. I slept building a new
picket fence. I slept replacing rotted floorboards on the porch where,
when the weather became fair, Muddy sat doing the needlework—
painfully, her fingers gnarled—that kept food on the table. But I
never thought about that. I never thought about any thing. I passed
hours thinking of absolutely nothing.

I kept the letters that came from Richmond in a growing stack
on my work table. She wrote a clear, an elegant hand. The ink was
blue, the stationery *écru*. I liked to look at the unopened letters. I
liked to touch them. But not to think about her.

I retreated to the places inside myself where I might hope to find
the essence that was me, but, hardly to my surprise, I found nothing.
I was the void before the beginning and after the end, the void
before the beginning began again. It perturbed me—too strong a
word; puzzled me—that I could think of absolutely nothing. But
wasn't puzzlement, I asked myself, something? Could anyone truly
think of absolutely nothing? Even to ask the question, was that not
a kind of thinking? I am puzzled, therefore I am.

The less I thought, the more acute became my hearing. I would
hear mice scurrying in the attic and the song of distant birds and
the far moan of a whistle that I knew was not the Fordham train.
From the orchard I would hear bacon frying in the pan. I would
hear Muddy plying her needle. Sometimes, I almost thought I could

hear people passing the time of day in the village. Hello, Edgar, they said; how are you today? It must have been a different Edgar. You are looking well, Mr. Poe. Writing, are you?

Well, I was. I had begun a story about a lighthouse keeper, an unnamed lighthouse keeper identified only as a noble of the realm (the realm itself unspecified) who had taken such employment in order to finish writing a book. My story* was the journal he kept. It had just three entries. Or four, if you count the date—the date and nothing more—on the top of the last page. The lighthouse was two hundred miles from the nearest land—a magical island, as it happened, but I did not write that. I could give no name to the island, and therefore could not write about it. Which was odd, because giving the narrator no name did not worry me. *He* worried. He worried that despite the lighthouse's massive, iron-riveted walls, it would not survive a violent tropical storm, but I did not write that. I had never experienced a tropical storm. Besides, I knew he should fear not a storm but a submarine earthquake. But I did not write that. I had never experienced an earthquake. The lighthouse keeper, no longer relieved to have left the world behind him, grew increasingly nervous in his isolation. The lighthouse, he kept reminding himself, was not invulnerable; nothing is. Would he live to complete the book? Would he live to complete his life?

After the first three entries in the journal, I was unsure what to write. By placing on the final page only the date, I meant to suggest that the lighthouse in fact was destroyed and the protagonist with it, thus side-stepping my inability to finish the tale. Perhaps if the lighthouse keeper had faced not a storm or an earthquake but a cholera epidemic, like the one then raging in New York City, I could have finished the story. But cholera claims no victims in a lighthouse two hundred miles from land. Appendicitis—what if he came down with appendicitis? I did not write that either.

---

* Among Poe's posthumous papers was found a fragment of an untitled tale whose narrator took employment as a lighthouse keeper two hundred miles from the nearest land in order to finish writing a book. (Editor's note)

I wrote a letter to New York, and a letter came back, and one spring afternoon I found myself in the dining room of the Astor House Hotel "cutting my mutton" with Rufus Griswold. We ate cantaloupe melon. We ate clear turtle soup. We ate roast chicken with oysters stuffed under the skin. We ate a joint of rare beef (no mutton). We ate Long Island duckling breasts in a tart-sweet sauce. We ate artichoke hearts and Oriental salad and out-of-season peaches. Or, rather, Rufus Griswold did; ate and smiled his moist smile while I spoke and just picked at my food. But I drank. I drank four kinds of wine and began to wonder how I would pay for this Lucullan feast, but when he heard all I had to say, Rufus Griswold frowned his happy frown and insisted on paying. He did so with crisp new folding money, enough for Muddy and me to live on for a month. I had more than a month in mind. After I returned to Fordham, Rufus Griswold made me wait. But finally the money came.* I gave most of it—sixty dollars—to Muddy. It would keep her in comfort were I to spend the entire summer away. For I was going. When I brought home the tickets for my journey, Muddy cried. She fretted about me. The cholera, Eddie, she said. Your accident in the railroad cars, she said. As Virginia's consumption had always been, for Muddy, bronchitis, so my swallowing an ounce of laudanum was my "accident in the cars." But all that lay behind me. I was well; I had returned from the wilderness of wherever I had been, as good as new.

In the morning Muddy walked with me to the station, and from the window of the car I watched her stout figure recede until it was a dot where the tracks came together in the distance.

From Manhattan I took the steamboat to Perth Amboy, and boarded the train for Philadelphia, the first stop on my journey. As the cars raced south through New Jersey, I was in splendid spirits. The late June day was fine. I wore my accustomed black, but in the trunk which I had shipped ahead to Richmond reposed a white linen

---

* Neither Poe nor Griswold made an account of their dinner meeting. But shortly thereafter, Griswold included three more poems by Poe in the tenth edition of his anthology. Moreover, Maria Clemm said it was then that Poe appointed Griswold his literary executor. (Editor's note)

suit, almost new, a gift from Muddy, to wear in the Southern summer heat while lecturing and, doubtless, doing obligatory readings of "The Raven."

I began to wonder if Elmira would like the Edgar Poe she saw. I had read her letters. I was very far from the "lovely boy" she remembered. Perhaps, I told myself, I should shave off my mustache. Might Elmira think my raven-black attire too artful, symbolic? But I would have the white suit. Bless Muddy. Would Elmira dislike my voice? It was soft, compelling; some said mesmerizing. Would my moods disturb her, swinging from bleak despair to wild elation and back? But that was over and done with, was it not?

Certain things about me, never the less, she might find difficult to accept. For example, my preternaturally acute hearing.

That morning on the steamboat I had heard a woman and her lover plotting the death of her husband—heard them from across the lounge, their clandestine conversation rising above the louder voices of other passengers. The plotters looked across the lounge at me. The man said, Who is he? and the woman said, I've no idea. The man said, I get the distinct impression he is eavesdropping on us. The woman said, Impossible. Still they looked at me. I did not like the way they were looking at me. I rose casually and went out onto the deck, just aft of the bridge, from where I would be seen. They did not follow.

The railroad car in which I rode was almost empty. There were just two other men, seated at the far end. It was hot. I opened the window near my seat. Smoke and soot blew in. The two men glanced at me. I shut the window. They were large disreputable-looking men in the sort of loud clothing worn by riverboat gamblers. Suddenly I could hear them, despite the clatter of the wheels.

One said, If he opens that window again, I swear I shall kill him.

The other said, You're joking.

The first said, I never joke.

The second asked, Do you know him?

Never saw him before. That is the beauty of it. I may kill him on a simple whim, and get clean away—a motiveless murder, and thus quite unsolvable.

It so happens *I* know him. He is the writer Edgar Poe. And I have a better motive than yours. Just the other day a man of my acquaintance offered me sixty dollars to kill him. That is a lot of money.

It would be a simple matter, to kill him.

How?

Soon after Bordentown there is a tunnel. When it is pitch dark, we hit him over the head, drag him to the platform between the cars, and throw him off. What do you say?

I could use the money.

With an effort of will so intense it left me trembling in every limb, I kept my seat as the train slowed for the Bordentown station. Nor did I move when, with a final lurch, it came to a stop. In the rear of my car the two men made no sound. It took an even greater effort not to turn and look at them. No one entered the car. Through the window I saw the conductor go by. " 'Board!" he called. "All aboard!" With another lurch, the train began to move. I seized my carpet-bag, sprinted for the door, wrenched it open, and leaped to the ground. Panting, I watched until the last car disappeared around a curve.

Then I entered the station and calmly inquired the time of the next south-bound train.

The shed of the Philadelphia Navy Yard loomed gigantically. You came out of a tavern and there it was, in daylight or darkness, dwarfing the city that dwarfed you, so you went into another tavern, but when you came out it was still there, it was always there, and in it, unseen men scraped and caulked and refitted ships for journeys to far places where, possibly, my brother Henry had been but where I would never go. I did not miss those places now. Richmond was where I was going, and Richmond seemed as distant as Panchatan. But where, pray, was Panchatan? It was no place I knew.

I walked into another tavern, and when I came out the two men from the train were waiting in the darkness. I need not say I ran. They gave chase but I proved fleeter, running north into the center of the city. The evening was hot. The doorman of the Congress Hall Hotel gave me a dubious look, but I went past him with hauteur. I was looking, I said at the reception desk, for Panchatan. No, for Thomas W. Frederick. No, for Frederick W. Thomas. The song writer. I was studied down the length of a long nose and told that Mr. Thomas had left Philadelphia that afternoon.

Outside, the two men from the train were waiting. Again I ran. By the time I lost them, I had left the gas lamps of the city center behind. I slowed to a walk along a street of red brick houses with marble stoops that gleamed in the moonlight. Except for the grid-iron streets, it could have been Baltimore. Or even New York. It could have been anywhere. A man came toward me. I tensed, but he was not one of them. We passed, he to my left, I to his right. No, that is not possible. It only seemed that way. In any event, we passed. Then I pretended not to hear him call my name. Then I felt his hand on my shoulder.

"Poe? It *is* you!"

In the moonlight I saw John Sartain, the illustrator.

"What are you doing here?" I demanded.

He took my arm. We walked together, stride for stride. This proved difficult for me, as I seemed to be wearing only one shoe.

"I live here," he said.

We went into a house and along a corridor to a cluttered studio. While he lit gas lamps, I surveyed the etching-covered walls. Then I turned nonchalantly away so he would not suspect me of looking for the oval portrait of Virginia.

"What brings you to Philadelphia?" he asked. He did not remark on the scruffy growth of beard on my chin, nor the sorry state of my once fastidious black attire.

"They are after me," I said.

Sartain raised an eyebrow. "Critics? Creditors? Jealous husbands?"

"The two men who planned to throw me off the train to my death. They are here in Philadelphia. They recognized me."

"But why would they want to, er—"

"Gratuitously, in the case of one; he must be deranged. For money in the case of his confederate."

"How do you know this?" John Sartain asked after a while. He had grown pale.

"My acute hearing," I told him. "It saved my life. For the time being."

My plight so dismayed him that he was speechless.

"Have you a razor?" I asked.

"A what, a razor?" He looked at me and licked his lips.

"A razor, yes."

"I regret that I have none."

Lying, of course. Why did he not want me to alter my appearance? Was he in league with them?

"I must shave off my mustache so they will not recognize me," I explained.

"Come inside with me and I'll remove it for you."

This he did with a pair of scissors. He brought me a hand mirror. The removal of my mustache made a considerable difference.

While I studied my new face, Sartain cut slices from a cold joint of lamb. He cleaned and put away the carving knife. He sliced some bread and put away the bread knife. He slathered the bread with butter and cleaned and put away that knife too and assembled a platter of sandwiches, which he set upon the table with two glasses and a pitcher of milk. We ate in companionable silence.

I pushed my chair back. "I am off to the reservoir."

"At this hour?"

"I like the cascades and the fountains. The roar of the water. I want to sleep there."

"You can sleep here."

"I want to go there first, no matter where I sleep."

He said the night air might be tonic for him too. "The cholera," he said. "Against the cholera." He sounded most nervous; a common enough state in times of pestilence.

As I had only one shoe, he gave me a pair of his own to wear, and off we went along streets that crossed other streets at right angles, always at right angles.

SARTAIN: (*to the Chevalier C. Auguste Dupin three months later, at the end of September*) I knew that Poe could not be left alone while he spoke first of men who wanted to kill him, then of taking his own life.

DUPIN: How was his voice? Earnest? Intense?

S: I should call it, rather, flat. You are an artist, John, he said; would you not agree that your work is your life? I told him it was *part* of my life. No, he said, we are what we do, John. And I have not written a complete tale since my accident in the cars. Since what? I asked. Since I almost died in the cars, he said. He looked terrible. He looked as if he had been to Hell and back. I could believe he had been near death. Were you injured? I asked. He repeated in the same flat voice, I suffered an accident in the cars. I asked, What kind of accident? He said, It could happen again. It is as simple to commit suicide as murder. Simpler, as the victim does not resist.

D: *Ciel!* You tried to distract him from such talk?

S: Without success. But when we reached the waterworks, he found his own distraction. The municipal authorities.

D: The municipal—ah, I see. The fountains would have been shut for the night.

S: Why have they turned off the fountains? he demanded. I told him they always did so at dusk. But they would look like liquid silver in the moonlight, he said. They knew we were coming—knew *I* was coming. So they shut them.

In that case, I said, there is no reason to stay here.

But Poe thought otherwise—*acted* otherwise. He made for the steep wooden staircase that ascends above the overflow to the top of the dam. I told him it was unsafe in the dark. Nonsense, he said, look at the moon; it is so bright, it casts shadows. It cast *his* shadow as he started upwards.

D: You followed?

S: I followed, fearing that he might hurl himself into space. He climbed swiftly. The staircase swayed. The lights of the city seemed to rise with us. I saw him above me, flailing for balance. The steps were slippery with spray from the overflow. Slow down! I shouted.

But he did not, and neither could I. Soon he achieved the top. He went to the edge, striding into the mist that rose from the overflow. She is all radiance, he cried, like silver dipped in light.

The moon shone through, effulgent, argental. He struck what seemed a listening attitude, head cocked and thrust forward. The moment extended. I stood close, ready to grab him should he try to hurl himself into the abyss. Abruptly he stepped back from the edge.

She is leaving, he said. She mistrusts this place. See? See how her wings trail in the water, all bedraggled?

I have never heard so sad a voice. I stared, almost expecting to see what he saw, to hear what he heard.

He raised his hands. For a terrifying instant I thought he intended to push me over the edge. But he turned, to race down the stairs no less recklessly than he had climbed them.

We walked home together. That night he slept in the drawing room, upon a sofa; I, upon the one opposite. I was still afraid to leave him alone. But in the morning . . .

D: He seemed normal?

S: As sane as you or I.

D: Did he remember climbing to the top of the dam?

S: Yes. He spoke of it as a child does of a madcap adventure. He laughed. How glorious to feel young again, he said.

D: He remained with you how long?

S: For ten days.

D: And during that time his behavior was normal?

S: (*smiling*) *Very* normal. He scoured the city for anyone who might lend him money. I myself lent him enough to reach Richmond. He was bursting with plans. To be reunited with his Elmira. Elmira Royster Shelton—the widow Shelton.

D: I know who Madame Shelton is.

S: For ten days there were just two topics of conversation—Elmira, and the *Stylus*, the magazine he intends to publish. A magazine of Southern literary excellence, he called it. With no toadying to smug New Yorkers or insufferable Bostonians. A magazine which would not own its writers.

D: A witty name, the *Stylus*. But the name of a magazine is rather like the title of a tale, or its first line: it is a beginning. Edgar Poe is very good at beginnings. It is endings that give him trouble. Well, we shall see.

S: He intended to travel as far as St. Louis and build a subscription list of Charlottesville and West Point alumni. With a list of five hundred he was sure he could get financial support in Richmond, where he intended to locate the magazine. He asked me if I would be interested in becoming his principal illustrator.

D: And were you?

S: Absolutely. Poe had—has—very sound ideas, you know. What he always lacked was money.

D: The widow Shelton, she is wealthy, is she not?

S: I believe so. But Poe mentioned a provision in her husband's will whereby, should she remarry, Elmira Shelton would forfeit three-fourths of her inheritance. He is no fortune-hunter, if that is what you imply.

D: (*mildly*) It is not my business to imply, only to infer. And I infer that the lady, even with a quarter of her wealth, can support our friend's magazine. Whether she can support his morbid moods as well—

S: We must hope they are a thing of the past. When I saw him off for Richmond, he had never looked so happy, so confident—so eager to confront the future.

Thirty-seven

I mourn not that the desolate
Are happier, sweet, than I,
But that *you* sorrow for *my* fate
Who am a passer by.

—"To ——"

I put up at the Swan Tavern on Broad Street. In my youth one of Richmond's fashionable hotels, it was so no longer.

My room under the eaves was suffocatingly hot, but offered a view of the dome of the capitol building designed by Jefferson and of the verdant islands in the James River. Outside, eight once-white columns fronted a sagging porch, where rocking chairs were occupied during the daylight hours and on into the dusk by men old enough to have lived through the entire history of the nation. They would sit, and rock, and spit brown unerring streams of tobacco juice into spittoons and appear always about to speak but in fact speak rarely. For they were listeners. They listened to the creak of the floorboards and the drum of hooves in the street and the buzz of a solitary bumblebee searching for blossoms dried up by the remorseless July sun and the clatter of a stick dragged by a small boy along a picket fence and, fainter, so far off that it could have been a moan of wind had there been any wind, the mournful singing of a coffle of slaves. Sometimes one of them would say "Y'all ever seen such heat?" with an air of having discoursed profoundly upon the worldly condition, and the rocking and the listening would resume until another would say "First lightning bug tonight" as the rockers creaked in place along the trail of their spent lives.

I was listening too. Did I hear things they could not hear? But at forty I was young enough to be the son of the youngest of them. So even if I did, it need not mean a recurrence of my acute, my preternatural hearing. I wanted no more of my acute hearing. Though not a fearsome thing in itself, it accompanied my hallucinations—which, at the time I suffered them, seemed no more hallucinatory than the heat or that first lightning bug.

I listened. I listened on the sagging porch and on Broad Street. I heard the creak of a carriage harness, very different from the creak of a floorboard, and I heard the snuffle of contentment a horse will make standing in dappled shade when the feed bag is placed over its muzzle, and I heard the shouts and laughter of boys splashing in the river. I could imagine their disbelief were I to tell them that once on a summer day no less hot than this one, the boy Eddie Poe had swum the six miles from Ludlam's wharf to Warwick against the tide. But I had done so. It was no hallucination, it was the outcome of a wager, and I walked home to Richmond afterwards, too.

This time, as befitting my mature years, I took a row-boat from Ludlam's wharf to the islands (heard the creak of oars in oarlocks, very different from the creak of a floorboard or of a carriage harness, but normal, it was normal) and went ashore to look through the heat haze over the water at the city rising on its hills. That was Church Hill there, where the Shelton house stood, and I heard her scolding her son Alex for opening the carriage door himself and saw her servant—had his name been Amos?—putting the feed bag in place, the horse snuffling with contentment again. None of this was hallucination, it was memory, and while memory can be as hurtful as hallucination, it is normal, as normal as old men rocking their lives away, locked so hard in their memories that speech is almost superfluous.

What if, seeing her, seeing that dark amber hair of hers, those clear blue eyes, that Indian face with its high cheek-bones and unexpectedly prim mouth, what if, seeing her, I heard with no warning things I could not possibly have heard and began again to hallucinate, with the absolute conviction that my fantasies were real?

No, I was not ready for the big house on Church Hill, not ready for Elmira Shelton. But I could go to Sanxay's book store and, seeing through the window that the clerk was no one I knew, venture inside to ascertain the reality of my own tenuous self. I found on the shelves three volumes verifying me, two of tales, one of poetry. I took down *Tales of the Grotesque and Arabesque* and flipped through the pages. After a while I became aware of the clerk standing at my side.

"A native son, you know," he said, "even if he was born in Boston. Grew up here in Richmond, yes sir, that's a fact. They tell me he is right famous as far away as Paris, France."

I replaced the volume on the shelf.

"Are we not acquainted, sir?" He set a pince-nez on his nose and looked at me. Then he took the same volume down from the shelf and opened it to the flyleaf and moistened the tip of a finger to lift the glazed paper from the etching.

"But my dear sir," he said, "you are Edgar Poe!"

Fleeing, I went down to the river and saw that the Alhambra Tavern was still there, where in return for washing up I had lived in the back room, all the food I could eat and all the gin I could drink, and soon less food and more gin. I wanted to go into the Alhambra but did not. I walked to the house of my boyhood friend Ebenezer Burling. A servant opened the door. The Burlings? Why, the Burlings done moved down to the Tidewater somewhere, seems like. I climbed Church Hill but avoided Grace Street, where she lived. At dusk I returned to the Swan. I saw a lightning bug, possibly the first of the evening. The old men were rocking. The lightning bug made no sound. A reporter from the *Daily Republican* was waiting in the lobby.

The interview appeared that Saturday, and on Sunday I donned my white suit and climbed Church Hill to Grace Street.

ELMIRA ROYSTER SHELTON: (*to the Chevalier C. Auguste Dupin, in early October*) But then, you have come all this way for nothing, monsieur.

DUPIN: He is gone—flown the coop, I believe one says?

E: I tried to stop him. He was in no state to travel.

D: He had been . . . indulging?

E: (*coolly*) No, monsieur; he was ill. He came here to bid me good-bye. This was last Thursday evening. He was pale, and his eyes had a yellowish cast. I felt his pulse. It would beat ten times, then stop.

It was quite alarming. And he was feverish. I begged him not to go until he felt better. But there was no dissuading him.

D: Had he accomplished what he came here to do?

E: His magazine will have ample backing when he returns. (*Blushes.*)

D: And the summer passed agreeably in other ways as well?

E: Very. Edgar found that the Richmonders hold him in great esteem. Entertainments were organized around him. He is a brilliant conversationalist, and he often, with an endearing show of reluctance, was prevailed upon to recite "The Raven." Reciting, he stands without moving. His voice is soft, compelling. He is mesmerizing! Richmonders could not help comparing him with the actor Edwin Booth, who performed here just this past spring. Edgar did not suffer by the comparison. Nor is he the less handsome. (*Blushes again.*)

(D *smiles encouragingly.*)

E: He was invited to lecture here in Richmond more than once, and in Norfolk. He passed several agreeable days at Old Point Comfort.

D: Old Point Comfort, what is that?

E: It is a resort near Norfolk. It piqued Edgar's fancy; one can bathe, sail, dance under the stars—not a quarter mile from the grim bastions of Fortress Monroe with its three hundred cannon. Edgar stayed at the Hygeia Hotel on the seafront. (*Gives a little laugh.*) Surrounded by scores of adoring adolescents, from a summer school for girls of good family. Edgar is *so* patient with children. I can see them, can almost see them swarming around him, all over him in their white organdie dresses while he recited "Ulalume" and "Annabel Lee."

D: And "The Raven"?

E: His preference is for his later poems. He *so* enjoys the company of young persons, Edgar does. He never talks down to them, never patronizes.

D: This Old Point Comfort, he was asked to speak there?

E: No. He was lucky to get a room at the Hygeia in the season. He was actually bound for Norfolk, when someone in the train stole his lecture notes. He repaired to Old Point Comfort to re-write them from memory, and was so entranced with the place that he stayed on.

D: Someone stole his lecture notes?

E: Rifled his bag and stole them, yes. Edgar tried to make light of it on his return to Richmond. Conspirators, he said; conspirators in the train stole his notes.

D: I see. Madame Shelton, is one permitted to ask whether you have an . . . understanding with Monsieur Poe?

E: The dear sweet man was so certain I would scorn him for his lack of worldly goods. But the serious artist wears poverty like a badge of honor, don't you agree?

D: (*dryly*) Edgar Poe would as soon cast off such a badge, I imagine.

E: Do you suggest that, in courting me, Edgar—

D: Your pardon, madame. I have suggested nothing.

E: Who are you really, monsieur? What do you want of me? What do you want of Edgar?

D: Information. It is always information I seek, *chère madame*. In Paris a long time ago something . . . *outré* happened, a series of events which I am determined to unravel. As to who I am, I have already presented my card.

E: The Chevalier C. Auguste Dupin. Please! The name of a character in one of Edgar's stories!

D: In three of them, actually.*

E: You expect me to believe it is your real name? It is as much a—a disguise as those green spectacles you wear.

D: Ah, but you are mistaken. Edgar and I met in Paris when we both were young. It is not odd that he used my name and my . . . avocation in his stories. In fact, he had asked my permission.

E: (*mollified*) Well, your accent is certainly French. And you have the manners of a *chevalier*. But—

D: (*Bows.*) It pleases me that you say so.

---

* "The Murders in the Rue Morgue," "The Mystery of Marie Rogêt," and "The Purloined Letter." (Editor's note)

E: But I did not know Edgar had been to Paris. Do you not mistake him for his brother?

D: It was Henry who bade him come to Paris. Edgar and I were introduced by their friend the writer Alexandre Dumas.

E: Dumas!

D: Indeed. And even were we strangers, I would not have imputed to Edgar Poe—or to anyone—a dishonorable motive for seeking your hand. One need only look at you to know better.

E: How gallant you are, monsieur! Half of Richmond thinks we shall marry when he returns from New York.

D: And you, *chère madame?* What do you think?

E: I am very different from the wife Edgar lost.

D: Is that not as well, madame?

E: I saw them once when they were newlyweds, you know. Here in Richmond. Edgar and his lovely tragic Virginia. She was so young. I saw them quite by chance. Without knowing why, I hid myself in a doorway as if—as if I were spying upon them. I felt an agonizing wrench as they walked by, arm in arm. I had to remind myself I was a married woman, a mother. I had to banish my feelings as I would a poisonous reptile. . . . Why am I telling you this?

D: Because I listen. Most people do not know how. It is the basis for my modest success as a *détective.*

E: A *détective?* I do not know the word.

D: One who detects.

E: Detects what?

D: (*archly*) One who is trying to detect, *chère madame,* what sort of arrangement you have with Edgar Poe.

E: (*after a silence*) When he asks, I shall consent.

D: And he will ask?

E: I believe he would have, before he left, had he not been so ill. Far too ill to travel. But he was determined to go. I passed a sleepless night. Before dawn I had Amos drive me to the Eighth Street station, where a rail line connects with the steamboat from Port Walthall for Norfolk and Baltimore. But the cars had already left. Amos drove me through the dawn to Port Walthall—recklessly, I fear; but to no avail. The steamboat had just cast off with my poor dear ill Edgar aboard.

Thirty-eight

Why this?—why not that?

—Marginalia

Election day dawns—if such is the appropriate word—more like a bleak December morning than one in early October. The storm-roiled waters of Chesapeake Bay slap and smash against pilings. The wind blows a fitful melancholy dirge, rattling rain like pebbles against the high small windows. Still, there is an air of excitement in the coop. Today we inmates, or whatever we are, shall be taken to vote—and then dispersed into the streets of the city to confront or flee whatever problems drove us here to this brief hiatus in our existence.

By mid-morning, half a dozen recruiters have come for their charges. This leaves only those of us brought to the coop by the man in the tall beaver hat and stone-gray topcoat, who is unaccountably missing. There is talk that he will not come, that he diddled the Whig politicians, that, possibly, he works in some capacity for the notorious Ryan.

It is therefore almost a letdown when, towards noon, carrying a large black umbrella, he appears.

"Almost did not know you without the white suit."

These words he addresses jocularly to me, and he has a similar greeting for each of his charges. Then he looks at me closely.

"Feeling poorly, are you?"

As a matter of fact, I am. My head throbs with pain, my eyes burn, and every joint in my body aches.

"I am capable of marking a ballot," I tell him.

"*Three* ballots, old man," he says.

Old man? Well, yes; I certainly walk like one as, trailing after the others, I follow him outside. But my decrepitude is hardly unique, for we are as ragtag-and-bobtail a group of derelicts as ever came out of hibernation to rejoin the world. Which is: a black sky, a cold wind whistling up a narrow empty street from the harbor, and in the water the same row-boat, half sunk, or half afloat.

As we hurry along unfamiliar streets through the rain, a chill grasps and shakes me. I begin to sweat profusely in the icy wind. Soon I am burning with fever. Stumbling along, I fall farther behind with every step.

The beaver hat bobs alongside. "We vote first in a Fourth Ward tavern. A hot drink will do wonders for you. Easy!"

I have almost fallen. He steadies me; walks at my side. "Come on, old man. A dollar each time you vote. Cash on the barrelhead. For both of us."

We turn into a street I recognize, East Lombard Street. A few militiamen stand anxiously at the corner. Ahead I see a sign swinging in the wind: Gunner's Hall. Men mill about in front of the tavern, red-faced and loud, many carrying two-by-fours. Taunts are hurled. I hear the incongruous sound of a brass band. The beaver hat leaves my side to converse with someone outside the tavern. A path is cleared to let us derelicts through.

The doorway is blocked by two men, one a huge Negro, the other white, hardly less large, with a livid sickle-shaped scar on his face. Suddenly a slender man emerges from the crowd, stands straddle-legged, and points at the doorway. What he is pointing with is a pistol. The huge Negro shouts, "Mister Thomas, now!" But the slender man looks this way and that, confused, and does not fire. I start forward, certain that, could I see his face, it would be one I know. But he dashes away through the rain with a companion, a tall woman in a riding habit. Watching them disappear into the crowd, I am pushed from behind by those seeking shelter in the tavern. I fall; am trampled upon; somehow regain my feet.

Inside, it is suffocatingly hot. Opposite the long bar I see a ballot box on a table, two men behind it, watching each other warily.

Voters file forward. An officious voice asks me my name. My name is—for the moment is—Phidias Peacock. It is Phidias Peacock he will find on his list of qualified voters. Does Phidias Peacock own property? Will I be asked where? My head swims. His address—I remember not even his address. Phidias Peacock's world has contracted until it is no more than the fever raging in my body.

"Steady there!"

"He's going to faint!"

Faces float above me on the surface of a blue cigar-smoke sea. One swims down.

"Edgar," it says.

The voice smells of whiskey; the red cheeks wear auburn side-whiskers. They belong to Joseph E. Snodgrass (E. for Evans, I tell myself, pleased I can remember something, any thing), Joseph Evans Snodgrass, erstwhile publisher of the erstwhile *Saturday Visiter*. We have often drunk together. A drinking man, Joseph Evans Snodgrass. Is that why the *Visiter* failed?

"Dr. Snodgrass," I say and raise a hand weakly.

A drinking man but resourceful, Joseph E. (for Evans) Snodgrass has turned to the practice of medicine. Owlishly he stares down, exhaling his whiskey breath. Voices consult.

I see a small square card, a pin. The pin pricks me. Eventually the card is attached to my filthy shirt. I am lifted, carried.

Someone speaks. "Damned waste of a talent."

"Of a life," says someone else. "Poor devil."

I look up. See the ribs of an umbrella, a curtain of rain. I am deposited in a cab.

"Hamstead and Broadway," says Joseph E. Snodgrass.

"The hospital?"

"You saw him, did you not?"

As the cab sways and starts forward, I reach down, fumbling no more than Snodgrass did, for the card. THIS MAN IS EDGAR A. POE THE WRITER. Printed in a not very steady hand. Little wonder Joseph Evans Snodgrass, M.D., has not accompanied me. Will he inform someone of my plight? Is being Edgar A. Poe the writer a plight? Whom will he inform? My cousin Neilson lives in Baltimore now.

He is a judge. Most respected. Will he judge me? A few years ago, as a director of the Baltimore & Ohio Railroad, he was the recipient of Samuel F. B. Morse's first commercial telegraph message, "What hath God wrought?" And what hath He wrought? Does even He know? Has Neilson Poe ever asked himself such questions? Would he recognize a plight if he saw one?

The cab climbs Hamstead Hill. As it turns to enter a driveway, I slide hard against the low door. This gives me a glimpse of a depressingly grim red building overburdened by a heavy off-center cupola. The roof bristles with chimneys, and through the rain in the dull light of the afternoon many of the vaulted windows appear to be barred.

Again the cab veers—this time in the opposite direction, in obedience to a clang of bells, brazen, clamorous bells—and again I slide inertly across the seat. We have stopped to allow a police wagon to pass us and pull up just ahead at the south entrance to the hospital, a door beside the too-grand staircase that climbs to a tall, pretentious portico. Two men remove a stretcher from the wagon bearing a woman clad in a riding habit. Her long hair hangs in thick ropy strands. With horror I realize that the ropiness can best be accounted for by blood. The woman's eyes are shut; her face is swollen. Her arms, encased in long narrow sleeves of a smoky gray, are folded, her fingers enlaced tightly atop the crown of a black silk hat that rests upon her bosom.

The men carry her inside. My driver climbs down from his box and starts to follow. But, turning, he leans in over me, says a gruffly concerned "Still alive, I reckon?" and removes THIS MAN IS EDGAR A. POE THE WRITER from my shirt. Taking my identity with him, he disappears into the building.

Thirty-nine

The human mind, no less than the body, may fall prey to dismemberment.

—"The Paradis Cure"

My name is C. Auguste Dupin.

In his tales based upon three of my more flamboyant investigations, Edgar Poe ascribes my prowess as a *détective* to unusual powers of ratiocination. Doubtless he has his reasons. I shall not attempt to understand *his* arcane profession. But the truth is, I think, more pedestrian. I am a good, a sympathetic, listener. People find it easy to talk to me, to confide in me, frequently answering questions I have not even thought to ask.

So acute a listener am I that I have been accused of mind-reading. Again the truth is simpler. Speech is not merely vocal. The face expresses much, and the hands. The body has its own language. These, not minds, are what I read.

There is also, finally, intuition.

Eh bien, enough about my modest skills.

Other business having brought me to America early in the autumn of 1849, I seized the opportunity to pursue the strange case of the Poe brothers.

The murder (or not) of Henry Poe in his rooms in the Rue de la Gaîté remained unsolved. The police would not even acknowledge my inquiries; they dislike being reminded of their little failures.

The manner of Edgar's departure from Paris also awaited explanation. I did not—could not—credit Count Dionisio di Tangeri's asseveration that Edgar Poe had vanished right before his eyes. And yet his lovely daughter Maia's disappearance, on the same date as Poe's, is indisputable. And the cavalry officer with whom she was to go riding is listed to this day as a deserter.

The effect upon the Count of this extraordinary concurrence of events was profound. He never again practiced hypnotism. Before long he was living in the twilight world of the opium addict.

Edgar Poe returned to America—so much for vanishing—and shortly thereafter published "How the Yaanek Lost Their God,"* which, as every reader of his *oeuvre* knows, relates a sequence of supernatural events following the shattering of a heathen idol in the unexplored uplands of the Malaysian island of Panchatan.

Edgar continued to publish tales of a general excellence—some of them, gratifyingly, about myself. So I thought of him with a fair regularity and, on the occasion of my voyage to America, I determined to meet again this man whose mind was singularly congenial with my own—and, not incidentally, to try to shed light on the unexplained events in Paris.

From his New York publisher George Putnam I learned that the author, after the death of his beloved young wife, had become virtually a recluse in the village of Fordham. Putnam, however, had recently had from Philadelphia a disturbing account of a visit by Edgar to the illustrator John Sartain.

At Fordham, a Mrs. Clemm, Edgar's aunt and mother-in-law, told me that her dear "Eddie" was absent on a lecture tour in the South, where his differences with the New York and Boston literati could only enhance his standing. Mrs. Clemm further intimated that Eddie intended, while there, to woo his childhood sweetheart Elmira Shelton *née* Royster. He would soon (averred Mrs. Clemm, citing a letter from Edgar which she did not produce) return north for his "Muddy," who would make her home in Richmond with Edgar and the second Mrs. Poe.

As I had completed my business in New York, I did not await Edgar's return, but set off to follow his itinerary.

You have seen how I broke my journey at Philadelphia to learn from John Sartain the particulars of Edgar's visit to that city. Alarmed, I proceeded to Richmond and my interview with the handsome widow Shelton. Her news sent me on to Port Walthall, to meet the steamboat *Columbus* on its next call there. After a show of

* Not in the Poe canon. (Editor's note)

reluctance, the captain, one Pompey Gliddon, informed me that my quarry had disembarked at Baltimore in a lamentable state of inebriation.

I sailed on the return journey. When we docked, Captain Gliddon recommended a lodging house run by a cousin in Amity Street. To this I repaired for a good day's sleep after a fruitless nocturnal round of Baltimore's more unsavory taverns, a search I resumed the next night to better avail.

By the evening of Thursday, October 4, 1849, Dr. John J. Moran, the young superintendent of Washington College Hospital, had gone some forty hours without sleep. At eight-fifty p.m.—it was another cold, blustery night—he flung himself fully clothed onto his bed. His wife, Mary, removed his shoes.

"You must be exhausted, darling."

"Utterly."

"Your two mystery cases? Are they any better?"

"The woman is dying. Fractured skull and pelvis, double compound fracture of the left femur, and God knows what internal injuries."

"Poor thing."

"Her mare caught a hoof in a chuck-hole and fell and rolled over on her. It broke a foreleg and was mercifully put down by the first policeman on the scene," said Dr. Moran, a frown creasing his pink-cheeked, boyish face. "The young woman was . . . less fortunate."

"Who is she?"

"No one has reported her missing, so we don't know yet."

"And the man? There is some hope?"

"The odds are against."

"An accident victim too?"

"He shows the effects of exposure, his breathing is short and oppressed, his pulse intermittent. There are signs of nervous collapse." After another frown, Dr. Moran went on, "I would have said *delirium tremens*, but there was no smell of alcohol on his breath. The tremors *are* pronounced, and his partial amnesia is symptomatic. Still, he has not been shrieking and flailing at phantoms. And the incoherent ramblings could be caused by the fever."

"Had he no identification?"

"There was only a card brought in by the hackie, but *that* was misplaced while we were dealing with the woman."

Mary sighed. "Then you've no idea who he is either?"

"I did not say that. We've had no end of ideas since he was admitted yesterday. In his conscious intervals, he claimed to be a Mr. Phidias Peacock of this city, and he supplied three addresses in as many hours. We learned that he was unknown at the first, a boarding house run by a Mrs. Gliddon—and then Sister Sparrow found the card among the dying woman's possessions."

"The woman's? How very odd," said Mary.

"Confusion is no stranger to this hospital," said Dr. Moran dryly. "At any rate, when we showed the card to him, the patient began at once to argue with himself."

"With himself?"

"Had you been there, Mary, you would have wagered your patrimony that the patient was two distinct people."

"I have no patrimony."

"Your sole flaw," smiled Dr. Moran.

"I assume Phidias Peacock was not the name on the card?"

"No, but that did not prevent Peacock from fighting to exist. 'You are so transparent,' he reproved his other self. 'You simply wish to be famous. Believe me, anonymity has its advantages.' "

Dr. Moran was reading these words from a note-book. He turned the page. " 'That may be,' the patient replied. His voice was different now, softer and more melodious. 'But it does not alter my identity.' They argued—and with each exchange the Phidias Peacock voice became fainter, less sure of itself, the Poe voice firmer, more obviously in command."

"Poe? Like the writer?"

"He *is* the writer," said Dr. John J. Moran.

"The patient is Edgar A. Poe?"

"So said the card, and so said his cousin Judge Neilson Poe this morning. But Poe the writer is a widower, I believe?"

"Yes. He married his niece—no, his first cousin—when she was very young. And she *died* young, of consumption. Three or four years ago."

"My patient Poe says he is married, and his wife is in Richmond, and he must go to New York to bring his mother south to live with them."

"His mother died when he was a babe," Mary said. "How much do you know about Edgar Poe?"

"About his work, nothing. I have no time to read fiction or poetry, Mary. About his life . . . only what is common knowledge, some of it rather unpleasant."

"I should not give *that* much credence. The Northern literati spread dreadful falsehoods about Poe's life because he prints dreadful truths about their writing."

"So it's all baseless innuendo?"

"Oh, not the part about the abject poverty. He tried to support the family with his pen, you see."

"And a writer cannot earn enough?"

"Apparently not. If Edgar Poe cannot do it."

"You have read his work?"

"Every story. Every poem. He is one of my favorites."

"Did he ever write of a character named Phidias Peacock?"

"I am almost certain he did not."

"It was too much to hope it would be that simple. Or a woman with the rather fanciful name of Nolie Mae Tangerie?"

Mary's smile was broad. "As in *noli me tangere*?"

"He did not?"

"I wish he had! Poe is very inventive naming his characters. Hugh Tarpaulin. Mr. Windenough. Thingum Bob, Esq. I should love to read a tale by Poe about a woman named Nolie Mae Tangerie."

"He seems to think this woman is in grave difficulty. Is trapped somewhere."

"Trapped? Literally cannot get out?"

"It is unclear. She seems to be trapped there, but still *here*."

"Now, that sounds like something Edgar Poe might have written," said Mary, and recited: " 'Is *all* that we see or seem but a dream within a dream?' "

"What an extraordinary notion. Not just 'see' but '*seem*,' " said Dr. Moran. "It has a way of resounding."

"A whole volume of metaphysical speculation," said Mary, "in just thirteen words—all of them a single syllable except one. But I've changed the subject, haven't I?"

"You have, Mary. It's what I love best about you—apart from your freckles—the way your mind darts. Can you hazard a guess why he would call this imaginary woman Nolie Mae Tangerie?"

"Mmm, the untouchable. It has been said of Edgar Poe—unfairly, I think, if you read his work—that his love for women is rather more spiritual than physical. That isn't very helpful, is it? Perhaps he will tell you himself."

"Perhaps," said Dr. Moran doubtfully.

Mary brought him a cup of herbal tea.

He stretched, stifled a yawn, waved the steaming cup away. "Believe me, I shall sleep."

But, to his frustration, he did not. Once or twice he dozed off, only to return with a start to wakefulness—and worry. No more than a short passage and a staircase separated him from the tower wing where lay dying the nameless woman and, one floor below, the stricken author of poems and tales which, to his regret, Dr. Moran had never had the time to read. A nursing sister was stationed outside each of their doors; in an emergency Dr. Moran would be summoned. Still, sleep eluded him. Mary was right. He should have taken the tea. Or a narcotic, just a light dose, enough to put him under for a few hours.

The bell clanged at the night entrance downstairs. There followed an utter, an eerie—later Dr. Moran would tell his wife a *preternatural*—silence. The bell clanged again; again it was succeeded by a soundless void.

Where was the night porter?

When the bell clanged a third time, Dr. Moran rose, hurried downstairs and across the dimly lit hall, and unlocked the door.

The slender man who stood in the doorway tipped his hat. He carried a malacca stick and wore spectacles that looked black in the gas light.

"Yes?" Dr. Moran said brusquely. The man appeared sound of wind and limb. What did he want at this hour?

"My name is C. Auguste Dupin." The accent, like the suggestion of a bow, was French.

"Is there some problem? Are you ill?" Dr. Moran demanded.

"I have come to inquire about, and when possible to see, my old friend Edgar Poe."

"Mr. Poe can receive no visitors."

"I understand—the hour is late. I shall wait. I have come a long way."

"You do *not* understand, sir. His condition is grave. Even his cousin Judge Poe was permitted but the briefest of visits—just long enough to identify the patient."

It began at that moment to rain.

"You had better come in," said Dr. Moran grudgingly, and led the visitor to the receiving room. Still grudgingly, he said, "You can stay here until the rain lets up. There is a cab stand at the bottom of the hill."

"Is he dying?"

"We are doing all that can be done."

"I must see him."

"That is not possible, sir. I bid you good night."

Two hours later it was still raining and Dr. Moran was still awake. He rose and tucked his nightshirt into a pair of rumpled trousers. He started for the passage to the tower stairs, then stopped and headed in the opposite direction.

The receiving room was empty.

Could he have slept after all, and dreamed the Frenchman with the odd name? But he never had dreams, or at least none he remembered.

At the night door the key was turned in the lock. The porter, reading a magazine in his cubicle, said he had opened for no one, coming or going.

With a shrug Dr. Moran returned to the east tower and mounted the stairs.

Sister Sparrow was dozing at her station outside Edgar Poe's room. Through the open door, Dr. Moran heard voices.

"How long have you been sleeping?" he asked Sparrow.

She stirred; her head jerked up. "I must have nodded for a moment. I'm sorry, Doctor."

Dr. Moran heard Poe say, "She is somewhere in this building. I'm sure of it."

"But you saw her only once, a long time ago, the last day *anyone* saw her. You think you would know her now?" This voice Dr. Moran recognized as the Frenchman's.

"She hasn't changed. She is as she was the day I met her leaving her father's house to go riding. She is here, I tell you!" Poe shouted. "She is here, Dupin. Will you not understand? She is in desperate trouble. Oh God—her hat! Find her for me, Dupin. Find her."

"You knew he was permitted no visitors," Dr. Moran told Sister Sparrow angrily.

"I did. I do. Your instructions were most explicit."

"Then how dare you disobey them?"

"But," insisted the nurse, "I most certainly have *not* disobeyed them. The patient may be speaking, but only to himself."

Dr. Moran heard the Frenchman say, "If she is here in this building, I will find her."

"Hurry, Dupin. Hurry."

Later Dr. Moran would tell Mary—but no one else—that he heard footsteps, rapid footsteps, approaching the doorway from within, and instinctively he stepped out of the way. Yet no one passed him. Then, he would tell Mary—but no one else—he heard the phantom footsteps receding along the passage.

Dr. Moran entered the room and in the dim glow of the lamp looked at his patient. Edgar Poe was sleeping deeply. Dr. Moran ran to the stairs. Above and below him there was only silence.

Forty

There are few persons, even among the calmest thinkers, who have not occasionally been startled into a vague yet thrilling half-credence in the supernatural, by *coincidences* of so seemingly marvellous a character that, as *mere* coincidences, the intellect has been unable to receive them.

—"The Mystery of Marie Rogêt"

The night before the lighthouse sank into the sea, Edgar dreamed of Maia Tangeri.

On horseback, she was racing up a cliffside path above a desolate, endless beach beneath a flaming sky. The saffron-colored sea heaved, boiled, flung itself upon the sand. The cliff trembled, swayed—

Edgar woke. The lighthouse was shaking. He heard the grinding of stone on stone. He heard an awesome roar, as if a gigantic mouth had opened in the sea, as if the sea were swallowing itself.

In the dawn light he saw cracks in the massive walls. The cracks widened, became fissures. Chair, table, bookcase—all juddered in a wild dance across the pitching floor. Books flew about the room like a flock of uncaged birds. What had been a snug apartment built into the shaft of the lighthouse was now hardly more than a platform suspended perilously in space.

Edgar raced for the spiral staircase and plunged down. His only thought was to get himself out of that fracturing column of stone, and the Devil take the rest. No time to worry about his books, his boots, his raincape, his—oh God!

His manuscript!

In three months at the lighthouse he had almost completely re-written his novel about the end of the world. Another day or two would have seen it finished. It was, Edgar knew, his masterpiece.

He turned and raced up again, past the living quarters, open now to the saffron sky. He could bundle his manuscript, he thought, in the oilcloth that covered the logbook table. The door to the clockworks room stood ajar, askew. He shouldered his way inside. Chains swung wildly about, pendular weights oscillated with the swaying of the great stone shaft, heavy ropes whipped through the air. Before he could reach the logbook table, a hundred-pound pendulum hurtled at him. He threw himself flat—and saw his manuscript scattered on the floor. The pendulum swung back. He heard the sound of a hundred millstones grinding. A section of curving wall fell away. Helpless, he watched the pages of his manuscript rise and flutter past his outstretched hands and through the emptiness where the wall had been.

He began to crawl back toward the door—a door previously ajar and askew, now absent. He picked his way across the splintering floor with the caution, and the haste, of an Alpinist traversing a field of crevasses.

At last he was at the doorway, at the stairhead, on the steep spiral itself. Down he plunged, and down, vaguely grateful for the helical form that afforded him overhead protection from the chips and chunks and solid slabs of masonry hurtling past him on every side, vaguely grateful for the sturdy iron construction that still held while the whole tower dilapidated. The staircase tossed him from side to side before disgorging him in a welter of crates and casks and debris that used to be the storeroom. He clambered through it, to where a jagged hole gaped in place of the iron door.

Outside on the landing stage, Edgar felt the air crackle. His hair stood on end. White water hurled him back against the shuddering wall. When it receded, he saw the row-boat, half sunk, or half afloat. This, somehow, did not surprise Edgar. Every thing around it, man's creation and God's, lighthouse and shoals and the very sea, was wrenched and riven by a mighty submarine earthquake—yet the row-boat sat steady and low in the water, quite undisturbed.

Edgar swam the few strokes to it, grasped the gunwale.

The boat was no longer half swamped. He saw instead casks and bundles, neatly stowed fore and aft; saw a small mast and a furled sail; saw, resting on the nearly dry bottom of the boat—the Shard.

He had little recollection of rowing past the disintegrating breakwater into the tumult of the open sea, but he would never forget the broad circle of spray, the ironic rainbow, the black and terrifying shape of the whirlpool. Into this vortex the lighthouse plunged.

Maia Tangeri stood at the taffrail of the steamship *Columbus*, Captain Pompey Gliddon commanding, out of Marseilles and bound for Panchatan.

Sunset had turned the sea a deep rose, in which the wake of the *Columbus* streamed. They had been making excellent time since leaving Singapore, where Monk had joined the ship four days ago. And of course, with Monk's arrival, exit Charles. Poor dear Charles, deserting from the cavalry to accompany her on her mad quest, for no better reason than passion—how naive he had been. But how useful! A woman does not journey halfway around the world on her own. At Singapore, Charles by now would have recovered from the effects of the drug. He was young, perhaps he would learn. *Caveat amator.*

The steady throb of the *Columbus*'s engines was punctuated by the slam of a door as Monk came out on deck. He carelessly kissed Maia's lips, and as he stepped back she raised a hand to her straw bonnet in an apparently unstudied movement that accentuated the contour of her bosom.

"You do that very well," Monk said with his cold grin.

Maia turned from him and drummed her fingers on the taffrail. She watched the tall black silhouette of a Chinese junk glide slowly across the disappearing rim of the sun.

"Impatient?" Monk asked.

"You know I am."

Monk leaned on the rail, his left profile to her, the side with the scar. For all Maia knew, he meant to call attention to it. That infuriating male smugness: if the scar repels you, leave; but you won't; you need me.

What a contrast to Will Henry he was! Both adventurers, both strivers, but Will's striving was that of the moth for the star, of Man for the Unattainable, while Monk's was simply the implacable pursuit of lucre.

A time would come, and soon, when she must choose between them. But for the moment Monk was right; she needed him.

Again she raised a hand to her straw bonnet.

"You needn't do that for my benefit," said Monk. "And I trust you know better than to do it for anyone else."

Insufferable! When she raised a hand this time, it was with the intention of slapping his smug face, but at that moment a voice rang out from the crow's nest.

"Small craft to starboard!"

Maia followed Monk along the promenade deck, half running to keep up with his long strides. Daylight was almost gone. Passengers and crew crowded the rail. Suddenly the *Columbus* changed her heading.

Did Maia see a speck far off against the darkening sea? She pointed. Monk saw nothing.

In the tropical night Maia, peering at the fast-fading speck that might have been a sail, felt an inexplicable sentiment so intense that it left her trembling.

For a full hour after sundown, Captain Pompey Gliddon searched, in hopes that a glimpse of the sail might be caught against the phosphorescence of the sea. Then for a further hour he lay hove-to in the middle of the search area, to allow the tiny craft a chance to make her own way to the *Columbus*'s side. Periodically the lookout aloft hailed, but there was no response. At last the engines throbbed again into life, and the ship resumed course for Panchatan.

On the walk aft to the dining saloon, Monk commented on the obvious difficulty, the near impossibility, of maritime rescue at night. "Still, the law of the sea is that the effort must be made," he said. "If nothing else, our supper will be the more welcome."

"You go, then, Monk," Maia said. "I—I'm really not very hungry."

Forty-one

At no time on Friday, October 5, Dr. John J. Moran would tell his wife, Mary, did Edgar Poe "converse" with the Chevalier C. Auguste Dupin or any other creature of his imagination.

"It would have been a restful day for him, if the Monk had not looked in," Dr. Moran said.

"Professor Monkur disturbed your patient?" J.C.S. Monkur, Professor of the Theory and Practice of Medicine, was senior physician at Washington College Hospital.

"The Monk always disturbs my patients. But this time at least he concurred in my diagnosis. Edgar Poe is suffering from excessive nervous prostration and loss of nerve power resulting from exposure and inflammation of the brain."

"Then it is not *delirium tremens?*"

"Probably not, although the hallucinations can be similar."

"I thought he was no longer talking with phantoms."

"That was yesterday. Tonight the Frenchman returned."

Mary smiled. "You almost seem to mean that literally."

Dr. Moran's usually frank and steady gaze wavered. He looked at the unremarkable doorway, then out the window at the unedifying darkness.

"John?"

"Those confounded footsteps! I heard them again, Mary."

"You are pushing yourself too hard, dear."

As superintendent at the hospital, Dr. John J. Moran was always on call.

"I think," he said after a while, "I would have heard those footsteps under any circumstances."

Mary slipped a hand into his. "Tell me about it, John."

"Sister Sparrow was on duty. Poe had been asking for someone named Doo-*pan* all evening, she said. A little after seven p.m. he became violent and she needed help restraining him. Just as she was telling me he had been calm since then, Poe called out, 'Dupin!' That was when I heard the footsteps, Mary. Confound it, I heard them! As if someone were hurrying past me into the room."

"Did Sister Sparrow hear any thing?"

"I did not ask. My attention was riveted on Poe. He was sitting up then, the first time since his admission, and smiling. He shouted, 'Dupin, Dupin, I have found her!'

"Then his Dupin voice said: 'Yes, my dear Edgar, so have I. She is, as you suspected, here in this building.'

"But the Poe voice went on as if the Dupin voice had not spoken. 'She is right here in Nieuw Aidenn.' "

"New Aden?" Mary asked. "Where on earth—"

"That's what Dupin wanted to know. Poe spelled it for him. The N-i-e-u-w is Dutch; the A-i-d-e-n-n I'd never heard of."

"Oh, but I have," said Mary. "Poe used that name in 'The Raven.' To rhyme with 'laden.' I think it must be a variant of Eden."

"If so, this Nieuw Aidenn is optimistically named," Dr. Moran observed. "From what Poe said, it seems to be a rather seedy seaport, the main European settlement on the island of Panchatan in the South China Sea."

"And Poe believes himself to be there?"

"Well, I missed the next hour of the conversation. There was an emergency upstairs. The woman was sinking fast. We expected her to die. But her will to live is enormous, and she rallied. When I could finally return to Poe's room, they were still talking."

"Sister Sparrow had been listening?"

"Sister Sparrow," Dr. Moran said, "was seated outside the door crocheting. The patient, she told me, had been speaking sporadically with an imaginary friend. I asked her what about, but she seemed not to understand the question. 'He has not been agitated, Doctor,' she assured me. I could have strangled her.

"I hurried into the room in time to hear Dupin say—"

"That is," smiled Mary, "to hear Poe in his Dupin voice say."

"Yes, certainly. He said, 'You must get on with your story, Edgar. Time and tide, as the proverb has it, tarry—'

"But Poe said, 'I am not sure that I wish to.'

"There was a longish silence, then Dupin said, 'Is it because you fear the end may be something you would rather avoid?'

" 'Perhaps,' said Poe in an uncertain voice.

" 'But it is *your* story. *You* are telling it. The ending is entirely for *you* to decide. Come, resume where you left off. You had been at sea for several days in the small boat when you saw the steamship. . . .' "

I shouted until I grew hoarse. I jumped up and down, rocking the little boat dangerously. The wind rose. I tried to turn the boat into it, but the sail luffed. It was full dark when the ship passed no more than a mile away. I could see her lights a long time after that. Then the night swallowed them.

Three days later, I drank the last of my water; ate my last rock-hard biscuit. I felt resigned, more than ready to surrender to the inevitable. I was too weak to row, and my sail was in tatters. I drifted, what remained of the sail protecting me from the savage sun. I have no idea how much time passed. But one morning bright-plumaged land birds flew past. In the afternoon I fished a leafy branch from the water. Just before night fell I saw a faint gray-green smudge on the horizon.

Forty-two

I have passed this day in a species of ecstasy that I find it impossible
to describe.

—untitled tale, posthumously called "The Lighthouse"

The Nieuw Aidenn port agent for the Compagnie Générale des
Phares d'Outre-Mer was a hulking, bald, bullet-headed man who,
according to the sign suspended over his door, also represented two
steamship companies, a dealer in tropical hardwoods, and a world-
renowned consortium of London insurers.

When I entered, he barely looked up. "We can settle no more
tidal-wave insurance claims until instructions arrive from London,"
he said.

"I am Edgar Poe," I said. "The lighthouse keeper?"

"How extraordinary. We had given you up for lost, like your
predecessor. You are a fortunate man, Mr. Poe."

"And my predecessor?" I asked.

"He *is* lost—no matter what rumors you may hear to the contrary.
You have the logbook?"

"What rumors have you heard about Will Henry?"

"That he has been seen at a settlement in the interior. It is not
possible."

"Why not?"

"Because ever since the Yaanek troubles, people do not go to
Eidolon, they flee from it. The place is dying. Is dead. You have the
logbook, Mr. Poe?"

"Eidolon," Mary asked, "is a *place*?"

"Apparently. Does it strike a chord?"

"There is a line in one of Poe's poems* about 'an Eidolon called

* Mrs. Moran refers to the poem "Dream-Land." (Editor's note)

Night.' But that was not a place; it was some kind of fearful ruler."

"In any case," said Dr. Moran, "the word is Greek. I looked it up. It means an image, or a phantom. Cognate with 'idol,' most likely. I couldn't find any Yoneck."

"Yaanek—double 'a.' Those are a tribe in Panchatan who worshiped a stone idol. Poe wrote two stories about them. I wonder— might the settlement have been named for the idol?"

"Perhaps. Poe did not say."

"Well, what *did* he say? For pity's sake, John, do go on!"

"You have the logbook, Mr. Poe?"

"I'm afraid not. The lighthouse was utterly destroyed."

"The logbook was your responsibility to save. You saved *yourself.*"

"By a miracle. With only the clothes on my back."

"How did you reach Panchatan?" the port agent asked.

I told him about the small boat, half sunk, or half afloat.

He assured me there was no such vessel in the lighthouse inventory. "Moreover," he said sternly, "you do not look like a man who crossed two hundred miles of sea in an open boat."

He had a point. My clothing seemed in good repair. I needed no shave. My hair felt combed.

Nor could I offer as evidence the boat itself. It had brought me safely to land, and then simply disappeared—and the Shard with it.

I cannot account for any of this, Dupin.

"Would you be attempting some diddle?" the agent asked.

I took umbrage. Never mind my exact words.

He was unmoved. "We cannot be too careful. Phares d'Outre-Mer, you see, is required to pay substantial indemnities to those of its employees who return from the dead. Not that this has ever happened in my experience."

"I returned from the lighthouse, not from the dead."

"We listed you on the books as dead. But now you are here. I must apply to head office for instructions."

"But it will be months before you get an answer."

"It is not *I* who claim to have returned from the dead. Good day, Mr. Poe."

I found work stripping the fitments from a small schooner that the tidal wave had driven aground near Nieuw Aidenn's only hotel worthy of the name.

At noon of my second day on the job I heard a woman's voice call from the hotel verandah:

"Monsieur Poe! Edgar Poe!"

I was rendered breathless on recognizing the lovely voice and beguiling accent, not quite French, not quite Italian, of Maia Tangeri. Climbing the wide stairs, I went to the table where she sat alone.

She looked no less beautiful—yet (such was my unworthy thought) somehow more attainable—than in Paris. As in Paris, she was dressed for riding: *habit d'amazone* and a *chapeau de forme* which, after signaling to the waiter, she clapped more firmly upon her blond head.

But what had brought her to Panchatan?

"What brings you to Panchatan?" she asked.

"I am searching for my brother."

My words surprised me—so much that I barely noticed, at the time, the appraising look she gave me.

Our drinks came: tall, cool, the color of sunrise. We touched glasses, and her hand brushed mine. Something I can only describe as a galvanic current surged between us, and it would charge all that followed.

"One hears stories of a man who speaks fluent French and English who went upriver," she said. "I believe that man could be Will Henry—your brother."

I dared not let my hopes surge. "Phares d'Outre-Mer have heard such rumors. Yet they list Will Henry unequivocally as lost—dead."

You often speak, Dupin, of the language of the body. For the first time I fully understood what you meant. Maia Tangeri recoiled from my words, as from a blow, and I knew that she and my brother had been lovers.

At that hour men crowded the verandah, drinking hard, talking loud—and casting covetous glances at my companion and envious ones at me. A tall fellow, his features shaded by a broad-brimmed hat, emerged from the hotel and made for our table, or seemed to, then abruptly changed course and disappeared around the corner of the L-shaped verandah.

Maia Tangeri sat forward in her rattan chair, as if she might rise, as if she might flee.

She said, "This is no place to talk."

Her small room faced the harbor, but rolled-down rattan blinds hid the chaos left in the wake of the tidal wave. In the narrow bands of sunlight, her eyes glowed like glass.

"Will you go upriver?"

"If there is any possibility of finding Henry, I must."

"Then take me with you."

"Into the wilds of Panchatan? Are you mad?"

"I can help. I know Will Henry—in ways you do not."

"Doubtless," I said dryly.

"I know about cometary stone too. I've read every word written about it."

"Many of which," I rejoined, "were written by me."

"*And* I have a fair idea of its value—something I suspect you have not."

"Value?"

"Yes, Edgar, value! Upriver in Yaanek country there may be more of it, maybe dozens of shards like the one I—the one we already know about. This is the Orient, Edgar, where pulverized rhinoceros horn goes for a king's ransom. What price then for a substance that *does* have unearthly powers?"

"So that is why you are here?"

"That is why your brother is here—if he is here. And you? Does the chance of such a fortune not tempt you?"

"Very much," I said frankly. "I have been poor all my life."

Did a shadow pass across her lovely face?

"I too am tempted," she said. "And yet—to sell such a rare and wondrous thing as if it were no more than mere gold or diamonds? Even if it is not as sacred as the Yaanek believe, must it not have some higher purpose?"

"What purpose?"

"Who can say? But we shall never find out, you and I, unless we go upriver together."

"Then," Dr. Moran told his wife, "they began—not Poe and the woman but Poe and Dupin—to discuss this 'shard.' Presumably the same 'shard' that vanished with Poe's little boat."

"And what is it, would you guess, John?"

"Some sort of talisman. Here, I've written it down. See what you make of it."

DUPIN: Did you ever tell her that you had experienced the shard's magic yourself?

POE: You mean the events in Paris? No.

D: I mean at the lighthouse. Do you not remember? You enclosed the shard in your hand, and you wished.

P: I remember, but—

D: You wished that your brother be still alive. And in Panchatan you heard rumors that he is. You wished to encounter again the captivating Maia Tangeri, and so you have. You wished also to complete your tale about the end of the world, and you did.

P: The manuscript was lost.

D: None the less, your wish was granted. Another of your wishes was for everlasting fame, and it will be yours.

P: With Rufus Griswold as my literary executor? Come now, Dupin. He will blacken my reputation at every opportunity.

D: Precisely so! Griswold has always envied you. His malice will accomplish what praise and puffery never could. He will make you notorious: Poe, the evil genius. By the time he is finished, the world will clamor to read every word you ever wrote—my countrymen no less than yours.

P: But—

D: It is a certainty.

P: I wished . . . I wished also to remain eternally young.

D: (*removing his green-tinted spectacles and staring at them*) To never grow old—ah! and who would not wish—

Mary Moran interrupted her husband. "You say the Frenchman removed his spectacles? You *saw* him do that?"

"No, of course not. How could I have?" said Dr. John Moran after a moment's hesitation. "I only meant that his tone of voice seemed to *suggest* that he removed his spectacles. At any rate, he changed the subject, saying, 'Get on with your narrative, my dear Edgar. The hour grows late.'"

The uncharted interior of the island of Panchatan was no place for a woman, and I was again telling Maia so when she bowed her head, removed her black silk hat, reached into it—and placed in my hand a hard, sharp-edged object a few degrees warmer than the ambient temperature.

For a long time we gazed at each other, the Shard between us.

No, Dupin, I did not ask the question which, to you, must seem so obvious. I think I may be forgiven for that. I find it harder to forgive myself for all that was to follow. Or was my role in it inseparable from hers? Or did I accept, even then, that when we journeyed together upriver what would happen would happen?

We did not speak of the Shard, nor of the Yaanek and their idol, nor of any thing.

Swiftly, hungrily, finally—for I had the uncanny conviction I had known her half my life—we fell into each other's arms.

Forty-three

Over the Mountains
Of the Moon,
Down the Valley of the Shadow,
Ride, boldly ride.

—"Eldorado"

It appeared that Maia was not without funds, for she hoped to hire
a boat. But we soon found that no craft suitable for the journey
upriver had escaped the fury of the tidal wave. Accordingly, through
the good offices of the Phares d'Outre-Mer port agent—did he wish
to rid himself of me?—we arranged for the hire of two Malay porters
and as many horses, and the purchase of what gear we would need
and, to err on the safe side, victuals for a full month.

From the little I had read on the subject, I had conceived of a
tropical rain forest as so dense and luxuriant that one had literally
to hack a path for himself. But not so—not, at any rate, in the forest
of Panchatan. Unimpeded by the undergrowth I had anticipated,
our Malays were indefatigable walkers even with heavy loads upon
their heads, and they set a steady pace for the horses Maia and I
rode, sometimes within view of the saffron-hued river, sometimes
leaving it for hours on end. The welcome lack of undergrowth I
attributed to the fact that no sunshine could penetrate the thick,
unbroken canopy spread high overhead by great ebony, teak, and
mahogany trees.

The atmosphere was, as a consequence, oppressive—so still and
sultry that we might have been walking our horses at the bottom
of a deep and stagnant sea, and so redolent of decay that I expected
at any moment to come upon the decomposing remains of animals
on which perhaps sat fat and torpid vultures, their beaks all bloody.

And yet—and yet! To dispel such gloomy thoughts I had merely
to observe the grace with which my companion sat her horse, right

knee hooked easily around the pommel of what in your country, Dupin, is called a *monte à l'amazone*; I had but to hear the music of her voice in even the most casual utterance; had but to observe the excitement in her smoke-gray eyes as our passage flushed a bird from cover, its wings a blur of iridescent green in the jungle half-light; had but to see the smile upon her face each day when the roar of the rain began, like that of railroad cars through an endless tunnel, though no rain fell until I had counted—slowly, in the portentous voice of a stage magician, Maia joining in the final counting—to thirty, whereupon the rain finally penetrated the dense foliage overhead. Maia would remove her hat and laugh, and afterwards wring out with both her hands her long blond hair, so sensuous a sight that at such times I wished our journey would never end.

Our little expedition proceeded in this fashion: the older Malay first, then Maia side-saddle upon a bay gelding and I astride a black, then the younger Malay bringing up the rear. Fastened at my saddle-bow was our only firearm, a lightweight rifle of Swedish manufacture very like the Hall carbine I had all but slept with at West Point. I shall have more, alas, to say about this presently.

Late in the afternoon of the sixth day the way grew steeper, and as we toiled upwards—our horses' hooves eerily soundless on the spongy ground—tendrils of mist drifted toward us. The older Malay raised his left arm. He turned to call something to the younger, a look of obvious concern on his wizened face. Then the fog came at us like a wall. I sat my horse in a ghostly world of white, and was startled when, like an apparition, Maia leaned close to grasp my hand.

"Why do you stop, John?" Mary Moran asked her husband.

"That was where his account was interrupted last night. The bells of the police wagon woke you?"

"I slept like a log."

"There was a knifing outside a tavern at Fell's Point. They brought the victim here."

"Of course. We get *all* the drunken sailors. Well, someone has to, I suppose."

"I'm afraid I hadn't much solicitude for this one. I just sewed him up as fast as I could and raced back to the tower. I found Poe sweating profusely. Before I could measure his temperature, however, he began to shiver with cold. I covered him with another blanket. His lips trembling, he said:

" 'Who would have thought that tropical heat could give way to arctic cold in a few seconds? Yet that was what happened when the fog enshrouded us.' "

Despite my exhortations the Malays would proceed no farther, and when after an hour the fog had not dispersed, they bent their steps back the way they had come.

We transferred to our saddle-bags the supplies they had left behind—an extra blanket, some lengths of rope, rice cakes and dried fish. As we worked, I saw tiny droplets of moisture glistening like diamonds on Maia's eyelashes.

Impulsively, to make amends for letting her down (though what could I have done?), I placed the Shard in her hand.

"You are giving it to me?"

"Say rather I am returning it."

At dusk the air became a silvery liquescence not without beauty —but it was a beauty that left us damp, cold, and miserable, so that when I say we spent the night in each other's arms you will know that we had no other desire than to share the warmth of our bodies.

Morning, except for a creature of the night like yourself, Dupin, is a time of restored spirits.

This was particularly true of Maia Tangeri, as I knew from five days of waking beside her. She would throw back her saddle blanket and rise from the jungle floor as if she had slept in the finest of half-tester beds upon a feather mattress under an eiderdown quilt. Her eyes would glow with eagerness as she made what toilette she could in the wilderness, and even more as she saddled the bay for the day's journey. To mount side-saddle is an operation that cannot be accomplished with the same verve as leaping astride, but Maia made it seem so. The beginning of her day, in short, was a time of great enthusiasm.

But not this day. Despite the mist, which had not abated overnight, I myself on setting out felt a surge of anticipation, as if I knew something of great moment would soon occur. Whistling one of my friend Frederick W. Thomas's well-known tunes, I expected Maia, as she usually did, to hum in harmony. But she rode at my side in silence. Her gloom was as palpable as the fog grasping us in its cold embrace, and I ascribed the one to the other. I was thus doubly heartened when finally we climbed into clear air.

I reined up and sat marveling at the view behind us, where, under the pellucid blue of the morning sky, lay banks of cloud so apparently solid that one might imagine we had walked here upon them. Ahead and far below I could see the gleam of the river through the trees and, at a great distance, the dazzle of sunlight on what might have been a lake.

Maia manifested not the slightest interest.

Confronted by her now unaccountable melancholy, my own high spirits wavered, and I challenged her with forced cheerfulness to a race down the slope to the river below. Her response was a shrug. Not wishing to lose what remained of my own enthusiasm, I spurred my horse, and soon was gratified to hear her coming hard behind me. At a bend in the trail she cut the corner sharply and pulled ahead, a maneuver I did not hinder, thinking a victory would uplift her spirits.

By the time I reached her, she had dismounted and knelt at the water's edge to drink from her cupped hands. Upstream of us the broad river ran swiftly between its banks, but here it opened into a still, clear lake which reflected with remarkable clarity the widespreading branches of the India-rubber trees which now dominated the woodland. The scene had a profound effect upon me: the sudden leap of a rainbow-hued fish; the flight low across the water of a bird of asphodel-red plumage; Maia's horse slaking its thirst a short distance downstream; and Maia—beautiful Maia—for an instant so motionless that she might have been a statue carved by Phidias himself. Beholding her perfection, I could not stifle a gasp of desire.

As she rose I enclosed her in my arms. But she stiffened and drew away.

To cover if not master my chagrin, I cast about for a task to occupy me. As the carbine had been subjected for twenty-four hours to the corrosive effects of the dense fog, I took the cleaning kit from my saddle-bag and went to work. Disassembling the short-barreled rifle with the ease of an old West Point man, I spread its parts upon a blanket and one by one cleaned them with an oily rag. I had threaded the rag through the barrel when Maia, who was watching my every move, said:

"Teach me how to shoot it." Before I could answer, she added with unassailable logic, "Were some accident to befall you, I should be helpless." I nodded, and for the first time that day she seemed more like herself. Watching me reassemble the firearm, she almost smiled.

As I explained how the chamber could be removed from the barrel to serve as an emergency side-arm, it occurred to me that Maia might more easily handle the smaller weapon. Accordingly, I did not fit the chamber back into place but loaded it from my bandoleer and proffered what was now a large pistol.

"That rock yonder would make a suitable target," I suggested.

She took the pistol and backed away. "Give me the bandoleer," she said.

I stared at her, nonplussed.

She was pointing the pistol unwaveringly at my heart.

"The bandoleer—no, don't hand it to me. Toss it over there."

She retrieved the bandoleer without taking her eyes off me and walked backwards toward the bay gelding. Grasping its bridle, she led it some distance away—far enough, apparently, to feel confident of mounting with no interference from me.

Still, I tried.

She fired the instant I moved, the bullet ricocheting off the rock I had proposed as a target. As I retreated, she tucked the pistol into the waistband of her *habit d'amazone*, gripped the pommel of her saddle, mounted, whistled three piercing notes that summoned the black, and rode off with both horses at a rapid trot, only to return moments later and toss at my feet a sack of victuals and a knife before wheeling again and disappearing through the trees.

"But my dear Edgar, what did you expect?"

"Had I known what to expect, I might have forestalled it."

"Think back, my friend, to your encounter with Maia in Nieuw Aidenn."

"What about it? I heard her call from the hotel verandah, and I—"

"Indeed. *She* called to *you*—and invited you to her table and, very soon, to her room. Why? You had met only once. If we set aside 'love at first sight,' what then—"

"Come now, Dupin. How can you, a Frenchman—"

"What, I ask, did she know of you?"

"Well, er, she was familiar with my writing. We had spoken a bit of 'How the Yaanek Found Their God' and its setting."

"Just so. She knew you had knowledge of the cometary stone of Panchatan—which, by the way, other readers of your tale would assume to be fictional. Within minutes of seeing you, was she not urging you to take her into the interior? *Mon dieu*, she pulled out all the stops. A shared concern for your brother, then the promise of turning the stone into riches, then that mystical talk of a 'higher purpose.' When still you wavered, she offered up the Shard—and her lovely self. Not that the latter cost her any thing. As for the Shard, if you had not made things easy by handing it back, she could have filched it any time after she sent the Malay porters away."

"Sent them away? They deserted us!"

"By prearrangement, I wager. Would natives be frightened off by a mere fog bank? No, the fair Maia intended all along that you escort her so far and no farther."

"All along? Even while we were—"

"If it is any solace, it distressed her to have to abandon you. That, not the fog, lowered her spirits."

"Distressed or not, she did it."

"It might have been worse. If she had listened to Monk, she might have shot you."

"Monk!"

"The man on the hotel verandah who turned aside abruptly when he saw you with Maia. Clearly a confederate. And in the absence of Henry, who more likely than the shipmate you told me about, the one who shared Henry's exploits on Panchatan, the scar-faced Monk?"

"But there you must be wrong, Dupin. If it was not Henry who died in the Rue de la Gaîté, it must have been Monk."

"Must it? The bloody wreckage of the apartment contained no body. A ruse still seems plausible."

"If Henry meant to throw off pursuit and keep the Shard, it didn't work. The Shard made its way first to me, then to Maia. Explain *that*, if you please."

"You ask me to apply rational thinking to the Shard? It does not even obey natural laws, we are told. Certainly for its possessor there comes a blurring of the distinction between memory and hallucination—which, anyway, are not so different one from the other as most people think. And perhaps, as you imply, the Shard has a will of its own."

"Then the Shard could have forced Maia to act as she did?"

"A good question. One of many which might be answered, *mon vieux*, by resuming your story at the point where the wench stranded you."

"I feel so sorry for him!" Mary Moran said. "He is in love with her, isn't he?"

"It would seem so."

"The poor man—his own loves as tragic as those of his heroes." A rueful smile dimpled her cheek. "Listen to me! Sometimes I have to remind myself that none of this really happened."

Their eyes met. "No, of course not," he said.

"Did Poe go on with his story?"

"I wish I could say. But Sister Sparrow came in then and told me the dying woman was trying to speak. It seemed to have something to do with a will."

"A will?"

"Or possibly, it occurred to me, a man *named* Will."

"Occurred to you because of Poe's brother."

Dr. Moran nodded. "Yes; Poe and Maia mentioned him often enough."

"There is no Maia," Mary said.

"Indeed not; no more than there is a Dupin."

Again their eyes met, this time in an exchange of sheepish glances.

"In any event, I hastened upstairs," Dr. Moran said, "in hopes of learning who the woman was."

Someone was there, in the darkness.

At first she thought it was Phidias. But it was not Phidias's voice she heard, it was Will Henry's.

"The worst thing I ever did in my life, you ask?"

She tried to tell him she had asked nothing, but she could not speak.

"I should not like to disillusion you," he said. "You know, Will Henry could never be mistaken for an angel.

"Would you not rather hear of the strangest experience I ever had? It will be of particular interest to you, because, you see, you were part of it. And, as you have not much time, it has the advantage of being brief.

"I was hurrying through the streets of Baltimore. It had been raining. I knew, without knowing how I knew, that I would soon see my brother Edgar, whom I had not seen in years. This certainty guided my steps unerringly to an unfamiliar house in an unfamiliar street, one of a row of unremarkable brick houses of two stories with marble stoops and white front doors. Just as I raised the wrought-iron door knocker, a wind sprang up and the door burst inwards. I saw a looking glass upon a wall, and candles that flared in the gust of wind, flared and flung across the opposite wall the shadow of Edgar with your own shadow collapsing in his arms. Before I could discover how you and my brother knew each other, or even make my presence known—your scream distracted me—the shadows disappeared in darkness. By the time I fumblingly lit a match, you were gone, you and my brother both, as if you had been figments of my imagination no more corporeal than your own vanished shadows, as if you had been ghosts. But I do not believe in ghosts."

She waited for him to say more, perhaps to say why he did not believe in ghosts. But no one was there.

"Tell me, John. What did you learn from the woman?"

"I was too late. She had lapsed into a coma. It is unlikely she will ever wake. But at least she broke the spell cast upon me by Poe."

"What ever do you mean?"

"I am responsible for two hundred patients, Mary. But I have been neglecting them to listen to the delirious ramblings of one."

"You did not return to his bedside?"

"I would not allow myself to do so until I passed what remained of the night in the wards."

"But you did go back, then?"

"And found Poe entering Eidolon on foot. It seems to have been one of those river towns that support planters—in this case, India-rubber planters—in that part of the world. But it fell on hard times and the planters left—except, as is usual, for a few eccentrics, and either they were killed by the natives or the jungle swallowed them."

"Then he was quite alone there? It sounds frightening."

"Not quite alone. You see, an attempt was made on his life."

Forty-four

We stand upon the brink of a precipice. We peer into the abyss—
we grow sick and dizzy. . . . Unaccountably we remain.
—"The Imp of the Perverse"

You would expect, Dupin, that when at last I entered the town of Eidolon there would be something to mark the exact place—perhaps an abandoned watch-tower, for like all river towns of any size in the

Malay Archipelago, Eidolon had been fortified; or perhaps a dwelling still essentially intact, façade painted a cheery yellow, window panes reflecting the purple blossoms of a flowering spikenard, doors wide open as if the return of its occupants were momently expected.

But no; the jungle did not "end"; the town did not "begin." I saw first pepper vines hanging from a lintel bereft of any door, and then no further sign that man had once lived here until I came upon a low fence festooned with lianas, and then the remains of a stone wall splotched with green mold like some huge decaying molar, and next a shutter hanging askew from a glass-less window that framed a fallen roof overgrown with gingery galangal, and finally a faintly red object, rectangular in shape and as big as a tram car. I walked around it and saw an axle, an iron wheel thick with rust. It *was* a tram car, and the tracks, equally rusted and barely visible through the brush, ran down a slight incline to where sunlight gleamed on the river across which lay the domain of the Yaanek, whose idol my brother Henry had shattered some twenty years before.

"At that point," Dr. Moran told Mary, "Dupin asked him why he said twenty years, and Poe said—but here, Mary, let me read you what I've jotted down."

POE: (*reflecting a moment*) Well, it must have happened during Henry's last voyage, because Monk told us in the Whig coop that his shipmate who destroyed the idol was punished with consumption. And the year Henry returned to Baltimore suffering from consumption was 1830.

DUPIN: (*dubiously*) I see. But you say his last voyage. How can it have been that, if we know your brother was in Paris some years later?

P: Was he? I . . . do not recall just when . . .

D: You will agree that our friend Alexandre Dumas's *La Tour de Nesle* was playing? And *that* was first produced in 1832.

P: (*agitated*) It was Dumas who knew Henry in Paris. I never saw him there. That is how we came to meet, you and I.

D: You wish me to believe your brother was *not* in Paris?

P: Yes—no—you are confusing me!

D: Nothing could be further from my intentions. I wish to solve the strange case of the Poe brothers, not to confound it.

P: (*uneasily*) I suppose, when I said his last voyage, I meant his last voyage as a seaman.

D: And he made no more after 1830?

P: No, he did not. A man suffering from consumption—

D: In Paris you never mentioned that Henry suffered from consumption. What else, I wonder, did you not mention?

P: I beg your pardon!

D: (*gently*) You know, Edgar, all I have to go on is your own account of events. If I am to make any sense of them, you ought not to be . . . less than forthcoming with me.

P: (*not meeting Dupin's eyes*) I assure you—

"John, really, 'not meeting Dupin's eyes'?" said Mary with a smile. "Soon you will have Dupin filling the room with smoke from his meerschaum pipe."

"How do you know he smokes one?" Dr. Moran asked.

"Because I read the Poe stories in which he appears." Mary looked puzzled; seemed about to ask a question of her own.

"Tell me, Mary," Dr. Moran said quickly, "what do you know of the brother?"

"Henry? His full name was William Henry Leonard Poe. He was some two years Edgar's senior. By profession, a sailor; by nature, a restless man, a compulsive wanderer who wished to be a writer— as, ironically, Edgar wished to be a world traveler, for Henry wrote little and Edgar was abroad only as a schoolboy in England. Henry died young, at the same age Virginia Poe died, and of the same disease. That would have been almost—"

"Twenty years ago?"

"Yes. Oh—I see."

"And was there a strong bond between the brothers?"

"They were as close as identical twins, for all that they saw each other rarely. It has even been suggested that Edgar Poe borrowed details from his brother's life to enliven accounts of his own."

The rusted, overgrown tramway led me to the edge of the river. There it was placid and wide, most of a mile across. A wharf green with algae lay awash near the shell of a three-story building with a long verandah fronting on the water, India-rubber trees growing through its roof. As I approached the wharf—for I was hot and filthy, and it was my intention to bathe fully clothed in the river—I felt a vague sense of disquietude. I looked about. Gentle wavelets lapped the shore. A large bird rather like a gull swooped toward the water, its gray head dipping at its own saffron reflection, so that it seemed to peck itself. The head emerged, a silvery fish wriggling in its beak. The bird flew off so low across the water that it seemed in danger of colliding with its own upside-down reflection.

From this riparian scene something made me turn. Had a sound upon the verandah called itself to my attention? Had I glimpsed movement in the deep shadows of the India-rubber trees?

All at once I smiled. How like a situation I might have used in a tale of terror! The half-heard sound, the barely seen movement; the gull as symbol of the predator that, unseen, was stalking *me*. Was it not likely that, stimulated by the aura of gloom that permeated the abandoned town of Eidolon as strongly as the spicy fragrance of galangal and cloves, my well-honed powers of invention were overtaking my common sense?

And yet even as I reassured myself, the disquietude, if any thing, heightened.

I began to feel foolish. My rational self was offended. You of all people will understand, Dupin.

Determined not to let my fancy get the better of me, I removed my boots and was wading out upon the submerged wharf when, hearing again and more unmistakably a sound from the verandah, I whirled to see a tall man raising to his shoulder a Kentucky—or, more properly, a Tennessee—rifle, down whose barrel he took dead aim at me.

My initial thought, most inappropriate, was one of relief that I had not, after all, been deceived by my own imagination—and, even more, relief that the weapon to which I would fall victim was not my own, of which Maia had so effortlessly disencumbered me!

My next thought was to wonder where Maia was.

Only then did I dive into the water, and just as I did so, I heard the crack of the rifle.

Monk, intent upon framing Edgar's head in the sights, knew nothing of Maia's coming at a silent barefoot run until she shoved his arm, spoiling his aim.

She saw Edgar dive into the murky, saffron-hued water; saw the ripples spread; saw hundreds of birds explode from both banks of the river crying raucously. She looked sidelong at Monk, waiting for him to explode too. She well knew his temper, his hot blood, his reckless rages.

But when finally he spoke, it was in a soft drawl. "Why did you do that?" His eyes had a drowsy look which he thought inspired fear in men, and excitement in women.

Maia said, "I did not wish to see him die."

"But that was why I ordered you to wait inside," he said, speaking slowly, explaining as he would to a child. This hardly surprised her. He was one of those men who thought all women childlike, or even childish. "Seeing a man die is never pleasant," he told her, his eyes intent upon the water.

"Must you kill him?"

"Stranding him," said Monk patiently, "did not work. Not that I blame you for trying. I appreciate your . . . sensibilities. But you see, my dear, with both Poe brothers here, I need to shorten the odds."

A soft breeze ruffled the water. Had it been two full minutes? Could anyone stay under that long?

She watched Monk lower the rifle. "It may be," he said, "that you were right, after all, to spare yourself the sight of him being shot. Because if he has not come up by now, it is safe to assume he has drowned."

Maia continued to look at him. She said under her breath, "I wish it had been you."

Monk smiled quizzically, a smile which he believed women found irresistible. "What? I did not hear you."

"Nothing," she said.

Was she trying to goad him? To punish him? How very foolish. Monk would not give a rap how she felt. It was she who needed *him*. Monk knew how to find the place. Nothing had changed.

Nothing . . . and every thing. Remembering her magical interlude in the jungle with Edgar, Maia knew she could not bear to stay with Monk, knew she had to get away from him *now*.

She could do it. She was the better rider. Surely there would be a place upstream where she could cross the river. Over there she would find Will Henry and . . .

And bring him the dreadful news that his brother had drowned.

Her eyes filled with tears. She blinked them back—and saw, far out across the water, much farther than she would have thought possible, Edgar's head breaking the surface.

Monk raised the rifle to his shoulder and swung it in a long, smooth arc. Three hundred yards out upon the river, Edgar's head rose and fell each time he gulped air. As Monk steadied the rifle, Maia grabbed the long barrel and yanked with all her might. The rifle went spinning into the underbrush. Monk reeled across the verandah and tumbled into the water.

Maia ran inside. Where had she left her boots? Had she time enough to saddle her horse? Unlikely. Hide somewhere? Wait until he . . . he what? She found her boots. She heard Monk's heavy footsteps on the verandah. He roared her name.

She put on her left boot; would lace it later. Her right boot looked strange. It looked wrong. A liquid leathery something was rising out of it. Was that a pair of eyes? A spreading hood? The head darted, and made a sound like a kettle hissing. She felt a stab of fire in her foot. Monk came in carrying the rifle just as she screamed.

"Snake," she managed.

"I saw," Monk said.

He brought the rifle to his shoulder and fired once.

Then he stood there staring at her.

"Make it bleed," she said. "It has to bleed."

Staring at her as if he had never seen her before.

"An incision, Monk. Hurry."

No, not as if he had never seen her before. Staring as if he had seen her once too often.

"Then suck the venom out. I would do it for you, Monk. You know I would."

Staring at her and saying, "He has got away."

"Monk, I'm begging you."

He went outside. Her foot throbbed with pain. She could see it swelling. Was he going for his knife? What was taking him so long? She heard the creak of leather, heard hoofbeats. She hobbled onto the verandah. It was very bright. Her eyes hurt. She swayed, almost fell. Her saddle-bag, she had a knife in her saddle-bag.

Monk was riding off with all three horses.

She looked at her leg. It was swollen shapeless below the knee. A chill shook her. Then she was hot, hot and parched—burning. It was difficult to swallow. She saw double. She saw two tiny hummingbirds hovering before her eyes, and she reached up instinctively. On blurring wings the hummingbirds flew away. She knocked her hat off.

Her hat—she dropped to her knees, crawled to it, reached inside, felt around the band.

The Shard was cool to the touch, but her own fever could account for that. She closed her hand on it and felt at first only the inertness of a stone. Help me, she pleaded. Whatever you are, please help me.

Did she feel a tingling? It might have been because she held the Shard so tightly. Then all at once, despite her fever, she felt warmth trapped in her fist and she was seized by a wild surge of hope.

But when she opened her hand, it was empty.

Forty-five

... from the gray ruins of memory a thousand tumultuous recollections are startled. ...

—"Berenice"

There are landscapes in the nightmares of even the most rational of men so inimical that they seem to preclude the possibility of human habitation under their baleful skies. Wading from the water, I found myself in such a place.

I stood not, as might have been expected, on the bank of a river but upon a surf-tormented shore at the edge of a shoreless sea, under a night sky aflame with the light of a comet that spanned half the zodiac, ten times brighter than the full moon. The tide was out, the sand black. I saw outcroppings of rock that had been carved into fantastical shapes by the action of the waves. Above the beach loomed a cliff of black rock of an impressive height, on which stood—brooded—a turreted castle, its windows like blank bloodshot eyes with the pupils rolled back, its battlements and crenellations glowing red in the comet-light. Below, gnarled trees writhed and clashed their dead limbs in the windless night.

I scooped up a handful of black sand and let it trickle through my fingers. The surf broke gigantically and raced up the beach. It came at a sibilant rush to my feet before running out again, taking with it those black grains of sand. And I shut my eyes so that I could see what was lost, and I saw worlds that had ceased at that moment to exist, and worlds that might have been, had time and circumstance followed a different course—I saw entire worlds with their seas and forests, their plains and mountains, their farms and cities, I saw the pageant of their history unroll before me, and, seeing it, I understood every thing and, as swiftly, forgot.

And the waves curled and broke, and the sky flamed, and the

gnarled trees writhed and clashed their limbs in the bright, windless night. And I could detect in that bleak, infinite region no living creature but myself. And my eyes were drawn to the castle, for I longed to discover if it were inhabited, if only by someone no less lost than I.

Through the tall vaulted windows of a dim and gloomy hall, shafts of comet-light illumined random parts of armorial trophies—here an iron gauntlet, there a visor, a pauldron, a breastplate, the leaf-shaped blade of a lance. On damp walls, mildewed tapestries depicted scenes from those worlds I lost forever when the sand trickled between my fingers to the waiting voracious surf.

The hall ended, rather anticlimactically, I could not help thinking, at a door of modest proportions which opened to my touch. I climbed a flight of stone stairs in darkness to a second hall, lofty, with fretted ceilings smoke-blackened and remote. Mullioned windows too high to reach, their leaded panes encrimsoned by comet-light, hurled images of themselves like barred gates upon an ebon floor. Hidden wall recesses held unseen artifacts from the worlds that might have been, had time and circumstance followed a different course. Between the recesses, the walls were lined with shelves overflowing with books. Scattered on scarred and broken tables were more books, and more spilled from every open chest and armoire; more were stacked in flat-topped pyramids like sacrificial altars or in precarious columns that threatened to fall and crush me. I walked faster. I began to run.

Outside I heard a muted explosion. Through a tall window I could see a fireball streak away from the head of the comet to sear a trail across the sky and leave a sound like the crisp crackle of a comb through hair, the long hair of a young and beautiful woman or ghost on a cold winter night.

There is amusement in my friend's eyes as they regard me over the rims of his green-tinted spectacles. "My dear Edgar, would you really have me believe that a castle such as you describe is to be found in the wilds of Panchatan?"

"Do you think I was not dumbfounded to find it there, let alone to discover what lay in its singular precincts?"

"But that is just my point. Your castle is not in any way 'singular.' There are—let me see—dim and gloomy halls; barely glimpsed armorial trophies; tapestries depicting scenes you virtually *admit* come from your own imagination; mysterious wall recesses hiding God knows what. In short, Edgar, this 'singular' castle of yours is a stock setting of a so-called German or Gothic tale—the sort for which, deservedly, you are famous. And how do you arrive at this castle? You dive into a river in broad daylight and emerge not on the far bank but on the shore of a paradoxically shoreless sea—under a night sky lit by a comet that strikingly resembles the comet of your tale 'The Conversation of Eiros and Charmion'—in a landscape that you yourself describe as 'nightmare.' "

"You think I was dreaming?" I protest.

"What else *can* I think? In dreams, we re-visit the events of our past and glimpse those still to come, and we combine them in ways that seem to exist 'out of space, out of time'—to use words which I believe you will find familiar.* You have furnished a castle—someone *else*'s castle—entirely with lumber out of your own mind. And how do you round it off? With books, books everywhere, books heaped to threatening heights! Is this not the besetting dream of a writer who cannot finish what he is writing?"

"But I *did* finish, or almost finish, what I wrote at the lighthouse."

"Only to lose it while escaping."

"Could I help that?"

Dupin blows an ambiguous cloud of smoke. He says, "No one can help what he dreams. Why not admit that you were dreaming? That, in fact, you are dreaming now, even as we speak."

"Then wake me," I tell him impatiently.

"Eh? Wake you?"

* The reader is referred to Poe's poem "Dream-Land." (Editor's note)

"You say I am dreaming. I say I am not. Very well. If, as you insist, I am dreaming, wake me."

Despite a library full of books, books of ancient lore and the occult sciences and the conventional palliations of philosophy, Count Dionisio di Tangeri increasingly turned for solace—curious solace!—to pondering those uncanny events when, under hypnosis, the young American author Edgar Poe had vanished. Yet how curious was it, really, that he found solace in those events, though they had destroyed his career? They were real. *They had happened.* They were no part of the twilight world of opium dreams. For too long the Count had sought to escape in that world, from which Poe could not vanish for the simple reason that, there, he did not exist!

But the Count was a rational man, a man of science, and could not surrender his essential nature forever to the insidious drug.

Abandoning it, he came to Panchatan, the island of which Poe had so memorably written and, under hypnosis, spoken. Here perhaps he might find some explanation for what had happened in Paris. Yet once on the island, he found that he still craved solitude. This *folie* of a castle, built in the last century by an immensely wealthy Dutch planter, supplied it.

Over and over Count Tangeri would re-live that dreadful day. Over and over he would feel with undiminished force the horror and then the anguish he had communicated in his letter to Dupin.

Monsieur Poe became deathly pale, literally taking on the dead-white hue of a cadaver. I bade him wake. I used all my skills as a hypnotist, to no avail. I could not wake him. I feared for his life. Yet when I felt his pulse it was strong, steady, one hundred forty beats to the minute, as if he were engaged in violent exercise. Even as I counted his pulse, his arm began to feel lighter. Soon it was quite weightless. By then the skin of his face had assumed the translucent look of a very old man's. Before my horrified eyes Monsieur Poe began to fade. Through him I could see the wall, and the Ingres portrait of my beloved Maia. And then only the wall and the Ingres. Monsieur Poe was no longer here.

Maia too is not here. She went this morning to ride in the Bois. She ought to have returned five hours ago. . . .

The Ingres portrait was, aside from his books, aside from his memories, all that remained of Count Tangeri's former life. Maia had sat for it in the drawing room of their *hôtel particulier* in the Rue St-Honoré, the golden spill of her hair set off dramatically by the silver-gray of the wallpaper, her gown of unbleached batiste contrasting no less dramatically with the crimson silk upholstery of the sofa. The subdued glow of a lamp on an octagonal table of gold-threaded marble highlighted her large smoke-gray eyes, which gazed not at the painter but at the folds of silver drapery framing a window to the left of the painting and adding a touch of mystery because whatever she saw there seemed to impart to Maia's lovely face a look of wonder and surprise.

Count Dionisio di Tangeri frowned. He peered at the canvas. He could have sworn that a shadow moved across the drapery, as if some incorporeal presence had entered the room within the painting. His imagination, of course. The self-imposed loneliness; the longing for his daughter; the glow of comet-light upon the portrait—a classic example, the Count assured himself, of that strange phenomenon auto-hypnosis, on which he had written the definitive monograph.

But then why did the shadow darken, why did it suggest so unmistakably the silhouette of a man?

"You!" Count Tangeri cried.

Believe me, Dupin, I was no less astonished.

In the Count's eyes, the same smoke-gray as his daughter's, I saw—replacing a momentary fright—a look of hope. "You have found her?"

How could I tell him that she had betrayed me to throw in her lot with a scoundrel like Monk?

"Found and lost her, I fear."

"Where is she? You said she was in great danger."

I had no memory of saying that, and told him so.

"No—no, perhaps you would not. You were under hypnosis, after all."

Of that day in Paris I could remember only the Count passing his hand before my eyes. The next thing I knew, I was at the offices of the Compagnie Générale des Phares d'Outre-Mer.

The Count crossed to a rosewood desk. "The transcript of your hypnosis," he said, holding up a few sheets of foolscap. "How often have I gone over its every word, hoping for some clue to her fate. But there is nothing. Listen."

And he began to read; or rather, to recite. It was obvious that he had committed the transcript to memory.

"POE: Your daughter Maia! She flees—is fleeing a very great danger. *(Poe rushed to the door.)*

"TANGERI: You will return to your chair and sit when I say now. Now.

"P: *(sitting)* But don't you see, I must help her!

"T: Tell me, what is the danger she faces?

"P: It cannot be described. I only know that I must rescue her . . . and save the Yaanek. . . .

"Those were your last words to me," the Count said. "They mean nothing to you now?"

"I'm sorry, no. Only—the Yaanek. In your transcript I seem to have said—"

"Did say."

"—that I wished to save the Yaanek. But as you are here on the island, you must know it is no longer possible to save them. They have become virtually extinct."

"You are saying, then, there is no hope—for the Yaanek, or for Maia?"

We looked at each other. He waited for me to speak.

"If you were to hypnotize me again," I said slowly, "we might discover what I meant."

"An excellent plan," says Dupin. "And did he?"

"Yes, but not without difficulty."

"Yet in Paris you were an ideal subject. Odd, is it not?"

"I'm no expert on hypnotism."

"Nor I. But I suggest that, *already dreaming*, a subject might be most resistant to a hypnotic trance."

"I thought we had been through all that. Surely you haven't forgotten how you tried to rouse me and could not."

"That proves nothing. As it is *your* dream, I could hardly be expected to wake you from it. Listen, Edgar. Can you deny that the trappings of the castle are all drawn from your own life? And what about the portrait? The room in which Ingres painted Maia Tangeri. Is that room not familiar to you?"

"No. Should it be?"

"Is it not the very room into which you carried Nolie Mae Tangerie when she fainted in Mechanics Row in Baltimore? And also the room where you read 'The Raven' at Miss Anne Charlotte Lynch's *conversazione* the night you met Fanny Osgood?"

"There are," I concede, "certain points of similarity."

"Ergo, you associate that room, in your dreams, with an attractive woman. If you accept the logic of that, will you at least grant that you *could* be dreaming?"

I consider. "You may be right," I say.

Dupin looks pleased, like a teacher with a clever pupil.

"But if you are right," I say, "why could not Fanny Osgood and New York be the dream, and *this* the reality?"

When the Count's efforts to put me into a hypnotic trance proved unavailing, he leaned across his desk and rummaged through the shelves behind it.

"A reflector is sometimes useful," he explained. "Or a gemstone dangling from a chain, focusing your attention as it swings slowly —where did *this* come from?"

We stared warily at each other, then at what was in his hand.

"Use it," I said.

"Use it?"

Was I thinking, even as I spoke, that the Shard could suspend natural laws?

"Never mind your reflector, your gemstone on a chain," I said. "Use the Shard to hypnotize me."

TANGERI: Now you are in a deep sleep. I want you to remember our first session, in Paris. What had you to say then about Panchatan?

POE: I said that thousands of years ago a comet struck the earth, destroying a vast continent and leaving the islands of the Malay Archipelago. Here on Panchatan a tribe called the Yaanek found some residue from the comet, and made of it an idol. It is written that when Europeans came—

T: Where is it written?

P: I told you then that it was in notes for a story I had yet to write. This story, called "How the Yaanek Lost Their God," tells how white men came and destroyed the idol, with fearful consequences. All that was left was—this.

T: The Shard?

P: The Shard. A single fragment of a shattered god. I began to wonder about the nature of the Shard. What god-like attributes did it possess? Would other shards, if any, be the same, or different? Was a single shard somehow dangerous? Or part of a miracle? Was part of a miracle valuable? Which part? If the idol was god-like enough to number among its attributes perfection—but was it?— would not a single shard necessarily be perfect? Was the god a wrathful one? Might such speculations, such doubts, anger it? Was that why . . . in the legends . . .

T: Yes?

P: While writing my tale, I did some research. Perhaps you know that on the islands of Sumatra, Borneo, Celebes, Java, and Panchatan, the people share a common written language derived from Sanskrit and Javanese. The oldest extant writing in that language is a compilation of folktales and legends. One, a prophetic or monitory legend, concerns a powerful deity destroyed by a mere mortal.

T: As in your tale?

P: Exactly. Once, this legend says, the Yaanek fished with nets that flashed silver in the sunlight, nets as gossamer as spiderweb. Once—

T: Then, it was about *this* island?

P: Panchatan, yes. Once, the legend says, the Yaanek could pluck ripe fruit from the nearest tree at any time of year. Once, men and women alike wore gaily patterned garments made from the inner bark of the paper mulberry tree. They were never ill, nor mean of spirit, nor jealous of one another. They danced, they sang, they bedded innocently with whom they desired. They loved children, which was the same as loving themselves, for they were as children.

In a secret glade, before a stone idol, they worshiped their god by recounting stories of such imagination that they glorified the entire world. For even out of distortion and deformity, out of disharmony, they could fashion beauty—until the night their idol was destroyed.

They became despondent, and one by one they abandoned their god's gifts. They abandoned their gossamer fishnets that flashed silver in the sunlight. They abandoned their orchards and let the fruit rot on the ground. They abandoned their gaily patterned garments of mulberry bark and went naked, hiding their shame from one another in dark places in hidden valleys. They became sickly in a land where disease had been unknown, and what meager possessions remained to them they guarded jealously from one another. Newborn children, of whom there were fewer each year, they abandoned. Their imaginations having withered and died, they spoke no stories to worship their god by glorifying the world, stories which took them anywhere they wished without setting foot off the island. That all ended when the idol disappeared in a blaze of light.

T: How beautiful a legend, and how sad . . .

P: It is both of those things. It is also incomplete.

T: Incomplete?

P: There is a darker version of the legend—verified by recent events. In this version the god of the Yaanek created the earth and its creatures, and went on to other things, leaving behind the idol —and an awesome responsibility.

T: What responsibility?

P: Were the people to stop speaking the glories of creation, the world would end.

T: (*smiling*) Then it is clear that they did not stop.

P: For a long time, no. The idol replaced the god in their devotions; *became* the god for them. Then the idol allowed itself to be destroyed.

T: *Allowed itself?*

P: What else could its worshipers think? Would an all-powerful deity suffer destruction at the hands of a mere man unless it *wished* to deprive its worshipers of itself?

T: Had they committed some transgression?

P: Not at all. Since time immemorial they had joyfully spoken the glory of creation in the glade where the idol stood. That was what so embittered them. They took their revenge by recounting instead legends of the destruction of the world.

T: As if that had actually happened? Of course—the comet! Are you saying it is happening again? That this comet . . .

P: Yes. Unless . . . unless the idol can somehow be . . .

T: Monsieur Poe, listen carefully. In a moment I shall bring you out of the trance. When I do, you will remember every thing that was said while you were in it. All right—you are now awake.

"My God, what an extraordinary experience. And what an extraordinary *idea*!" I cried.

"Indeed."

"And yet—does it not make a kind of sense? Consider, Count. Have you ever seen a Yaanek tribesman? Even one?"

"No, never. As you say, they might as well be extinct."

"When you mesmerized me the first time—"

"Hypnotized. I hypnotized you. Mesmer was a fraud."

"—I said that I must rescue your daughter and save the Yaanek."

The Count turned from me to gaze at the Ingres portrait of Maia.

"Is it not obvious, Count, that I cannot do so unless you help me to go—"

"Impossible! I was trained as a medical doctor. I took an oath. First, do no harm . . ."

"But you will do irreparable harm if you refuse."

"Yet I must."

I raised a hand toward the portrait. "Even if her life hangs in the balance? Believe me, Count, I have as great a stake in this as you. You see, the man who shattered the idol was my brother."

A charged silence filled the room until I said:

"If I am willing to attempt it, why not you?"

"It's not the difficulty, I assure you. I cede to no one in the pursuit of knowledge. But," Count Tangeri gave the Shard a worried look, "if what you say about this is true—"

"It must be. Or we are all lost."

TANGERI: You are in a sleep so deep that all memory is unlocked. You can call up at will any time, any place. When I speak a word or a name, you will let that word take you to whatever time and place it summons. Let us begin. *Maia Tangeri . . .*

POE: I have come to the Rue St-Honoré, bearing a card from the Chevalier C. Auguste Dupin, to seek the Conte di Tangeri. On his doorstep I encounter a young woman of breathtaking beauty, clad in a riding costume the exact smoke-gray color of her eyes and a hat of—

T: Yes, I am aware of that encounter. Let us move to another time and place. *You are with Miss Tangeri. . . .*

P: We are in Baltimore, in a church; no, aboard a ship; no, it is both—a seamen's bethel. Rain drums on the roof. The preacher's voice is indistinct. Miss Tangerie says, "You would have shot him. You would have shot Monk. And if you had, who could lead us to the Shard?" I say nothing. "For the first time," she says, "I am able to believe that you *are* Will Henry's brother."

T: She talks of Henry, of the Shard? Excellent. Go on.

P: But she says no more of that. She becomes confused and distraught, believing herself to be trapped, trapped in an alien and frightening place, unable to get out. I try to calm her, telling her that as she is here with me in Baltimore, it is evident she has got out. But Nolie Mae says, "Why can't you understand? I did *not* get out. I am still trapped here."

T: Nolie Mae? You call her Nolie Mae?

P: *She* calls herself Nolie Mae Tangerie. I have wondered whether the name is "made up." If a woman is alone, and if her name is Tangerie *or* Nolie Mae, she might adopt the other part as a signal that advances would be unwelcome. But I don't really know. This is only the second time I have seen her.

T: Hmm. Now, let your memory take you back. *You would have shot Monk. . . .*

P: I am outside a tavern called Gunner's Hall. Obadiah, my former slave, emerges with Monk, the man who has killed my family. I raise my Colt pistol. Obadiah shouts, "Now!" but Miss Tangerie cries out, "Phidias, no!" and I do not shoot.

T: Why does she call you Phidias?

P: I do not know. It confuses me, for I know my name is Thomas W. Frederick.

T: (*sighs*) You are going back, further in memory, to your first meeting. *You are with Miss Tangerie. . . .*

P: We are in an opulent room, furnished in rosewood and crimson upholstery and silver drapes—

T: The room in the portrait above my head?

P: Yes, that is the room. That is the woman. She asks how I cannot remember how my own brother died. She goes on, "Am I likewise to believe you remember nothing Will might have said about Panchatan?" I have never heard the name. She runs out, returns for her hat, says I will not find the Shard without her help. I say, "What shard?" and she says, "Tell me you would not kill for it. Anyone would. *I* would."

T: Now another memory, another time and place. *Henry . . .*

P: It is night in the Rue de la Gaîté, Paris. With Alexandre Dumas and a gendarme, I have climbed the stairs to my brother's apartment. Furniture is overturned, upholstery shredded, blood everywhere—

T: You have told me of these events in Paris. Go further back. *Henry . . .*

P: He pulls from behind his pillows a bar-hammer pepperbox pistol. He calls it his good-luck piece. I ask why. He says, "When

I was in Marseilles I survived its best efforts to kill me. There was a girl, a most beautiful girl named Nola. . . . Well, I shall tell you about it some time."

T: Go to that time. *Henry tells you the story.* . . .

P: But he never did.

T: Very well. Let us seek other memories. *Monk* . . .

P: Dozens of men are sitting around trading stories. No one expects Monk to join in, but he does. He tells how, on an island in the Malay Archipelago, he and a shipmate heard of an aboriginal people reputed to possess a great treasure. In the interior they found the Yaanek, a tribe who worshiped a stone idol that resembled a statue of Poseidon except that it carried a parang. During their stay Monk and his shipmate found no treasure, but one of the Yaanek stole a bar-hammer pepperbox pistol belonging to the shipmate, who, on recovering it, vengefully shot the idol to smithereens, to the accompaniment of a blinding light. Immediately thereafter Monk found on his face a parang-shaped scar, and the shipmate began to cough blood. As for the Yaanek, deprived of their idol, they sank into such apathy that it threatened their very existence.

T: Very good. Now, *Monk in another time and place* . . .

P: (*after a pause*) I'm sorry, I find no more.

T: . . . *idol* . . .

P: (*Shakes his head and says nothing.*)

T: . . . *comet* . . .

P: I am with my wife in her sick-room. Virginia has found letters another woman wrote to me. I expect recriminations, but there are none. Virginia tells me she is not jealous; tells me she has no life of her own, *can have* no life of her own; tells me she wants to live her life through me. Then she cries: "Eddie, I want something to *happen*! Any thing! I lie here all day, or sit at the window watching people walk by and wondering where they are going and if, perhaps today, their lives will change. I want . . . I want the roof to fall in or the street to flood or a comet to strike the earth—"

T: . . . *shard* . . .

P: I am at the President's House in Washington City, at a levée.

I have been drinking heavily, and am seized by vertigo. With an effort I hold myself motionless in the middle of the madly whirling room. Then I find that I can stop and start the whirling, as if I were twisting the tube of a kaleidoscope. One by one I inspect the colorful shards. The shards are segments of faces—angry eyes, a nose bent off true, sallow—"

T: No, this memory is not helpful. Go to another time and place. *Shard . . .*

P: John Allan has forbidden me to play with the kaleidoscope that his wife, Frances, gave me for my birthday. A kaleidoscope needs light, and light can damage the eyes of a child with measles. But I am restless and bored, and what harm can a little light do? I steal silently to the window and roll the shade up a hand-span. I return to bed, remove the kaleidoscope from under the pillow—and wait.

For I am convinced that a single twist of the tube will show me something so strange and wonderful as to transcend any thing one might expect of shards of glass reflected in mirrors. Waiting, postponing this vision, I am giddy with excitement.

When finally I twist the tube and see the shards begin to tumble, John Allan shouts: "Give that to me!" but before he can snatch the kaleidoscope from me, I hurl it against the wall.

Later, Frances Allan finds me seated on the floor amid the fragments. I hold a single shard in my hand, roughly hexagonal and of a brilliant golden color. I can feel its sharp edges. I can also feel its warmth, like the warmth of a living thing. I clutch the shard more tightly. Suddenly I am crying.

"I shall get you another," Frances Allan tells me. "With a brass tube, like a spy-glass."

"I don't want another."

And with all my strength I close my fist on the golden shard and watch blood seep between my fingers.

T: You have gone back too far. Try again. *Shard . . .*

P: I clutch the shard more tightly. Suddenly I am crying. "I shall get you another," Frances Allan tells me. "With a brass tube, like a spy-glass."

T: You are resisting me, Monsieur Poe. You will *leave* that time and place, you will go to another. *Now.*

P: In the fading light I see two horsemen galloping up from the river.

The sun has burnished the water to the color of saffron, saffron blotched with gloomy shadows cast by the overhanging trees. Scrub grows in a profuse tangle here; the horsemen disappear into it, reappear, disappear again. Sometimes only their broad-brimmed hats are visible, jouncing above the slate-green brush behind their horses' disembodied heads. They rein up fifty paces from where I stand. One of them peers through a brass spy-glass. He exclaims, and passes it to his companion. The second man looks. They seem isolated from every thing familiar, every thing they or I have ever known before, as if they are forever lost in some alien, other place, searching for a way out which they will never find. They spur their horses forward, and for an instant the first man looks straight at where I stand in the shadow of a clove tree. I shout my brother's name, but the rapid beat of hooves quickly fades. I race in pursuit. The earth is loamy underfoot, the hoofprints deep. It is like running on sand, black sand. . . .

Forty-six

It is evident that we are hurrying onward to some exciting knowledge—some never-to-be-imparted secret, whose attainment is destruction.

—"MS. Found in a Bottle"

In the bedroom window Mary Moran could see reflected her tousled chestnut hair, her wide-spaced eyes, the freckles on the bridge of her nose. It was an hour before dawn. The stars were still bright in a velvety black sky.

Why is it black, the sky at night? Why does it not blaze—dazzle—blind with the light from an infinitude of stars in an infinite universe? Edgar Poe posed that question, and answered it:* When we look out into the far reaches of space we look also back to the dawn of time before the stars were born.

Poe—was there any question he left unasked, no matter how audacious? Now he was dying, and Mary felt a wave of sorrow not only for the man whose days were running out so prematurely but for the world soon to be deprived of his genius.

Mary listened to her husband's slumbrous breathing. He was sleeping finally, poor darling. With the comforter drawn to his chin, he looked like a little boy. The responsibility that weighed so heavily on him was, for a time, lifted.

Dear John, so conscientious and sober, so unlike her too romantic self. They were cut from different cloth, and a good thing too! Still, John had hardly seemed the same man these past few days; had, in fact, surrendered himself to flights of fancy that quite took Mary's breath away. It was almost as if the presence of the dying Edgar Poe had imparted to him Poe's own tumultuous imagination.

Mary saw a shooting star. Who was it, what Roman with poetry in his soul, who said there is a star in the firmament for every human being who ever lived or ever will, a star that shines dim or bright according to his lot and that will fall when he dies? Pliny—it was Pliny the Elder. Poetry in his soul, yes, but twinned with a scientist's fatal curiosity. For Pliny, wishing to observe the eruption of Mount Vesuvius in A.D. 79, went to Pompeii. Was he suffocated by toxic gases? Buried under volcanic ash? Crushed by a hurtling boulder even as he raised his arms stiffly in final defiance, a shout of outrage forever silent on his lips? Did a star fall?

John stirred and murmured in his sleep. He was frowning. Was he dreaming? He never mentioned his dreams. Crossing to the bed, she lightly kissed his brow. Dreaming of what?

Mary heard, muted by the closed window, the beat of hooves. She sighed and waited for the night bell to wake her husband. What

* See *Eureka: A Prose Poem.* (Editor's note)

other business would bring riders to the crest of Hamstead Hill before dawn on Sunday morning?

But the hoofbeats passed close and receded, and when Mary returned to the window she saw no one. Opening the casement, she heard again, faintly now, hoofbeats. She leaned out and peered in both directions, again seeing no one. She had the ineffable feeling that some unknown truth had passed her by.

She hurried from the room, following an impulse that took her along the passage to the east tower, where Edgar Poe's life, the reach of his life, had been reduced to a bed in a small, Spartan hospital room. But, to her surprise, after exchanging greetings with silver-haired Sister Margaret at Poe's doorway, she found herself climbing the stairs to the next floor. The same open door, the same dim night lamp, but no greeting from Sister Sparrow, who was dozing beside the unknown woman's bed. Mary approached slowly. A bandage swathed the woman's head. Her face was swollen, discolored, her breathing shallow and rapid. Like Poe, she was dying. Was there someone, now, out there in the indifferent night, in the anonymous city, frantic with worry because she had disappeared? But surely by now they would have inquired of the police, the hospitals.

Mary sat on the edge of the bed and took the unknown woman's hand in her own. The hand was cold. Mary squeezed it gently, as if to say, someone is here, someone cares. Whoever you are, you are not dying alone.

Was it Mary's imagination, or did she feel the slightest pressure in return from the long, slim fingers?

My name is Nola May Frederick. The family, except sometimes Tom, always called me Nola. But I suffered through a series of name-stages in childhood, after Uncle Thaddeus sent me off to the Tarr School at Baltimore. Not that I blame him. It was just bad luck that my parents died in a boating accident at Hampton Roads, making him my guardian. That was no reason for him to stop galli-vanting all over the world. He reckoned he was placing me in good, if experimental, hands.

The Tarr School may have been experimental (it had both boy

and girl students, though outside of class hours we were strictly separated, at least in theory), but it was not so experimental as to stint on the classics. Latin commenced early. By the time my first feminine curves were visible—these also commenced early—we had reached the verb *nolle*, which sounds like Nola and means "to not want to" and earned me the nickname Miss I-Prefer-Not. I, preferring not to seem "stuck up," asked to be called the friendlier Nolie-May. But a classmate, playing on *noli me tangere*, transformed my nickname to Miss Touch-Me-Not, and after that there was hardly a boy who did not try—to touch me, that is. My next idea, to call myself simply May, was no better. Apparently it had a permissive ring! So then I decreed flatly that my name was Freddie. This I backed up with words (Anglo-Saxon) and fists, the use of which Uncle Thaddeus had taught me when he heard of my trials.

That was not all Uncle Thaddeus taught me. During school vacations he made a point of being at home on his plantation, called Panchatan, on the Chickahominy near Williamsburg. There I learned to ride—side-saddle *and* astride—to swim and to fence and even to handle firearms. Uncle Thaddeus taught me what he could, in short, and trusted that I would "pick up the girl-things" somehow. He was hard-drinking and hot-tempered and cantankerous, and I think he loved me as much as I loved him.

When word came of his death in the Iowa Territories, I felt more orphaned than the first time.

The plantation passed to the only surviving brother, my uncle Thomas—who also inherited me. This meant no more Tarr School. I continued my studies from the eclectic library Uncle Thaddeus left, and from the books my boy cousins brought home from their colleges. From my girl cousins I did "pick up the girl-things," although I found it a trifle absurd to be called "a little lady" when I was already as tall as Uncle Thomas. And I would still, sometimes, when I was missing Uncle Thaddeus most acutely, grab a horse and a gun and ride out to hunt in Panchatan's woodlands. My girl cousins called me an impossible hoyden, but they were secretly envious. Even my boy cousins were awed by the way I could plink bottles off the fence at a hundred yards with a .22 varmint rifle. My favorite cousin, Thomas Jr., just two years older than me, often used to say I should have been a boy, and as often added, "But I for one am mighty pleased that you are not."

Uncle Thaddeus left to me only a small sea chest full of potsherds from the island of Panchatan, that distant place from which he had derived his fortune, and the plantation its name. This eccentric bequest I somehow knew was meant as a token of his faith in my resourcefulness.

Besides, to say Uncle Thaddeus left me only the chest of potsherds is not entirely accurate, for he also left a letter with a firm of attorneys in Baltimore, to be opened on my coming of age—an event which went unmarked, occurring as it did so soon after my uncle Thomas—Thomas W. Frederick, Sr.—and my cousins Thad, Lizzy, and Ginny were murdered in their beds by an unknown intruder. Cousin Tom escaped their fate because he was away at William & Mary studying the law, and I escaped because, there being a full moon that night, I had decided to gallop Tom's mare Jewelweed along the towpath.

Dear Cousin Thomas! After brooding more than was good for him, he freed the slaves and sold the plantation (to a disagreeable Richmonder named Allan) and made provision for me (a handsome bank account and his spirited mare Jewelweed to boot), and determined to sail to Panchatan to learn the provenance of the potsherds that had been stolen on the terrible night of his family's death.

As it happened, I went to Baltimore not long after Tom did—he to seek a berth on a ship bound for the South China Sea and I to claim my letter at Uncle Thaddeus's attorneys.

Their offices were in the Fourth Ward. After I made an appointment for that afternoon, I set out, it being an Election Day, to see the festivities attendant upon electing congressmen. Soon learning that the festivities consisted chiefly of drunken brawls, I went—prompted by nostalgia—to visit the Tarr School. But it was no longer there; nor could anyone in the neighborhood, at the very top of Hamstead Hill where a hospital now stands, remember it. Cities change so fast.

Returning to the Fourth Ward, I caught sight of my cousin Thomas outside the polling place. Poor Tom! He might have been capable of killing in hot blood but not in cold—and when our former slave Obadiah led him to the murderer of our kin he just stood in the rain weeping, a revolver dangling from his hand. I understand he has said I struck the weapon aside before he could fire. I shall not object if he insists this was so, but I do not recall the events as he describes them.

The upshot of all this was that Tom, having confronted the murderer and found that he was not one himself, was relieved of his obsession. I, on the other hand, after reading Uncle Thaddeus's letter, became obsessed with Panchatan.

How very like Uncle Thaddeus that letter was! It even lacked a salutation, unless you count its second word.

Well, sprout, you will not be reading this letter unless your old uncle has departed this life. Weep no tears. I enjoyed every minute and mile of the time I had, and that is more than most people can say. My only regret is, I never did return to Panchatan.

If you have had your legacy appraised by the perfessers at Williamsburg, you know—to your considerable consternation, I bet—that it is worth a heap of loot, enough for the rest of your natural life.

[I had *not* had it appraised! It had never occurred to me that a chest full of broken crockery could be worth any thing, except sentimentally. And by the time I read Uncle Thaddeus's letter, of course, it was too late.]

Have the perfessers told you how old those pot-sherds are? My bet is a thousand years, even more. What you see on them is writ in an ancient language, part Sanskrit, part Javanese. Now here is some advice, which as you know I have always been free with. Don't you wait for the perfessers to put together those pot-sherds like a jigsaw puzzle so they can translate every word. It will take them years, perfessers are like that, and you will not be young forever.

Well, here it is, sprout. Like I said, I never did return to Panchatan. I want you to go for me, back where that idol is, whose history is writ on the pot-sherds. (Quite a story, something about how a comet came and sank a continent and left the idol that the natives have to worship or it will all happen again. I forget the details.)

You will see that one piece has no writing on it but a design that looks like a fan. It depicts, they tell me, part of the tail of a peacock. A young fellow that goes by the cognomen of Will Henry has the other half. He saved my life once on the island of Borneo when some head-hunters . . . but that is another story. The two halfs of the peacock, they form a talisman that ought to get you and him out of tight spots, assuming you get into any, with the natives, called the Yaanek, assuming you run into any.

Being a rare fellow, one who will not find you too much woman for him, Will Henry will like you. I write this as a warning, for I reckon you will like him too. Will Henry is a gallivanter, same as me. Be prudent, sprout.

But forgive my rambling. My attorneys are holding in trust for you ample money to pay your passage to the Orient. Will Henry should not be difficult to find. He is known by every harbormaster and saloon keeper and pretty woman from Aden to Zamboanga and beyond, if it comes to that, but he is unlikely to be very far from Panchatan, for he has become obsessed with the idol. Now, obsession comes in a lot of shapes, so best not jump to the conclusion that he aims to steal the idol. Could be that he wants only to stare it in its diamond eye and ask, what in tarnation is so special about you? *Which is all I did, as I told him. But he is young and manful and . . . well, you will see what kind of a person he is when you join up with him.*

There is the chance, of course, that you are too late. It has been a while since we last saw each other, and he may figure I am dead. Which I am, come to think of it, so don't you go holding that against him, sprout!

You are wondering why I never went back there, why I kept putting it off. It pains me to tell you that I did not trust myself to do the right thing. Now, the rightest *right thing would have been, I reckon, to take that chest full of pot-sherds straight back where I got them. But I never could bring myself to do that, and I am surely not minded to ask you to do it for me. What I found was already smashed to smithereens, which is hardly the same as the Elgin Marbles that were lifted off of the Parthenon in Athens, much of the sculpture being the work of the great Phidias himself. So that is a whole different kettle of fish.*

But I am rambling again. Go find Will Henry for me, sprout. Maybe the two of you can discover for me what I should have done. If you are too late, at least you will have seen something of the world.

I did, of course. I only wish I could remember it all. You see, shortly after leaving the attorneys' offices in Baltimore, I was thrown by my horse, and suffered a blow to the head, and after that things went missing from my memory. For instance, I cannot recall how I set about looking for Will Henry. But whatever I did, it was effective.

I tracked him down in Paris—a considerable distance, I need not say, from Panchatan.

He was living under the name of William Henry Leonard Poe in a rather *louche* outlying street, appropriately called the Rue de la Gaîté. There I contrived to make the acquaintance of a lad who ran errands for him. The errands consisted largely of carrying messages to a wide variety of women, and I formed a picture of Will Henry as a nocturnal sybarite. But further cultivation of the errand boy yielded more intriguing information. Will Henry, erstwhile seaman, had come to Paris not so much for its licentiousness as for its literary life. When he was not pursuing women, he was seeking the company of poets and playwrights. And in the silent nighttime hours, when the carousing was over, he himself tried to write. According to my informant, he littered the floor with discarded pages even more numerous than his discarded mistresses.

Eager to meet this complex and fascinating man, I was approaching his apartment one evening with the intention of presenting myself when I heard fearful noises from above.

I saw the boy emerging from the building and detained him, but he said he could not stop as he had a message to deliver. When pressed, he insisted he "didn't know nothing" about the noises. I said that, from the sound of it, his master might need him here and that, as I was going into the city myself, I would carry the message. To this he acceded.

I slipped around the corner and opened the message, addressed to one Edgar Poe at a café in the Rue de la Paix. It read:

Eddie,

Sorry, I cannot meet you tonight. I am busy concocting my own murder. (If you're around when it is discovered, do be a good fellow and act shocked and grieved. And above all do not tell Alexandre I am alive, or le tout Paris will know.) Tonight I am off to embark on life's greatest adventure. If you don't mind how long it takes, why not join me? I'll be in Marseilles until the 12th, at l'Auberge des Marins, then I depart for the island of Panchatan.

A bientôt?

Henry

Taking care not to be seen, I remained in the Rue de la Gaîté until the noises from the apartment ceased and the police belatedly arrived. I mingled in the crowd and heard the rumors: The apartment was a bloody ruin, the occupant had clearly been slain, but no body had been found.

More eager than ever to meet the intriguing Will Henry, I put the undelivered message in my pocket and set off to find a railroad timetable for Marseilles.

I had grown up in a seaport, but Marseilles was a tougher town than Baltimore, and the waterfront area was no place for a respectable woman. So I entered it dressed as a man.

The Auberge des Marins had cheap rooms above, and a cheap tavern below filled with rowdy sailors. Will Henry was not among them. A blowsy bar-maid said he usually came in around this hour, so I bought a beer and took it to a quiet corner.

Presently I saw that I was being watched with disquieting intensity by a swarthy lascar with drooping mustaches. Had he seen through my disguise? Had he a taste for effeminate boys? Either way, as he approached, I could foresee an ugly situation. I was considering whether to extricate myself from it at gunpoint (I carried in my pocket a small single-shot pistol designed by Uncle Thaddeus's friend Mr. Deringer) when Will Henry finally appeared.

Casting myself in the role of damsel in distress, a role to which I did not feel entirely suited, I let him rescue me. This took some doing, as the lascar got in the first blow, which sent my rescuer tumbling to the floor. Had I not intervened, the lascar would have stomped him, quite possibly to death, but fortunately I was within reach of those drooping mustaches and, grasping the right one, I ran the howling lascar across the room, giving Will Henry time to regain his feet.

The ensuing brawl left the lascar with a broken nose and three teeth knocked from his head (and his right mustache torn out at the roots)—and left the bruised and bloodied Will Henry in possession of the lascar's firearm, a cumbersome affair with a long hammer and a cluster of barrels.

The attraction between Will Henry and me was immediate and intense, but how we spent the next few days (and nights) does not bear on this tale. Suffice it to say I learned that shortly before leaving Paris, Will Henry had received a letter from a man called Monk enclosing a sketch of the half-a-peacock potsherd, which this Monk said he had received from the hands of Thaddeus Frederick. Monk also wrote that he had narrowly escaped with his life from an attempted robbery, and warned Will Henry to guard against a like attack upon himself. They should meet, he said, as soon as possible in Panchatan.

In the face of this, I had no countervailing proofs to offer. Even granting I was the niece of Thaddeus Frederick—and my descriptions of my uncle satisfied Will Henry that we spoke of the same man—why would Thaddeus entrust such a mission to someone so unsuitable? I produced my uncle's letter, and it gave Will Henry pause. But he had never seen Thaddeus Frederick's handwriting. He could only, he said, go partners with whoever had the peacock potsherd. We argued, but he was a stubborn man. I could not help feeling that while he found his uses for me, these did not include taking part in the search for the Yaanek idol. I was, after all, only a woman.

On the 12th, as his message to his brother had said, he was gone from Marseilles.

Having learned on what vessel Will Henry was working his passage east, and how long it might take, I, with letters of credit in my pocket-book and steel in my soul, determined to be there on his arrival. I sailed on the first fast ship bound for the Orient.

Forty-seven

There comes a blurring of the distinction between memory and hallucination—which, anyway, are not so different one from the other as most people think.
—*The Lighthouse at the End of the World*

It was like running on sand, black sand. And mind you, Dupin, I am no tireless tracker, no real-life Natty Bumppo. Still, I could follow the hoofprints of their two horses by the light of a moon one day off the full.

I was driven by a sense of extreme urgency, for I knew what must inevitably follow should I fail to prevent the theft of my brother's revolver.

First, Monk would apprehend the thief, administer a beating, and return the weapon to Henry. Then Henry, incited either by anger or by what I have called the imp of the perverse or by some motive unknown to me, would empty all seven chambers of the cumbersome revolver at the Yaanek idol, shattering it. Next (as Monk told it in Baltimore) a scar in the shape of a Malay parang would appear on his face, and Henry would begin coughing blood. And the Yaanek, believing their god had unjustly deserted them, would speak no more the glories of creation but instead its annihilation, threatening with extinction not only themselves but . . .

"Why do you pause?"

"Because it is absurd. How could the destruction of a primitive idol in the jungle of a faraway island lead to the destruction of the world? Anyhow, the fact that you and I are here discussing it proves it did not happen."

"Yes," says Dupin with a smile, "but *why* did it not? Did you prevent the theft? Or is the so-called legend of the Yaanek idol no more than a tale of the imagination, a Gothic tale of the sort you yourself write?"

"You are suggesting that I made it up—under the sway, perhaps, of some morbid mental state?"

"Morbid?" Dupin asks, surprised. "To be sure, many of your tales derive their effect from a *narrator's* morbid mental state, but why should this imply that the *author* is similarly afflicted? No, Edgar —let the absurd take care of itself. Finish your story."

Would I be too late? In an hour the moon would set behind the hills to the west. Henry and Monk could not continue in darkness. They would make camp. What better time for the thief to strike?

Imagine my relief when, stopping to regain my breath, I heard hoofbeats. They must, I told myself, have rested their horses a while; I had almost overtaken them. So eager was I to believe this that it was some time before I perceived that the hoofbeats were not receding into the night ahead of me but *gaining on me from behind.*

I whirled and saw a single rider astride a roan stallion, its white-tipped hairs like silver in the moonlight as it galloped straight at me.

I tried to leap aside, but tripped on an exposed root and fell. The stallion, rearing, came down almost on top of me. I rolled over twice to escape its hooves.

The rider, already brandishing a small pistol, perhaps a derringer, snatched from the saddle-bow a Malay parang, that formidable native weapon with its heavy, curved blade.

As I scrambled to my feet the rider dismounted and raised the parang in a forbidding manner, then abruptly let it drop to the ground.

"Phidias!" she cried. "Oh my God, Phidias Peacock!"

"You also were astonished?"

"I never expected to see her again. Nor did I know until then, actually *know*, that they were one and the same person."

"One finds doppelgängers in the pages of German tales, not in real life," says Dupin with a dismissive Gallic shrug. "Still, we *are* dealing with illusion—in the sense that love is always in part illusion. I have a theory about love, my friend; I am, after all, a Frenchman. It is this: Every man has his ideal woman. She is imaginary; can only *be* imaginary. But sometimes he meets a woman who reminds him of her in some way—her walk perhaps, or a dimple when she smiles, an accent he finds delightful, the color of her eyes, a way she has of holding her head . . . well, it can be any thing. A flirtation follows, or a love affair, or marriage—but the woman of flesh and blood, when compared with the ideal, must always suffer. Because he always seeks the woman of his fantasy, man can never be contentedly monogamous. As for you, my dear Edgar, you with your prodigious imagination believed you had found not just an approximation but the ideal woman herself—more than once."

"But she *was* flesh and blood. I held her in my arms. I kissed her. I tasted the salt of her tears. I—"

"She is young, this ideal of yours, eternally young. She is tall, she is blond, she is beautiful, her eyes are like gray smoke. She is in many ways as capable as a man, albeit the very essence of femininity." Dupin fills and lights his meerschaum. "Of the women who in one way or another remind you of her, I had the opportunity to meet one."

"Who?" Without knowing why, I am instantly wary.

"The handsome widow Shelton. She is not young, not tall, not blond. Yet in some way she must resemble . . . But of course, how foolish of me! It was the way she drove recklessly through the dawn the morning you left Richmond."

"She did? Why on earth—"

"To try to stop you. You were ill. She was worried. Why did you leave?"

"I . . . had to go north to put my affairs in order."

"Affairs? You mean property, stock certificates, bank accounts? You have none of these."

"I was going north to bring Muddy back with me."

"But you could have waited until you were well. So I ask again, why did you leave? You were courting the widow Shelton. It was your intention to marry her, was it not?"

Dupin's green-tinted spectacles glitter more brightly than can be accounted for by the feeble glow of the bedside lamp. Looking at him, I have the alarming notion that if I am not careful he will absorb me, or rather my thoughts, into his own more logical ones, and I will cease to exist.

"Of course I intended marrying her."

"But you left. Had you decided, after all, that you did not love her?"

"I loved her! Must you go on asking these infernal questions?"

"No, not if they disturb you," Dupin says calmly.

There is a long silence. I break it by saying:

"It was *because* I loved her that I had to get away, don't you see? How could I marry her if I knew I had not long to . . ."

"To what?"

"Enough!" I shout.

Dupin says, "Forgive me," and busies himself unnecessarily with relighting his meerschaum. Presently he says, as if there had been no interruption, "Your ideal woman, although passionate, is untouchable by any man who does not conform in some way to *her* ideal. This man, we know, is dark, he is well-knit, he is handsome (when not glowering), he is sensitive. He often lacks confidence but never courage. He cuts a dashing figure—when he cares to. He drinks more than is good for him. She loves him as much for what he is not as for what he is. She thinks him a genius. She will never find him. And never stop looking. Since, however, she appears to be two people, or even three," Dupin smiled, "there is a greater chance of her stumbling upon *you*."

"Are you saying that I dreamed her—invented her—created her, as I would a character in a story?" I demand.

"I am. Because you did. In exactly the same way that she dreamed—invented—created you."

I look at him, shocked into silence. He is wrong, of course. But I cannot say how.

Forty-eight

> I cannot help thinking that romance-writers might [take] a hint from the Chinese, who, in spite of building their houses downwards, have still sense enough to *begin their books at the end.*
>
> —*Marginalia*

An arresting epigram, is it not, my dear Alexandre? Edgar quoted it to me ten minutes ago, just before he dozed off.

I then took up my pen to resume this account. I did so with no reluctance but, rather, with gratitude to you for requesting it. I find that setting down Edgar's words, and my own thoughts, helps me as I grope toward an understanding of the Strange Case of the Poe Brothers (although, of course, I do not pretend to write with the inventiveness and intensity of a Poe, *nor* with the fluidity and *élan* of a Dumas!). Yet for ten minutes my pen was idle as I sat pondering that epigram.

To build a house downwards! What can Edgar have meant? Surely not to build in defiance of gravity, the upper stories suspended in air while the lowest is not yet in place to support them. Perhaps Henry, in his travels, made some observations of Chinese architecture, and passed them somewhat ambiguously to Edgar? Perhaps he meant that the Chinese erect a skeleton of a building and put a roof on, then finish the work under its shelter? Now *that* might make some sense.

But what has it to do with beginning a book at its end?

I wish you were here, *mon vieux*. You might cast some light. Not on where a book should begin—I know perfectly well your views on that ("Begin at the beginning and end at the end," although you sometimes don't; *The Three Musketeers* did not end at the end but continued in *Twenty Years After* and now I hear, even if you think it a secret, that you are writing a sequel-to-the-sequel!). No, what I should like to ask is whether you ever happened to discuss with Edgar Poe this tangled subject of beginnings and ends. If so, you will know how it troubles him. He recently said he was uncertain whether he had commenced his longest narrative, his only autobiographical narrative, at its beginning or close to its end. And if he himself cannot say, who can?

I think that Edgar has been seeking some way to write a novel in which beginning and end become more than merely a place to start and a place to finish. For here is something else he said to me recently, another of his epigrams (aphorisms?):

"A narrative is not a horse race."

Now what do we make of *that*? If a horse race is run on a circular track, the start and finish lines are arbitrary, and are likely to be the same place. Did Edgar mean that in a narrative the beginning and end, unlike those on the racetrack, are *not* the same? But that is elementary. Or did he mean a book's ending is not, as some have argued, inherent in its beginning? No, intuition tells me that Edgar had in mind something far more subtle. I submit he meant this: When an ending circles back to the beginning, the beginning is not what it was in the first place, and the changed beginning will lead to a no less changed end, which in turn . . .

Eh bien, mon cher Alexandre, we now approach the end of the narrative of Edgar Allan Poe. You, as a creator of fictions, will know far better than I, with my formal logic, what Edgar was attempting and to what degree he succeeded.

Ever since I suggested that he and the woman had, in effect, invented each other, Edgar has been noticeably more evasive. He seems to weigh every question, and to answer at times so obliquely as to leave me wondering what, precisely, I asked.

He has never said whether it was Nola Frederick or Maia Tangeri he encountered on the climactic night of his life. Here I shall refer to her as Maia, because you were acquainted with that charming person and I myself know the enigmatic Nolie Mae or Nola only by hearsay.

But perhaps in accusing Edgar of evasiveness I am too harsh. Perhaps in his final hours he is, rather, impatient with my questions.

I questioned Maia too, in her room above Edgar's in the east tower of the hospital in the pre-dawn hours of that gloomy Sunday, hoping she might clarify what Edgar left obscure. Alas, her answers were often as equivocal as his own, leaving me obliged to reconstruct the events I here set forth.

He held her in his arms. He kissed her. He tasted the salt of her tears. They must have spoken, but neither would say what words passed between them. Was "love" among them? I prefer to think so.

Did they discuss what had to be done? He never told me, nor did she, but in the light of what follows it is apparent that she knew, at least, what the problem was.

Would Edgar be content to warn Henry that the fateful weapon might be stolen—when Edgar knew that, if events followed their course, it *would* be stolen? I think not. Writers, I hardly need tell you, my dear Alexandre, are accustomed to exerting control over the worlds they create. So they are inclined to assert it over the world in which, *faute de mieux*, they must live.

They walked side by side, Maia leading the roan stallion. The moon had set. The way began to climb steeply. Far below they could see starlight glinting on water. Edgar would mention a waterfall like a veil of silver against the dark face of a distantly looming cliff; she would not. Both would say that they left the trees behind and entered a desolate region of boulders and wind-stunted shrubs.

The roan stallion whickered softly. Maia turned and stroked its muzzle. A moment later they saw two hobbled horses. Their quarry could not be far off.

Searching for the camp, Edgar and Maia became separated. Was this their intention? To separate was efficient, each would say—possibly in defense of the other—but was it wise? Together they could have dealt better with the unexpected.

It was Maia who found the camp.

She saw first the gleam of leather in the starlight. In the lee of a large boulder, two men slept, heads pillowed on their saddles. The wind keened; it reminded Maia of a baby crying. She stood stock-still looking at the men wrapped in their saddle blankets. William Henry Leonard Poe's sleeping face gave her a start. So alike were the two brothers that it could have been Edgar she saw. The other man was Monk. He moved in his sleep, turning on his side and facing Maia. She held her breath. But his eyes were shut.

What Maia would afterwards refer to as the lascar pistol lay on the ground between them.

Where was Edgar? Should she try to find him?

Her eyes returned to the lascar pistol.

The wind would cover any sound she made. She took a step, and another. She dropped into a crouch, the Malay parang gripped in one hand. She was reaching for the lascar pistol when Monk rolled out of his blanket and stood up.

He looked gigantic in the night.

According to Maia, the wind dropped then. For the first time she could hear Will Henry's deep, regular breathing. She was in no danger, she knew. She had only to wake Will.

But she did not.

Monk groped his way sleepily around the boulder. She could not see him. She heard the splash of water on rock.

She picked up the lascar pistol and ran.

The ground—as it was described to me—dropped away twenty yards or so beyond the camp. It might have been the edge of a cliff, for all Maia knew. But she chose to run in that direction. There she found a trail that plunged down a steep slope into woods. Undergrowth impeded her way.

She heard something heavy crashing through the brush behind her.

———

I am at a loss, my dear Alexandre, to explain Maia's behavior.

Did she, presented with the opportunity, decide to take the fateful weapon, intending to give it to Edgar?

But then why did she flee directly away from where she had last seen him?

There was light there, she would say, like the full moon seen through a pane of ground glass. What was that light? Did it exert some compelling power over her, drawing her as a moth to a candle flame?

The analogy at first seems apt. But does it bear scrutiny? Maia was fleeing through woods along a trail so overgrown that she called it a verdant tunnel. How could such diffuse light as she described have reached her? She would say that, later, it became blinding.

Have we now, through Maia's eyes, our first look at the Yaanek idol? A diffuse light impossibly spread over a broad horizon in a narrow, overgrown trail? A light that would become hardly less bright than the tropical sun at noon, if we are to believe Maia?

There is, alas, reason to doubt her.

Hers was, after all, *not* our first glimpse of the idol. Monk described it at the Whig coop, did he not? It reminded him, he said, of a statue he had seen in Athens of the ancient Greek god Poseidon, lord of the sea and earthquakes—but instead of a trident this statue held a Malay parang in his hand.

True, Monk did mention a blinding flash. It came when the idol was destroyed, he said. So did his companion's hemorrhage—and Monk's own crescent-shaped scar, ascribable to no natural cause.

Are we to believe *him*?

Is there not a simpler explanation for Monk's disfigurement?

At the Whig coop, Monk made no mention of Maia. But how credible is his account? To chase and overpower an armed heathen robber in the unknown interior of an island on the other side of the world, Monk cuts a heroic figure. To chase and overpower Maia, he is little more than a bully.

He was, we may assume, pursuing an unknown thief through the darkness. At what point did he know it was Maia? Did he ever know?

A light, at first diffuse, then blinding . . .

The stone likeness of an immemorial god . . .

Which am I to believe, if either?

You, my dear Alexandre, I am sure would say, "Never mind weighing contradictory statements. Just tell me what happens, it is what my readers want."

Edgar's readers, however, might be harder to satisfy.

I sit in my accustomed shadowy corner of Edgar's room smoking a meerschaum, my first of the day—or last of the night—writing these words. It is an hour I have always found unsettling, when the faintest light of dawn touches the window, disturbing the tranquillity of the darkness. The hospital, for all that it should be a quiet place suited to calm reflection, sounds and resounds with noise. This being a Sunday morning, it is the more annoying because unanticipated. Something rolls heavily overhead. Something else bangs. A voice shouts. In the corridor outside I hear brisk footsteps.

These belong to J.C.S. Monkur, Professor of the Theory and Practice of Medicine, and his entourage. Sister Margaret rises from her chair at Edgar's bedside and opens the door. Professor Monkur marches in followed by Dr. Moran and two young men who, I assume, are staff physicians, one of them carrying a lamp. The four surround the bed and peer down at the patient.

"Good morning, Edgar," says Dr. Moran.

"He cannot hear you," says Professor Monkur impatiently. Monkur has one of those faces aglow with an indecent health and a self-confidence that verges on arrogance. With thumb and forefinger, he pries apart the lids of Edgar's left eye and bids the others observe the pronounced pupillary dilation and contraction. Inflammation of the brain, he lectures them; terminal loss of nerve power. "He will not survive the dawn," pronounces Professor Monkur.

They march out briskly. Dr. Moran pauses to look back at Edgar, then hurries to join the others.

I wait expectantly. This daily pre-dawn visit usually leaves Edgar in a mood to talk.

"They have gone?"

"Yes."

Sister Margaret is smoothing the counterpane.

"I hate that fellow Monkur," Edgar says. "So overbearing."

Sister Margaret says, "There. There now," and resumes her seat.

Edgar says, "I was dreaming when they came."

I misunderstand his tone of voice. "Nightmare?"

"In a way. I dreamt I was at the lighthouse. The night before the storm destroyed it." He lets out a long breath. "Why couldn't I have persevered?"

"You had no way to know."

"I could have finished my novel that night instead of deciding to sleep and get a fresh start in the morning. To come so close to the end, only to have the very elements conspire against me! So close! Nola Frederick—Maia, if you insist—had already hurried off through the woods with what she called the lascar pistol, had already heard a crashing in the underbrush behind her.

"She turned. She turned at bay, Dupin, when it was apparent she could not outrun her pursuer, and saw Monk. Did she shoot him in his tracks as he rushed at her? No, she raised the parang in an instinctive gesture of defense. His arm came up to parry it, and the razor-sharp blade sliced his face open from the corner of his eye to his chin. Then he was upon her. Could he see her in the darkness? Did he know who she was? At the lighthouse, I had not made up my mind on that point. It was only a first draft; I would, I told myself, work it out later.

"He knocked her down and the lascar pistol flew from her grasp. He could easily have taken it and gone. But he straddled her; he beat her about the head with his fists until she lay quite still. Then he picked up the pistol, stepped across her inert form, and was gone.

"And I? Meanwhile, I wrote, I had stumbled upon the abandoned camp; stumbled literally, for I tripped over a saddle, one of two I found there. Looking about for some sign of what might have happened, I noticed, some twenty yards from where I stood, that the terrain dropped away abruptly. I went to the edge, expecting an abyss, but saw a wooded slope steeply descending.

"I wrote that I felt a sense of dread, as if I saw in the darkness below a harrowing vision of myself as both victim and e.

"Never the less, or for that very reason, I started do slope—only to see a figure loom directly in my path.

"That was as far as I wrote, having taught myself always to stop in the middle of things.

"But in the morning the sea rose mountainously, the lighthouse broke apart and sank, and I barely escaped with my life. My life, yes; but not the manuscript."

You will have observed, my dear Alexandre, how Edgar by now is confusing the story—which has come to obsess him the more, the more its ending eludes him—with the events of his own life. Who are we to gainsay him? A writer like Edgar writes from his secret dreams to banish irksome reality. But can anyone say where one leaves off and the other begins?

A light, at first diffuse, then blinding . . .
The stone likeness of an immemorial god . . .
What did *Edgar* see?
I do not mean upon the path; we shall come to that. I mean the idol. What was the idol, in his eyes?

He wishes me not to know. How else can I interpret his cryptic answer?

"Nothing," he said. "I saw nothing at all, Dupin. *Rien du tout,*" he repeated, as if doubtful of my command of English.

(Here let me append my scribbled notes of the ensuing conversation.)

POE: Why do you keep asking? There is nothing unusual about seeing nothing.

DUPIN: Perhaps what I fail to see is the metaphor.

P: There is no metaphor.

D: An empty canvas? The empty canvas that confronts the artist, is that the metaphor?

P: I told you, I saw nothing. Not any thing. An utter blank.

D: Ah! The blank paper that every writer must deal with. That is the metaphor.

P: Must you insist upon a metaphor? We should be talking about Henry. He was worried. He knew Monk meant to shoot the idol.

D: To *shoot* it? Yes, I see—chip off some fragments.

P: They had argued about it. Monk called Henry a fool to feel bound by the sanctimonious moralizing of an adventurer no better than themselves, and dead to boot.

D: Thaddeus Frederick, I presume?

P: *(Nods.)* Monk said he had not come ten thousand miles just to catch a glimpse through a spy-glass of what was down there.

D: What was it? Did Henry describe it to you?

P: Henry told Monk the Yaanek might not take kindly to their idol being damaged.

D: Where were they, these Yaanek?

P: The argument grew heated. They might have come to blows had Henry not proposed they sleep on it and settle their differences in the clear light of day.

D: Daylight would not have helped. It never does.

P: In any event, Monk chose not to wait. When Henry woke, some time toward dawn, he was alone. He had barely started down the slope to find Monk when—

D: Why in that direction? From the camp it looked like the edge of a cliff.

P: *(testily)* I suppose that if they knew the route this far, they knew it the whole way. For pity's sake, Dupin, stop interrupting! Henry, as I say, had barely started down the slope when he heard someone behind him.

D: You?

P: Together we found Maia.

Edgar saw her just as she was regaining her feet, and ran to her with a glad cry. She responded by springing at him with the parang. I asked her about this. The light, she told me; the light was blinding and she assumed her attacker had returned.

Edgar caught her wrist but she resisted with such strength that, but for Henry's help, he could not have disarmed her. Struggling, she never made a sound. There were two of them, she told me; all she could think was that now there were two of them. I asked Edgar how he could have recognized her in that blinding light, and he replied without hesitation that he not only recognized her but saw on her face evidence of a brutal beating—contusions, an eye swollen half shut, split and bloody lips.

Light? he then said. What light? It was still night.

I asked him how, if that were so, he was able to see her at all.

With no difficulty, he replied. You of all people, Dupin, should not dispute that.

The moment they released her, she bolted. This is hardly surprising given what *she* thought was happening. However, it surprised *them*. Henry, ever the man of action, recovered first, shoving the derringer into his pocket and hurrying in pursuit. Edgar, snatching up the parang, followed.

The entire experience, as you will have noted, partakes of what Edgar, in one of his tales, has called "the unmistakable idiosyncrasy of the dream."

Why, for example, did they not speak? A few words from the brothers would have let Maia know she was in safe hands.

Their versions of what followed differ.

Edgar would say that when light first touched the horizon (one cannot help wondering what horizon, if they were plunging through a narrow track in the jungle), he heard birds calling tentatively, as if fearful they might be expelled from the only reality in which they could exist. The only reality in which they could exist!—is this not an overt admission by Edgar that he was dreaming and that his dream-self might decide, like some petulant demiurge, that these dream-birds were superfluous to the dream-world he had created?

Maia would remark only the beauty of the birdsong—which in itself is suspect. Tropical birds scream raucously. Their beauty is a beauty of plumage.

Both agree that the trail debouched upon a vast and circular space. Edgar describes it as a huge basin enclosed by stupendous ramparts of black rock towering into the desolate pre-dawn sky like walls enclosing the universe. He speaks of countless six-sided columns, black as the ramparts and twice the height of a tall man, that ran in rows from the center of the great basin toward its rim, like spokes from the hub of a wheel. The basin he estimates as two miles across, with a clearing in its center of perhaps a hundred yards. Here and there among the radiating rows of six-sided columns could be seen tarns or small lakes, their dark, clear waters girt by tall sedges rustling in the wind and reflecting distorted images of the columns.

Maia alludes to no wind but speaks at length of a silvery mist rising from those dark tarns, swirling about the columns and partially obscuring them while, however, their reflections remained perfectly clear, giving her the extraordinary feeling that reality was to be found not above but within those watery depths.

When I call Edgar's attention to Maia's description of a silvery mist, he at once puts it into service as, if you will, a *deus ex machina* of his dream, a device to lead Maia out of harm's way. He says that before long, a tendril of that mist touched—or, he corrects himself, caressed—Maia, whereupon she was drawn into the silvery cloud and herself became radiant, like silver dipped in light. He remembers running to her, raising both hands to grasp her, but the mist swirled and she was gone.

Here in this other-worldly landscape, for all its specific detail, one is confronted again by the unmistakable idiosyncrasy of the dream. For has not Edgar conflated two separate geological phenomena, one glacial and the other volcanic?

What he describes as a vast basin surrounded by high walls is, apparently, a cirque. Cirques are formed over thousands of years by the erosion of snow and ice and, geology tells us, are quite typically filled by numerous small lakes or tarns. All well and good—until we remember that snow and ice, let alone glaciation, are unknown at the tropical latitude of Panchatan.

As for those dark, specifically hexagonal columns, they can only have resulted from the solidification of lava.

Now, we know that Edgar's travels were limited. He never saw a range of high mountains, like the Alps or Pyrenees, where one could expect to find a cirque. And columns of solidified lava are not found in the settled regions of America, but only in the Rocky Mountains far to the west. Edgar has written of those little-explored highlands, you say? And so he has*—without once having been anywhere near them.

I am, moreover, unaware of such six-sided columns in continental Europe. But an example may be seen on the northern coast of Ireland, where it is called the Giant's Causeway—and *Henry* more than once visited the Emerald Isle.

What do we conclude? That Henry, in recounting his travels, described both cirques and the Giant's Causeway, and that Edgar, dreaming, superimposed one landscape upon the other.

Yet he insists none of it is a dream, and half of me strains to believe. . . .

I know, my dear Alexandre, I know! You prefer that I eschew such speculation and get on with the tale. Very well.

After Maia disap

Forty-nine

> You will say now, of course, that I dreamed; but not so. What I saw—what I heard—what I felt—what I thought—had about it nothing of the unmistakable idiosyncrasy of the dream.
> —"A Tale of the Ragged Mountains"

I wake. On the night stand the lamp is turned low. I can see the barest glimmer of first light outside the window. The silver-haired sister sits quietly beside my bed. From the far corner I hear a familiar voice—Dupin's. He is muttering a mild scatological oath, and, as my eyes grow used to the dimness in his corner, I see that he is shaking his right hand up and down impatiently.

* See *The Journal of Julius Rodman*. (Editor's note)

"*Merde, et encore merde,*" he says, more loudly.

A mild oath, yes; yet foreign to Dupin's lips.

"Bone dry," he shouts. "The confounded thing has run out."

Dimly I can see in his hand a reservoir pen, stubby, of a bilious yellow color.

"There, there, Mr. Poe," says the silver-haired sister. "It is going to be all right."

"I prefer, anyway," I tell Dupin, "that you write no more of that."

He stops shaking the empty pen. "How do you know what I am writing?" he demands.

"There, there," says the sister. I feel her cool hand on my brow. I should tell her to leave us. But I do not.

"I know every word of it," I tell Dupin instead.

"*Zut!* How? You have not stirred from your bed."

"And how can *you* explain to Alexandre Dumas a situation you yourself fail to grasp? You insist that I dream, and, to bolster this contention, you write that Nola Frederick is simultaneously living her own somewhat different version of the same dream."

I expect him to contradict me—or at least to say that the woman is Maia. But the empty pen concerns him more.

"I must find some ink," he says, rising.

"Sit down. Listen to me, Dupin. You have written enough of those . . . ratiocinative maunderings of yours."

"Maunderings!"

"There, there, Mr. Poe, we must try to remain calm."

"Yes, maunderings! Your sort of reasoning may be internally valid. But it is useless if it is based on erroneous assumptions."

Dupin sits heavily. He looks at the pages of foolscap he has written, then folds them and tucks them away.

"How have I erred?"

"You are writing to Dumas of a dream that resembles reality, while I have been living a reality that resembles a dream."

"We must discuss this further," says Dupin eagerly.

"Why? Because it is now *you* who fear the ending, *you* who wish to delay it? How long has it been since you urged me to finish my tale?"

Dupin sighs. "Very well," he says. "Finish it."

She faded into the mist. Among the barely visible black columns she looked like silver dipped in light; looked like light itself. I ran after her, but it was no use. Who can capture a will-o'-the-wisp, a *fata morgana*, a dream that belongs to someone else?

I thought I heard hoofbeats; but mist can distort sound just as wind can distort an image on water, and I could not discern where they came from. I did, however, hear Maia's distinctive whistle somewhere off to my left. The hoofbeats grew louder, thundering so close that I was amazed I could see no horse. Then the sound receded.

The mist, having accomplished its purpose, was soon blown into tatters by the wind, and I found myself looking down into a dark tarn where I saw, instead of the familiar six-sided column, a reflection of the lighthouse where I had gone to finish writing the story that had so obsessed me. From the high balcony girdling the lamp someone had just fallen, or jumped. I ran in terror from that image to another tarn, but it too cast up a reflection of the lighthouse. The body had plunged halfway down the tower; had turned over; was caught, in this image, falling head-first—for all the world like a daguerreotype, if these could somehow capture motion. I pushed my way through the clattering sedges at the edge of a third tarn. There the body had fallen farther yet, from deep within the tarn almost to its dark and gleaming surface, and I could clearly make out the face of my brother Henry.

I heard two reports, one loud, one less so, and ran toward the clearing at the center of the vast basin. Monk stood at its edge, holding the bar-hammer pepperbox pistol. Henry's body lay crumpled nearby, the useless little derringer at his side, blood pouring from his mouth.

Looking up, Monk cocked the pistol with which he had killed my brother.

———

"It is time," Dupin tells me firmly, "to address the nature of that firearm."

"What about it?"

" 'Bar-hammer,' 'pepperbox.' You are always calling attention to its singularity. Yet if I suggest it might be a metaphor—"

"Henry had one like it in Baltimore," I say impatiently. "He took it off a drunken lascar the night he met Nola Frederick, and brought it home as a reminder of his luck. You see, that firearm almost killed him."

"The firearm? Not the lascar? How revealing that you put it that way! As if to imply a mechanistic universe in which neither you nor your brother has the power to change, in even the smallest detail, your destiny. In which case, what could you hope to accomplish in Panchatan? No, I am more certain than ever that you are dreaming. And, if you are," Dupin ponders, "if you are, then that means I . . ."

He sinks into distracted silence, and I resume my narrative.

I ran straight along Monk's line of sight as he pointed the lascar pistol at me, and I bellowed wordlessly as I ran. (This touch pleases Dupin, who observes that a carnivore, in the instant before it pounces, attempts with a frightful roar to immobilize its prey.)

At my wild shouting, Monk looked frantically about. This at first made no sense to me. His eyes sweeping from side to side could only mean that he was trying to find where my voice was coming from—could only mean that he heard me but did not see me.

He began to circle slowly to his own left, as if negotiating an obstacle that stood between us. Unsure of what was happening, I swung the parang, a prodigious blow that, had nothing stopped it, would have decapitated him.

The blade rang—on metal? on stone?—the impact almost tearing the weapon from my grasp. I swung again, and again the blade rang. Monk looked terrified. It may be that he cried out. I cannot be certain, for I was striking a third time, a fourth, a fifth; the blade rang, sparks flew, my hand went numb. I gripped the parang in my left hand and attacked anew. Monk looked up, shielding his head with his arms. Something struck him above one eye, drawing blood; a stone, it was a small stone, a shard. Others fell from nowhere— dozens, hundreds, thousands, with a clattering roar like a railroad train rushing through a tunnel after an accident in the cars. And I swung the parang, could not stop swinging it, not even after Monk lay buried under a cairn of shards.

Later—who can say how much later?—I watched as that vast basin, surrounded by those high ramparts like walls enclosing the universe, blazed with the fierce light of the new day.

But when I walked to where my brother had fallen I saw that what rose behind those ramparts was not the sun.

I stood upon a surf-tormented shore at the edge of a shoreless sea, under a sky aflame with the light of a comet that spanned half the zodiac. Above the black sand beach loomed a cliff on which brooded a turreted castle, its windows like eyes, blank bloodshot eyes with their pupils rolled back, its battlements and crenellations glowing red in the comet-light. Below, gnarled trees writhed and clashed their dead limbs in the windless night.

I scooped up a handful of black sand and let it trickle through my fingers. The surf broke and came up the beach at a sibilant rush, and I shut my eyes so that I might see what I had lost.

Well, I had lost the idol. But the idol was nothing. It was nothing, and yet I had destroyed it. Would I have destroyed it any less —or more—had it been a blinding light, or the stone likeness of a god?

Had I lost the Yaanek? It seemed so. Otherwise, where were they? Were the Yaanek, like their idol, beyond my comprehension? But I knew the legend. I had written of it. Had the knowing come first, or the writing? Did it matter, now that I had lost the manuscript? I never saw the Yaanek, not once. When I destroyed their idol— which, according to the legend, desired its own destruction—why did they not come out from their huts to flee into the jungle, or along this beach? I saw no huts, no Yaanek village, no Yaanek tribe, no tribesman who could have stolen Henry's pistol. Would any thing have been different had I not come here? Would my not coming have changed the legend?

What legend? What I knew, what I wrote of at the light-house, was an immemorial myth known to the peoples of the ar-chipelago, a myth that had as its subject the Yaanek. What I mean to say, Dupin, is that it was a legend *about* the Yaanek, not one passed down *by* the Yaanek. Had the Yaanek legends of their own? Did they tell of a flawed hero who came to their island to right a terrible wrong, only to cause the very events he wished to prevent? Did they curse him, vilify him?

I walked, listening to the slap and hiss of the surf. Far out to sea, beyond the horizon where I could not see it, a huge wave was form-ing. I became conscious of someone walking at my side.

"No, I will tell you," said my brother Henry. "It was like this."

Had he been there long? He seemed to be replying to a question I did not recall asking. He was no ghost. He was simply *there*, as I was.

"I always longed to write," he said.

"I remember."

"As much as you longed to travel." For a moment he was silent. "Sometimes I can't help thinking I have lived your life, and you mine," he said then. "I wonder, what would have happened had we changed places?"

He smiled; or seemed to. "I was absolutely convinced there was a story in me, if only I could find the words. Often at night in some distant port I dreamed I saw those words flowing like a magisterial river across a world of pages. But in the morning they were gone, and I wrote nothing. Well, almost nothing. I wrote a single line— 'My name is William Henry Leonard Poe.' Only that, and nothing more."

We had fallen into step side by side on the wet black sand at the water's edge. "In desperation, I sought solitude, finding it as the keeper of a lighthouse two hundred miles from the nearest land. But even there, I was unable to remember my dream and could

write nothing. Oh, you will never understand this, you who effortlessly—"

I did not contradict him.

"—have completed so many tales from first line to last."

"What were you trying to write?" I asked him.

But I knew.

"It was the story of a man much like myself who became tormented by a tale he wished to, but could not, write. When the
torment became insupportable he traveled the world, fleeing from
himself. Finally, in desperation, he sought the solitude of a lighthouse. But he wrote nothing. He did not know where the story was
going. Its ending eluded him. Was his plot, like my own, too doom-
laden? Was his vision, like my own, too limited?"

"Well, that was then," Henry said, raising his voice. "And now?
Now, when it is too late, I can see every word of my story, down
to its last lines."

And I held my breath.

"How beautiful they are! The beauty not of a closing, not a finishing, but of an opening, a new beginning, like a vast and awesome
silence waiting to be filled. Listen . . ."

And, still breathless, forgetting that Henry said it was too late, I
listened. But he said no more.

Across the blaze of sky the comet arched its parang blade. Shooting stars streaked earthward. There came a muted explosion, and
another. The ground began to shake. A fireball broke away from the
comet's head, followed by a sound like the crisp crackle of a comb
run through hair, the long hair of a young and beautiful woman or
ghost on a cold winter night.

From beyond the horizon a huge wave raced toward the shore, its
crest shattering the sea-borne reflection of the comet into floating
splinters of light. When I could tear my eyes from them, I saw that
I stood alone on the beach.

Long and straight on the wet black sand behind me was the trail
of only one pair of footprints.

The wave broke gigantically, the shards of cometary light flying like shivered glass, and I ran, I ran for my life, hoping to gain the heights of the path which, once, I had climbed to the castle, before the flood could reach me.

"And did you?" Dupin asks.

No, but she did. Nola—Maia, if you insist—did, urging the roan stallion up the steep path until she chanced to look back and see me. She reined up and wheeled about. As she raced headlong in my direction, the sky seemed to draw a breath, a long and shuddering breath like the rattle of continuous thunder, and the castle began to sway, and in the sightless eyes of its windows I saw the comet reflected—as red, as blood-red, as the ruby asphodel. Then the great hewn stones came apart and seemed to hang suspended in air while, at my feet, a fissure ran zigzag across the ground, widening as I watched.

Was there ever a time, an instant, some last fraction of a second, when either of us might have crossed?

Maia's roan stallion, on the far side, balked at jumping. She turned it, rode back up the path, came down again full-tilt. But by then the fissure was ten feet across, perhaps fifteen, and again the stallion balked. I shouted for her to leave me, to escape while—I might better have said if—she could. But she tried a third time, again to no avail.

I stood on the very edge of the abyss. I had an impulse to jump, as if I could clear in a single bound and by a sheer effort of will what was then a gap of almost fifty feet. She dismounted. We called to each other. The sky crackled and flashed. A building block from the castle smashed down not far from me, splitting open, splashing liquid fire.

What was it she called to me? Why am I left thinking she blamed herself for what went wrong, when it was my fault? I tried to tell her, but she could hear me no more than I could hear her.

We reached out, both of us, as if to touch across a hundred-foot chasm. Neither of us would leave, neither of us wanted to be the first to go—until the ground jolted underfoot and took on the semblance of crazed pottery, until the edge of the abyss began to crumble and fall away. Then she looked at me one last time, disconsolately, and mounted.

As she turned the stallion and rode up the path, new rifts forced me to retreat ever farther back toward the surf—where I was toppled by the undertow and swept into that turbulent sea.

I went under, I swallowed sea water, I fought my way to the surface, I came up gasping, I caught sight of something in the water ahead of me and swam to it. Even a log would help me stay afloat. But it was no log, it was a small boat. With my last strength I clambered over the gunwale. The boat rocked, water sloshed in its bottom. I despaired, thinking that it would sink. But the level of the water rose no higher. I fell exhausted across the thwart and saw, floating in the water below it, a package wrapped in oilcloth. I opened it. A glance was enough to recognize my own handwriting. The pages were out of order; the one my eyes fell on belonged near the end. *This* page.

A steamship appeared out of nowhere. I found strength to stand, to wave my arms, to shout. The ship grew larger. Its whistle blew. Soon it loomed like the black cliff above the beach. A Jacob's ladder came rattling down the hull and a sailor swiftly descended to the row-boat bobbing below. He asked in American-accented English if I needed help climbing aboard. He offered to take the oilcloth-wrapped package. But I wanted to finish the adventure as I had begun it, alone. I tucked the manuscript under one arm and slowly climbed the Jacob's ladder. Eager hands helped me over the rail.

I was given a hot bath and a suit of nautical whites. A young ship's officer asked if I wished the use of a bunk until dinner, but, having just escaped a watery grave, I felt too wrought up to even think of resting. "In that case," the young officer said, "Captain Gliddon presents his compliments, and requests the pleasure of your company in the saloon."

It was raining. The saloon deck was slippery underfoot. As we reached the bat-wing doors, they swung open and a corpulent man stood in the doorway. He had a patch over one eye and the red, convivial face of a drinker. My face, I am sure, was haggard with fatigue. Never the less, he recognized me, or thought he did, for he said something about having recently seen my likeness in a magazine and asked:

"You are Mr. Edgar Allan Poe, are you not?"

Fifty

> Together, they effected their escape to their own country; for neither was seen again.
>
> —"Hop-Frog"

This morning what engages my attention until Dupin bestirs himself is the constant to-ing and fro-ing. One does not expect such on a Sunday.

Dupin seems oblivious to it all—and to the fierce wind that rattles the casement and blows a draft into his accustomed corner. Every now and then he rolls his reservoir pen across the small table at which he sits, or strokes the yellowed bowl of his meerschaum. Except for these rituals, so characteristic of him when lost in thought, he could be mistaken for a dead man.

They have all been here in my room at one time or another since dawn, all but that Professor Monkur that none of the others like. You would expect his absence to impart to the hospital staff a relaxed air, but, to the contrary, brisk solemnity is the order of the day.

Dr. Moran comes and goes, his boyish face drawn with lack of sleep. Both nursing sisters bustle in and out. Once, briefly, they stand together at my bedside, blocking Dupin from view.

"Within moments of each other," says Sister Margaret.

"You might know, a Sunday morning, when most of the orderlies are off," says Sister Sparrow.

"We shall manage," says Sister Margaret, and asks Dr. Moran, who has just looked in for perhaps the third time, "Is this yours, Doctor?"

"What is it?—oh, a fountain pen. It's not mine, no."

"You don't see many of them," says Sister Margaret. "I found it on the floor over there."

I cannot help smiling. When he emerges from his distracted state, Dupin is going to wonder what happened to that pen.

"Yes, well," says Dr. Moran. "Put it with the patient's effects. He *was* a writer, you know." He turns away. Usually a courteous man, he clearly has no time to spend on a lost reservoir pen. "Where is my wife? Has anyone seen—ah, there you are, Mary."

Mrs. Moran is dressed for church in a high-necked frock with what I believe is called a lingerie collar, but it seems the Lord will have to wait, for, like the others, she has an errand in my room.

"His clothes?" Dr. Moran asks. "What about them?"

"See for yourself, dear. He cannot be viewed in them."

Dr. Moran opens the small wardrobe. "Clean," he says. "They have been cleaned."

"But they are still rags." Mrs. Moran looks at her husband. "You are about the same size."

Dr. Moran nods. "The brown suit," he says.

"I'll bring it directly. Then if you need me, I'll be upstairs."

"Upstairs?"

"I should like to go through her belongings. Something may have been overlooked that could tell us who the poor woman was."

Mrs. Moran pauses at the side of my bed. She looks so solemn that I think it inappropriate to smile at her. Indeed, I see tears in her eyes. She dabs at them with a handkerchief. Then she hurries out, and a moment later an orderly comes to inform Dr. Moran that someone from the Health Commission is here.

"Tell him he may certify that it was exposure and *encephalitis lethargica*."

"And a reporter from the *Sun*."

"Already? Tell him the rotunda. In an hour or so. There will be others. Serve coffee."

The orderly leaves and Dr. Moran leaves and so does Sister Margaret. Sister Sparrow sits in the bedside chair and soon dozes.

I will say this for Dupin. He might occasionally act out of character—as in his absurd insistence that I have been dreaming. But he cannot long remain untrue to his logical nature.

"Pascal put it best," he says without preamble as he gets up and approaches the bed, "in his argument for why one should believe in God."

Dupin's mind is superb at making inspired connections. I can see he is his old self again.

"Pascal said there are four possibilities. God exists and I believe He does. God does not exist and I do not believe. God does not exist although I do believe. God exists but I do *not* believe. You see?" And he paces back and forth, head down, hands clasped behind his back, most pleased with himself.

"Not exactly," I say.

"In the first two cases, no conflict arises. In the third, believing costs me nothing. But in the fourth, I become immeasurably the loser. And when one deals with eternity, twenty-five per cent is too great a risk to take."

"You are saying—"

"That I still think you have been dreaming. But I will not take the twenty-five per cent risk. Only a fool would refuse, under the circumstances, to believe."

"Believe what?"

"That your narrative is something more than a dream." Dupin peers at me through his green-tinted spectacles. "But it requires quite a leap of faith. In dreams there are always answers, if one knows where—or rather how—to look. The same, alas, cannot be said of reality. Questions abound. Answers do not. Why did Monk come to your rescue twice in the Whig coop? Why were you unable to see the Yaanek—not to mention the idol? And if Maia, when she was bitten by a poisonous snake at the ghost town of—what was its name?"

"Eidolon," I say.

"If she called upon the Shard to save her, and if it is as powerful as we are told, why did it not? Or the island—how did it come to be called Panchatan? As anyone with a knowledge of Oriental lore can tell you, the simple addition of three letters turns Panchatan into—"

"Please!" I interrupt. "One question at a time. The Shard *did* save Maia—by burying Monk under thousands of replicas of itself. If Monk was already dead, you see, he could not have gone with Maia to Eidolon. And if she was there without him, the circumstances would not have been the same."

"From this you would have me conclude—?"

"That the Shard saved Maia from dying of snake-bite."

"There may be a certain logic in what you say," Dupin admits. "But when last seen, Maia was making a hopeless attempt to ride up a crumbling trail to a disintegrating castle under a burning sky—not much of an improvement."

That was Nola, I am about to say. But it comes to the same and I say nothing.

"And your brother," Dupin muses. "This is a *most* baffling question."

He sticks his meerschaum in his mouth. He pats his pockets. "No tobacco, no ink . . ." he grumbles. "You were saying?"

"*You* were saying."

"If your brother died neither in Baltimore where he told you of the Shard—"

"He never mentioned the Shard in Baltimore. Just the pistol."

"—nor in Paris at the scene of the 'murder' where you *found* the Shard—if in reality he died on the island of Panchatan when the idol was destroyed—he could not have left the Shard in Paris for you to find. And if he did not, if it is only the subject of a legend—"

"It was *there*, I tell you, Dupin," I protest. "I held it in my hand. So did you."

"Don't misunderstand, Edgar. I argued earlier that you were dreaming, but now I am defending the opposing viewpoint." He sucks on his empty meerschaum, removes it from his mouth, scowls at it, puts it in his pocket. "Why did you go to Panchatan?"

"It was not my idea to go to Panchatan. If it was my idea to go anywhere—and I was under hypnosis, don't forget—it was to the lighthouse. I wished to finish my book there. But the lighthouse was destroyed and by some miracle I managed to reach Panchatan in the row-boat."

"And while you were in Panchatan you were again in the presence of the Shard, hypnotized. With what purpose?"

"To prevent the destruction of the idol."

"That is, to alter events that had already happened. And you think you failed?"

"Utterly," I say in a dispirited voice.

"But Edgar," says Dupin, "you *did* bring about changes—notably to the fate of your brother and Monk. And did not Maia too alter events by stealing Henry's pistol so that a Yaanek thief could not?"

"It was still stolen."

"And was Henry not absolved of destroying the idol—because you did?"

"Nobody but Monk ever said Henry did it. And, you know, we looked alike, my brother and I. Monk could have confused me with him."

"Monk is dead," Dupin reminds me. "No, my friend, you did effect changes—not the ones you wished, but significant changes none the less. Which brings us full circle to Pascal. I repeat: I cannot afford to believe you are dreaming."

"Because you think that might have a bearing on your own existence?" I ask tartly. "But you have it backwards. Even if you were only a creature of my imagination, you yourself assured me I shall have everlasting fame. So you too will be immortal."

"I should prefer something a shade more active for a while yet," Dupin says. "And even immortality will not last long, if the destruction of the world is at hand."

"Frankly, Dupin," I tell him, "you were much cheerier when you were triumphantly 'proving' it was all a dream in which you had no part."

"No part indeed, more's the pity." His voice takes on an aggrieved tone. "If I had been with you in Panchatan, things might not have proceeded with such disastrous illogic—and we might not now, as a consequence of the destruction of the idol, be facing the destruction of the world. I hope you will show more sense next time."

"Next time? What next time?" I say listlessly.

"Think. If it is more than a dream—as you insist, and as Pascal tells me to believe—what must you do?"

I shrug. I have not the faintest idea.

"You must return to Panchatan and, armed with the knowledge that you can alter events, try again."

"Go back there?"

"Of course. If it is true—or even possible—that the world will end if you don't, how can you not?"

I look at him, at how the daylight coming in through the window makes his spectacles glitter like emeralds.

"How can I?" I say. A lassitude has crept over me. I feel incapable of moving as much as a finger.

"With the Shard's help, of course."

"But the last time I saw it, it was in Count Tangeri's castle on Panchatan."

"Then perhaps Maia has it."

I lie there not moving, unable to move; not thinking, unable to think. And then my heart begins to pound.

"Did you—did you tell me once she was right here in this building?"

"I did. She is."

"Go to her. Hurry. Before it is too late. Get the Shard. The whole world—"

"If she has it, I'll get it."

He runs for the door.

Dr. John J. Moran hurried along the passage. *Three* reporters already, and the orderly was mistaken—not a man from the Health Commissioner's Office, it was the Commissioner himself. On a Sunday morning. But why not? One of the deceased was a celebrity, after all.

Dr. Moran heard footsteps pounding toward him. In the dim and narrow passage he saw no one. Yet, as he had once before, he stepped out of the way. This time he was too late. Something sent him crashing back against the wall, where he reeled and fell. He thought he heard the footsteps fading.

As he climbed to hands and knees, he saw an object on the floor. He picked it up. A pair of spectacles, their wire frames twisted, their green glass lenses shattered.

In the room upstairs, Mary held the unknown woman's black silk hat in one hand and a stone, or rather a fragment of stone, in the other. She had found the fragment of stone inside the hat.

The fragment of stone was warm to the touch.

A cold draft came from the window.

Why was the woman carrying a fragment of stone in the band of her hat?

They could not ask her now, poor dear. They could not ask her any thing. The riding habit was torn and mud-stained, the crown of the hat crumpled. The woman's clothing—she had no other possessions—made a sad little heap on the foot of the bed. There was nothing to tell who she was.

Mary walked to the bed to place the hat on top of the rest. She saw that the woman's face, uncovered, was fixed in a faint smile. But, surely, she would have noticed that before?

As Mary reached to draw the counterpane up, the wind rattled the casement, and it burst open. Mary cried out. She would always tell herself, afterwards, that but for her cry, she would have known whether she heard then only the wind or the words she imagined the wind carried to her.

—Give it to him? Why should I? Do you think I would dream of missing this? I will take it. I will take it and go with him.

Mary stood absolutely still and listened, afraid that she would hear more, afraid that she would not.

The stone was no longer in her hand. The stone was nowhere.

She heard only the silence between the words.

· A NOTE ON THE TYPE ·

The typeface used in this book is one of many versions of Garamond, a modern homage to—rather than, strictly speaking, a
revival of—the celebrated fonts of Claude Garamond (c.1480–
1561), the first founder to produce type on a large scale. Garamond's type was inspired by Francesco Griffo's *De Ætna* type (cut
in the 1490s for Venetian printer Aldus Manutius and revived in
the 1920s as Bembo), but its letter forms were cleaner and the
fit between pieces of type improved. It therefore gave text a more
harmonious overall appearance than its predecessors had, becoming the basis of all romans created on the continent for the next
two hundred years; it was itself still in use through the eighteenth
century. Besides the many "Garamonds" in use today, other type-
faces derived from his fonts are Granjon and Sabon (despite their
being named after other printers).